The E

A TRAVERS AND REDMOND ARCHEOLOGICAL THRILLER

By

DESMOND G. PALMER

THE EYE OF NINEVEH

First edition. January 4, 2022.

Copyright © 2022 D G Palmer.

ISBN: 978-1739759308

Written by D G Palmer.

THE EYE OF NINEVEH

DESMOND G. PALMER

Also by D.G. Palmer
The Chronicles of Daniel Welsh
Birth of The Mortokai
Rise of The Mortokai
Magic of The Mortokai
Short Stories
The Choices of Man

Prologue

6 1 2 **BC, Nineveh, capital of the Assyrian Empire.**
King Sin-shar-ishkun was deeply troubled.
Ever since deposing his weak brother as the ruler of the
mighty Assyrian empire, he had faced revolt after revolt.
First from his brother's chief general, Sin-shumu-lishir, and
then by Nabopolassar.

The king slammed his fist against the city wall as he
gazed out from its battlements. His mistake had given the
Chaldean the opportunity to stake his claim to the
Babylonian crown, and that lapse in judgement had come
back to haunt him.

'Stay strong, father,' Ashur-uballit pleaded.

'How can I? My mistakes have brought disaster
knocking at our front door.' Two times, he had made the
wrong choice. The first had been choosing to face
Sin-shumu-lishir instead of going to Babylonia to be
coronated king of Babylon. This had caused years of political
instability, until the rebel king, Nabopolassar, rose to power.
The second had been when he had met that same false ruler
on the battlefield, had victory in his grasp, but instead of
driving forward his advantage, Sin-shar-ishkun had returned
to Nineveh, the Assyrian capital, to quell yet another
uprising.

As he looked out at all the banners, it was likely that he
would not be given the chance to make a third. The enemies
of Assyria: Persia, Scythia, Chaldea, Elam, had all joined the
alliance of Babylon and Medes.

'Look at them all. Like vultures swarming around a carcass.'

'We are far from finished, father. Do not forget that we are the righteous. Look at the atrocities Cyaxares committed in the holy city, Assur? The great god Assur himself will bless us so we might smite the defilers.'

'The king of the tribes of Medes deserves no less. He inflicted brutal destruction upon my people, destroyed the temples, he left none alive, not even the children escaped his wrath.'

Suddenly, a soldier came running towards the king and his heir. 'Majesty, they have breached the wall!'

Sin-shar-ishkun turned to his son and placed a hand on his shoulder. 'Now is the time, my son. We will make our ancestors proud this day.'

• • • •

THE BATTLE WAS FEROCIOUS. Despite having superior weapons and armour, which was key to the Assyrian empire's dominance of the region for two thousand years, the sheer numbers of their enemies was just too much to cope with.

Sin-shar-ishkun was there fighting amongst his men, trying to rally them the best he could, berating his enemy kings who were nowhere to be seen, but it was hard to do when they could see parts of the city being razed to the ground, their morale was taking a beating, their fighting spirit was waning. The unthinkable was happening. The great Assyrian war machine, the chariots and cavalry that had won them countless wars, was ineffectual within the walls of the city.

The Assyrians were losing. Only the Eye of Nineveh could save them now.

The king, with his son and several of his royal guard, fought their way to the north palace. Sin-shar-ishkun was disgusted to see that soldiers of the Babylonian-Medes coalition were there pillaging. He made sure that his sword tasted their blood.

They arrived at the royal quarters; the king glad that he had got his wives to safety before the siege of Nineveh began. He led them through a hidden door and down a secret passage, telling his son to pick up one of the many unlit torches that lined the walls. Using stone and flint, he lit it and they continued on their way.

'I know you must think I should have used the power of the eye long ago, my son, but I didn't want to rely on it as our ancestors did. We are Assyrian. We are the dominant nation.'

'And we would surely have been victorious if it were one or two armies, father. But the numbers are against us.'

'Sire! The men of Cyaxares have followed us!'

'Of course they have. He would want nothing more than to parade my head among his Median soldiers. But I will not give him the satisfaction of doing that or doing what he did to Assur, even if it will cost my life.' Then he spoke directly to his guards. 'You must hold them back. Give me time and make sure my son gets through.'

They all nodded, and with a determined look on their faces, ran off to do their duty.

With torch in hand, the king lit more torches that were in the antechamber. Ashur-uballit was enthralled. He had not seen the glory of this temple since he was a child. This would be the first time he would see the legendary gemstone put to use, however.

Ashur-uballit stood between the two huge Lamassu to gather his resolve then, with his father, pushed open the enormous doors of cedar wood which were adorned with decorated copper bands and walked into a brightly coloured antechamber. A statue of the goddess Sammu-ramat stood in the centre, waiting for an offering so that she might bestow her divine blessing.

King Sin-shar-ishkun pulled a ring from a pouch and held it up for his son to see. 'This is the key, my son. Present it to ...'

The sound of the skirmish was close, very close. The king that he had little time to explain everything to his son; he would just have to hope that he would be able to manage, would be able to rebuild the empire. And what better way to help than to give him a clean slate to work from.

Ashur-uballit was watching the great gateway, expecting to see soldiers at any moment. His father called, and he turned to see the king disappearing into a formally hidden room. The crown prince caught up and there on a stand was a roughly cut, pale-pink crystal, which seemed to have an imperfection inside of it, a teal-coloured metallic sliver, the Eye of Nineveh.

'Take this ring, my son. When the time comes, use it and return glory to our people.'

He reached out and took the iron circlet before he tried to hide the tears building in his eyes.

'I wish I had more time, Ashur-uballit. I could have taught you so much more, been a better father.'

'You were... are the best father I could ever have hoped for.'

'And you the best son.' They embraced one last time before king Sin-shar-ishkun turned to face the Eye of Nineveh. 'Now you must leave, go to Harran reunite with our family.'

The crown prince had barely taken a reluctant step when soldiers of Babylon and Medes appeared at the entrance, breathing heavily from their exertions and covered in Assyrian blood. They smiled viciously with wicked intent on their minds.

Although Sin-shar-ishkun could not see the looks on the faces of his assassins, he could imagine it easily. Just as he could visualise their expressions when he held his arms aloft and recited a prayer in Akkadian.

Flame shot from the Eye of Nineveh, engulfing them in its cleansing fire, leaving nothing behind, not even ash.

'Go now, my son. Run and don't look back, for I am about to unlock the destructive power of the gem.'

With a final goodbye, just as the wall that hid the chamber of the gemstone closed once more, Ashur-uballit began to run. By the time he had reached the surface, chaos had ensued.

He saw madness in the eyes of men. Coalition soldiers once allies, now cutting each other down, maniacal grins plastered across their faces. When there were no opposing army soldiers to attack, they would kill their own. But to Ashur-uballit even more mind bending was the void of complete blackness above the city. It spewed forth more of the cleansing fire he had just seen first-hand, but this was even more devastating.

Rotating columns of fire roamed the streets, anyone that was caught within its flames was reduced to nothing. Fireballs rained down from within the void, exploding on impact. And finally, to complete the destruction, a tidal wave of fire, twelve metres in height rolled through the seven hundred hectares of Nineveh, destroying everything in its wake.

It was a scene that would haunt Ashur-uballit for the rest of his life, the only sane person in a city gone crazy. He had seen a man push his thumbs into the eyes of another before they were both swept up by a flaming column, their flesh melting away, the skin sliding off their bodies, right before his very eyes.

As he watched the destruction, agape, the crown prince collided with a soldier. He picked himself up and carried on, desperate to get beyond the wall before the wave of fire could complete its cleansing.

Ashur-uballit got beyond the wall and escaped to freedom, survived the destruction of Nineveh, but it would be several days before he would find out that during his escape, the ring of Sammu-ramat was gone, and so was his chance of ever returning to, not only, claim the throne of Assyria but also to possess the Eye of Nineveh.

Chapter 1

Mosul, Northern Iraq, 2016

Most people know Mosul as a war-torn city, the battlefield of many conflicts, past and present, dubbed as one of the most dangerous cities in the world. A hub for terrorist activity, a place where kidnappings, assassinations, and roadside bombings are the norm.

And so ends the general public's knowledge of the resilient city, not knowing that it has a long history and was once regarded as the centre of civilisation.

Despite the dangers, it was once the site of the ancient capital of the Assyrian Empire, Nineveh. Some scholars also believed that the Hanging Gardens of Babylon were located here, despite the name, since the fortified city was nestled beside the life-giving Tigris River. One believer of this theory was Natasha Travers.

'What do you have there, Anan?' Natasha asked as she stared wide-eyed at the innocuous piece of material her assistant was dusting off with a small brush.

'I'm not sure, Natasha. I think it's a piece of a jar; see how it curves? And look here,' the Iraqi archaeologist turned the piece over. 'It has some sort of engraving on it, a bit of it anyway.'

Natasha accepted the offered piece of history and scrutinised it. After a moment, a smile appeared on her face. 'It's a fish,' she whispered. 'it's a fish!'

'Are you sure?' Anan questioned, unable to see it.

'Without a doubt,' Natasha replied through a broad grin as she put the artifact down on a piece of paper and proceeded to trace what she believed would have been the rest of the engraving. 'Do you see it now? And for the record, it's not a jar, although I can understand why you'd think that, given that one side is more tarnished than the other, but the dimensions are all wrong.' She proudly pointed out, always happy to share knowledge at a given moment. 'No, this is a piece of a cylinder. A bronze water pipe, I'd say. And the fish must be the insignia of Sammu-ramat.'

'This is it, Natasha!' Anan threw her arms around her. 'You were right about the gardens being here.'

'Yeah.' Natasha couldn't hide her smile, but in her heart, she knew that she would need more than just a fragment. Until she could find more definitive proof, this was all still her unpopular hypothesis.

The Cambridge University graduate had written her thesis about the Hanging Gardens and whether they were in Babylon, or as she believed, Nineveh. Upon obtaining a First in Archaeology and rapidly making waves and discoveries amongst the community, she approached the curator of the British Museum, Dr Robert Jones, encouraged by her university mentor. Dr Jones liked her style, though many didn't, and he backed her on many of her expeditions, including this one, to Iraq. Now she was on the verge of paying him back with the biggest find of both their lives.

'Well, well, well, look at this. Your boyfriend is coming,' Anan teased. 'The perfect time to share your excellent news, don't you think? And share a little something extra with him too,' she winked.

'What are you are talking about?' Natasha asked as she turned and glanced over her shoulder to see the muscled frame of Lucas Redmond striding towards them, his L119A1CQB carbine rifle held across his midriff. She shielded her eyes from the sun. The sweat on the SAS lieutenant's uncovered arms and shaved head accentuated his dark complexion and she couldn't help but give a little smile of admiration, which she quickly hid.

'You see something you like?' Lucas asked with a smile.

Getting a protection detail for the joint excavation venture between the British Museum and the Iraqi Department of Antiquities and Heritage had not been an easy feat. There had been a lot of red tape to negotiate. Some members of parliament were against the whole idea. Pulling troops from the frontline to do shepherding work was deemed a waste of resources in these trying times. Especially for what these MPs thought was nothing but old bricks and a garden that may or may not have existed.

Some of the chosen soldiers had similar sentiments, preferring to stay where the action was. Others were glad for the respite from the hardships of the battlefield. Lucas Redmond began in the first camp, preferring to have stayed in an active role in the war, but once he was on the excavation site, amongst the archaeologists, he quickly changed his mind about the assignment, due in no small part to Natasha Travers.

'What are you two so happy about?' Lucas asked as he cleaned his standard issue wrap-around sunglasses, the perfect tool for hiding his eyes from a crowd that may be hiding an enemy combatant.

'Well? Aren't you going to tell him?' Anan urged, and pushed Natasha into the soldier. She had seen the two of them flirting with one another since day one, but neither of them had taken that decisive step. It was frustrating her. This was a real-life romantic drama. Anan was living vicariously through them, and she was desperate for a happy ever after.

Natasha looked at her in mock surprise. 'Tell him what?'

'Fine! I'll do it myself. She was right, Lucas. She was right all along! This *is* the site of the Hanging Gardens.'

'What? That's amazing, Nat. Now you get to prove all your doubters wrong.'

'Well, it's only a small fragment of what looks like bronze pipe, but the evidence fits. I was actually about to head back to the tent, to get away from the noise, and video call London to let them know about the find, if you'd like to accompany me.'

'No problem. I'll go with you. Just give me a sec.' Lucas used signs to signal his nearby comrade and let him know he would shadow Natasha. Then the pair set off in the direction of the expedition's campsite, towards the south wall of the ancient city.

'Don't forget to show them the other thing we found,' Anan called out.

• • • •

AS THEY WALKED IN THE blazing heat, a group of kids suddenly ran up to them, holding their hands out, asking for alms. Lucas had started moving them along when Natasha suddenly knelt and started handing out money. Some of the girls in the group played with the large, loose curls of her brown hair, the result of her Afro/Latino heritage.

Natasha undid the scrunchy that held her shoulder length hair and let the giggling children play with it a bit more as she smiled up at her protector. After a few moments, she spoke some words in Arabic, which brought groans of disappointment from her little friends, before they waved and ran off.

'You didn't approve of that much, did you?' Natasha asked as she re-tied her hair.

Lucas didn't respond immediately but continued to stoically scan their surroundings. 'There are some organisations out there that use kids like that to get close to targets.'

'They're harmless.'

'And that's why they use them; they avoid suspicion. I'm here to protect you, Nat. But I can't if you're going to be so careless.'

He hadn't spoken to her like that before, and Natasha was about to give him the sharpness of her tongue, but she held back. There had been banter between them for some time now, a little flirtatious remark here and there. But he had never shown concern for her. She nodded slightly and smiled as her cheeks warmed. 'Okay, Lucas. This is your area of expertise. I'll listen to you from here on.'

Lucas cleared his throat as he tried to regain his composure; that wasn't the response he was expecting. 'Well, you just make sure you do,' he replied.

• • • •

AS HE WAITED OUTSIDE the command tent, Lucas wondered if anything could really happen between Natasha and himself. After all, they were from vastly different backgrounds, and he doubted she would still show signs of interest if she knew everything about his past.

There was no point worrying about that now, though. Things were still in the early, fun stages of attraction and he fully intended to explore it a bit more and keep the veil of mystery well and truly up.

Even though Natasha had said it was all right for him to come inside the tent, Lucas had opted to stand guard outside, to give her some privacy whilst she made her report to London, but he might as well not have bothered. Her side of the conversation was so loud that he was sure her colleagues, back at the dig site, could have heard every syllable of her escalating tirade.

Natasha slammed the mobile phone down, and a few moments later, stormed out of the tent in a huff. She paced back and forth, fists clenched, all the while muttering to herself.

'I've heard less course language in the Mess,' commented Lucas with a smirk. 'Is that what they teach at Cambridge University these days?'

'What?' Natasha snapped, then sighed, realising it wasn't Lucas she was mad at. 'How do you know I went to Cambridge? Oh yeah, they gave you a file on me,' she remembered. 'So, what else does it say?'

'Well, your dad is a tax lawyer, by all accounts a particularly good one, cited for a knighthood. Your mother is a top surgeon, originally from Puerto Rico. It also said that you like to dress up like Cleopatra in your spare time and go shopping.'

'What?' She punched Lucas playfully, and he feigned injury. His ploy had worked – she couldn't help but smile. The levity was only a momentary distraction, however. 'They want to pull us out,' Natasha revealed. 'Apparently, they're getting pressure from government; something about wasting time, money, and manpower, i.e., you lot. They want you back on the frontline and they won't let us stay here without a guard.'

'What about the piece of pipe?'

'Too insignificant in size and not definitive proof, either. If I find a piece significant enough, I'll be sure to shove it straight up their –'

'Hey, come on now. You've got plenty of time to find something.'

'I showed them this too,' Natasha said and presented a ring-shaped piece of rock she pulled from her pocket.

'What is it?'

'Who knows? But you can just make out a fish which was the insignia of Sammu-ramat.'

'The Mesopotamian queen?'

'I'm surprised you've heard of her! Yes, the Mesopotamian queen, but they weren't interested. They've given me a week ... tops, to find something significant. They even want me to downsize the excavation now, such is their faith.' Natasha shrugged her shoulders, unable to hide her dismay as she slid her hands into her pockets and began the slow walk back.

'Cheer up, Nat. It's not the end of the world, just the end of this dig.'

'You're right. I love the field work, searching for ancient artefacts, experiencing different cultures. It's an adventure. There are a lot more historic items in the world just waiting to be discovered. If only I could have a business doing just that, life would be perfect.'

'Well,' began Lucas, 'why don't you?'

'Huh?' Natasha scoffed. 'You're kidding, right?'

'Seriously. Why don't you? In fact, why don't *we*? I know a bit about rare items and historical treasures, ancient artifacts—'

'You do?'

'Yeah. My mum was into obtaining and selling items; I learnt a bit from her.'

'Was it a family business?'

'You could say that.'

'Nice. Is she still doing it?'

He looked down briefly. 'She's been gone a long time.'

'Oh, god. I'm so sorry.'

'Don't be. You weren't to know. So, as I said, I know a bit about interesting historical items, but I'm sure you could teach me some of the fundamentals of archaeology and, in return, I can teach you how to use a gun and how to handle yourself.'

'I don't like guns.'

'You don't have to,' Lucas replied as he slipped his rifle over his shoulder and placed it on a nearby crate of artifacts. 'Now, hold your arms like this.'

Lucas demonstrated several wristlocks with Natasha, as well as ways to escape the holds. Natasha had been a bit reluctant, to begin with, but after a few tries, and successes, her interest grew.

This was the closest they had been to each other, in this not so formal way, feeling his hands on her one moment and then his arms wrapped around her the next. Natasha couldn't deny the attraction between them was obvious. She hoped it was his sense of duty that had held Lucas back from making advances. After all, he was meant to be guarding her body and not doing the things that were running through her mind.

'That's great, Nat. Now, I'm going to show you what to do if someone were to grab hold of your hair,' he said as he reached out and took hold of her ponytail. 'It could be a target, especially if you're trying to run away. What you would do is raise your arm that is closest to the one holding you, and bring your elbow down on theirs with as much force as you can –'

'Like this?' Natasha said as she followed through the instruction before Lucas had finished his explanation.

It was an unbalanced mess. She had overcooked her spin, and since he hadn't had time to get a firm grip of her hair, it just slipped out of his hand, meaning that when she brought down her elbow, there was nothing but air. Natasha fell into him, and they crashed to the ground in a heap.

'Not exactly what I had in mind, but I'm not complaining about the result either,' admitted Lucas.

They gazed into each other's eyes expectantly, each waiting for the other to show their intent and make a move. His hands slowly slid down her back as she licked her lips in anticipation. They had both secretly waited for this moment and now it had arrived.

Then the moment was shattered, and all hell broke loose as they heard terrified screams and machine gunfire ring out at the dig site.

Chapter 2

Lucas immediately rolled on top of Natasha to protect her with his own body, if necessary. The gunfire they heard were in short, controlled bursts. He had a suspicion as to what it meant. As he and Natasha were in a prone position, Lucas hoped that they wouldn't be in the line of sight of the assailants, that they would have enough cover to keep their position hidden.

He slowly raised his head and got confirmation of what he already knew in his mind.

'What's happening?' Natasha asked, the panic in her voice unintentionally raised the volume of her query.

Lucas slapped his hand over her mouth and put a finger to his lips. 'Be quiet.' The whisper was harsh, but it got his point across. 'There are four truckloads of masked combatants, heavily armed, mowing down the rest of my team and the Iraqi troops.'

Natasha looked up at him in alarm, her eyes wide with terror. 'What about my group? My assistants?' Her concern was palpable. She had pushed to make this expedition happen. Despite the dangers of the region, she had chased glory and, as team leader, these people's lives were her responsibility.

He stared into her watery gaze and didn't have the heart to tell her they had been cut down, some where they stood, others as they ran. 'I don't know. I only had a quick look.'

'Then we need to go and help them.'

'Not a chance. I need to get you to safety.'

'What?'

'That was the deal the higher-ups made; the Iraqis would look after their people, and we'd look after ours.'

'You have got to be kidding me?' The look she received from Lucas told her he wasn't.

'Now, what we're going to do is stay low, out of their line of sight and head towards the South Gate and make a break for it from there. Have you got that?' When she didn't reply, he repeated the question more firmly.

'Okay, okay, I got it,' she replied, despite still being against the idea. It wouldn't be him that had to deal with the guilt of the consequences. That burden would fall squarely on her shoulders.

'Good. In a moment, I'm going to retrieve my rifle and then we're going to –'

A sudden scream interrupted Lucas. It was a woman's voice, all too familiar to Natasha.

'Anan?' Before she could stop herself, Natasha popped up from behind the crate, shouting and waving her friend to safety. But it was only then that she discovered Anan wasn't alone. She was being chased by one of the gunmen.

The masked man shouted in a language that she surprisingly couldn't place, despite being somewhat of a polyglot. He spoke briefly into a radio, then shouted at the two women again, this time pointing his AK-47 at them threateningly. That's when several bullets from Lucas's rifle thudded into his chest, killing him.

As they embraced, Natasha could feel her friend trembling uncontrollably. Her face was streaked with tears and her voice shrill as she struggled to explain what had happened.

'What do you mean "they want us"?'

'He had a picture of you and me. After they killed the soldiers, they started killing the others when I didn't tell them where you were.'

Lucas searched the dead man's body. He flinched hearing the news that the other members of his team were dead; friends that had become brothers to this only child. He continued his search, looking for clues to find out which terrorist organisation the man was affiliated with. There wasn't much of anything except the fanged snake tattoo on the back of his hand, the tail of which coiled around his arm.

Suddenly, as it sparked into life, a message came over the radio, in the unknown language. When there was no reply, the message repeated. Lucas got to his feet and hurried the two women along. 'They're looking for this guy. They'll come searching any minute. We need to move. *Now*.'

They headed south, as the original plan had been, trying to stay ahead of their enemies and create as much distance between them. It might have worked, save for the fact that the assailants had off-road vehicles, giving them an advantage over the uneven terrain.

As they ran, in the back of his mind, Lucas knew the odds were against them. He also knew that if they carried on together, it wouldn't be long before they were all killed. If it really was Natasha and Anan that they were after, it made sense not to keep them together, and perhaps double their chances of getting to safety.

Bullets whizzed past as the trio reached their target, the southern wall of Nineveh, and took cover in one of the many archways of the ancient, ruined city, Lucas and Anan on one side, Natasha the other.

He returned fire as the enemy combatants pulled up in their vehicles, unable to proceed any further. Lucas kept them pinned behind the opened doors of their off-roader and delivered the news that his companions wouldn't like. 'We need to split up,' he stated.

'Are you crazy?' Natasha shouted over the gunfire.

'Nope. You two are going to get out of here whilst I give you cover.'

She stepped out from her cover, so angry that Lucas would even consider such a thing that she momentarily forgot they were under fire. That was until bullets pinged around her, forcing her back behind the wall. 'We're not leaving you. What happens if you run out of bullets?'

Lucas didn't reply. He took it as a rhetorical question. She knew what would happen as well as he did. 'You'll be long gone by then. Besides, Anan knows this city better than either of us.'

'I know where we can go for help,' answered Anan.

'Good! On the count of three, I'll lay down suppressing fire and the two of you run like hell and don't look back.' With his back pressed against the strut of the arch, Lucas took several deep breaths and steeled himself. If this were indeed the way the Celestial Being intended for him to meet his end, he was going to make sure that he wouldn't be travelling alone, that he'll be taking with him as many of the bastards as he could.

'One ... two ... three!'

Despite the laid-out plan, in just a split second, it had gone to shot. Lucas stepped out from his cover and squeezed the trigger of his rifle. He sprayed the burst of bullets in a wide arc and riddled a terrorist with them as, out of the corner of his eye, he saw Anan take off. Natasha, however, was slow off the mark. As he shouted at her to move, one of the masked men came out from behind the back of the 4x4 holding an M32 grenade launcher, then the distinctive thump, thump, thump sound of it being fired.

The familiar noise fired Lucas into action. As the first grenade exploded against the archway above Natasha, he launched himself at her. The second and third grenades followed almost instantly, bringing the piece of wall that had stood for over two thousand years crashing down. Great plumes of dust billowed into the air.

Anan flinched as she heard the explosions, hesitated momentarily, the temptation to turn back strong within her. But she knew she had to continue, knew that if Natasha and Lucas had somehow survived the collapse of the wall, the only way that she could be of assistance was to bring back help. With tears in her eyes, Anan ran on.

• • • •

NATASHA COUGHED AND spluttered, blinking rapidly. Wherever it was that Natasha found herself, it was pitch black, and she was hurting. Her body ached all over. Her shirt stuck to her in places where she could feel the sting of cuts. To top it all off, she was having difficulty breathing, a heavy weight crushing her chest.

As felt around to blindly check the seriousness of her injuries, Natasha discovered that the weight on top of her was none other than Lucas. Using all her strength, Natasha wriggled out from under him. As she checked on him, how they came to be in this predicament replayed in her mind.

Lucas had just completed his three second count, and she hadn't been able to move. The sounds of the gun battle were deafening, and Natasha had frozen in fear. It wasn't until she had heard Lucas shout at her to move that she regained her senses. But then the explosions came. The next thing she knew, her bodyguard was diving at her, knocking the wind out of her, but in so doing, he had saved her life. However, with much of the strut gone, the ancient wall had collapsed under its own weight. Large chunks of stone had fallen all around the pair and ultimately crashed through the ground, which had covered a hidden door, taking Natasha and Lucas along with it.

'I can't believe this,' Natasha exacerbated. 'This could be the find of the century and I can't see a damn thing.' She looked up at the two or three little slivers of sunlight that squeezed between the piles of rock that had now blocked the once hidden trapdoor. By all accounts, there was no going back.

Suddenly, Natasha felt a short cylindrical shape through one of the many pockets of Lucas's vest. She fished her hand inside and came out with a lifesaver, a flashlight. Clicking it on, Natasha let out a small sigh of relief as the cold, white light shone out of the torch. She wasn't afraid of the dark, not by a long stretch. Natasha had crawled through plenty of small, dark tunnels in her short career as an archaeologist.

But, despite that, it was still a welcome delight to be able to see again.

Using the torch, Natasha could give Lucas a better check-up. Apart from some minor cuts and bruises, he was okay, just unconscious. Seeing him there, knowing what he did, brought a smile to her face and a warmth inside.

After she had made sure Lucas was comfortable, Natasha stood and had a quick look at her surroundings. Her heart pounded, giddy as a child, knowing that she was the first person to have stepped foot here in thousands of years.

There was a passageway, but what the torch illuminated in the chamber drew Natasha's attention. Sealed for so long, the reliefs that adorned the walls were still covered in vivid colours. They depicted scenes of everyday life, people carrying items with the reeded Tigris River as a backdrop. Natasha could almost visualise the ancient Assyrians that did the work down there.

Her mind raced as she thought about the day she would return with a new team, with full government backing, and not what little Robert Jones could muster from the board. He supported her, he always had, invariably coming up trumps more often than not helped matters. But not with everyone within the archaeological community. Some branded her brash and arrogant. She couldn't wait for them to see this little find. 'More than significant, I'd say.' She smirked.

Whatever the chamber was, Natasha knew it wasn't a tomb; there were no declarations of a king or royalty that would normally be found. In fact, there was no cuneiform writing of any kind, which she found rather peculiar since the Assyrians, much like the Egyptians, loved to document their achievements for prosperity.

'Okay, Natasha,' she said to herself, 'we know what it's not. Now let's try to figure out what it is.'

Moving around the twelve-by-twelve-foot chamber, she carefully scrutinised each image under the torch light. 'So, we have all these figures holding things, foods of different kinds, wheat, livestock, bundles of fish, all this except one holding nothing. Maybe then it was some kind of storeroom?' Natasha thought it over as she played with a loose strand of hair, then realised her mistake. 'No, they had granaries for the wheat, they wouldn't store it down here.' She turned around and shone the light on the ragged column of rubble which now blocked their way in, stone from the city wall mixed with the stone of the chamber roof. 'Besides, there's no stairwell or anything. The way we entered this room was not the intentional way. So, it seems that the only way in would be through that passageway, the same way all these people in the carvings are facing.'

Talking out loud, verbalising a problem, always seemed to help her focus when she really needed it. And it did so again. She had concluded that this passageway, judging by its direction, led back towards the centre of Nineveh.

Then the idea formulated further in her mind. 'So, everybody is carrying something except for this one individual. In a period of time when every citizen had to work hard for the greater good, everyone that is, except the king.'

Natasha hurried to Lucas and took another item from his many pockets. A compass. 'If this passage continued to the north of the city,' she mused, 'then perhaps its start began at the North Palace, the royal residence of the last kings of Assyria.' Natasha shone the torchlight on the compass as she turned on the spot, watching the needle intently until it came to a stop. The passage was indeed heading north. 'It has to be a secret escape passage. Ashurbanipal must have had it added when he built the palace, in the event the city was sacked.'

Natasha spun around and rushed to the back wall. She needed to be sure. When she and Lucas fell here, they had been standing to the south of Nineveh. She knew that, if her hypothesise was correct, the passage should continue behind the rocks. She scrambled up the debris, and sure enough, Natasha could just make out the corner of what must have been the continuation of the escape tunnel, leading south beyond the walls of Nineveh, leading the royal family to freedom.

Suddenly, before Natasha celebrate her discovery, she heard muffled shouting from above, the same language she couldn't place before, although the more she thought about it, the more she thought it sounded somewhat Polynesian, but not one she recognised.

Then there was a gunshot, which was shortly followed by the sound of machinery, something akin to a jackhammer. Dust and stone-chipping began to fall, caused by the vibrations from above. The stones themselves were becoming dislodged and one rolled down, narrowly missing Lucas.

The whole makeshift mountain was now dangerously unstable. Natasha leapt down and grabbed Lucas by the shoulders of his vest. As more and more of the boulders rained down, she pulled, but he had some 50lbs of weight on her 145lbs frame, and right now it was a dead weight. Try as she might, she couldn't budge him. But she kept at it, she had to.

She had seen a large, jagged section of wall, teetering on the edge, rocking back and forth with each pounding of the jackhammer above. With all her might and adrenaline pumping through her body, Natasha yelled and leant backwards. Then the jagged piece of Assyrian masonry tumbled towards them.

Chapter 3

The conking sound of rock striking rock grew louder as impending death drew closer. In her haste to get clear, Natasha slipped and lost her footing before she eventually dug her feet in for extra purchase, and with a great heave was able to take several steps back, pulling Lucas out of the way of the huge boulder that crushed the ground where he had laid only moments before.

Exhausted from her efforts, Natasha collapsed to the ground, panting for air, vowing that, as soon she got back home to London, she would sign up to the local gym. As she lay there, looking up at the ceiling, thinking of what would happen after she told Lucas that she saved his life, the collapsed wall and rock that had been blocking the hole was finally cleared.

A masked head came into view. 'Natasha Travers? I am Baron and I believe you have something I want.' Although she couldn't tell, she was sure he was grinning down at her. 'Get the ropes ready,' he said to his men as he retreated from the opening.

Although she had intended to allow Lucas time to regain consciousness on his own, that was a luxury they no longer had. 'Hey,' Natasha yelled at him. But it wasn't until she slapped him that she got a response.

'Stop it. I'm awake, I'm awake,' Lucas said, somewhat groggy. 'What's going on?'

'I'll tell you on the way,' she urged, dragging him to his feet.

'Where are we going?' He shook his head, desperately trying to clear his senses.

'Down there,' Natasha said as she pointed the torch towards the passageway.

The sound of four ropes hitting the ground, lowered from the makeshift hole, compounded her urgency. Then the first of the Baron's men rappelled down, only to be met by bullets from Lucas's Sig Sauer P228 handgun. An AK was blindly fired into the cavern, forcing the pair to take cover.

'Okay, Nat, lead the way, and double time, we're going to have company any second.'

• • • •

DURING ALL HER YEARS at Cambridge, not one of her professors had once told her that there would be days like this out in the field. The days of the great adventurer, Giuseppe Belzoni, one of her inspirations for pursuing this career, dealing with bandits whilst digging up antiquities was supposed to be a thing of the past. Yet here she was, sprinting down an Assyrian passage, dodging bullets. But what annoyed her the most was the fact that she couldn't stop and study her surroundings more.

Not until they came to a crossroads in the tunnel.

'Which way, Nat?' Lucas asked as they hid behind opposite corners. Every now and then he would pop out, let off a couple of rounds, using their own torches as targets, before taking cover once more.

'I don't know?' Natasha admitted, as she swept left and right with the flashlight, desperately looking for some clue to point the way.

'You're going to have to hurry!' The odds were stacking up against Lucas. Staying in one place had allowed additional men to regroup and the extra guns to pin him back.

'Okay, okay!' She didn't like being rushed in ordinary circumstances, but these were anything but ordinary. Natasha let out a groan of frustration. One wall looked just the same as another, nothing indicating which way to go. Then by chance she glanced up, almost as if to ask the heavens for help. And they answered.

'Wait, isn't that Sammu-ramat?'

Lucas, with his back pressed to the wall, replaced the empty cartridge he ejected from his gun, with his last remaining full one. He'd have to make every shot count from here on out.

He looked up at where Natasha shone the beam of light and saw the image of a woman, an arm held aloft, two birds above her head and several fish around her feet.

'Many believed that she was the daughter of Derketo, the goddess of fish, amongst other things. That would explain the fish. The story goes that her mother abandoned Sammu-ramat as a baby and she was fed by doves, hence the birds.'

'Okay,' Lucas started before he paused to reach round the corner and fire two shots. One missed its target, the second, however, struck true. 'I got it. She was a demigoddess. But how does that help us get out of here?'

'If we continue north,' Natasha said, thinking out loud again. 'We should end up where Ashurbanipal's North palace was. There's no guarantee that we'll be able to exit there because it's rubble and we haven't dug deep enough there to reveal anything … '

'Come on! Come on!'

The constant gunfire was making the thought process harder for Natasha. 'Okay. Okay. Just give me a second. This relief of Sammu-ramat must mean something. She's going from west to east … left to right … birds or fish … '

'Which way?' Lucas urged.

'I don't know! You might as well flip a coin.'

'Then flip a damn coin.'

She looked down the left passage, then the right. Then Natasha made her choice and sprinted left. Lucas waited for the moment their assailants reloaded before chasing after her.

· · · ·

IT WASN'T LONG BEFORE the pair saw a large, wooden, double door at the end of the passage, flanked by two huge Lamassu, the protective spirit with the body of a winged bull and a human head, customarily used at entrances of important places.

Natasha looked around in awe. 'This place is very intriguing. You know, there was a professor at Cambridge, who specialised in Mesopotamian history. He always told us that everything that Egypt became was because of The Assyrians. But they weren't really known for hiding away significant structures, tunnelling underground. There was no evidence for it. "Just because it hasn't been found, doesn't mean it doesn't exist" is all he would say.'

'And yet these statues are here, guarding something,' Lucas pointed out.

'Exactly. His contemporaries never believed him. He said that it would be down to students like me, adventurous with plenty of curiosity and a hint of the analytical, to make the discovery.'

'Can't say that I've seen you show any of those attributes,' Lucas joked. 'But we can't dilly dally wondering credibility right now. Those guys won't be far behind us and I'm almost out of ammo, so we need to get through this door ASAP and hope it leads us out of here.'

Natasha agreed, and they both put a shoulder to one of the doors and pushed. Slowly, inch by inch, the door moved. Then bullets struck the statues as the group, known as J, announced their arrival. Lucas unceremoniously shoved Natasha through the gap before struggling through the small space himself.

As Lucas went around the large hall, snapping and distributing glow sticks to give them better light, their reactions to the room couldn't have been more different. Whilst Natasha skipped around, like an excited child, from one golden object to the next, stopping occasionally to admire the glazed reliefs on the walls, Lucas knew they were in trouble. Although he could appreciate all the gold, there was an important fact about the room; they had just entered it through the only door in or out.

Chapter 4

'I don't believe this,' Natasha exclaimed as she circled the statue that stood at the centre of the room. It was of a woman with her hand outstretched over her head with a golden dove resting in it.

'Believe it,' replied Lucas as he heard their pursuers taking up positions outside. 'We're in it deep.'

'No, I'm talking about this,' Natasha corrected him, oblivious to the imminent danger. 'This is a statue of Sammu-ramat. And look at these dishes,' she bent down to pick up some of the contents, 'coins, little cuneiform tablets. They're tributes and prayers. This one, for instance, is asking for her to open the eye and let its gaze lay waste to their enemies. This was a temple to her. A secret underground temple used by the Assyrian royal family! You don't know how important this find is.'

Lucas put his arm around her. 'Yeah, I do, but right now, I think it's more important for us to find a way out of here, so that you get the chance to tell everybody about your discovery.'

Suddenly, there was a shout from outside. 'You can't keep running, Miss Travers. You're outnumbered and your guard will run out of bullets sooner rather than later. All the Baron wants is the artefact. We've checked everything from the dig, he just wants that, and we will let you go.'

Lucas scowled. He wasn't about to fall for that, then whispered to Natasha. 'Do you know what he's talking about?'

'No, not a clue,' she said with a shrug and a shake of her head. She patted herself down, just to be sure, and felt something in her pocket. Inside, she found the stone circle and remembered that after her disappointing phone call to London, she had forgotten to put it back with the other pieces before the chaos descended. 'You don't think they mean this, do you?'

Taking the object, Lucas shrugged, turned it over in his hand and scrutinised it for a bit. He could see nothing special about it, except maybe the short, gear-like teeth on its inside. He yelled back to the man. 'What does this artefact look like?'

'A small stone ring.'

'Yeah, they mean this,' Lucas whispered to Natasha. 'Which also means they can't have it.' Then he addressed their antagonist again. 'Are you sure you looked everywhere? I mean, there's lots of crates. It'd be quite easy for something small to have fallen in between something. Perhaps you should go back and double check. We'll just wait here for you to return. How does that sound?'

There was no answer from the Baron's man.

'I don't think he's a big fan of your idea.'

'No, neither do I. Luckily, thanks to these heavy doors, we're at a stalemate, unless their boss gives them the go ahead to blow them down and storm the place. Until then, we need to figure a way out of this.'

They searched everywhere knowing that, as time ticked by, the slide rule of the impasse was moving further and further away from being in their favour. This sense of urgency, however, didn't stop Natasha from being gentle with the millennia old artefacts. Lucas, however, was slightly less discerning, making the passionate archaeologist cringe every time she heard clattering across the tiled floor.

'This is getting us nowhere,' Natasha said, her optimism waning.

'Yeah, I'm starting to think old Sammu stitched us up.'

Natasha glanced up at the statue of the demigoddess, thinking that maybe Lucas was right. It had been a fifty-fifty chance. This time they picked wrong. But she couldn't bring herself to put that at the feet of a woman from antiquity that she admired. Her name had been tarnished enough by others, as so many strong women in history have been.

During her short rule, she brought stability to the region of Mesopotamia as a military leader and builder. In a time of patriarchal rule, she was celebrated for things ordinarily associated with male rulers, military triumphs, building wonders and ruling with wisdom. And yet, by the Middle Ages, Dante had placed her in the second circle of hell, along with Cleopatra and Helen of Troy, in his divine comedy.

She reached out and touched the statue, as if trying to commune with the legend herself. Natasha stroked the statue's left hand, which was positioned across its torso, and discovered something that felt like grooves on the ring finger of the effigy. On the back of the statue's hand, she felt wedge-shaped indentations, and ducked underneath to have a closer look. 'Cuneiform,' Natasha exclaimed.

'What does it say?'

'Hold on,' she dusted off the ancient writing and began to read. '"*It fastens two people yet touches only one, starts where it ends, yet never ends.*"'

'It's a ring,' Lucas replied instantly.

'What? How...'

'Well, I'm not just a pretty face,' smirked Lucas.

After a moment, Natasha had a revelation. 'No way! Give me the ring, Lucas. I think I found something.'

The SAS Lieutenant placed the artefact in her hand, and she immediately slipped it onto the ring finger of the statue. After a little jiggly about, Natasha was able to slot the ring in position, like a couple of gears.

They both took a step back, but nothing. 'Now what?' Lucas asked.

Natasha shrugged and went back to fiddle with the ring again, making sure it was firmly in position. That's when she found out that the ring could rotate around the finger. As she turned it, there was a click followed by a loud series of clunks, and finally the sound of the back wall of the temple moving aside.

Lucas punched the air. 'Yes! I knew old Sammu wouldn't let us down!' It dawned on him that the members of J, outside the door, had also heard moving machinery, when their next radio calls contained a hint of panic in them. 'I think they may be getting ready to blast their way in,' he said to Natasha, who had already made her way into the new room.

It was filled with all kinds of weapons and armour used by the Assyrians of the time. Shields, swords, spears, helmets. They were stacked up against two walls, surrounding a single pedestal. Laying in front of it was a skeleton, still wearing the armour he wore the day he would have died. On the stand was a roughly cut, pale-pink crystal, which seemed to have an imperfection inside of it, a teal-coloured metallic sliver. At the back was a large stone tablet covered in cuneiform script, which Natasha was reading, despite the dust and cobwebs.

Whilst she did, Lucas took a closer look at the human and noticed something. 'There doesn't seem to be any kind of the injuries on these bones, you know, chips from swords, and the like. I guess he must have been poisoned.'

'Or he locked himself in here to stop this gem from falling into the wrong hands.'

'Why would he do that? Was he a priest?'

Natasha barely heard him as she studied the gemstone, the tablet, and the body. 'We need to get out of here,' she said in hushed tones.

Lucas laughed. 'What do you think I've been trying to do?'

'I'm serious, Lucas. We need to get out, and we need to take this with us. If it is what I think it is, it would explain everything that's happened today.'

'It's a fair size, I'll give you that, but I've seen better looking gems. What's the big deal?'

'That's no priest, Lucas. That's the last king of Assyria, Sin-shar-ishkun. Mesopotamia is known as the cradle of civilisation,' she began. 'Many of the most important developments in human history are said to have started there; the invention of the wheel, the planting of the first cereal crops, irrigation, the development of cursive script, maths, astronomy, the Archimedes screw before. And then, of course, there was the advent of iron. Imagine being the first to develop iron weapons in the Bronze Age.'

'And what's this got to do with that?' Lucas asked, pointing at the gem.

'The thing is, when these advances happened, they literally happened over night. Some people say it was aliens, coming down and bestowing knowledge ... '

'What?'

'... But they're not far wrong. That green stone inside is a piece of –'

'Your time is up, Miss Travers! It didn't have to be like this, but you made your choice. The Baron has told us to take what we want by force! And we will!'

'Okay, Nat,' Lucas slammed his cartridge with his last remaining bullets back into his gun. He had popped it out to see how many bullets he had left, and he wasn't encouraged by what he saw. 'Things are about to get hairy. We might have to put some of this gear to the use.' He grabbed a javelin and tested its balance.

'I've got a crazy idea.'

'I'm listening. Right now I think I'd take crazy.'

'According to the tablet, this is The Eye of Nineveh and if it really is the source of the Assyrians' rise to power, it could protect us.'

Lucas looked quizzical. 'Protect us how?'

Natasha shrugged. 'I don't know. It does mention something about being impervious, though. The piece of stone inside of it is supposed to be Chintamani stone, which is purported to be from a meteor that landed on Earth thousands of years ago and could bestow immortality, amongst other things.'

Lucas rubbed his brow in disbelief. 'This isn't a crazy idea! Getting married at first sight is a crazy idea. *This* is completely nuts.'

'Well, yeah! No need to tell me that!'

'If we do get out of this alive, you and I are setting up that business.'

'Damn! If we get out of this alive, Lucas, I'll marry you.'

'Well, you'd better put this on,' he said and took off his bullet-proof vest and fastened it on her.

Natasha grabbed the eye and read aloud one of the cuneiform prayers from the large tablet. As she did, the stone inside the gem emitted a green glow. It caught Lucas's eye as he reached out and took a convex shield, an Assyrian design that the Romans would later adapt, intent on putting it to good use.

Just then, an explosion blew one of the heavy doors off its hinges and the final group of Natasha and Lucas's pursuers charged in. The first was taken out as the SAS Lieutenant emptied his clip. Another was almost taken out when a javelin narrowly missed his head.

'When I say run, you run! Stay behind me and stay close!' Lucas said to Natasha as he picked up and threw another two javelins. One of the assailants screamed as the projectile impaled his leg, whilst his comrades momentarily took cover to avoid the other one. 'Now!'

They took off! Lucas held up the shield and ran straight for the two men that stepped out from their protection. They didn't have enough time to pull the triggers of their guns they had raised before they were steamrolled over.

The pair charged out of the secret temple with bullets pinging all around them on. They headed straight across for the opposite passage. Almost immediately, there was a sudden decline, which caused Lucas to stumble and Natasha to crash into the back of him. They both fell onto the shield, and it flew down the ever-steepening slope, leaving their enemies behind, but not knowing where they were being taken.

The speeds they reached was immense and before they knew it, they were coming up to what looked like a dead end. 'Damn!' They both let out the prolonged scream as they smashed through the roots that had grown across exit and flew through the air. Neither of them able to hold on any longer as Lucas, Natasha and the shield splashed heavily into the Tigris River.

When Lucas surfaced, there was no sign of Natasha anywhere. He called her name several times and was thinking that maybe she got caught in the fast underwater current of the river or, worse yet, come upon by one of the crocodiles that frequent the area.

Lucas had just started to swim towards the west bank of the Tigris when something caught his leg. He flipped around, knife in hand, only to see the Eye of Nineveh break the surface clasped by Natasha.

'I dropped it,' she grinned.

To say he was ecstatic to see her unharmed would have been an understatement, so he pulled her towards him and kissed her deeply, in the hopes that his actions would get his emotions across louder and clearer than any words he could have used.

She beamed, her cheeks glowing. 'Well,' Natasha began after taking a few moments to regaining her breath, more from the knee weakening kiss than the swim. 'We got out alive, so I guess we'll be going into business together.'

Lucas smirked. 'Yup, I guess The Acquirers are opening for business, Mrs Redmond.'

'What? I may have said that I'd marry you, but at which point did I say I'd be taking your name?'

Lucas leaned in and they kissed again.

'Fine! Natasha Travers-Redmond is all you're getting.'

He smiled contently. 'I can live with that.'

As they gently floated along, their arms wrapped around each other, Natasha's head resting on Lucas's chest, she sighed, happy to appreciate the calm, tranquil and somewhat romantic setting they now found themselves, especially after all the madness they had just been through. She had never felt such security before. 'Do you know that, according to the bible, the Tigris is one of the four rivers that flowed from Eden?' Natasha said with a soft voice, her eyes closed, as she enjoyed the scene..

'Do you know the Tigris has crocodiles?'

She thought for a moment. 'Perhaps we should get out,' Natasha said before swimming briskly to the shore.

Chapter 5

Present day.

Dr Robert Jones, a well-respected curator of the British Museum, smiled broadly as he continued with his routine pre-opening checks. Ever since he took the position, many moons ago, he had always taken it upon himself to ensure that the museum was in its best possible shape before it opened to the public. This was a position of pride for him, as a lover of history as well as a patriot. He wanted every person who walked up the steps and into the Great Court of the Grade I listed building, be they staycation tourists or from further afield, to leave with the same impressions; that the British Museum was not just one of the best places to visit in the United Kingdom, but one of the best in the world.

As always, he had started his check at the top, beginning in the Japan Galleries, working his way through the past of different cultures, Ancient Greece and Rome to Ancient Egypt, Asia to the Middle East.

It was as he walked through Room 6, where some of the museum's Assyrian sculptures were on display, that the curator put on his biggest smile. He patted the muscular legs of one of the two colossal, winged human-headed lamassu, as if it were the real leg of a powerful lion. Before him were the enormous Balawat gates. Although they were reconstructions, at 6.8 metres high, they were no less impressive. The originals had been made from cedar and had rotted away long before they were discovered in the late nineteenth century by Hormuzd Rassam, the first Assyrian archaeologist.

Seeing the large wooden doors, Dr Jones reminisced about the first time he had seen them as a child. The bands of bronze that were mounted on them, eight on each door, were embossed with scenes of warfare and hunting, giving people today an insight into a long-gone civilisation. Gazing at them as an eight-year-old boy, he had been fascinated by the images of chariots bearing archers, of Assyrians attacking a city and ultimately receiving tribute from the defeated. It was almost as if he were reading an adventure novel. It was the moment he fell in love with history and archaeology.

And one thing that was true about the world of archaeology was that there was always something else to find.

The gates may have been his favourite piece amongst all the collections of the British Museum for a long time. But that all changed the day an upstart young girl, fresh out of Cambridge University, with a recommendation from his good friend, Marcus Madison, came to him with a passionate story about the Hanging Garden of Babylon not being in Babylon at all. He had listened to her impassioned tale; her zeal had reminded him of his own at that age. Giving her an audience was the wisest decision he had ever made.

Although Natasha Travers hadn't yet proven definitively that the Hanging Gardens were actually in Nineveh, she had found some very compelling pieces to suggest that further excavation was necessary. What she did discover, however, was a find so important that it was on par with the discoveries of Howard Carter and Tutankhamun and

Pierre-François Bouchard finding the Rosetta Stone. Even though the secret temple of Sammu-ramat, wasn't as gold laden as the tomb of Tutankhamun and it didn't decipher a long-lost language, it held something believed to have caused the uprising of a civilisation and an empire, the Eye of Nineveh.

As the excavation, at the time, had been a joint venture between the Iraqi Museum and the British Museum, there had been a lot of disputes as to who the artefact belonged to. The arrangement that was finally agreed upon was for each museum to hold the eye for five years, before passing it to the other. It had been five years since the agreement and the gemstone was on British soil for the first time.

There had been a private unveiling to VIPs, and it had gone well. Today was the first day that it would be shown to the public, and Robert Jones couldn't wait for them to see the special exhibit.

'Good morning, Dr Jones,' a cashier said as she opened the museum shop.

'Good morning, Alison,' he sang with a gleam in his eyes. 'And what a wonderful morning it is.' There was still some fifteen minutes before the heavy doors of the museum would be opened for the day, and Robert Jones had one last stop to make to inspect the new Eye of Nineveh exhibition.

On his way to room 30, at the back of the ground floor, where all the temporary paid exhibits were held, Robert Jones's phone binged. Someone must have been trying to get hold of me whilst I was downstairs, he thought. He listened to the voicemail and heard the agitated voice of Marcus Madison.

'Damn it, Robert. You and your damned slow checks. Um, fine. I wanted to tell you I must go. I'm being followed. I have to disappear, but, ah, I had to say sorry to you. I, ah, know how important this thing was going to be for you, but I had to do it. I couldn't let them have it. Um, maybe we'll see each other again, old friend. Oh, and for god's sake, don't tell Natasha. Oh, Christ! They've found me!'

Robert looked at his phone as the voicemail became a dial tone. 'What the hell was that all about?' He listened to the message two more times. Although he and Marcus had the kind of friendship where they were forever pulling pranks on each other, even at their age, Robert felt that this time was somewhat different; it sounded genuine, unless his friend had become an Oscar-winning actor overnight. The concerned curator tried to call Marcus back a few times, remembering that even when he had seen him the night before, he seemed a bit off. After getting no answer each time, Robert slipped his mobile phone back into his inside pocket, intent on trying to get hold of his friend again later, before continuing on his way.

The long hall room was atmospherically lit, with spotlights highlighting particular pieces. On display were a vast array of items found by the team, but it was the artefacts found by Natasha in the secret temple, which took pride of place. Weapons and equipment had been brought, as well as the prayer tablets and coins.

And on a shiny black Dias, at the back of the hall, the main piece of the exhibit, the Eye of Nineveh. Or that's where it should have been, but the mystical gemstone was gone.

. . . .

NATASHA THREW DOWN her sports bag on the bench in the women's changing room of Haven Sports Club in Covent Garden and sat in a huff next to it. Jennifer Moore, Natasha's university friend and lawyer, finished their weekly squash match, showered and dressed before a bombshell was dropped.

'You have got to be kidding me,' Natasha yelled, startling the other women that occupied the facility. 'You told him the offer, right, Jenny?'

'Of course I did,' she replied as she put on her lipstick before they made for the exit of the club. 'Exactly as we discussed. He gets everything, except the business.'

'And he wouldn't accept?' Natasha thought it was a great deal. They both loved their place in St Katherine's dock, as well as the duplex in Port Saplaya, Valencia. She was certain he'd go for it, but she should have known better, after all, Lucas had developed a knack of disappointing her.

'Nope. His lawyer actually came back with a counteroffer.'

'Which was?'

'He gets The Acquirers, and you get everything else. He says it was his idea.'

'Okay, maybe it was, but I've put in just as much into the business as he has.'

'Well, according to his lawyer, Lucas has brought in ten times the amount of revenue as you have.'

Natasha put her hands on her hips 'What? That's bull!.

Jenny shrugged and lit a cigarette. 'He seemed pretty convinced. I assume you won't be taking the offer?' Natasha shook her head and her friend continued. 'Well, if the two of you can't come to some arrangement, why don't you just stay business partners? That's surely better than the company going into dissolution. Just saying.'

The lawyer flagged a taxi for them and just as Natasha was about to enter, she paused as someone she knew exited an exclusive bar further down the road. 'You take it Jen; I've just seen my dad. I'll speak to you later.'

'Okay, but just you think about what I said.'

Natasha nodded as she shut the door and waved her friend off. As she walked towards her father, she found herself admiring the man in his company. She wouldn't claim to know all her dad's clients, and if the man was indeed one of his patrons, he was by far the most stylish one she'd seen. He wore a single buttoned grey suit, judging by the way it showed off his shape. It was probably tailor-made. He completed the look with a purple tie. The way he carried himself exuded confidence, and that self-assuredness was topped off by the fresh and energising scent of his aftershave, which she breathed deeply, before she even realised she'd done it.

'Natasha? What are you doing here?' her father asked.

'Is this one of your ploys, John?' The man pushed his glasses up the bridge of his nose and smiled at the new company. 'I tell you I was invited to the British Museum last night to see the Eye of Nineveh and the person who found it, your daughter, just happens to turn up here. John, I told you, you already have my business.'

'I can assure you that my father had no idea that I'd be here today.' Natasha smiled.

'Peter Armitage, this is my daughter, Dr Natasha Travers,' John Travers said, standing tall with his chest puffed out.

'I was just telling your father that I was a bit of an amateur collector of antiques myself,' Peter said as he shook hands with Natasha. 'You have such incredibly soft hands for someone who plays in the dirt.'

'I moisturise,' came her reply as they locked eyes. 'So, what kind of a collection do you have?'

'Why don't you save that for later. I've invited Peter to dinner. You can make it right, Natasha?'

She had planned on just vegging out in front of the TV in her comfy sweats with a tub of ice cream, but the prospect of spending the evening getting to know Peter was hard to refuse. Natasha nodded and smiled. 'Of course I can make it!'

Suddenly, Dua Lipa's *Break My Heart* played, and Natasha could feel her cheeks warming as she answered her mobile phone. 'Hello? Whoa, slow down Robert, breathe. No, why would I know where that idiot is? What? Why would they want to speak to us? What about the eye? Stolen? You're kidding me. How is that even possible?'

Chapter 6

The morning sun streamed through the floor-to-ceiling windows of Lucas's apartment in Chelsea Harbour. He squinted at the beams of light before he pulled the bedsheet over his head to shield his eyes; he wasn't ready to get up just yet.

His action had wafted the scent of Cartier around his head. It was the favourite perfume of the woman that, at that moment, was showering in the en-suite. The thought of joining her in the walk-in cubicle flashed through his mind, but just as it did, the shower was switched off and moments later, a tall woman with an athletic build stepped out with a towel on her head and nothing else but a few droplets of water. She had a sleek, catlike walk which drew the eye. It was that walk that hooked Lucas when he had seen her at the Fox and Bear bar.

'Now, that's a view worth getting out of bed for,' Lucas said with his head slightly tilted to the side.

'Is it a view worth making breakfast for?' she asked in her slight Australian lilt and unwrapped her waist-length hair.

'What was that?' Lucas mocked. '"Making breakfast"? I don't understand that term, Chiara. This is the age of delivery, love.'

'Then maybe you can deliver yourself another woman to share your bed with tonight.'

'Well, since you mention it ... ' Chiara's wet towel hit Lucas's head with some force, making him laugh. 'Come on,

I was only joking. Of course I'll make you breakfast; you know I'm the king of scrambled eggs.'

'That's why I asked. You know how much I love them,' she said and blew him a kiss. A little ego stroking was a small price for the fluffiest, buttery eggs she'd ever eaten, something he'd picked up from his time in the military. 'Your phone has been ringing like crazy, by the way.'

'Probably Natasha having a go at me for not accepting her offer and giving her The Acquirers.' Sure enough, there were a couple of calls and messages from his estranged wife, but curiously, there were several voicemails from Robert Jones. As Lucas listened to each message, his demeanour progressively turned to one of concern, until he jumped up and hurriedly got ready to leave. 'We're going to have to take a rain check on breakfast, hon. I've got to go.'

'Something wrong?'

'Sounds like there's a problem at the museum.'

'Well, hurry up and I'll drop you on my way to work.'

· · · ·

A CROWD, MADE UP OF people who had planned a visit, as well as those that had been passing by when they saw the police activity, was growing outside the museum gates.

Luckily, Natasha had been nearby when she received the call from Dr Jones, and had arrived before the police to lend support to her friend and help in police enquiries. They had responded quickly to the curator's call, having a theft from a London museum wasn't an everyday occurrence, and having that crime happen at the world-famous venue was bound to attract significant international press attention the moment the news was officially released. Under that kind of spotlight, the police commissioner needed this to go without a hitch, so she made sure to put one of their best on the case, Detective Jake Russell.

They called him "The Terrier" due to his tenacious attitude in not letting his quarry escape, and he was already on the hunt. As soon as he had arrived at the scene, he set up interviews for all the employees that were there, whilst he examined the CCTV. When the detective returned from viewing the footage, his questioning became more focussed and decisive.

'Where is Lucas Redmond?' The detective spoke in a firm voice, standing in a wide, open stance with his hands behind his back.

'How should I know?' Natasha replied, unfazed by the detective's intimidation.

His eyes were unwavering. 'Well, you're married to him, are you not?'

She folded her arms across her chest and stared at him with narrowed eyes. 'We're getting a divorce, actually.'

'Sorry to hear that. May I ask why?'

'No, you may not,' she responded bluntly. 'I don't see what that has to do with what's happened here. Do you?'

He dismissed question and continued with his inquiry unabated. 'What do you know about his parents?'

At that moment, a constable came up to them. He made a point of turning his back on Natasha and Dr Jones and whispered in the detective's ear and then returned to his position outside.

'Okay, bring him in,' the detective said to the officer, before turning his attention back to Natasha and the doctor. 'It would seem as though we can call off the search for your husband, Mrs Travers-Redmond. He is outside.'

Natasha rolled her eyes upon hearing the news whilst Detective Russell smiled broadly like the cat that got the cream, before turning on his heel and, with a direct stride, headed off to converse with a group of officers.

'I have to warn Lucas,' she said to the doctor as soon as no one could overhear.

'Warn him about what?'

'I don't know, but this Russell guy seems to think that he has something on him.'

'And why do you care?'

'I don't.'

Doctor Jones creased his eyebrows, noting the complete lack of enthusiasm in Natasha's tone. She in turn opened and closed her mouth, struggling to find the words to explain why she wanted to help the man that had broken her heart, so she left and walked towards the museum entrance.

A red Audi R8 Quattro coupe had pulled up outside the British Museum. The car's roof was down, showing off the palomino brown leather seats and interior that surrounded its occupants.

'Thanks babe,' Lucas said, leaning over to kiss Chiara. 'Judging by all the police presence, I guess this is something serious after all.'

'You sure you should be going in there? It could be a bomb scare.'

'The doc is a friend. If I can help, then I will.'

'Just be careful, okay? Shall I come over tonight?'

Before Lucas had the chance to reply, he heard a familiar voice in a familiar, if barely controlled tone, behind him.

'What the hell is wrong with you, Lucas?' Natasha said.

'Look, Nat, I'm not giving up my half of the business, so you have to either give up yours or just get over the fact that you'll still have me in your life.'

'What? You insufferable ... ' she swallowed the last word. 'I'm not talking about that. Didn't you listen to your messages? Robert said he left you a voicemail telling you that the police asked about us.'

'So? I haven't done anything. Have you?'

'Don't be ridiculous.'

'Then we have nothing to hide.'

'This Detective Russell certainly thinks you have. When he questioned me, he brought up your parents.'

'Really? That's interesting,' Lucas responded. His voice was even as he looked off into the distance. The thoughts percolating in his mind were only interrupted when he heard Chiara telling him to call her later before she drove off, at which point a police constable accompanied Natasha and Lucas to the Great Court.

'New flavour of the month? She Australian?'

'What? Oh, her. Yeah. We met at Dré's place.'

'No prospects of a long-term thing then?'

'What's it to you? You looking to give us a second go?'

Natasha recoiled and wrinkled her nose. 'You must be joking. Been there, done that, got the T-shirt to prove it.'

'Then why does it matter if it's long-term or not?'

'It doesn't. At least I don't have to worry about finding another woman's hair and makeup on my pillow,' she stated in a matter-of-fact tone.

'My mind wasn't in the right place when that happened.'

'And why wasn't it? You never did tell me why you did it. I know it had something to do with that letter you got; you changed after you read it. And you didn't even tell me what was in it.'

Lucas played with the wedding band he still wore. It had become his tic, a quirky trait, just like Natasha, when she was in deep thought, played with her hair. He never had the habit before he got with her, such was the influence they had on each other. 'You're right, you should know what was in that letter.' He paused a moment as he looked for the words. 'It was about my parents —'

'Mr Redmond? I'm Detective Russell,' he injected as he approached the pair. 'I'm so glad you're here. You've saved us the time and trouble of having to track you down.'

'Why would you have to track me down? Just pick up a phone and dial.'

'I have some questions for you, that's all, Mr Redmond.'

'Actually,' a man in a slick blue suit and red tie suddenly said. 'I have some questions too.'

'And who might you be?' the detective asked. The man handed him his card in response. 'Kallum Taylor. Insurance investigator?'

'From Barrington's?' Dr Jones asked. 'That was quick!'

'Well, as I'm sure you can understand,' Kallum began, taking off his sunglasses and putting them in his breast pocket, 'this is a very delicate situation, on an international scale, so our response was expedited. Being the insurers of such a remarkable artefact, obviously for Barrington's, a rapid conclusion would be most welcome, so let's not waste any more time, Detective. Lucas Redmond, can you tell us why you stole the Eye of Nineveh?'

'That's one hell of an accusation to bandy about for someone that just got here and without a shred of evidence,' Natasha stated. She'd been around her lawyer friend, Jenny Moore, long enough at university to have picked up a few things.

'I tend to be of the same opinion,' the Detective revealed, 'and I've seen evidence. Well, Mr Redmond, are you going to answer the question?'

'I won't even waste my time.'

'Perhaps you would like to see the CCTV footage before you make any further comments?'

'You're being serious?' Doctor Jones suddenly asked with surprise. 'I thought you were playing some sort of joke. These allegations don't make an ounce of sense. You do know that it was these two that found the eye in the first place, right?'

'And you do know how many millions that gem was insured for? It would make the Frankfurt art heist pay-out look like a drop in the ocean.'

'What Frankfurt art heist?' Natasha asked.

'Back in 1994, the Tate Gallery loaned two Turner paintings to the Kunsthalle Schirn in Frankfurt,' explained Lucas. 'They were stolen, and the Tate was paid something in the region of £26 million by insurers for the theft. They paid some of that back to ensure that Tate retained title of ownership in the paintings if they ever resurfaced. They did and the Tate paid to get them back. So, the Tate Gallery not only got their paintings, but they also ended up being around £16 million in the black.'

'Trust you to know the story,' Kallum said.

'I read.'

'Or perhaps it's because your mother was implicated as the mastermind behind it all?'

'Implication isn't proof of guilt.'

Lucas and Kallum glared at each other, neither one of them willing to concede to the other and avert their eyes.

Dr Jones was aghast. 'Are you implying that the British Museum is behind this robbery? For the insurance pay-out?'

'£100 million is one hell of a chunk of dough,' replied the investigator as he turned to face the curator.

The doctor drew himself up in an erect posture, and with a tight jaw, replied, 'And my integrity is worth a hundred times more.'

'Calm down, doctor, I'm just putting it out there, that's all. You being friends with someone that has a history and thievery in their blood kind of sets off alarm bells.'

'What are you talking about? Lucas's mother was an antiques dealer, buying and selling.'

'Selling, yes. Buying? Now, that claim is a bit of a stretch, isn't it Lucas?'

Lucas took a determined step towards Kallum, who didn't back away. Detective Russell insinuated himself between them so things wouldn't get physical, but he was still being pushed back by the powerful physique of the former SAS soldier.

'Why don't I show you what we got before you make things worse for yourself, son?' The detective led the way to the security room, where he asked the guard there to play the CCTV footage from the previous night. 'This is right at the beginning when everybody is taking their seats.'

Sure enough, on the screen was the palm-sized Eye of Nineveh, perched on a replica stand of the original one found in the Sammu-ramat temple. Arranged in a circle around the artefact were four rows of seats that were filling up with VIPs. Natasha recognised Peter Armitage as he sat in one of the front seats, next to a man in tinted glasses, and there was Lucas, with Chiara, one of the last to take their seat in a back row. She rolled her eyes, seeing them together. Then she saw one last guest arrive.

'Marcus?' Natasha couldn't believe that she hadn't known he was there. 'Why didn't he come and say hello?'

'No idea, and when he phoned this morning, he sounded really strange. Seemed to think he was being followed.'

Now that Dr Jones said it, Natasha did think he looked a little jumpy on the screen. The detective and the inspector paid no attention to the old man as they continued to focus on Lucas.

'Ah, here we go,' Jake Russell said as, on the monitor, Lucas and Chiara were seen whispering before leaving, during Natasha's recount of the expedition, which drew an icy stare from her. 'Would you mind telling me where you went, Mr Redmond?'

'Well we,' he saw his estranged wife's glare and felt a little uneasy. 'We, uh, went to stretch our legs.'

'And you just so happened to be heading toward this very room,' the detective said after having the security guard punch up the camera feed. 'You didn't come in here, did you? Maybe set a timer to shut off the camera?'

'No, I didn't, and this direction also just happens to take you to the toilets, which is where we went to ... '

The room fell silent for a moment as Lucas's revelation sunk in.

'Okay,' Detective Russell cut through the awkwardness. 'Let's forward it to 23:26. Now, everything is winding down. Everybody has had their fill of the free food and alcohol. People are getting a last look at the remarkable gem before they leave.

That's when both Natasha and Lucas saw different things in the same frame on the CCTV. What she noticed was the fact that Marcus Masterson looked terrified. As the crowd dwindled, he hovered in front of the eye for a few moments, before the blood seemed to drain from his face and he exited to the right, the opposite direction of everybody else.

What happened next caught Lucas' eye. The man in the tinted glasses followed right, at a determined pace, and as he adjusted his suit, the former elite soldier glimpsed what looked like a familiar tattoo.

'Stop. Replay that,' Lucas blurted out.

'No,' Detective Russell ordered. 'Forward it to 23:48. Now, Mr Redmond, can you tell me why, several minutes after everyone had left, you returned?' On the video, Lucas was there standing in front of the gem. Then the video feed cut off.

'Where's the rest of it?' Lucas asked.

'That's all that's left on the recording. The rest has been conveniently erased.'

'Not for me, or else you would have seen me return to my seat and search for Chiara's missing earring.'

'A likely story,' Kallum scoffed.

'At this time, Mr Lucas Redmond, I'd like to take you down to the station for further questioning.'

'You're arresting me?'

'If you want me too.'

'Fine, let me just speak to my wife first.' Lucas leaned close to Natasha and whispered in her ear. 'You need to get a copy of that recording to Ellen. Look at the man in the glasses, try to get her to enhance the image of his hand. I'm not completely sure, but I think our old friends from Mosul may have returned.'

Chapter 7

Natasha ran her hands through her hair, holding it back a moment before releasing the natural curls as she let out a huff. She didn't know what the police were thinking. It was as if they wanted to pin the theft on anyone, regardless of how circumstantial the evidence was, just because it was a high-profile case.

Lucas didn't deserve to be the scapegoat.

Despite the way things between them had deteriorated in the last year, the previous five had been nothing short of blissful. Although some people, her dad mainly, were a little surprised at how swiftly things progressed with them, Natasha always stated that falling in love in times of crisis didn't mean it wasn't real love.

She and Robert Jones looked on as Detective Russell led Lucas Redmond away. Despite his flaws, when he turned back and winked, she felt herself get warmer as her body temperature rose. Then he was ushered into the back of the police car and driven off.

'What was that?' Natasha asked as she suddenly realised that Dr Jones had been talking to her.

'I said, this whole thing is ridiculous. Lucas is no more guilty of the theft than either of us. And for that insurance investigator to suggest that I played any part in this heist is simply outrageous.'

'Where is he anyway?'

The curator looked around, trying to spot Kallum Taylor but shrugged when he couldn't see him anywhere. 'He's probably off reporting to Barrington's. I have a good mind to put in a complaint about him.'

'Before you do, I'd like a copy of that CCTV footage; there's something on there. I'd like to take another look at.'

'The police took that as evidence, but the system makes two recordings. Wait here, I'll be right back.'

As Robert Jones re-entered the British Museum to retrieve the security recording for Natasha, she took out her mobile phone and made a call. 'Hi, Jenny. I need you to do me a favour.'

• • • •

IN WEST SILVERTOWN, on the south side of Royal Victoria docks in London, stood the Millennium Mills flour mill. It had a turbulent, relatively short existence since it was built in 1905. It was destroyed in 1917 when a neighbouring munitions factory, a supplier for Britain's WWI effort, exploded, flattening 900 homes, factories, and warehouses, killing 73 people. The death toll would have been much higher if it had happened during working hours.

The art déco building was rebuilt only to be a casualty of war once again when it suffered severe damage during The Blitz, when the German Luftwaffe targeted the East End of London.

The mill was in steep decline during the eighties and finally closed down in 1992. Abandoned and derelict, the graded, ten storey building dominated the local landscape and had been the subject of many redevelopment proposals, but with no progress made, a private buyer appeared and offered the council more money than the previous developers, and more on top of that when the council wanted to know what they intended for the site.

Natasha stepped out of her Range Rover Evoque and checked the GPS on her mobile phone several times to make sure she was at the right address. She stood on the spot and rotated in a circle until the blue cone indicated the direction she was facing, and sure enough, it pointed towards the building with the smashed windows and security fencing surrounding it. Her eyebrows raised involuntarily. 'You have got to be kidding me.'

Natasha had never met Ellen; she was a contact of Lucas's who preferred to stay unseen. As far as she knew, Lucas was her only true friend. By his accounts, she wasn't short of a penny either, so to think that this was where she lived was a bit of a shock, unless you wanted to be off the grid.

Her talents were in high demand, he had told Natasha, mostly by people in certain undesirable circles, but not exclusively; if you had the money, you could hire Ellen. She was a free agent, which made her the kind of person who all intelligence agencies both feared and respected in equal measure, for the simple fact that she had no allegiance to any government or cause, beholden to no one but herself.

Ellen was only loyal to Lucas. The few times Natasha had heard him on the phone to Ellen, he had called her maestro. He explained it was because she could make computers sing and perform like no one else. Ellen was a computer genius.

With her hands on her hips, Natasha looked up and down the length and height of the security fencing. 'Now how am I supposed to get into this place?'

'Why would you want to? Does it look inviting?'

Natasha jumped at the electronic voice. But it did make a valid point. The site was anything but welcoming. In random spots across the courtyard, tall weeds had sprouted between the cracks of the paving stones, as nature tried to reclaim the space. 'Not particularly,' she replied, not knowing where the voice had come from. 'My name is Nata —'

'I know who you are, Natasha Travers-Redmond. Soon to revert to plain Natasha Travers, thankfully.'

'I don't want to be here anymore than you want me to be here, but Lucas sent me to give you this,' she held up the flash-drive, assuming that Ellen could see as well as hear her. 'He wants you to enhance an image.'

'Why didn't he come himself?' Ellen asked.

'The police have him. They think he stole the Eye of Nineveh, but I've sent my lawyer to get him out.'

There was silence, then a thunk as the powerful magnet that held the gate closed was released, allowing a cautious Natasha to push it open and enter.

* * * *

ONCE NATASHA HAD ENTERED the old mill, she was confronted by the smell of bird droppings and the sight of feathers blowing around, with graffiti covering every bit of the huge space. The only way up seemed to be a narrow staircase she thought looked so precarious that it might well collapse if she so much as breathed on it. It was like she had stepped into a dystopian reality. Natasha looked around, half expecting a gang from Mad Max to jump out at any moment.

'Now, turn left and walk towards the wall,' Ellen said over the PA system she had installed throughout the structure.

It was the end of the building that Natasha had initially thought was a bit strange when she had seen it from the outside. Every window of the derelict old mill had been smashed, but this one solitary section of the edifice had no windows. It had the frames where glass was meant to go, but there was nothing there but plastered over brick.

She came to a stop in front of the wall, heavily graffitied like all the rest, but in a different style. It had what was commonly known as a magic eye painting, a random dot autosterogram, a visual illusion that revealed a three-dimensional image within a two-dimensional painting. Natasha stared at it. A smile was just beginning to spread on her face as the image of a dolphin breaking the water came into view.

Then the picture split apart, down the middle, until it was revealed that the wall was hiding a lift; the whole west section, which had no visible windows, was in fact, a lift shaft calling at all ten storeys of the Millennium Mills.

If the ground floor had looked dystopian, then the level the lift finally came to a stop at was nothing less than sci-fi. Large monitors displayed various areas of and around the building. Both long walls of windows, which ran the floor's length, were blocked off from the main floor with a false corridor. On that were attached ultra-thin OLED monitors which displayed what would have been seen from those windows.

'That's the feed from the cameras outside by the windows,' Ellen explained from behind a rather impressive desktop setup.

'So you still have a room with a view,' replied Natasha. She was a bit taken aback. She never expected the person who Lucas spoke so highly of to be so young. The girl looked as though she was barely out of her teens, no more than twenty-one.

'A better view.' She went on to display the powerful zoom capabilities the cameras had. 'The flash drive?'

Natasha tossed it over and Ellen slipped it into place.

'Do you know the time stamp?'

'It's around 23:26. Will this take long?' Natasha gazed around at all the electronic components and equipment. She wasn't a tech genius, by any stretch of the imagination, but neither was Natasha a technophobe, so she had a begrudging respect for the setup, despite Ellen's veiled hostility towards her.

'That all depends on whose definition of long you're using as a frame of reference. If it's mine, then I'd tell you I'm done.'

'Really?'

'Take a look yourself.'

Natasha walked around the desk and looked at the screens. It was what she had seen at the British Museum, but a much sharper, clearer picture. 'Wow, that was quick!'

'I'm good at what I do,' Ellen said with a shrug. 'Now what is it you want me to enhance.'

'It's coming up. He was following my university professor.' They watched on until Natasha said stop and pointed out what she wanted enhanced and with a tight zoom. They had reached the spot where the man in the tinted glasses adjusted the cuffs of his suit, revealing the fanged snake head tattoo on the back of his hand. 'Damn! Lucas was right, it is the same people that ambushed us in Nineveh.'

Ellen sat up in her chair. 'The ones that killed the rest of Lucas's CP team?'

'Yeah. They all but executed the Close Protection team, the Iraqi military, and people I worked with. They were led by someone called ... what was his name?' It came to her, after a few moments, like a lightning bolt. 'Ah yes! He said his name was The Baron.'

Ellen's fingers flew across her keyboard and opened the FBI Most Wanted list as well as Interpol's Red List. 'Aliases, unknown. Age, unknown. Height, unknown. Weight, unknown. They know nothing about this guy except the name and terrorist actions he and his group, J, have taken credit for. Are you sure this is him?'

'I didn't say this was The Baron. The man that spoke to me wore a mask. They all did. They all had the same tattoo as well, so I'm not surprised these agencies have nothing to go on.'

Ellen could barely hide her disappointment at the news. 'Are you okay?'

'Did you know Nikos Petravaki?'

'He was one of the SAS soldiers assigned to my dig team. He was killed at the excavation site.'

'He was my brother. When he died, I had no family left. I was put in a foster home ... I had just turned fifteen when ...

' Ellen couldn't bring herself to speak about the things that happened to her. The memories were too painful. 'Lucas was there for me. He helped me a lot. He became my big brother. I used to blame you for the death of Nikos; he was only there because of you. But now I know that this man,' Ellen pointed at the screen, 'might be the man in charge, or the one that pulled the trigger. I can focus my efforts on them.'

'I had no idea.'

'Just because I told you this doesn't mean you're my favourite person, you know. You should have stuck with Lucas.'

Natasha's eyes widened. 'Excuse me?'

'He's not as tough and all together as he likes to make people believe.'

'He cheated on me, in our own bed!'

'Like I said, he's not altogether. But it's not my place to say.' Ellen took the opportunity to change the subject, thinking that she might have already said too much. 'So, what about this old guy? Why is he being followed?'

'That's a good question, and one that I don't know the answer to yet. Maybe I should go and ask him. His name's Professor Marcus Masterson. He's the head of the archaeology department at Cambridge University.'

'Do you know where he lives?' As soon as Natasha shook her head, Ellen was already typing away at her keyboard. A few moments later, she got a result. 'According to his credit card records, he's paid for an apartment at the Savoy Hotel, room 116.'

'The Savoy? Where'd he get that kind of money from?'

'I think you better get over there and ask him. Oh, and stay in touch, I think you might need me.'

. . . .

NATASHA ARRIVED AT the world-renowned Savoy Hotel and headed straight for the lounge to the right of the foyer. There were only half a dozen people in the room at the time, it was still early, and a waiter came up to quietly tell her they were still serving breakfast.

'It's all right, I'm supposed to meet someone. I'll have a look if he's here yet, then I'll get a menu.' She walked to an alcove in the farthest corner of the elaborately decorated restaurant, which afforded her a total view of the room. From here, she could determine that Marcus Masterson was not one of the diners and made to leave the restaurant. 'He must still be upstairs,' Natasha said to the waiter as she walked across the foyer towards the lifts. Unbeknownst to her, she was being watched every step of the way by the waiter.

'Waiter,' came the voice of a man standing behind the servant. 'Excuse me, waiter!' He said a little louder after getting no response.

The waiter gave the man a glare so cold that he came out in goosebumps, and he swallowed hard as he slowly backed away terrified.

The man in the waiter's uniform turned back in time to see Natasha Travers enter the lift. He took out a mobile phone and dialled a number. 'She has entered the lift and is going up as we speak,' he said when the other end was picked up. 'As ordered, I will continue surveillance until the strike team has arrived.' He ended the call and made his way toward the stairs.

When Natasha arrived at room 116, she knew something wasn't right. The door wasn't closed properly. She looked around the corner, up and down the corridor, thinking that maybe it was a housekeeper. But there was no one there.

She returned to the room, slowly entered, and called out the professor's name. There was no reply which prompted her to search the suite for him. The room was decorated in a traditional Edwardian English décor, with clear views of the River Thames through full length French windows, which led onto a balcony that overlooked the historical river which had spawned the City of London. In the bedroom were a chaise lounge and a king-sized bed, which had a reproduction Victorian head and foot with huge ornamental brass knobs, polished and gleaming. The spacious living room continued the traditional style with its sofa and two armchairs, a well-equipped working desk, a circular glass table, a fully stocked mini fridge bar with a decorative glass front and ADSL high speed internet access.

Natasha sat down on the chaise lounge, bemused by the Marcus' absence. In fact, she found nothing in there to suggest that he had been living here at all, except for several pairs of shoes that caught her eye as she slumped in her seat.

Her mind was about to formulate a new plan of action when there was a sudden knock at the door. Room service. Natasha didn't know what to do. Perhaps Professor Masterson had made the order and then stepped out. She opened the door.

'Room service, madam,' a man in a waiter's uniform said as he wheeled in his food-covered trolley.

'Who ordered this food?' Natasha asked as she stepped back to give the waiter space.

He silently closed the door and bent down beside the food cart. When he rose, the waiter pointed a silenced gun at her and Natasha heard the distinctive click of a gun hammer being pulled back and realised, perhaps too late, that things were not as they seemed, and that she had made a mistake, possibly a fatal one. Whatever this man was delivering, it definitely was not food.

'Don't make any sudden movements, Travers, or I will be forced to kill you.'

Chapter 8

Natasha held her hands up. She could feel her pulse racing, her heart thumping in her chest. She was rooted to the spot, unable to move as she stared at the gun pointing at her. On the back of his hand, she could just make out the fanged snake tattoo. The terrorist group, J, were most definitely back.

During their years together, Lucas had insisted on training Natasha in ways to handle herself. What he had taught her six years ago, in the ruins of Nineveh, had only been the beginning. He was of the opinion that since a lot of the excursions they'd be going on as The Acquirers, would send them to dangerous, and often lawless regions of the world, it only made sense for her to be able to protect herself.

'Tell me where Professor Marcus Masterson is?'

'I don't know! I'm trying to find him myself,' Natasha replied. In a situation like this, there were only two courses of action to take. Either comply with the demands of the gunman or attempt to disarm the enemy. This was obviously dangerous since she didn't know what kind of man she was dealing with, nor if he would stick to his threat and kill her if she moved. But she would have to if she were to put any of the disarming techniques she'd been shown into effect. She took several deep breaths to steel her nerves before she slowly took small steps toward the phoney waiter.

He stepped back, attempting to keep the distance between them, and barked instructions at her. 'Stop moving or I'll blow your head off!' But she took no notice and continued to move toward him.

Even to her inexperienced ears, she could hear the anxiety in his voice and knew that he was probably a rookie and didn't yet have the mettle to pull the trigger, nothing like the men she had met in Mosul. Either that or he had orders not to kill her. Eventually, he backed up into the door and could go no further. That was when a banging came from the other side.

'Natasha. Are you in there?'

It was Lucas. The unexpected arrival startled the gunman and Natasha made her move. She took a step to the right, away from the path of the gun, and grabbed his wrist before he could aim it at her again. They tussled for a moment, but as his superior strength began to tell, the little confidence she had, which had been bolstered by a surge of adrenalin, began to wane. Everything Lucas had taught her about self-defence faded as fear asserted its dominance. Training was one thing, but this was a real fight, with real consequences if she lost.

The barrel of the gun was slowly turning to face her. Natasha knew that there wasn't much time to think of anything else. The banging on the door became heavier blows as Lucas tried to break it down. She wished him more strength, believing that he was her only saviour.

Thinking of Lucas triggered something. A final bit of training he had given her after everything else. A desperate measure. Even at the time, she had asked him why he hadn't taught her that from the beginning. "You wanted to learn how to defend yourself, not kick somebody in the nuts. Besides, not everyone you'll be facing will be a man."

Luckily for Natasha, this was a man, and with all of her strength, she put her knee into his groin with such crunching force that he dropped the gun and buckled over, leaving him in the perfect position for another knee to the side of the head, which was enough to render the waiter unconscious, and he collapsed to the ground in a heap.

Natasha panted hard. The excitement of the encounter had given her a buzz; now she knew how Lucas felt when he beat people up. Then she remembered he was outside and opened the door for him.

He bounded in, ready for combat. 'Who the hell is that?' Lucas asked, seeing the waiter on the floor.

'I don't know, but look,' Natasha replied as she bent down to show Lucas the back of the waiter's hand.

'J,' he said, then he noticed the gun and saw that it had a silencer attached to it and he suddenly blew up at Natasha, catching her completely off guard. 'What the hell were you doing fighting this guy? If the man had the nerve to follow through with his threats, then no one would have heard the gunshots. I couldn't have saved you!'

It had been a while since Natasha had heard concern like this in his voice, especially towards her, and now it dawned on her just how lucky she was that her gamble had paid off.

'He may not be alone,' Lucas said as he retrieved the gun. He checked the clip, saw that it was full and put back in. 'We'd better get out of here.' He opened the door a crack and looked up and down the corridor. 'You did good, Nat.'

She smiled proudly behind him as they left the missing professor's suite.

. . . .

THEY WALKED TOWARDS the lifts, with Lucas explaining that Jenny had been able to get him released from police custody with ease. She had threatened to sue them for damages, stating that the evidence against Lucas was so flimsy, that it wouldn't stand up in any court.

'And when I left the station and saw the missed calls and voice message from Ellen, telling me what she'd found and what you were up to, Jenny had given me a lift, hoping to get here in time,' he explained.

As Natasha listened, she was about to press the button to call the lift when Lucas grabbed hold of her hand and pointed to the floor indicator. It was moving up.

'Come on,' Lucas said, not wanting to wait around and find out who was coming up. 'We'd better take the stairs, just to be on the safe side. There's a fire exit, first left and at the end of the corridor,' he said, reading the evacuation plan.

They ran toward the passage that led to the stairwell. But when they turned the corner, they came to quick halt. At the end of the hallway was another waiter walking out of a room carrying plates and cutlery, which he placed on his waiting trolley. The estranged couple cautiously made their way down the hallway. Lucas held the gun behind his back, ready for action, when and if the need arose. The waiter seemed to notice them for the first time, smiled and greeted them as he wheeled his trolley toward them.

There was a strange, silent tension in the air, broken only by the rhythmic squeak coming from the trolley's wheels. Lucas suspected this waiter was a colleague of the man

Natasha had left unconscious in the professor's room when his keen eye caught sight of his tattooed hand, slowly sliding down the handle of the trolley, trying desperately to seem innocuous.

Lucas was about to raise the gun he held behind his back and stop the waiter dead. But, he had not heard the forty-two-year-old woman from Hampshire, who was staying at the hotel to attend a series of business meetings, leave her room and begin to make her way down the hallway towards the lift.

The woman, Elizabeth Stadler, had not wanted to come to London because she had to leave her six-year-old son behind. Today was his special day, but she had not yet phoned to wish him a happy birthday and tell him how much she loved him. Elizabeth had decided not to call him first thing in the morning, hoping that he would think that she had forgotten. She wished she could see his face when she did finally call. As she continued walking, she passed an adjoining corridor and from the corner of her eye; she saw something that she wished she had not; three people, a waiter, a brunette woman, and a shaven headed man. What scared Elizabeth though was the fact that the shaven headed man had a gun held behind his back, and she could not stop herself from shouting, 'Oh my god! He's got a gun!'

Lucas spun around when he heard the scream and saw the frightened woman standing in the hallway. The distraction gave the waiter all the time he needed to slip his gun out of the holster that was fastened underneath the food cart. The former SAS soldier had made a cardinal error by turning away from his enemy. When he turned back to face the waiter, a silenced handgun was pointed at him.

He had no time to think, just act. As the first bullets escaped from the terrorist's suppressed barrel, Lucas pushed Natasha against the wall and threw himself against the opposite side. The bullets flew past, missing their intended target. But anything in the path of a bullet instantly becomes the object cited for destruction. And their new target was struck with deadly force and accuracy.

Elizabeth lay on the ground. Her blood slowly pulsed out of the wounds in her stomach. 'Oh god ... it ... hurts ... so much ... please ... let the ... pain ... stop ... please ... plea...'

Seeing what had happened to the innocent woman angered Lucas to the point where he disregarded his own safety. He stepped out into the middle of the hallway and strode purposefully toward the waiter. The terrorist was totally thrown by this action and didn't know how to react. All he could do was hesitantly raise his gun. But this indecision had already cost him.

While the enemy gun was still trained towards the spot where Elizabeth once stood, Lucas's stolen gun was already pointed at the terrorist and fired four times, each bullet landing in his chest with a thud.

Natasha was completely still, her eyes swivelled left and right as she took in the violence going on around her. It had started and ended in a matter of seconds, although it felt so much longer. Then her arm was gripped, and she was being pulled along behind Lucas, down the stairs, the image of the dead woman burned into her memory.

• • • •

THE COUPLE BLASTED out of the Savoy hotel entrance, almost knocking over a pile of suitcases which the hotel Porter was removing from the waiting cab with a family of tourists.

'Where did you park?' Lucas asked as they reached the junction of Savoy Close, the short road that led to the hotel, and The Strand.

'A couple of roads down. This way,' Natasha said, taking the lead.

Three of the tearoom patrons Natasha saw when she first arrived at the nineteenth century luxury lodgings had followed them out and in mere moments, those same men had been picked up by two black BMW 4 series coupés and were giving chase.

'Who are these people?' Natasha queried as they made their escape.

'I wish I knew, but it looks like your professor was in something up to his neck.'

The high engine revs and insistent honking alerted Lucas to their pursuers, as Natasha took a left and led them down a side road. Seconds later, they arrived at her Portofino-blue, Range Rover Evoque HST.

'What are you doing?' Natasha asked Lucas as they both went to the driver's side.

'Unless you've become a boy racer in the past months, I'm getting us out of here,' he replied and pointed back the way they had come, 'because we've got company.'

Natasha looked in the direction Lucas indicated and saw the two black cars skidding around the corner. Her mouth dropped open, and she pressed the door release on the key fob, then jumped in the back, whilst the engine roared as Lucas fired it up.

As Natasha climbed into the passenger seat, she immediately regretted letting him behind the wheel of her new car. Instead of taking the right back to the Strand, Lucas veered left.

'Are you nuts? This is a one-way street!'

'Relax, it's empty.' A car suddenly pulled out of a side road, forcing Lucas to take evasive action. 'Alright, it's a little empty.' He smiled. 'You'd better buckle up. Pull it tight.'

She did just that, then she gripped her seat, just as tight, as if it were a stress ball. Seeing cars hurtling towards them, Lucas zigzagging to avoid a collision, would be enough to stress anyone; Natasha was just thankful she'd had a light breakfast that morning.

In the side mirrors, she could see their pursuers doing their best to replicate his manoeuvres, but they continued to fall behind. When they turned right onto Westminster Bridge, then left into Millbank, hurtling past Big Ben and the Houses of Parliament, she hoped they were driving too fast for the police to have caught sight of her license plate, as Lucas floored the accelerator down the long straight.

Horns were honked frantically as he performed a handbrake turn onto Lambeth bridge with a sly smile and a glint in his eye.

The Range Rover thundered around the Lambeth Road roundabout, with the two BMWs following suit. On their second rotation, Lucas had one of the terrorists in his sights. He intended to crash into it, hopefully taking it out of commission.

When Natasha realised what his plan involved, she reached over and yanked down on the steering wheel, sending her car to the left, down the Albert Embankment, narrowly missing the rear of the black BMW. 'You are not smashing up my car.'

'What the hell are you doing?' Lucas yelled as he regained control of the HST. 'What's the problem? You've got insurance.'

'Yeah, but are you paying it?'

Lucas shrugged, then a new strategy formulated in his mind, as the Vauxhall bus station came into view, and he headed towards it.

A reduce speed sign flashed into operation as Lucas and Natasha came into the station at least ten times faster than a bus would. The Range Rover's breaks were tested to the max as they negotiated the hairpin turn. Buses pulled out from their stands and Lucas swerved in and out between them. As he passed each bus, he leaned out of the window, aimed the silenced gun at a front tire, and fired twice. With the sudden punctures, the two buses lost control, almost colliding, but more importantly, blocking the road behind the blue SUV. The BMWs skidded to a halt and made to reverse out, but the one-way route was already blocked by other buses.

Lucas smiled triumphantly at Natasha as they drove off, having ditched their pursuers. He turned away from her not so impressed scowl.

'Where to, your ladyship?'

'Take me home.'

Chapter 9

After the excitement of the chase, Natasha's and Lucas's adrenaline levels dropped back to normal, and the awkwardness of their current relationship status resurfaced. In an attempt to drown out the silence that prevailed, she switched on the car radio, but that didn't help matters either; too many songs that played over the airwaves evoked memories of happier times. Natasha was desperate to question Lucas about the things Ellen had said, but knew that she couldn't, not without exposing her.

The unnatural reticent continued all the way to Ivory House, St Katherine's Dock where their top floor warehouse apartment was situated. They left the Range Rover in the underground car park and, as they entered the marina's iconic building, they were greeted by the porter.

'Good morning, Miss Travers,' Simon Rhodes said. Then he saw Lucas walk in behind her and got excited. 'And Mr Redmond? Together? Does this mean that ... ? I guess you were right after all. Took a little longer than you said it would though.'

Lucas' eyes shot open as he frantically shook his head and put a finger to his lips. The porter read the gesture but all too late, as Natasha halted mid stride.

'What took longer than he said it would?' Natasha queried without turning around.

Simon mouthed a sorry to Lucas before he explained that a wager had been made between them.

'What kind of wager?'

'Well, Lucas said that he'd be moving back here in no time.'

'Did he now?' Natasha stormed off to the lift and when Lucas tried to follow, she stopped him. 'Take the stairs,' she said pointedly as the doors closed.

Lucas threw a glance at Simon, who tried to make himself look busy, and then made his way upstairs.

· · · ·

AFTER HE RANG THE DOORBELL for a fourth time, Natasha finally relented and let Lucas in. As he took a step, their xoloitzcuintli dog, named Solo, pounced on him, wagging his tail excitedly. The Mexican breed of dog was the third party in the relationship who they had bought when they first got together. Natasha had chosen the breed, because of its history with the Mayan and Aztecs as well as its uncanny resemblance to Anubis, the Egyptian god of death, which was understandable as it was cross breed with a pharaoh hound. The dog's name, Solo, came from Lucas's favourite character from the Star Wars franchise. That's what he told people, anyway. It sounded better than it coming from him giving up on trying to pronounce the whole name of the breed.

'Any chance of a drink?' Lucas asked as he played with Solo.

'A bit early, isn't it?'

'I think we deserve it.'

'Then make it yourself,' Natasha she scowled, still seething from the recent revelation. She didn't like the idea that people thought she was easily manipulated.

Lucas opened the drinks cabinet and was pleasantly surprised to see that his selection of spirits and liquors were still there and hadn't been poured down the drain. He needed to calm her down a touch, and he knew just the drink.

'Here, you might like this,' Lucas said, handing her a drink.

She cautiously took it and had a sip. 'That's not bad,' she begrudgingly admitted after letting the liquid swirl around her tastebuds for a moment. 'What is it?'

'A Peach Martini, Trey taught me.'

She smiled at hearing the name of Lucas's military friend. 'How's he and his bar doing?'

'The Fox and Bear? The bar with the pub name?' Lucas quipped. 'They're both doing good. He's always asking after you.'

A couple more rounds of martinis, and the tension had eased sufficiently to allow conversation to flow pleasantly with no hang-ups. It was like old times, but neither one would dare be the first to let on to the other just how much they'd missed it.

Lucas sighed. 'What a crazy morning. Despite Jenny getting me out, you know I'm still Detective Russell's number one suspect, right? Even though you and I both know that your professor friend has a lot to answer for.' Natasha shot Lucas a look. 'Don't look at me like that, Nat. You were the one snooping around his apartment.'

'I just wanted to find out why he was being followed.'

'Because he has the Eye of Nineveh, he has to. This Baron guy and his cronies are fixated with it. They've tried to perforate us multiple times to get it, and now they're after your professor, who just happens to be the leading authority on all things Assyrian, according to you. It's not a coincidence.'

'I agree, but there was nothing at his place, no clues as to where he is or what he's up to; we're at a dead end.'

'What's the big deal about this eye, anyway? It's a decent gem size, and I'm sure the Baron could get a good amount of money on the black market to fund his terrorist activities, but I've seen bigger and better.'

'What? When?' Natasha asked, bemused, but continued without waiting for an answer. 'The legends about The Eye of Nineveh portray it as no ordinary gem. The Chintamani stone inside it is said to grant amazing powers. It's like the eastern equivalent of the philosopher's stone. It's talked about in Hindu and Buddhist traditions, it is said to have been in Shambala, the legendary kingdom in the Himalayas.'

'But we found it in Iraq. How could it have gone to places and come back?'

'Because there's more than one. It came from a meteor that crashed on Earth fifteen million years ago, so who knows how many there are out there, or what would happen if several were brought together. The legends say it can enhance psychic and healing energies, purify water, and even grant wishes. In Hindu scriptures, it mentions a jewel that belonged to the sun god. It says whichever land possessed the jewel would never encounter droughts, floods, earthquakes or famines, and would always experience prosperity.'

'Are you serious?'

'Very. The ring of King Solomon is said to have been made from it. Alexander the Great and Akbar I are both supposed to have had some of the Chintamani stone. And of course, the Assyrians who dominated Mesopotamia because they had advanced technology, Iron Age weapons in the Bronze Age.'

'This is all a bit fantastical to believe, don't you think?'

'Maybe it is, maybe it isn't. The thing is, the Baron believes. The idea of such an artefact fires up the imagination. Even Henry Wallace, Secretary of Agriculture, during the Roosevelt administration, funded an expedition to find Shambala and the Chintamani stone.'

'Really? They believed in this supernatural stuff?'

'Why not? Hitler did. Let me show you something else,' Natasha said with a sparkle in her eye as she took out her mobile phone. Moments later, she handed it to Lucas. The screen showed a painting of Jesus wearing a crown and a mantle, surrounded by angels. 'This is called Christ Surrounded by Singing and Music-making Angels by the 15th century painter, Hans Memling.' She took the phone back and showed him another image. 'This triptych is Earthly Vanity and Divine Salvation by the same artist. As you can see, the portrait of Jesus is almost identical, wouldn't you say?'

'Yeah, pretty much. Even the clasp with the three coloured stones looks the same.'

'Okay, now look at this.'

Lucas was shown a picture of three circles grouped in a triangle. The similarities to the amulets were uncanny, even down to their colours. 'And what's this?'

'A very sacred symbol in Buddhism. It's the Tibetan symbol for the "mani stone". According to legend, the stone is one of four relics that came in a chest that fell from the sky in Tibet. It is also their name for the Chintamani stone.'

'Okay, but what's that got to do with Jesus?'

'He went to Shambala, where he was given a Chintamani stone.'

'What? Come on, are you serious?'

'How familiar are you with the New Testament?'

'I know of it.'

'As a chronicle of Jesus' life, it's incomplete. From age twelve until he's thirty is not written about. That's eighteen years. Important years, arguably his formative years, which are not there.'

'It is a bit odd; I'll give you that.'

'I think it was written, but it was taken out at the Council of Nicaea along with everything else that went against their narrative of a divine being.'

'When did he start performing miracles?'

Natasha smiled. 'When he was thirty, after he returned with the stone. Turning water into wine was his first miracle.'

'Jesus ... I mean damn.' Lucas played with his wedding ring as he slowly digested everything that Natasha had told him about the Chintamani stone and the Eye of Nineveh. His head was spinning; there were just too many coincidences for it to *be* a coincidence. He looked up and saw Natasha watching him absentmindedly twist the ring around his finger. He immediately stopped and took out a cigar from his pocket. 'Don't worry,' Lucas said, seeing Natasha's expression. 'I'm not smoking it here. I'm going to dash to the apartment because we've got things to do. We need to find your professor and the eye before the Baron does. A terrorist like him having something like this artefact in his possession really could usher in a New World Order.'

'People keep bandying that term about, but what exactly is it?'

'Well, to be honest, this is more Ellen's area of expertise. The concept of family will be gone, as children will be raised by the government. All land will be owned by the government so there'll be no right to private property.'

'Jesus...'

'Which brings us to their next mandate. The right to worship will no longer exist because the act of worshipping a God will be a crime. Religious people will be deprogrammed. Those that won't change their belief will be put in concentration camps or just killed.'

'Wow, this is deep. I had no idea. I thought it just meant that there would be one world government.'

'This is Orwell's Nineteen Eighty-Four on overdrive. It'll be a world where people no longer think for themselves, but have their decisions made by others.'

Natasha looked at Lucas with a slack jaw.

'What? Ellen talks about this shit all the time.'

'The Assyrians used the power of the eye to gain advantage in their era. If someone used it today, everything you just said would be possible. It doesn't bear thinking about.'

Chapter 10

It hadn't been long since Lucas left the apartment, but Natasha still felt somewhat bad. She wasn't accustomed to having a drink so early in the day, and she didn't know why she had given in so easily to Lucas's offer of a refill. He always was able to get her to step out of her comfort zone.

She wouldn't lie and say that she hadn't enjoyed it because she had. It reminded her of how things used to be between them, easy flowing, fun, laughter. At one point, she was tempted to suggest that they continued things in the bedroom. But then the images of him with another woman in there ran through her mind and shattered that idea. Natasha wondered if she'd ever be able to forgive and forget, she supposed that she would have to, if neither one of them was willing to sell their half of the Acquirers business, and they ended up working together day to day, like Jenny suggested.

The feelings she had for him weren't gone, but she didn't know if she could trust him with that knowledge. And she didn't know how he felt. He was with someone else now after all. But even at the best of times, he had difficulty sharing his feelings and telling her what he was thinking.

Just then, Natasha's phone rang. It was a number she didn't recognise, but when she answered, she did know the voice.

'Peter?'

'Hello, Natasha. I hope you don't mind, but I got your number from your father.'

'Oh, okay,' she replied, more than a little confused.

'I wanted to tell you personally that I won't be at your parents' for dinner tonight.'

'I'm sure my parents will be fine with it.'

'The thing is, I was really hoping I would get to see you, Natasha.'

'You were?'

'Definitely. I felt a certain affinity towards you.'

'Oh.' Natasha had certainly felt an attraction for Peter. There was something about his clean-cut, dashing image which had appealed to her, but it had just been a fleeting, throwaway introduction they'd had. She didn't think that she had made any sort of impression on him.

'So, I'd like to take you to lunch if you're not busy.'

Natasha looked at her watch. It was coming up to 11:30. 'You mean right now?'

'Sure. Come to the office and we'll leave from here. I'll send you the address.'

Before Natasha could reply, Peter Armitage had ended the call. Seconds later, the address of his offices came through The Shard, London Bridge.

Her interest was certainly piqued, and she was somewhat flattered by the attention from someone of his status, and even though she was supposed to meet up with Lucas, to find Professor Masterson, a part of her felt that she deserved a bit of attention.

After a quick freshen up and change of clothes, she was on her way.

Natasha made the journey on foot. It was only a twenty-minute walk to The Shard, and the fresh air would do her good. She was halfway across the iconic Tower Bridge when she heard someone behind her calling her name.

'Nice to see you again, Mrs Travers-Redmond,' Kallum Taylor said as he fell into stride beside her.

'Are you following me, Mr Taylor?'

'Kallum, please, and yes, of course I am.'

Natasha came to a stop. 'Excuse me?'

'Your husband is my prime suspect in the theft of the Eye of Nineveh, and I just saw him leaving the apartment you own together, so it only makes sense that I should watch you, too. It wouldn't be a stretch to see you as his accomplice. Maybe he was there stashing the gem.'

'Like you said, he's my husband. He has a right to be there.'

'But aren't you two currently going through a divorce? I would have thought there'd be nothing to say between you without your lawyers present, unless, of course, it was about illegal activities one or both of you might have taken part in.'

Natasha rolled her eyes. 'What is your fixation with Lucas? You seem determined to pin this heist on him. Have you even looked into how the footage was erased?'

'No doubt an accomplice,' he said, eyeing her with suspicion.

'Oh, good god.' She'd had enough and started walking to her lunch appointment again. It was like talking to a brick wall. He didn't seem open to the idea of anyone else being a possible suspect.

'If not you, perhaps his new lady friend; Chiara Harris, was it?' Kallum caught up with the power walking Natasha and, as they completed crossing Tower Bridge, he tried a different tact. 'You think I'm barking up the wrong tree, don't you?' She didn't reply. 'I'll take your silence as a yes. How much do you know about your husband's parents, Gary and Donna Redmond?' Her strides slowed a touch. 'Criminals, the both of them.' She came to a stop. 'Thieves, actually. So, the apple wouldn't have to fall far from the tree, would it?'

'And that's your reasoning for accusing Lucas? A bit flimsy, don't you think? Children don't always follow in their parents' footsteps, you know. My dad is a tax lawyer, my mother a surgeon, yet I'm an archaeologist.'

'Fair point.' He paused to gather his thoughts before he continued. 'Let me ask you this, have you heard of Sebastian Jericho?'

'No. Should I have?'

'Maybe, maybe not. They call him The Ghost because he can get in and out of places like he walks through walls.'

'Who does?'

'Criminals and police alike. Actually, some dignitaries and high-powered individuals as well. You see, it's not just antiques this Sebastian Jericho steals. It's whatever the customer wants as long as the customer can pay.'

'Okay, so why are you telling me this?'

'Because I have reason to believe that Lucas is The Ghost.'

Natasha stifled a laugh. 'You're joking, right? Didn't I tell you before about throwing out wild accusations?'

'And I didn't have time to reveal my evidence then.'

'And what? You can now?' Natasha replied, her patience fast running out as she crossed her arms.

'Do you remember a Morgan Spivey?'

She thought for a moment. 'Yes, I remember him. Swiss born; Imperial College educated. He made a fair bit of money on stocks and shares but lost it all, which forced him to pawn a lot of his pieces, including a clock, a family heirloom. He came to us claiming that when he got back on his feet and was in a position to buy back the clock, the pawnbroker gave him a forgery.'

'But you turned down the job.'

'Yes. It's not the kind of thing we do at the Acquirers.'

'But you went to Switzerland, anyway.'

'For something completely different; a romantic getaway.'

'Really? So, I take it you had no idea that a pawn broker was robbed during your time there? He claimed Morgan Spivey was behind it, but why would he steal a clock that he had a receipt for? Obviously, the police never investigated it further.'

'That's it? That's your evidence?'

'That and three other similar cases; Berlin, Monaco, Cartagena.'

'Now wait a minute. That trip to Colombia was to help a friend of mine.'

'Maybe it was, but Sebastian Jericho has associates and contacts across the globe.'

'I've had enough of this,' Natasha said abruptly, turning on her heel. 'I've somewhere I need to be.'

'Okay, Mrs Travers-Redmond. Just think about what I've told you,' Kallum called over his shoulder as he walked back across the bridge.

• • • •

NATASHA ARRIVED AT the 72-storey glass-skyscraper, with her mind reeling. Things were adding up in her head, and she wasn't liking the result of the equation. Maybe it was a coincidence that they happened to be in the same city as a high-profile theft. Things were stolen in cities all the time, but for it to happen four times was a bit much. And then there were the claims his divorce lawyer made about Lucas bringing in more revenue for the business than her. Theft of high value items would certainly provide that. But Jenny told her that the invoices all looked above board, no evidence of criminality. 'Why am I even entertaining this nonsense?' She sighed.

Armitage Holdings occupied the thirty-fourth and thirty-fifth floors of the United Kingdom's tallest building, and as the lift Natasha was in arrived on the latter of the two, she had come to a decision. Now wasn't the time for lunches with admirers, as much as she was tempted. Professor Marcus Masterson was missing, and so was the Eye of Nineveh. Finding them both had to be her priority, and she thought that Peter at least deserved to hear it from her.

The receptionist met Natasha and led her to an office, then left, closing the door behind her as she did so. There was a double door at the opposite end of the office, but she was taken by the floor to ceiling windows, which afforded spectacular views over the city. She wasn't quite up in the clouds, but she was halfway there. With all this glass, and it being a sunny day, Natasha, had always thought that being within the eye-catching structure might have felt a bit like being in a greenhouse, but it was pleasantly cool. No doubt due to a high spec air conditioning system working overtime to keep the working environment at a steady, manageable level.

As Natasha strolled around the spacious office, she noted the many paintings and archaeological pieces that were in display cabinets placed around the walls of the office. At first, she thought they were exceptional fakes, but when she came to a chipped clay plate, she inspected it and was almost certain that it was a genuine Iron Age artefact, possibly from the Dobunni tribe of Somerset.

Suddenly, the double doors opened, and Natasha was surprised to see Chiara Harris walk out. Natasha blinked rapidly as she tried to process what she was seeing. She had no idea that this was where the hussy worked. Behind her, Peter Armitage was having a heated conversation on his mobile as he paced back and forth. Before she could get any idea as to what the urgent call was about, Chiara closed the doors.

'I'm afraid Mr Armitage won't be able to have lunch with you today, he's quite busy, but he was hoping that you'd be able to reschedule for the same time, the day after tomorrow?'

'I was actually here for the same reason. Something's come up, but I just wanted to tell Peter in person.'

'I will be sure to let him know,' Chiara replied as she directed Natasha back to the lifts.

'So, you work for Peter, huh?'

'Yes, I do.'

'What, are you like his secretary or something?'

'His executive assistant, actually,' Chiara said with narrowed eyes.

'Potato, potaato,' replied Natasha nonchalantly. 'Lucas never actually said what you did.'

'I'm not sure he remembers. There isn't much talking being done when we're together,' she replied with a smirk.

'No need to tell me. Been there, done that, got the ring to prove it,' Natasha said as she flashed her ring finger in the tall woman's face. 'I'll be sure to ask him since I'm on my way to meet him now.'

They glared at each other. Natasha was some three inches shorter, but her back was up and she was in no mood to backdown. The receptionist looked from one to the other, with no idea what was going on, but she knew that Chiara Harris was not one to be messed with.

The lift arrived.

'Well,' Natasha began, not breaking eye contact with Chiara for a second. 'It looks like my ride's here.' She stepped into the lift and just as the doors closed, her phone rang. It flashed up as an unknown number. Then it stopped. Seconds later, several pictures of her parents and then of her, taken from various times of the morning, including her entering The Shard, appeared on her phone.

The phone rang again. This time Natasha answered immediately. 'Hello?'

'Natasha Travers? This is Baron. I will keep this short and get straight to the point. As you can see, I have your parents, as well as you, under surveillance.' His polite manner suddenly became very menacing. 'Marcus Masterson said you are a talent. Now is the time to prove it. You found the gem before, now find it again. If you do not get me the Eye of Nineveh in thirty-six hours, I will kill your father, then your mother, and finally, you. And don't waste your time contacting the police. I will know if you do, and your parents will die.

Chapter 11

Having returned to his Chelsea Harbour apartment, Lucas sorted out a quick, basic tactical bag or go-bag. Within, were carried essentials of a survival pack: torch, extra batteries, zip ties, foil blanket, window breaker etc. It was a far cry from the tactical bags he would usually take out in the field; those would usually have guns, munitions and other weapons thrown in, too.

It was coming up to midday and, as Lucas stood by his large window overlooking the Thames River, he reflected on the eventful morning he'd had thus far, culminating in morning cocktails at St Katherine's dock. He had enjoyed it a lot. Lucas even thought that things might have progressed a bit further, but even the usually cocksure Lucas was hesitant, knowing that it was in that bed that he had first slept with Chiara. Knowing that the makeup discovered on those bedsheets had tipped off Natasha to his affair.

But Chiara hadn't been the first, nor the only one. Ever since he had received that letter, a switch had been flicked on in his mind, and a side of him he thought had gone resurfaced. The side that distrusted women that were close to him. The side that believed the twisted mantra, do unto others before they do unto you.

He never wanted to hurt Natasha, but he was a complicated and conflicted man. Even her love couldn't change that.

Lucas's phone flickered to life as it rang. 'Hey, Nat. Everything okay?' Instead of a concise answer, he got a bunch of hysterics and knew something wasn't right. 'Whoa. Slow down. Say that again.'

'The Baron, he's got people watching my parents. Watching *me*.'

It had been some time since Lucas had last heard her like this. The panic was there in her voice. He could almost sense that she was near to tears. 'Try to calm yourself, Nat. I won't let anything happen to them, or you. Just tell me everything he said.'

She relayed everything to him between hyperventilated gasps. 'How am I supposed to find the gem? I wouldn't know where to start looking.'

'You had some idea earlier when you went looking for your professor.'

'Not really. I was just trying to find out why a J terrorist was following him. On the CCTV you get the impression that Marcus knew who he was.'

'Well let's continue with that lead.'

A thought suddenly struck Natasha. 'Wait a minute. Robert got a message from him this morning. He was saying something about being sorry.'

'It's worth checking out.'

'I can't. I have to see my parents!'

'Look, Nat, you're the only one that can find the gem; leave your parents to me.'

'My dad hates you,' she stated.

'Your fault for being a daddy's girl. Just imagine how I feel having to save him.' He heard her try to stifle a laugh. 'I'm doing this for you, Nat. Don't worry, I won't let you down.'

The fact that Natasha had instinctively turned to Lucas in her time of need wasn't lost on either of them. But neither knew how to handle it; emotions were still raw on one side and on the other hand, neither of them wanted to force things too soon.

'I ... uh ... I have to go,' she stammered, breaking the silence that had descended.

'Wait, Nat. There's something we need to clarify. You know we can't give them the Eye of Nineveh, right?'

'Of course not. It belongs in a museum. And that's *if* I can find it.'

'That's not exactly what I meant.' He sighed. 'If half of what you told me about this gem is true, it could spell disaster for the entire world.'

'But I can't refuse their demands either.'

'Just watch your back. I don't trust them. It's more than likely that if you do find it, whoever they have following you will try to snatch it. Once I've dealt with the ones watching your parents, I'll come find you, Nat.'

• • • •

NATASHA RUSHED HOME and changed into loose-fitting clothes, more akin to what she would wear out in the field. By the time she arrived back at the British Museum, the crowds that were there in the morning had swollen to include journalists and news crews. Somehow they had gotten wind of the Eye of Nineveh heist, despite the best efforts of Robert Jones.

'It's alright, officers, she's with me,' he said as he approached the gates of the museum. The constables were under strict instructions from Inspector Jake Russell, not to let anyone in unless under Dr Jones's supervision.

As soon as journalists spotted the museum curator, they fired a barrage of questions at him.

'Was it an inside job?'

'What has this done to international relations between the UK and Iraq?'

'Is your job now in jeopardy, Dr Jones?'

Robert Jones ignored every one of them and led Natasha up the steps and into the Great Hall of the British Museum. The afternoon sun streamed through the spectacular glass roof as the sounds of their footsteps echoed around. The staff were being sent home, after being questioned, since the chances of opening today were very slim. Only security and the forensic police remained.

'The journos started turning up not long after you left,' he explained as they took a seat inside the Hall of Enlightenment. 'I don't know how they found out. They must have scanned the police frequencies because they even knew about Lucas' arrest.'

'He's been released now.'

'Of course he has. He had nothing to do with this.'

'No, he didn't,' she agreed before she took a moment to figure out how to broach the delicate subject. 'But I think Marcus may have.'

'What? That's just as preposterous as Lucas having committed the crime.'

'I'm not so sure, Robert. I was able to blow-up part of the CCTV footage; that man following him was from the same terrorist organisation that attacked my expedition and it looked like Marcus knew that. And when I went to Marcus's room at the Savoy, another terrorist attacked me.'

'Wait. The Savoy? How could he afford that? Besides, he has his own place near Lambeth North.'

'He does? I don't suppose I could get the address?'

'Sure, I'll write it down for you.'

'And can I have a listen of that message he left you?'

He skipped through his voicemails until he found the right message and played it for Natasha.

'Damn it, Robert. You and your damned slow checks. Um, fine. I wanted to tell you that I must go. I'm being followed. I have to disappear, but, ah, I had to say sorry to you. I, ah, know how important this thing was going to be for you, but I had to do it. I couldn't let them have it. Um, maybe we'll see each other again, old friend. Oh, and for god's sake, don't tell Natasha. Oh, Christ. They've found me!'

She listened to the voicemail from Marcus again and let out an exasperated sigh when it finished. 'Jesus, Robert. This is basically Marcus's confession.'

'I thought it was a joke at first, so I thought nothing of it. Then I saw the Eye was missing ... ' it had been a stressful morning for the curator. 'I don't know what to think anymore, but I'll need more evidence before I believe he was involved with the disappearance.

'So, he did know who they were!' Things were falling into place, but the more Natasha learnt, the more questions popped up. 'Just what kind of trouble has Professor Masterson got himself involved in? And why the hell didn't he want me to know?'

'I don't know, but there must be a reason. Either one of us would have helped him. Anyway, here's his address. If he's not there, he has a spare key taped behind the doorbell. Just slide it up.'

'Hopefully I'll be able to find something at his place; a clue of what he was up to, or where he was going, anything. If I do, I'll let you know. Don't worry, Robert, I'm sure he's fine.'

She couldn't know that for certain, but she wanted to give some hope to her friend. But in her heart, she knew that if this terrorist group caught up with him, there would be only one outcome: a bullet to the head.

· · · ·

THE JOURNEY TOOK THIRTY minutes and Natasha was acutely aware that time was ticking away. She hadn't watched the clock so intently since she sat her exams at university.

She arrived at the Lambeth Road address. After receiving no answer from frantically pressing the doorbell several times, Natasha did as Dr Jones had told her, and pushed it up. The key was there, and she entered the house.

It was like stepping into the past. Everywhere she looked, there were pieces of history, carvings here, a collection of coins there. They would have been gathered from his years in the field before he accepted his tenement at Cambridge.

Natasha didn't think that she would ever stop being a field archaeologist. For her, that was where the true fun was, and the true connection to history. Walking in the footsteps of people thousands of years ago was of far more interest to her than reading about someone else that did it, unless it was Giovanni Belzoni, of course.

Just like her, the adventurer had been an influence on Professor Masterson and, by his own accounts, had somewhat modelled himself on the Italian archaeologist in his youth. Judging by all the artefacts she was seeing; Natasha finally saw that it hadn't all been the hot air she had believed it was as one of his students.

But this wasn't helping her. She didn't have time for a tour; she needed to remain focussed on finding a clue. One single bit of information to not only help her find the professor but also the Eye of Nineveh, and ultimately, save her parents.

It was coming up to one o'clock. The afternoon sun had passed its zenith. Having found nothing of significance, Natasha threw herself down on the bed in frustration. The force of the action moved the bed and nudged the bedside cabinet. A picture that had been standing on it toppled and fell to the ground. Luckily, the glass didn't break on the thick carpeting.

Natasha scooted over to the edge of the bed. As she leant down to retrieve the photograph, she saw something that she initially took no notice of. But as Natasha sat up, she thought it was rather odd, a single pair of shoes.

She took another look under the bed, to make sure that she hadn't missed a pair by mistake, but she hadn't. There were no other shoes anywhere else, not in the wardrobe, under the desk, nowhere.

Natasha reached for them and pulled them out. A look of puzzlement came across her face. She put one down on the bed in order to inspect them individually. They were brogues with a vintage burnished, tanned leather finish. Not really his style, from what she could recall.

She frowned and turned it over. Stitched at the rounded tip was the maker's name and logo. Judging by the condition of that, and the sole in general, it became evident that the shoes had never been worn. Natasha sat heavily on Marcus's bed with a sigh. Her eye was drawn to the framed photo she had lain there, but hadn't yet looked at properly.

Until now.

'Marcus was a Freemason?' The photo showed a gathering of men, all dressed in their full Masonic regalia: white gloves, apron with embroidered badges. It seemed to have been taken in a hall, judging by the number of seats there, some of which were golden, such as the one Marcus Masterson was seated on.

Natasha flipped the frame over and took the photo out. On the back of it was written the date it was taken, a few years ago, and the location, Freemasons' Hall, London. She knew where it was. Ironically, it wasn't far from the British Museum. 'I wonder if Marcus is hiding out there. Or perhaps he's stashed the gem there?'

As she put the picture back, her gaze fell onto the shoes again. Sure, it was weird, she thought as she walked downstairs to make her way to the Freemasons' Hall, but it was hardly enough to spend any more time thinking about it, especially when time was such an expensive commodity right now.

Natasha was losing faith in finding any sort of clue and threw herself backwards on the bed in frustration, with such force that she bounced up and down. It was a problem that she couldn't figure out, and it was killing her.

From a young age, Natasha always felt that she had to prove herself; because of her skin colour, because of her gender, her looks, her parents' money. Being able to deduce archaeological conundrums and problem solving was what made her who she was proved that she was more than what her genetics made her look like. She had worked hard to make her mind the phenomenon it was; it made her special. Without it, she felt...ordinary.

But now it was failing her, because her subconscious mind wouldn't let her drop the unusual fact of the lone pair of shoes.

As the bed became still once more, she grabbed a shoe again, flipped it over several times, poked and prodded it. Nothing happened. She picked up the second shoe and did the same. There was a click, and the heel moved slightly.

When she heard that sound, she had a moment of recollection and it brought the information she needed to the forefront of her mind. Marcus Masterson was once a Cold War spy. Being an archaeologist gave him reason to travel to the far corners of the planet without drawing attention. He had told her about some of the spy-craft he had used in those days. One in particular was the false-heeled shoe.

The heel swivelled on a hinge and hidden inside the cavity was a piece of a note, part of a longer message. On this ripped shred of paper was written, "Curiosity will kill you, Natasha."

Chapter 12

The red Alfa Romeo Guilia GTA, of Lucas Redmond, pulled into the St Mary's hospital car park. He stepped out and although he wasn't expecting it, he had a cursory scan of the area to see if anything or anyone seemed out of place. As he assumed, there was nothing; this organisation didn't hire complete idiots. Even the ones he had encountered at The Savoy would have been competent enough for most.

As he entered the hospital, famous for being the choice for royal births, he realised it had been some time since he had last seen Natasha's mum. Fortunately he got on a lot better with her than he did with her dad.

Lucas headed towards the office of Sofia-Valentina Travers. He turned a corner and could hear her distinctive accent down the hallway. Despite being in England for most of her life, Sophia's South American origins were still evident in her speech.

Born in Medellin, Colombia, she grew up during the time of Pablo Escobar and the Medellin Cartel. She saw many atrocities. Violence on a scale you'd expect in a war zone, and at times that was exactly what it was; bombings, shout-outs, assassinations were the norm. It instilled in her the drive and determination to excel and strive for a better life, all traits she passed on to her daughter.

'Yes, Graeme, I'm on my way to my office now. Please let them know that we can begin the video conference soon.' Through her Dior glasses, she saw Lucas standing in the middle of the hallway. 'Okay, Graeme, I have to go. Speak to you soon.' Sofia ended the call and slipped her mobile into her suit pocket. 'Qué diablos crees que estás haciendo aquí?'

'It's good to see you too, Mrs Travers.'

'Ugh. Will you stop calling me that.' She smiled as she wrapped her arms around him.

'Well, it was your idea.'

'Si, but only when people that know my husband are around. He still hates your guts, you know.'

'I figured.'

She linked her arm with his and leisurely strolled along towards her office. 'How are things with Natasha?'

'She's still intent on going ahead with the divorce.'

'Don't worry. I still believe that she'll come around, eventually. You two were good for each other, you just have to show her the Lucas Redmond that she fell for. You still want to be with her, right?'

'Yeah! She makes me a better person; I just made a mistake.'

'Several of them, from what I've heard.'

'Come on, that's not true.'

'Probably not. The info did come from the wounded party, after all. All I know is that my daughter has never been happier than when she was with you. You just have to let her know how you feel. Don't shut her out, and don't make me regret giving you my blessing.'

'She met the other woman today,' he admitted sheepishly.

Sofia slapped his arm. 'Madre de Dios! ¿Qué diablos estabas pensando?'

'It wasn't planned; she was dropping me off at the museum and Natasha came to meet me at the gate.'

They arrived at her smartly decorated office. Sofia ushered him in and, as Lucas took a seat, admiring his surroundings, she made them both a drink. 'No wonder she's not softening to you. You need to get rid of this home wrecker, Lucas.'

They sipped their drinks. Lucas deliberated over the choice he would have to make, and how he would deliver his decision. Getting a gun and running into a battlefield would be a lot easier.

As Sofia watched him, she reflected on his initial question. 'So, why are you here anyway?'

If she hadn't had the upbringing she'd been subjected to, Lucas knew he probably wouldn't have told Sofia a thing. But knowing that she was unlikely to become hysterical, he calmly took out his phone and showed her the pictures Natasha had sent him. 'You're being followed.'

'What? That's this morning when I came to work.'

'They're out there somewhere,' he said, gesturing to the window with a slight flick of his head. 'Probably watching us right now.'

'Who are they? What do they want?'

'The terrorist organisation me and Natasha crossed paths with back in Iraq.'

'You mean J?'

Lucas nodded. 'They're forcing Natasha to do something for them, and by threatening you and John they're making sure she does it.'

'Mierda.' Sofia handed Lucas back his phone before downing the rest of her drink and pouring another. 'I suppose we can't go to the police?'

He shook his head. 'Don't need them. Besides, they're too busy trying to fit me up for a crime. Don't worry, I'm sure Natasha will bring you up to speed,' he added after seeing her bemused look.

'How will you find him?'

'Going by the angle of the photo, I'd say he's more than likely holed up somewhere in that construction site across the way. Just carry on with your day as normal, Sofia, and I'll phone you when it's all clear.'

• • • •

'OH MY GOD,' ELLEN SCREAMED down her intercom at Natasha. 'What the hell are you doing back here? Just because I helped you once. It doesn't mean we're best buds, you know? This is why I don't give people my address.'

'You gave me your number.'

'Yes, my number. It wasn't an invitation to drop by whenever you wanted.'

'I need your help ... '

'I figured that.'

'I need your help to get into a room at the Savoy hotel.'

The intercom went silent.

'Hello? Are you still there?'

Ellen's interest piqued. 'Come up.'

The lift was already waiting when Natasha entered the derelict building, which Ellen called home. When the doors opened on the upper level, the young hacker was waiting eagerly.

'So, you went to see that old guy and you end up in a murder scene. You still think he's innocent? I heard all about it on my police scanner,' she added, guessing Natasha was about to ask how she knew.

'I still think there's some explanation for it.'

'There is. He's a bloody thief. A criminal!'

'You can talk. I've heard about some of the things you've done.'

Ellen grinned. 'I'm no thief. I think of myself as being more like Robin Hood, or Robina Hood in this case.'

'Yeah, but didn't he steal from the rich to give to the poor? You seem to steal from the rich and keep for yourself.'

'Semantics. But let's not harp on about me. What about your dodgy professor? I thought you already went to the hotel?'

'I did, but I've come across some new information, a partial message, and I need to get back in there to find the rest of it.'

'And now it's a crime scene crawling with police.'

'And that's not all. The Baron has given me 36hrs,' Natasha checked her watch, 'Thirty-five hours, now, to find the missing Eye of Nineveh, so I kind of need to get in there fast.'

Ellen leapt out of her chair and grabbed a nearby backpack. The challenge of the task, put to her, motivated Ellen greatly. Sneaking into the Savoy, right under the nose of the police was a caper she had to be a part of. She slipped her high-spec laptop into it and a few more bits and pieces, electrical components that she thought she might need and finally a taser, which she tested to make sure it was fully charged. Then she bounded upstairs, returning a few moments later. She'd changed into a sporty outfit and grabbed a long, light-fabric coat which, when zipped up all the way, passed her nose.

Natasha stood there speechless as the tech-genius walked past her, hoisted her bag onto her shoulders and entered the lift.

'Well? We doing this or what?' Ellen said as she prepared to send the lift down.

• • • •

LUCAS STOOD AT THE entrance of the hospital, pretending to speak on his phone, all the while he scrutinised everything and everyone in the area on St Mary's. He paid close attention to the building site opposite the office of Sofia Valentina Travers. It was an obvious place for a sniper's nest.

He put his phone away as he crossed the road, intent on searching the site thoroughly for any suspicious activity. There was nothing at the front entrance. It was securely padlocked, no work was taking place today. So, when Lucas turned into the side alley of the hospital wing, he felt vindicated in his belief that this was the right place. Halfway down the road, a man stood at a side entrance of the closed off building, smoking a cigarette.

He could just as easily have been a security guard, posted there to watch-over any left equipment and other easy pickings for opportunistic thieves. As Lucas nonchalantly approached him, however, he could see that the man was anything but security; the way he carried himself and seemed alert were a dead giveaway.

'Hey, buddy,' Lucas said as he got closer to the man, 'I don't suppose I could get a light?' The man shook his head. 'Come on, I'll just use your butt.' Lucas reached up to take the cigarette from between his lips. The man grabbed Lucas's wrist, revealing a familiar tattoo on the back of his hand. He realised too late that the action was just a diversion as Lucas head-butted him squarely on the bridge of his nose. Blood burst across his face. He didn't have to worry about his appearance for long as Lucas quickly stepped behind him and wrapped his arms around his neck in a sleeper hold. He squeezed until the snake tattooed hand that was trying to pull Lucas's arm away became limp as he fell unconscious.

These were the times when regularly hitting the gym paid off for Lucas, not that dragging a knocked-out terrorist was a daily occurrence, but it certainly helped as he dumped the body inside, before he slowly and quietly searched for any of the man's friends.

He instinctively and stealthily headed to the floor opposite to Sofia-Valentina's office, knowing that from that position it would be just as easy to photograph her entering the hospital as it would be to shoot her in her seat.

Lucas reached the top of the stairwell and peered around the large, partially empty space. Wiring hung down through exposed parts of the ceiling and there were several partition walls in place, perfect for hiding behind. As he ventured further in, he soon discovered exactly how much cover they provided when he was suddenly struck from behind.

He fell to his knees, clutching the back of his head. Lucas berated himself; he'd been sloppy. He had barely heard the creaky footstep behind him, but he'd been able to move just enough so he wasn't completely knocked out. It still hurt like hell, though. Lucas checked his hand. There wasn't any blood, but he was sure he'd have a lump there tomorrow. He couldn't hear his assailant's demands at first, due to the ringing in his head. When they were accompanied by forceful kicks in the chest, however, the words came through loud and clear.

'I said, tell me who you are? Who else knows you are here?'

'You want to know who I am?' Lucas replied after taking another kick. 'I'm the last mistake you'll ever make.'

The terrorist paid him no mind, determined to beat a proper answer out of his captive. His repeated actions played right into Lucas's hands, as the former SAS soldier jumped to his feet and grabbed the leg, then drove his elbow down on his assailant's knee, sending it the wrong way. The J terrorist screamed in agony as his knee was shattered, but he was quickly silenced with a swift blow to his trachea. He immediately had difficulty breathing and was wheezing until he had no breath at all. His eyes bulged, and he collapsed to the ground.

Lucas rubbed his chest as he rang a number on his phone. 'Sofia? You're all clear.'

• • • •

'I'M ALL DONE,' ELLEN suddenly announced. They had made the almost forty-minute drive in silence, which was only penetrated by the sound of Ellen's rapid tapping of her laptop keyboard as she sat in the back of Natasha's Range Rover. 'We should have no problem getting access now. I've changed the name on their system to yours. We'll just rock up and tell them you've lost your key-card. Simple.'

Natasha parked on the same road she had before, and as the two women made their way to the famous hotel, the memories of a few hours ago came rushing back. It wasn't the first time she'd been shot at, that was at the Nineveh excavation, and it had happened plenty of times since she and Lucas started up The Acquirers business but being shot at in one of London's best-known hotels was a huge step from being shot at in some of the war-torn countries they'd been too.

After explaining to the constable at the entrance that they were staying there, Natasha and Ellen headed for the check-in desk.

'I'm sorry, and somewhat embarrassed to tell you this,' Ellen began in a well-spoken manner that caught Natasha off guard. 'My step-mother seems to have lost our key-card and my father is busy at a conference.'

'Okay, I can get you a new card. What room was that?'

'116,' replied Ellen. 'The Masterson's.'

Natasha almost made to protest, but Ellen waved her off.

'Oh, here we are,' replied the receptionist as she looked at digital copies of their passports, which Ellen had uploaded to the system. 'I'll get that replacement for you.'

'So, what's going on here? Why all the police?'

'Oh my god, it was crazy! A man and woman were shot this morning, on your floor, actually. The police reckon it was some kind of shoot out.'

'You're kidding me.' Ellen feigned surprise. 'Are we safe here?'

'I sure hope so. They don't know if the shooter was a guest or not, but they may have some questions for you at some point though.'

'Thanks for all you help. Now, take the key mother, and try not to lose this one.'

Natasha smiled thinly as she took the card. When they had entered the lift, she turned to Ellen. 'Mother? What the hell!'

'Stepmother, actually, it would look kind of unrealistic if you had a kid at ten years old.'

'But me being married to someone that's almost seventy is alright?'

'Of course. You look the type.'

'What the hell's that supposed to mean?'

The doors of the lift opened before Ellen replied. There was understandably a significant police presence there, and they headed to Marcus Masterson's room, the opposite direction of where the shootings had taken place.

Natasha opened the door and made straight for the bedroom, with Ellen following behind, whistling her appreciation of the suite. She touched and investigated everything and when the archaeologist threw the key-card on the bed, she swiped it up.

Natasha looked at her quizzically. 'What are you doing?'

'Making a duplicate of the coding for this card. I could use a place like this when I'm meeting my guy friends.'

'Guy friends?'

'What? You don't think I have guy friends?'

'It's none of my business, what you have, but you're loaded. You could just buy it when you need to.'

'Yeah, of course, but this is more fun,' Ellen smiled as she unpacked her bag.

All Natasha could do was shake her head as she began to collect the professor's shoes. One by one, she tested her theory about the shoes. She was right. Each heel contained a fragment of the message.

She laid them out, rearranging them like a jigsaw until she believed she had the message solved. It just needed the final piece she took from her pocket.

If you're reading this
Then something has gone horribly wrong
I had to hide the eye from them
I didn't want you to know to protect you
Because you have an innate hunger for knowledge
Your curiosity will kill you Natasha
But now you mustn't let the
Eye of Nineveh fall into the wrong hands
Look where my brothers sit.

'Well, well, well,' Natasha said, rubbing her hands. 'It looks like we got a little treasure hunt.'

'All because your professor knows you're a nosey bitch.'

'A determined bitch that gets the job done, you mean.'

Chapter 13

Natasha read out the message a few more times as she nonchalantly twisted a strand of her hair around her finger. Try as she might, she couldn't figure out what the professor had gotten himself involved in, nothing she believed he would be involved in, at any rate.

'Why are you wasting your time?' Ellen said as she finished the key-card duplication and started to pack away her things. 'Why don't you just heed his warning and let it go? He obviously hid it for a reason. We could just chill out here for a bit, order some room service and see if it's up to scratch.'

'He wants me to find it,' Natasha replied in a matter-of-fact manner and held up two strips of the message as evidence. '"But now you must not let the Eye of Nineveh fall into the wrong hands" and I don't intend to. I don't really have a choice in the matter either. I have to find it if I want to save my parents.'

'You're just like he said.'

Natasha spun in her seat. 'Who?'

'Lucas,' Ellen replied. 'He said that you have this tenacious attitude when it comes to old things and unlocking history.'

'Perhaps I do.' She smiled at the compliment.

'He also said that it gets the two of you into loads of trouble,' laughed Ellen as she remembered some of the adventures Lucas had told her about.

Natasha scoffed at the accusation. 'Yeah, well, some artefacts should be in museums, not private collections!'

'So they can be stolen?'

'Museum heists aren't as common as you think they are. And I'm not so sure this was a heist either. Something is a bit off about the whole thing. We know that Professor Masterson, in his own words, has hidden the Eye of Nineveh, and yet on the CCTV, the stone was still there after he left.

'Okay, since you have to do this, solve your mystery, recover the artefact, save your parents, save yourself, save the world, I suppose we should start with his brothers, like he said. So, where are they?'

'He doesn't have any, he's an only child,' Natasha replied, then pondered for a moment. 'But he does have a brotherhood, a fraternity. He's a Freemason!'

Ellen rolled her eyes. 'Of course he is,' she replied. She picked up her bag, ready to leave. On her way out, she stopped at the minibar and emptied its contents into her backpack. 'Okay, now I'm ready to go!'

It was a ten-minute walk to Freemasons Hall in Bloomsbury. For the entire journey, Ellen waxed lyrical about the reasons why she wouldn't be setting a foot inside the temple. Natasha couldn't believe the amount of information the young woman retained about the society, be it right or wrong.

'When you get in there, they're going to tell you all about Freemasonry being a fraternity of free and accepted men enjoined to devote themselves to ethical, educational, fraternal, patriotic and humanitarian concerns.'

'And what's wrong with that? It sounds like a group focussed on camaraderie.'

'You're supposed to think that. That's the visible aspect of the society. But there is also an invisible aspect, an inner society which is the masons true beating heart.'

'I see.'

'Yeah, well you can be as sceptical as you want but answer me this, why did Adam Weishaupt, the man that began the Illuminati say that "the strength of the Order was in its concealment; let it never appear in any place in its own name, but always covered by another name. None is fitter than the degrees of Freemasonry."'

'So, you're saying Freemasons and the Illuminati are one and the same?'

'No, aren't you listening to a word I'm saying? You have your visible Freemasons, the camaraderie crap you were going on about, but only the illuminated Masons, those indoctrinated into both organisations, know the true secrets of the Masonic lodges. And don't get me started on the Rosicrucians.'

'And how do you know all of this?'

'You don't really expect me to tell you that, do you? You're entering the world of secret societies, get used to not knowing shit.'

Natasha looked at her in disbelief. 'So, you're not coming in then?'

Ellen shook her head and rummaged in her bag.

'Fine. Just don't go anywhere, I won't be long.'

'No problem. I'll sit here having a party,' Ellen replied as she lit one of her special roll ups and opened a miniature she took from the hotel.

· · · ·

AS NATASHA ENTERED the art déco building known as Freemasons Hall, she was immediately struck by its opulence. The marble staircase was wide with plush red carpeting. Grand paintings of significant members of the past lined the walls.

'If you're here for the tour,' the receptionist at the front suddenly said, 'you'd better hurry up. It's about to start.'

'Oh, yes, thank you,' Natasha replied, and she picked up one of their free magazines, attempting to appear as nothing but a curious tourist. 'Where do I go?'

'Up the stairs and to the left. The meeting point is in the shop.'

Natasha thanked her and set off up the impressive stairs. When she arrived, the guide was already explaining the origins of the society. Although she wasn't really paying attention, Natasha was more interested in locating the clue she was expecting to find here, she overheard some of the spiel the guide was delivering and to her surprise, it was just as Ellen had said, word for word.

She shook her head at the coincidence and continued to look around. The Royal Grand Masters throne, a huge, gilded lime wood chair with thick royal blue padding, was impossible to miss as the small tour group was led around. Natasha thought it would be the perfect place for Professor

Masterson to have hidden something. It wasn't as if it didn't have enough space to squirrel something away.

As the party moved on, Natasha walked all around the throne, scrutinising every inch of the seat. Seeing nothing out of the ordinary, she took the bold move of stepping over the rope for a closer look. She ran her hand over the arms and legs but found nothing. The underneath revealed nothing as well. Just as Natasha reached up to check the globes and crown that were on either side and above the symbol of the masons, the set square and ruler, there was a cough behind her, and the cashier glared at her.

Natasha smiled weakly and rushed off to re-join the tour, passing a large portrait of King George IV which seemed to smirk down at her and her failed attempts of discovering Marcus's secret.

The slow walk around the edifice was an interesting one, to say the least. With all the stained-glass windows adorned with Freemason iconography, it was hard not to be. The guide revealed that the building was built to honour the Freemason brothers of the United Grand Lodge of England, who had fallen during World War I. An impressive shrine which housed a scroll with all their names was of particular importance to the lodge as, not only did it have four golden statues on the top, representing the four branches of the armed forces, but on its front, it also had four figures that were important to freemasonry: Moses, Joshua, King Solomon, and Saint George.

They moved onto the Grand Temple, the jewel in the crown of the lodge. Its doorway was two, solid bronze doors, each weighing one and quarter tonnes. Depicted on them was King Solomon overseeing the building of his temple. After the guide asked for a volunteer, she asked them to try pushing a door open with a single finger. Natasha was not as impressed as the rest of the group, knowing that such things were being done hundreds of years before. She believed it might well have been utilised in the grand palaces of the Assyrian empire.

Inside the Grand Hall, itself could only be described as an iconographer's dream. The extraordinary mosaic ceiling displayed symbols from many different faiths, pagan and orthodox alike. Six pointed stars along with five pointed stars, Saint George next to Helios, an Ouroboros opposite Jacobs ladder, mathematical signs, and stars of the cosmos.

This is it, Natasha thought. If Professor Masterson left a clue, it must be somewhere in the hall. As the tour ended, the guide allowed the group to explore on their own. Many took pictures of themselves sitting on the Grand Master's throne and as Natasha waited for an opportunity to investigate it herself, she walked and looked among the other rows of seats, hoping that Marcus hadn't hidden it somewhere in the freestanding balcony's as they were out of bounds during the tour.

Soon, the rest of the tour party moved away from the golden throne. Natasha stepped up on the dais and get a closer look at the opulent chair. She ran her hands all around it, looking for any kind of hidden panel or raised button, anything that shouldn't be there or was out of the ordinary. Natasha came back around to the front, sat in it, and checked the sides of the cushioning. Still, she found nothing.

As Natasha squirmed about in the throne, searching every nook and cranny of it, the magazine she had picked up from the front desk fell out of her pocket. She reached down to retrieve it and noticed that it had fallen open on a group photo of a small lodge in Wales. The image immediately evoked memories of the picture at Professor Masterson's home, of him and his "brothers".

In her mind's eye, she could see it perfectly. He was seated on the dais, perhaps his position within the society bestowed a particular seat that was his alone, she thought. Natasha stood up from the Grand Master's throne and stood at the bottom of the steps, and turned to face it. She closed her eyes, visualised the photograph in her mind, saw where the professor was seated, and quickly headed to the chair.

The guide had gathered everyone together to leave, prompting Natasha to hurry. She searched thoroughly, and yet again, found nothing. Her mind was in turmoil as she thought through every scrap of info she had. As Natasha grasped the arms of the chair, feeling the intricate carving under her fingers, she leaned back, hoping that the mosaic cosmos above might shed a little light on her problem.

Then there was an almost indistinguishable click.

Natasha's ears twitched at the sound, and reaching underneath the seat of the chair, she discovered that a small hatch had been unlocked. Inside it was a small scrap of paper, barely big enough for the message that was written on both its sides.

'"Look to the light. The shadow of the gates holds the key." Damn it, Marcus. Could you be more cryptic?'

'Excuse me,' the guide said, suddenly coming up to Natasha. 'It's time for us to go. You seem rather taken with it all. Have you ever considered joining the Freemasons?'

'It is all very of interesting. I actually know a member, Marcus Masterson.'

'Oh, Marcus has been wonderful to the Grand Lodge. He helped design one of the stained-glass windows we passed and even paid for its recent repair, even though no one knew it was damaged. Unfortunately, he wouldn't be able to give you an invitation to join the Freemasons. Since the male and female lodges are separate, it would have to come from a woman, but if you are interested, I can put an invitation for you.'

Natasha had barely heard a thing the guide had said, not since she mentioned the stain glass windows. Look to the light. Maybe there was something there. 'I'll think about it,' she replied, just to placate her. 'I don't suppose you could point out the window you were talking about?'

'Of course, it's just outside. Okay, everyone, let's make our way back to the shop.'

They all passed the enormous bronze doors once more. The guide closed the door behind them and caught Natasha's attention. 'That's the one Marcus had done. Rather an abstract design compared to the others throughout the lodge, but those are from the twenties, and this is the twenty-first century, so a bit of modernisation is welcomed.'

The guide was right, the pattern was a bit different. There were no religious figures or other Masonic iconography. The pattern was a series of straight panels of varying lengths and colours, all placed at different angles as if it were a cubist's interpretation of a sunburst.

Natasha couldn't see anything special about the stained-glass window, no inscriptions or anything. Then she turned to walk away from it, and, at that exact moment, the sun moved from behind a stray cloud. The afternoon sun's rays shone through the coloured glass. The pattern that was created on the tiled marble floor was made up of only certain parts of the window itself.

'Is ... is that a map?' Natasha whispered as she stared at the shadowy image that was mysteriously projected on the ground.

Chapter 14

The Square Mile never looked so daunting to Lucas. He was sure that in all the offices surrounding him, all those people making million-pound transactions were less nervous than he was right now. Of all the combat situations He had been in, none of them made him feel as uneasy as he felt right now.

Sir John Travers never made any attempt to hide the fact that the former SAS soldier wasn't good enough for his daughter. She was his pride and joy, and Lucas was the man taking her to bed each night.

At the beginning of their relationship, he had been against it because Lucas was an active soldier, likely to get blown up at any moment. He didn't want her going through that. When they got married and opened The Acquirers, he said that Lucas was a bad influence on her, not only was he going to get himself killed with their treasure hunting, but he was putting her in dangerous situations too, although it was usually her hard headedness that frequently got them into trouble. If he ever told him about what happened in Peru, he'd never look at his daughter the same way again.

He smiled at the recollection of that particular adventure.

Natasha's dad felt his low opinion of Lucas was vindicated the day he found out about his affair. He wasn't sure, but it wasn't too much of a stretch for Lucas to imagine him cracking open the champagne and having a celebration.

And yet here he was, not far from Liverpool Street station, looking for anyone suspicious that screamed terrorists-R-us, and that might also be paying more attention than was necessary, to John's office block.

He sat by the coffee shop window, sipping his tea. He'd seen three likely suspects. One was wearing similar clothing to the sniper he had already taken out, and that had been watching Sofia-Valentina. He assumed the man with him was also part of their organisation, judging by their conspiratorial manner.

Lucas deduced that they were handling this target differently than they had Sofia. Having that construction site opposite her office had been a no-brainer for them to exploit. However, this was the financial district for the City of London; most of these offices would be occupied 24/7 because of all the different times zones of the major markets.

Their change in tactics made things slightly more difficult for Lucas. Now he had to contend with everyday pedestrians. It was a little after 15:00 and the office workers that had a late lunch were heading back to their cubicles and offices. If he were to take down John Travers's stalkers, he'd have to wait until the right moment. And when that time came, he'd have to strike quickly so they wouldn't have time to alert anyone.

Time ticked by. Lucas wondered if Natasha had spoken to Sofia yet. Although the archaeologist liked to give the impression that she was in total control of her emotions, he knew she was worried about her parents, and rightly so.

Just as he was about to take out his mobile phone and check up on the woman, who for the time being, he could still call his wife, Lucas suddenly saw movement across the street. One of the two men was having a heated discussion on his phone, perhaps with the third man down the road, who was also on a mobile. He was a lot calmer. No doubt the one giving the orders for this little group, Lucas deduced. Suddenly, the two men walked away, heading north towards Travers's law firm, whilst the third remained on the street corner.

Lucas watched them as he sipped the last of his tea and decided what his next plan of action should be; stick with the one in charge or follow the grunts? He made up his mind as he threw his disposable cup in the bin before he left the shop and followed the two men.

They were the ones that he was here for. The two-man watcher team assigned to keep tabs on John Travers, Natasha's dad. Except this was a three-man group. What if the ones that had been watching Sofia had a third man too? 'Damn it,' Lucas said under his breath and quickly dialled her number. He'd been cocky. 'You should have checked more thoroughly to make sure they didn't have a handler,' he berated himself.

By the time Lucas had informed her of the situation, the two terrorists had entered the building. He rushed after them. 'Hold the lift,' Lucas yelled as they stepped into it. Neither of them did as requested, but Lucas arrived just in time to slip his arm between the doors, forcing them to reopen. He stepped inside the lift and the doors closed slowly behind him.

They glared at him. Lucas stared back, wondering if they knew who he was; if they had an ace of spades in their pocket with his face on it. They knew who Natasha was. They had specifically targeted her family to get her to do their bidding, so it only made sense that they would know of him, too. He smiled. Even if they didn't, a few more beat downs would go a long way to introducing himself.

The inside of a lift was not the ideal place for a fight, especially with three large men. Even though Lucas was trained in close quarters combat, the confined space they were in desired a different fighting style, extreme close quarters. Punches and kicks were next to useless since it was difficult to get a full range of motion. Elbows and knees took precedence, as well as the tried and tested headbutt.

There was a flurry of motion. The J terrorists looked at each other, and Lucas launched his attack. They may have been proficient enough at hand-to-hand combat, but this combat environment was obviously not part of their training. Even using their numerical advantage, they were still effectively at a disadvantage.

Their blows had none of the strength behind them, whilst his were devastating. In a frenetic sixty seconds of violence, it was all over. The two terrorists lay unconscious at Lucas's feet as the lift doors opened and he stepped out.

'You should have held the door,' he smirked as he moved the "closed for cleaning" sign from a neighbouring lift and placed it in front of the one he had just exited.

Lucas felt pleased with himself. Two down, one to go, he said to himself and turned to head for the stairs. Then he heard a familiar voice.

'Lucas? What are you doing here?'

'Chiara?' He was stunned. Not being able to tell her the truth, he grabbed at the most likely story, no matter how unlikely it actually was. 'Uhm ... nothing much. I was passing by and thought that I might come and see John.'

'John Travers? Natasha's dad? The man that hates you?' she asked with a raised eyebrow.

Before Lucas could respond, the man in question and his guest, Peter Armitage, joined them.

'I thought I could hear your voice, but I assumed I was hearing things, and yet here you are. What do you want, Lucas?'

'So this is the man that I have heard so much about?' Peter queried as he looked him up and down. 'Aren't you going to introduce me, Chiara?'

'Yes, of course. Lucas, this is the man I work for, Peter Armitage. Peter, this is Lucas Redmond.'

'The infamous Lucas Redmond,' Peter corrected, putting his hands together.

'You two know each other?' John was a little surprised at the familiarity between Lucas and Chiara.

'Oh, didn't you know? It was Chiara that I was with when Natasha found out about the affair,' Lucas stated.

'What?' John Travers was taken aback by the news.

'Well, John,' interjected Peter. 'I see what you mean about him not being good enough for your daughter. Having such disregard for the honour of not only Natasha but Chiara too is no way for a man to act.'

'You're right. She's better off without him and you'd do well to steer clear also, Chiara,' sneered John.

'Tomorrow, I'll show Natasha how a real man is supposed to act in the presence of a lady, John.'

'Oh, didn't you know?' John began, responding to the confused look on Lucas's face. 'Peter and Natasha have arranged to have lunch together tomorrow. And with any luck, this will be the beginning of something that will see the end of you haunting my daughter's life with your presence.'

Lucas was so tempted to tell him about the men that were following Sofia and himself. Then tell him he was the one protecting his condescending ass. If he were alone, maybe he would have, but he couldn't, with Chiara and Peter hanging around. 'Anyway, I have things to take care of,' he announced as he turned to leave. 'I'll see you later, Chiara. And as for you, Armitage, Natasha is no fool, she'll see through whatever you and her dad have planned.

Lucas returned to the street, only to see that his fears had been realised. The third terrorist had gone. He cursed under his breath and, standing where he had last seen the man, looked all around, hoping to catch a glimpse of him.

Lucas suddenly spotted his prey crossing the road. The terrorist was on the phone again, possibly trying to get hold of his comrades or, as Lucas hoped, talking to The Baron himself, in the off chance that he'd lead him straight to the leader of the terrorist group.

Lucas kept a safe distance between the terrorist handler and himself as he followed him. He knew that this could turn out to be a solid lead, so he was intent on making sure that the phone wielding man didn't make him and get spooked.

The man finally hung up his phone as he turned onto a side road. Lucas jogged up to the corner, so as not to lose sight of him, only to have his way suddenly blocked by a man.

'Fancy meeting you here,' Kallum Taylor announced. 'Quite the coincidence, wouldn't you say?'

The man Lucas was following was getting further and further away, which prompted the former soldier to pursue. He tried to walk past the insurance investigator, but Kallum stopped Lucas by putting a hand on his chest.

'Just a second. I've got some questions for you.'

Lucas craned his head to see if he could still see the terrorist, but to no avail. He'd disappeared. Frustrated, Lucas brushed Kallum's hand away. 'What the hell do you want! I'm busy.'

'Really? Is The Ghost planning his next job?'

Lucas shook his head, tired of these accusations. 'When exactly are you going to produce any proof of your claims?'

'In time, Lucas, or do you prefer to be called Sebastian?'

'I'd prefer you not to talk to me at all.'

'Quite the opposite of Natasha. She was extremely interested in what I had to say, especially about your parents.'

That was the final straw, all Lucas could bear, as he grabbed hold of Kallum. 'What have you said to her?'

'Only the truth, Lucas, only the truth. In fact, do you know where she is? I have a few more things to say to her. In fact, don't worry, I have people looking for her.'

'Who are you really? What do you want?'

'I'm just a humble man doing his job.'

'Bullshit. You're part of the J organisation, aren't you?'

Kallum looked puzzled. 'Who?'

Lucas stared at him hard. He couldn't tell if he was being truthful or not. Which disconcerted him. There was something that didn't quite feel right about him. For a start, he didn't act like any insurance investigator that he'd ever seen before. He was just too slick, almost like a conman overplaying their role, a not very good conman. 'Play all the games you want; I'll find out who you are.'

'Is that before or after you go to jail?' Kallum's phone suddenly rang. He struggled to free himself from Lucas's tight grip, then took out his phone. He didn't say a word. It was a short, one-sided conversation. 'Looks like I don't need your help to find Natasha after all. My men have already found her.'

Chapter 15

It didn't matter which way she looked at the picture, Natasha couldn't see what it was supposed to be. She was sure it was a map, but a map of what or where, she had no idea. She glanced at the time and threw her phone down. Seconds later, it automatically switched off and the image vanished. It was already 16:00. Four hours had already passed, and she felt no closer to finding the Eye of Nineveh.

After they had left Freemasons Hall, Natasha had driven back to her apartment in St Katherine's Dock, with Ellen in tow. The young hacker had fired question after question at her, giving the occasional disbelieving scoff when Natasha answered them. 'That's what they tell the uninitiated,' she would say, before going into delivering her "truths".

At the time, Natasha had been glad to get home and put an end to Ellen's conspiracy tirade. Finding the map was the top priority. But they were getting nowhere fast, and it was frustrating them both.

'Can I ask you a question, Natasha?' Ellen asked as she played with Solo.

The delivery was so polite that she was caught off guard. 'Uhm, sure.'

'What the hell is wrong with your professor?' Ellen yelled. 'What kind of crazy old fool leaves a goddamn line as a clue?'

'He's not an old fool. You don't know him. He is a skilled teacher that knows how to inspire his students to excel.'

'And he also thinks you're a nosey bitch. Just saying.'

Natasha frowned at the very thought. 'He does not.'

'Yeah, he does. You forgot the message in his shoes? I don't need to be a cryptographer to know that "innate hunger for knowledge" translates into nosey bitch,' Ellen stated as she opened a miniature.

'Don't you think you've had enough of those?'

'Nope,' replied Ellen, and tossed one of the little bottles over to Natasha. 'You're right, I don't know this guy, but you do, and he knows you. That message was for you. You were his contingency plan. So this line, whatever it is, must mean something, something that he knew you would recognise.'

Natasha didn't want to say, but Ellen's hypothesise made sense. She twisted the top of the tiny bottle of whiskey and took a swig. The golden liquid warmed her chest. It wasn't her favourite spirit, but it would do in a pinch; she'd take anything to deal with the stress of the day she was having.

She let her mind correlate and sift through every scrap of information she could remember about Marcus Masterson; the excavations he'd been a part of in his youth, the artefacts he'd found. They had talked a lot over the years, but nothing was coming to mind as to what this crooked line represented.

'I can't think of anything it could be.' It felt like a fruitless exercise, a waste of time, something that she was running out of as it continued to run down unabated. But she couldn't give up. She had to solve it to protect her parents. With her resolve strengthened, Natasha put her mind back to the task.

'What about at his apartment? Was there anything there?'

'No, just his shoes and the books he's written. It wasn't as sparse as his room in The Savoy, but ... '

'What is it?' Ellen asked as Natasha suddenly sat up straight in her chair with a wide-eyed look.

Natasha grabbed the picture she had taken of the pattern the sunshine had made when it had shone through the stained-glass window at Freemasons Hall. A smile of recognition slowly crept across her face. 'You idiot, Natasha,' she whispered.

'You figured it out?'

'Yeah, I have,' Natasha replied triumphantly. Her winning mentality was sated once more. 'Marcus is one of the leading authorities on The Eye of Nineveh and the Chintamani Stone. He believed that every great empire of antiquity had possessed it, because they seemed to fall as swiftly as they rose.'

'Okay. What's that got to do with this crooked line though?'

'Marcus was in the process of writing a new book; he showed me the manuscript the last time I saw him. It was about the Roman Empire. He was trying to prove that the reason they could become such a strong, dominant force was because they had a Chintamani Stone. In the book, Marcus goes about proving that the fall of Rome began when Mark Anthony was defeated by Octavian.'

'The whole Cleopatra thing? Wasn't that for love?'

'I'm sure there was some love involved, but first and foremost, for her at least, was her love for Egypt and her people. She seduced Julius Caesar to secure her country's future, but he was just as canny an operator as she was and refused to bring the stone to Egypt. When he was betrayed, she worked on Mark Anthony. The story is that he had the Chintamani Stone when he lost the battle of Actium, and it was lost at sea.'

'That's all well and good, but again, what's that got to do with that line?' Ellen asked, pointing at the image Natasha held in her hand.

'This isn't just any line. This represents the old roman wall that once surrounded the City of London! And it makes sense really. That line in the message, "the shadow of the gates holds the key" must refer to the seven entry gates that were part of the wall, well, most likely only the five original gates; Ludgate, Newgate, Cripplegate, Bishopsgate and Aldgate.'

'That's it then. This quest is solved!'

'Not quite. There aren't any of the gates left, just bits of the walls along the route. Besides, we have no idea what we're supposed to be looking for.'

'Well, the quicker you get a move on, the quicker you'll find out.'

'What happened to "we"?'

'I'm not really a field agent, more like tech support and fixer, so I think I'm going to be staying here.'

Natasha scrutinised her closely. 'You're drunk, aren't you?'

Ellen scoffed. 'Who do you think I am? Natasha Travers? Of course I'm not drunk. You should be happy I'm staying here to look after your dog!'

'Fine,' Natasha replied as she prepared to head out again. 'And don't smoke any of your stuff in here either,' she added over her shoulder as Ellen began to make a roll up.

• • • •

IT WAS EARLY EVENING and the restaurants within the trendy marina were already filling with patrons. Many a night, when Natasha and Lucas lived in St Katherine's dock together, they would be out here having a meal themselves. The memories they created were so vivid to her that she could almost feel him caress her cheek and smell the Paco Rabane eau de toilette he would wear. It had been a Christmas present from her, a few years ago, but he'd loved it so much, he had continued to buy it for himself.

Out of the blue, her phone rang. When she saw Lucas's name on the caller display, she couldn't stop herself from smiling.

After Natasha composed herself, she answered the call and was subjected to an agitated barrage from the other end of the line. 'Whoa! Lucas, slow down, I can't understand you.'

'You have to watch yourself. Kallum is looking for you!'

'Kallum? But I spoke to him a few hours ago.'

'I don't know. What I do know is that he was near your dad's office, and he stopped me from following one of the terrorists.'

'Is Dad okay? What about Mum?'

'Don't worry, they're both fine. After stopping me, Kallum asked me where you were and when I said I didn't know, he told me he had people following you. I'm beginning to think that Kallum might be The Baron.'

'What? That's crazy,' Natasha replied, and had a quick look around. The people at the restaurants were busily eating and chatting. As she continued to turn, there was only one person paying her any attention. A man across the marina who watched her intently. Others had always complemented Natasha on her good looks. Although she considered herself to be quite ordinary, she tended to catch men glancing at her. But this was different. This was an intense stare, which made her uneasy, especially since she was sure that she had seen him before, on Tower Bridge when she had been stopped by Kallum. 'I think I see the man who's following me,' she whispered into the phone.

'You have to get out of there, Natasha. Head to London Bridge!'

'Lucas! Lucas!' Natasha said urgently into her phone, but he had already hung up. She put her phone away into her bag and made a move.

As Natasha crossed a couple of the bridges in the marina, heading towards St Katherine's way, she took a quick look over her shoulder and saw that the man had also moved to leave. The moment she was out of his line of sight, she sprinted.

She headed onto Tower Wharf, sidestepping tourists who were snapping pictures of the Tower of London and the neighbouring iconic bridge. Natasha glanced over her shoulder and saw her pursuer in the distance.

Natasha pumped her fists as she ran and in no time, she was joining the main road at Lower Thames Street, ironically not far from London Wall, the first stop on her trek to follow the remaining sections of the roman wall.

Her heart raced. Natasha was relatively fit, exercised regularly; played squash, tennis, she even recently took up mixed martial arts, to get rid of some of the anger about her broken marriage she had pent up. But that was all nothing compared to prolonged sprinting. Even Olympic sprinters hated running at top speed for long and struggled to do so. Another look over her shoulder and she could see that the man chasing her was still there, and even though he was gaining on her, she was spent and slowed down.

Natasha was just passing Old Billingsgate, the former Victorian fish market, when a tall, mysterious man suddenly stepped out in front of her. He grabbed her in a vice like grip. She couldn't believe that her pursuer had a compatriot. At no point had she seen him. As much as she struggled, she couldn't break free of his grip. Just as Natasha was about to scream, his big hand clamped over her mouth.

'Stop struggling. Don't make this any more difficult than it has to be Natasha,' he growled in a deep voice.

Chapter 16

Lucas glimpsed at the clock on his car's dashboard; It read 17:00, the middle of rush hour, although these days it felt like rush hour was at least three hours long. He wished happy hour would be so lax with its concept of time. The way this day was progressing, he knew he'd be needing a few by the end of it.

After his phone call to Natasha, he'd made a couple more afterwards, the last of which was to Sofia-Valentina. When he received no answer, Lucas had thought the worst, thought that maybe the terrorist he had missed, had made good on their threats to Natasha and done something to her mother. He had rushed back to the hospital, only to be informed that she had already left for home.

Although the Travers family home was on Bishops Walk in Surrey, Lucas knew that their townhouse on Primrose Hill was where they lived most weekdays, mainly because it was closer to their places of employment.

He parked his Alfa and ran to Natasha's parents' home. He was relieved to see her car parked outside, and even more so when she opened the door.

'Come on in, why don't you,' Sofia said sarcastically as Lucas all but pushed past her.

He urgently searched all the rooms. The voice in the back of his mind telling him he was probably being over cautious, but better to be that than lax. 'How long have you been back here?' Lucas finally asked once he was satisfied that they were alone.

'Not long,' she replied as she poured them a drink in the living room. 'Five or ten minutes, maybe. Why? What's this all about?'

'It's likely that there were more than the two men that I took out at the hospital following you. There were three at John's office and it's possible that they may have had a similar sized group tailing you too. Did you see anybody suspicious after I'd gone?'

She shook her head. 'No, not that I can think of.'

'Nothing at all? No one loitering about trying to avoid looking at you?'

'No, nothing like that. But there was ... '

'What is it?'

'Well, when I came back, I could have sworn I saw movement at the house across the road, at the Devonshire's, number 48.'

'And?'

'They're supposed to be on holiday. I saw them this morning packing their bags into their car.'

'What do they drive?'

'A Mercedes Maybach.'

'Colour?'

'Like a wine red, I suppose.'

Lucas pulled the curtain aside a looked up and down the street. 'There's no sign of the car. Maybe they have gone, but I'll check it out all the same. They got a garden round the back?' When Sofia nodded, Lucas rummaged through his bag until he found what he was looking for; a small aerosol can.

He shook it and sprayed it on each of his palms, waiting for it to dry before doing the other. Sofia looked at him cockeyed, like he was crazy, but Lucas knew what she was thinking. 'It's not glue. It's a silicone resin that remains mailable but covers my fingerprints.' He silently thanked Ellen for sourcing them for him.

Lucas was ready for action. At the door, they hugged and kissed both of the other's cheeks, as was the Latin way. He told her to carry on as normal, to keep up the pretence that she was non-the-wiser. Then Lucas jumped into his Alfa Romeo and took off down the road.

Once he had taken a corner and was out of sight of number 48, Lucas parked again and jumped out. He took a few steps and then paused. Something had caught his eye. On another corner was a dark red car. As Lucas walked further into the middle of the road, the car's make came into view. It was a Maybach. 'I guess they didn't make their holiday after all,' Lucas said to himself. He hoped he was wrong, but he was sure he could guess their fate.

At the back of the row of houses was a three-metre-high wall. With a bit of a run up, Lucas scrambled up it, and hanging from the top, was able to peer over. When he saw the coast was clear, he pulled himself up the rest of the way, climbed over and landed softly on the grass. He stayed in a crouched position behind a well-manicured bush and took stock of his surroundings.

There were a few possible entryways, the most obvious one being the large bi-folding doors that led to the open-plan kitchen. It would also be the easiest way to enter, if it was unlocked, that is. Lucas spotted a motion activated light above the glass doors, but since it wasn't yet dark enough to draw attention to his movement when it came on, he paid it no mind and crept up to the door.

Now that he was up close to the folding doors, Lucas could see that they weren't closed at all. There was a slight gap. When he investigated further, he found a dented, spent 9mm shell in the runners. His hope for the Devonshire's plummeted.

Lucas quietly slid the door open and closed it behind him. He was expecting three men to be here, but he couldn't count on there not being more. Ideally, he wanted to pick them off, one by one, quickly and silently, so that he could get back to Natasha. He had made a promise to Natasha that he would always be there for her if she needed him, no matter what. Lucas wasn't about to renege on that pledge now that she did, despite their estrangement.

As he left the kitchen, it became apparent to him that this house was pretty much a mirror image of the Travers's home across the road. It would make navigation of the property a touch easier, although if he were to hazard a guess, the stalkers were no doubt holed up somewhere in the street facing rooms of the house, so they could watch Sofia and John come and go.

He eased along the wall, glancing upstairs as he passed them, until he reached the edge of the doorframe to the living room. He glanced around the corner and upon seeing nothing out of the ordinary, Lucas slipped into the contemporary decorated room. It wasn't until he was further inside the room that he heard the soft rhythmic sounds of someone sleeping.

The breathing was coming from the large "L" shaped, dark-blue sofa which faced away from the door. He gave the adjoining room a cursory look to begin with, but when he saw the naked woman smoking a cigarette whilst going through the Devonshire's wine rack, Lucas stopped and stared.

He couldn't help but admire her body; her sinewy, lean muscles, the curve of her buttocks. Then, as she turned around, he saw the tattoo of a fanged snake on her arm. Lucas was stunned. Although he knew he shouldn't have been, terrorist organisations were well known for recruiting women and even children. Just because, until now, he hadn't encountered any, didn't mean they were any different from any other radical group.

The girl, who wasn't much older than Ellen, stood there glaring at Lucas with her left hand on her hip. She brought the cigarette she held in her right hand slowly up to her mouth and took a long drag of the white stick. As the clouds of smoke escaped her mouth, she smiled and slowly walked towards Lucas. The glare in her eyes became a leering one. Then Lucas caught something almost imperceptible. Her eyes quickly darted over his shoulder and then back.

Someone was behind him.

Strong arms came around his neck from behind. Fortunately, despite her distraction, Lucas had been fast enough to stop his unseen assailant from getting their sleeper hold locked in, but still had an arm around his neck to contend with. Whilst he struggled with the man behind him, the naked woman threw down her cigarette and rushed into the fray, repeatedly throwing punch after punch into Lucas's unprotected midsection.

He raised his foot and pushed the girl away, sending her crashing into the counter behind. Lucas looked on wide-eyed as she grabbed a bottle of wine and came at him again, intent on using it as a weapon. Before she could deliver the blow to him, Lucas twisted around just enough for the man grappling him to have the bottle smashed over his head. Claret exploded everywhere and mingled with the blood that flowed from the deep wound on his head.

The hold around Lucas's neck loosened instantly, allowing him to flip the man over his shoulder and, by keeping hold of the assailant's arm, dislocate it from its socket with a violent wrench of the joint.

Seeing that the man was also naked, Lucas assumed he was the one dozing on the sofa and thought the two of them must have been having some fun when he had left the Travers home.

Lucas saw that the woman hadn't given up on her attempted assault yet as she thrust the broken bottle at him with each step she took towards him. So single-minded had she become that she didn't even flinch as she walked through the broken glass with her bare feet.

Telegraphing her next thrust of the makeshift weapon, Lucas grabbed her wrist, twisted her arm until she released the bottle, and he delivered a punch, knocking her out cold.

Lucas turned back to check on the terrorist lothario. He saw him reaching out with his good arm for the discarded pile of clothes that belonged to the lovers, moving shirts and underwear. Then Lucas saw for the silenced gun. Without a second thought, he sprinted over, landing a knee thrust to the side of the terrorist's head. It was a concussive blow.

After he retrieved the gun, Lucas listened at the open door. He was more than certain that the scuffle had made enough noise to alert whoever was upstairs. Even though he knew they had set a trap for him, he had no choice but to spring it. He just wanted to even the odds a touch.

He looked around, desperately searching for something he could use to spring the trap. Then the naked woman stirred, and he got an idea. Lucas grabbed her and roughly dragged her to her feet, hoping the rough treatment would clear her cobwebs, just enough so that he wouldn't have to carry her.

With her arm draped over his shoulder and her legs almost moving independently of each other, Lucas slowly and deliberately led them upstairs. Just before stepping onto the landing, he paused and prepared himself. 'You were so good at your diversion,' he whispered to the semi-conscious girl, 'that I think I'd like to see it again.' With that Lucas pushed the girl up the rest of the stairs.

Almost instantly, he heard of suppressed gunfire as two terrorists stepped out from behind closed doors, one from either side of the landing, and riddled the girl with bullets. They had taken the bait and revealed their positions.

All too soon, the shooter on the lefts gun clicked empty, and Lucas jumped into action, pinning himself against the wall opposite. He fired three shots to the right in quick succession, knowing that there would nothing coming from behind, for a few seconds at least.

The three shots landed in a close grouping in the centre of the man's chest. Before the body had landed, he had dropped to a knee. A bullet ricocheted where Lucas's head had been. He squeezed the trigger three times, but there was only one bullet left. It struck the remaining terrorist in the shoulder, jerking him back and relieving him of his gun.

Lucas recognised him. It was the man that had escaped him, thanks to Kallum. The man drew a knife out of his belt and came at Lucas with gritted teeth. It was a foolhardy move. He was easily disarmed and thrown through a door into the bathroom.

Slowly walking in, Lucas loomed over him like an angel of death. It was then that he saw the bloody bodies of a middle-aged man and woman unceremoniously dumped in the bathtub, the unfortunate Devonshire's. The fate of the man crawling on the floor had been set as Lucas watched with an intense gaze. The J terrorist had taken his phone from his pocket and was calling for help from the person on the other end. Let him tell whoever he wanted, Lucas thought as he had a quick glance around until he found something suitable.

Then he heard someone saying his name. The wounded terrorist had turned on the speaker on his phone. 'Lucas Redmond. This is The Baron. I know what you have been doing. Interfering when you were not invited. Look at your phone.'

The phone in his pocket buzzed, and he checked it. There were four videos which he watched in turned. Each was of someone being recorded; John Travers, Sofia-Valentina, Peter Armitage and Chiara Harris.

'I will find you and when I do, I will kill you,' Lucas spat with venom.

'Is that so? Then maybe we should speed up this little game of mine and Natasha's.'

Lucas was barely listening by now. He had picked up the cistern lid, weighed it in his hands, before going to stand over the prone man. The pleas for clemency from the terrorist fell on deaf ears. Lucas was intent on sending a message, and he rammed the heavy ceramic lid into the terrorist's throat, crushing his windpipe. It wasn't as though he enjoyed killing, it was just one of the many things that he had become talented at. He let the dying man's final escaping breaths be heard over the phone before Lucas smashed it, dramatically ending the call, then he left with haste, rushing to aid Natasha.

Chapter 17

Everything had been meticulously planned, to a minute level. Plan and prepare. That was how it was done in the special forces, in their unrelenting pursuit of excellence. It had been drilled into him, and those teachings still served him. It was how you reduced the casualties of your regiment and how you increased your chances of success. But there were always things you can't plan for. That's when you activate your contingency plans.

The Baron was being forced to activate his now.

Because of Lucas Redmond's interference, he was having to show that his threats were not idle. Both Lucas and Natasha would soon know that what The Baron said, he meant.

He had reconciled his mind with the possibility of collateral losses a long time ago. He avoided them when he could, but sometimes it wasn't possible. Sometimes you had to do the unthinkable, so people knew that anything was possible. The people in charge were more motivated to respond when atrocities were committed and realised that the bluster wasn't sabre waving.

The Baron calmly sat in the plush office and lit his highly aromatic Turkish tobacco cigarette. Oriental tobacco was one of the most expensive types, but when you're being bankrolled by people with deep pockets, things like the price of pure tobacco don't faze you.

Even though he preferred to work from the shadows, remaining incognito, having his troops carry out his wishes,

He was more than capable of getting his hands dirty, if need be. The fact that few people knew what the terrorist looked like, allowed him to walk the streets unmolested, without causing a stir. And here he sat, waiting.

'Excuse me,' John Travers said, his face stern as he opened the door of his office and found a stranger sitting at his desk. 'You can't be here!'

The Baron continued to smoke his cigarette. 'You have quite a beautiful family, Sir John.'

'Thank you. Now, if you wouldn't mind leaving, I'd like to get to my family. You're not really supposed to smoke in here either.'

'I'm an associate of Natasha's. We both have a deep passion for Assyrian artefacts.'

'That's nice! If you wanted help with your taxes, I'd be more than happy to help, but I'd have to insist that you returned tomorrow.'

'And I have to insist that you take a seat, Sir John.' The Baron drew the gun from his shoulder holster and lay it on the table.

John was temporarily frozen like a deer in headlights, but when his fear allowed him, he took the seat opposite. 'What's this about? I'm a respectable lawyer —'

'Come on, Sir John,' the terrorist scoffed. 'We both know that's not entirely true. Just as your daughter has a knack for finding lost treasures, you have a knack of losing taxes. But I don't care about that, I'm here for something else.'

John visibly swallowed. 'Then ... what is it ... you want?'

'Natasha and Lucas,' The Baron began as he stood up and outed his cigarette before wrapping it in a tissue and putting it in his pocket.

'I ... I don't know where they are?'

The Baron took a pouch from his pocket and unzipped it, opening it flat. 'That doesn't matter. They are supposed to be doing something for me, but it seems like they need some extra incentive.' He picked up a syringe from the opened pouch and removed its lid before squeezing it, sending a quick jet of the clear liquid through the air.

John began to fidget, moments from gathering the strength of will to run. But he became still when The Baron's hand hovered over the gun.

'You don't have to do this.'

'But I do,' The Baron corrected, as he moved closer. 'Just as I had to do with your wife, Sofia-Valentine, and Chiara Harris. Don't move, or you'll break the needle in your neck, and that would be very bad for you. Now, shhhh.'

The Baron injected John Travers and emptied the contents of the syringe into the neck of Natasha Travers' father.

· · · ·

NATASHA FOUGHT TO FREE herself from the tall man's grip, tried to be as much of a nuisance as she could. It was an almost impossible battle, but she never gave up, despite the odds, as he dragged her off of the main road.

He was taller than any man she had seen before, almost freakishly so. He man-handled her with ease, lifting her off the ground like she was nothing but a doll. His big hand still covered her mouth, preventing Natasha from screaming out for help. But the scene was attracting attention anyway, as she heard the voice of a male passer-by shout at her would-be abductor.

'Oi! What the hell are you doing to that woman?'

The unwanted attention was enough of a deterrent for the tall man and his hold on Natasha eased ever so slightly, but it was more than enough to reinvigorate her attempts to break free. She thrashed about wildly, and Natasha finally made her escape when the hand over her mouth loosened, and she bit it as hard as she could. Once she was free, and with all of her strength, Natasha pushed her attacker over and made to run.

'This way!' The man that had come to Natasha's aid said.

She was hesitant, and rightly so. He wasn't the terrorist that had chased her from St Katherine's dock, that much she knew. But then again, neither was the giant that grabbed her. She had seen his right hand, closer than she would have liked, and there had been no tattoo of a snake bearing its fangs.

'Quickly. Before he gets up.' He tried to hurry her, but it was already too late. The tall man was getting to his feet.

'You know what? I think I'll be alright from here,' Natasha said as she moved away. 'Thank you for all your help though.'

The man suddenly grabbed her wrist. 'What made you think this was an invitation, Natasha?'

'What? How do you know my name? Who are you?'

'Someone that wants to know what's happened to the Eye of Nineveh. Where is it?'

'So, you work for The Baron?'

Before he could answer, the tall man was bearing down on them. He threw Natasha against the wall before he turned to square up against his foe. He attacked first, hoping to take the advantage with a flurry of blows against the taller man. But it had little effect, as the difference in fighting prowess was instantly apparent. When the smaller man realised that he couldn't match up in unarmed combat, he pulled out a knife. That just made things worse, however, and moments later, he was unconscious on the floor.

It was over so quickly that Natasha barely had time to run, but now that it was, she planned to get the hell out of there, and the tall man knew it.

'Don't run, Natasha,' he said. 'My name's Lyndsay Alperton. Lucas sent me to look after you.'

She pulled up in mid stride, turned and gave him a sceptical look. 'Lucas? Why didn't you say anything before, then?'

'You never gave me a chance. I had to hide you from the man that was chasing you, and you were making so much noise. Then this idiot turned up.'

'Okay, let's say I believe you. How did you know where I was? Lucas didn't know.'

'But he did tell you to go to London Bridge. I work nearby and Ellen has pinged your phone, so she was able to tell me where you were.'

'You know Ellen too?'

'Of course. I served with her brother.'

That's when the penny dropped. 'You're an SAS trooper too? How come I've never met you before?'

'Lucky, I guess,' Lyndsay laughed. 'I was on a mission when you had that fracas in Mosul, and I was deployed when the two of you got married. We just kept missing each other.'

'Until now. It's nice to finally meet you, Lyndsay,' Natasha said as they shook hands.

'Likewise. So, who is this guy?'

'No idea,' she admitted as she inspected his right hand. 'He doesn't have a snake tattoo, though, so he might not be part of The Baron's organisation.'

'Then who? Just a crazy knife wielding passer-by?'

'Lucas warned me that Kallum Taylor, the insurance investigator, had people looking for me.'

'What kind of investigator has someone like this on their payroll?'

Natasha shrugged. 'Lucas thinks Kallum might actually be The Baron. No one knows what he looks like, after all, and he seems to have the hump with Lucas too.'

'I could give you a list of people that would have the hump with Lucas.'

'Fair point. Could it really be Kallum behind everything, though?' Natasha remembered that every time she had heard The Baron's voice, it had a hint of the antipodean about it, perhaps even South African. Kallum, however, was straight up American. But then again, it was possible to fake an accent too. At that moment, Natasha's mobile phone rang. She read the name on the screen, then showed it to Lyndsay.

It was The Baron. 'Perhaps his ears were burning.'

'What do you want?' Natasha said in a harsh tone. His constant ringing grated on her. She hated the fact that he even had her number.

'Now, now, Natasha, that's no way to answer a phone call, especially when I'm the one that should be pissed.'

'What do you mean?'

'Don't play stupid, Natasha, you're an educated girl. Did you really think that I wouldn't discover what Lucas has been up to? Did you really think that the J organisation only has a hand full of soldiers?'

'I don't really care to be honest.'

'Well, you should. Thanks to Lucas's interference, I've decided to demonstrate to you both that neither of you are in control of this situation. I am the one in control. If you don't believe me, accept the video call.'

Natasha did as she was told. On the screen, she saw her parents tied to chairs, their heads lolled lifelessly. '*No*,' she screamed before The Baron, off screen, informed her they were only drugged.

The realisation that this was a very serious situation struck her hard, and she stared at the masked man that now came into view through her blurred vision.

'Now, who is in control here?' The Baron asked.

'You are,' Natasha replied reluctantly.

'Good. Now that we have reaffirmed that, I want you to know that no harm will come to you parents. Unless, of course, you fail to deliver the Eye of Nineveh to me. You have fourteen hours to get me the gem. If you don't then ... ' The Baron held up a gun to let Natasha know the consequences for failure.

'What? Fourteen? I should have at least thirty hours left!'

'You didn't think your husband's actions would go unpunished, did you?'

'But I don't even know what I'm looking for.'

'Then don't waste time, Natasha. Tick tock, tick tock.'

'I'll get Lucas to help me. The extra eyes will speed things up.'

'Unfortunately, he has to be punished too. So, he will be too busy to be of any help to you from now on. Unless he is successful in his task. And if he isn't, then you won't be seeing Lucas for a long time, perhaps twenty-five years to life.'

Chapter 18

Lucas gripped the steering wheel of his Alfa. The plan was to link up with Natasha as soon as he had finished at the Devonshire's house. That all changed the moment he watched the video of Chiara sent by The Baron.

She was innocent in all of this. Her being put in danger because of him, because of actions he had taken, gave Lucas a feeling of guilt that he didn't like. Peter Armitage, on the other, he couldn't really give a damn about, but he couldn't help wondering if Natasha did.

The whole point of leveraging someone in this way was to threaten somebody that they cared about. Natasha's parents and Chiara all made sense. Not that he liked it, but it made sense that they would be a target. The only reason Lucas could understand Peter being grouped in with the others was if things between him and Natasha were further along than he knew.

He balked at the idea. Not out of jealousy or some notion that if he can't have her, no one can. It was out of the fact that he knew her and knew that this guy wasn't her type. This was the type of man her dad had always wanted for her.

Instead of heading directly to London Bridge, Lucas had phoned his friend and former comrade, Lyndsay Alperton, and asked him to meet up with Natasha, letting him know she was in trouble. In the meantime, he would head home to Chelsea Harbour.

In The Baron's video, Lucas had recognised the surroundings, and remembered that Chiara was supposed to come to his again that night. He became anxious when he had tried to call her but kept getting her voicemail. When he arrived, the car had barely stopped moving before he was rushing up to his apartment to see if she was there.

'Chiara! Chiara!' Lucas shouted as he threw open the door. When she'd suggested he should give her a key to his apartment, since she spent so much time there, Lucas had been a little reluctant, to say the least. He had eventually submitted, although he hadn't told Natasha this nugget of information, nor did he intend to. But with the imminent danger, he was glad that he had given in, because he'd be able to keep her here safe.

Just as Lucas was about to check the upper floor of the duplex, his phone rang. 'Chiara? Are you okay?'

'Of course I am. Why wouldn't I be?'

'I've been trying to get hold of you.'

'Oh, you must have called when I was in the office basement. You have a tough time getting a signal down there. What did you want anyway?'

'I thought you were going to be here.'

'You're at the Harbour? I was on my way, but I was called back to the office so I'm going to be back later than I thought.'

'That's okay. I haven't finished that thing yet.'

'Thing? You mean the Natasha thing? That girl has issues, you know. I don't know how you put up with her.'

'It must be my superpower.'

'Clearly. Anyway, I'll see you later tonight, babe.'

Lucas hung up the phone and left out a sigh of relief. He suspected that she was still being shadowed, but as long as he didn't rock the boat anymore, The Baron would have no reason to harm her. He called a halt to trying to stay ahead of the terrorist and playthings his way for the time being. The best bet now would be to contact Natasha, find out where she was and link up with her and Lyndsay.

First, he wanted to check out his wounds, see if any of them needed treating or not. Apart from the slight swelling under his dark-brown eyes, he wasn't as banged up as he thought he was. If he had been on the end of that bottle of claret, things might have been different, however.

Lucas smiled at his reflection in the mirror. To say he was enjoying the thrill of the action would have been an understatement. He was an unashamed adrenaline junkie. This was his lifeblood. That was why he was so keen to keep a hand in The Acquirers. That, and to stay close to Natasha.

She provided the legitimacy to the name, as well as her archaeological nous and knack at finding things. He brought the muscle and tactical knowledge to get them out of the hairy situations they invariably found themselves in.

Either one of them, truthfully, could have walked away during the divorce proceedings and set up a new rival business, but Lucas secretly suspected that, deep inside, Natasha knew as well as he, that what they had could be replicated, but never bettered.

With his thoughts resting on his wife, Lucas turned to leave the bathroom and noticed something that, if he hadn't been married for years to someone that insisted on having a spotless bathroom, he might have missed.

Natasha liked things to be a certain way in that particular room of the apartment, things Lucas had subsequently picked up as a habit; toilet paper going over rather than under, the toilet seat being down when not in use, face cloths dried on the bar-radiator and not the side of the bath. That last custom was something that Chiara didn't do either.

So, when Lucas saw the damp cloth on the bath, he knew straight away that someone had been there.

His phone suddenly rang. It came up as an unknown number. He let it ring; if it was important, they'd leave a message. They did. He listened to the short voicemail and discovered that it was The Baron. 'Answer my call.' A few moments later, the phone rang again, this time Lucas pressed the accept button.

'What do you want?'

'Lucas Redmond, you have been troublesome. No, scratch that. To be honest, you have been barely bothersome, but bothersome all the same. Because of you I have had to punish Natasha.'

'What have you done to her?' demanded Lucas, his nostrils flared.

'I just let her know who was in charge here and upped the stakes so that we'll have no more of your heroics. Her parents are with me now, and she only has fourteen hours to get me The Eye of Nineveh, all because of you, Lucas.'

'That's not enough time!'

'Maybe you're right. To show that I will be a benevolent leader when I have the eye in my hands, I will give you the chance to gain her more time.'

'Okay, I'm listening. What do I have to do?'

'Have you heard of the Brienne box?'

'The four-hundred-year-old postmasters' box of undelivered seventeenth century letters? I've heard of it.'

'It's more than that. It's a time capsule, a snapshot of everyday life. The worries and concerns of people today were mirrored by ordinary French and Dutch citizens from the late seventeenth century'

'You sound like a gushing documentary presenter. What's this got to do with anything?'

'I want you to get a particular Brienne letter for me.'

'Are you out of your mind? They're in The Hague. I'm not going to Holland. I need to help Natasha.'

'Yes, they're in the museum voot communicatie. You interfered too much and now you're being taken out of the game, Lucas. Natasha will have to do without your help.'

The former SAS trooper mulled things over in his mind. Although he would rather be with Natasha in her time of need, he knew that doing this for The Baron would help her in the long run, gaining her valuable time in her search for The Eye of Nineveh.

'You seem uncertain of what to do, Lucas. Before you decide to do anything stupid, let me help you. Maybe you should check upstairs.'

Lucas stared at his phone, unsure of what to expect from this calculating man. He did as he was told and slowly made his way up. With each step, his sense of apprehension grew, and he prepared himself for anything. Except for what was in the second bedroom.

On the bed, a man lay in a pool of blood, his chest open and his heart cut out and placed on his face. Lucas couldn't look away from the gruesome scene. His fist shook, and he almost crushed his phone in his hand.

'Who is this?'

'Nobody,' The Baron replied. 'But he will become somebody if you don't do as I tell you; he will be the man that sends you to jail. One call is all it will take.'

'Another life you will pay for,' Lucas replied in a controlled tone.

'If you say so. Now, will you do the job?'

'Do I have a choice?'

'Good! I will send you the details of the letter, and a number to call when you have it. The faster you get this done, the sooner my men can dispose of all the evidence that would link you to that poor man's death.'

'For something like this, I need time to plan. The security level around the box must be pretty high, and I'll most likely need to recruit a team.'

'Time is something you have very little of, Lucas. I don't care how you get it done, but I expect a call from you sooner rather than later. Tick tock, Lucas, tick tock.'

The Baron hung up the phone. Lucas cursed under his breath as the pounding in his ears subsided. Once he had his emotions under control, Lucas made a call, which was answered almost immediately.

'Ellen, I need your help.'

Chapter 19

Natasha stood completely still. She glanced around with dull eyes, desperately searching for answers. She didn't respond when Lyndsay talked to her, and she was slow to react when he touched her shoulder.

'Huh?'

'I asked what that bastard wants now?'

'He's ... he's taken my parents. He said he'll kill them if I don't bring the Eye of Nineveh to him. He said I only had fourteen hours to do it. I'm worried about Lucas, too. The Baron said he won't be able to help me because he has him doing something to punish him.'

'This guy is a real piece of work. Look, don't worry about Lucas; the captain is very resourceful. Until he gets here, I'm at your disposal.'

She smiled up at Lyndsay. The reassurance that she wouldn't be going through this alone was exactly what she needed. Even though she had found herself in many dire situations, in the past, in many countries around the world, Peru, Bolivia, Mali to name a few, she had always had Lucas with her, or nearby. She had to admit to herself that, right about now, she missed his presence.

'So, what's the plan, Natasha? Where do we begin?'

The question forced her to switch mindsets. To become the determined, problem-solving archaeologist, who had a knack for finding things. It wasn't that she did things others couldn't, more times than not, it was because she did things others wouldn't. 'Well, I figured out that the old London

Roman wall is somehow involved. I don't know what Professor Masterson has done there, or what I'm looking for, but it's a start.'

Lyndsay rubbed his hands together. 'Okay, so where do we start?'

'Tower Hill.'

• • • •

NATASHA HAD ALWAYS marvelled at how London at night became two distinct and different cities. The West End was busy until the early mornings, being the location of London's nightlife, clubs, bars, cinemas, theatres. The area known as the City was more of a business district, and as such, the streets were all but deserted by six pm, just a few tourists left taking pictures of London's famous landmarks, lit up at night.

She checked the time and sighed; It was almost seven-thirty. The Baron had given her thirteen hours, and she felt it was never going to be enough time, that it was an impossible task. Archaeological finds take months, years, sometimes even a lifetime to be discovered, not hours!

'You okay?' Lyndsay asked, hearing the sounds of exasperation coming from Natasha.

'Yeah, it's just dawning on me how daunting this whole situation is. What if I can't find the gem? What if I can't save my parents?'

'Come on, Natasha. From what Lucas told me about you, that won't be a problem. You've got this, no doubt.'

She smiled to herself. 'When did Lucas tell you about me?'

'After the first day of his protection duty. Just before I was deployed, he called me and told me that he'd met the one, that he was going to try and get out of his deployment.'

'The one?'

'Yup. His exact words ... well, not quite. He said he'd found his unicorn.'

'Unicorn?'

'Yeah, back at Sandhurst military academy, me, Lucas and Dré used to talk about finding our perfect woman. We each ended up with a long list of requirements that we eventually said that we'd have more luck finding a unicorn than finding someone to fit the bill.'

Natasha was incredulous. In Mosul, at the Nineveh site, she eventually recognised the fact that he was attracted to her, but she didn't really know how deeply it went. Even after they were married, he had never told her. 'I was his unicorn?'

'Big time. He would talk about how intelligent you were and your studious and analytical mind, not mention your kind heart and trusting nature and, of course, your looks.'

She could feel her cheeks warming up dramatically. It was one thing to have Lucas telling her these things, which he did, but to know that he was telling other people, gave her ego a little stroke.

They arrived at Tower Hill station and could immediately see the section of the Roman wall. Even at just a fraction of its original size, it was still impressive enough to give you goosebumps; if you knew what it was, that is.

Lyndsay flicked a loose hand at the ruin and shrugged. 'Is this it?'

Natasha looked at him cockeyed. 'What do you mean "is this it?" This is eighteen-hundred years old, just think of everything it's seen. It predates Alfred the Great. It was here before that was,' she said, pointing to the nearby Tower of London. 'Just because it's not complete and it may not be as aesthetically pleasing as the White Tower, doesn't mean it's not important. You can't turn your nose up at history like this.'

The former SAS trooper grinned. 'Lucas did say you were passionate too.'

With Lyndsay thoroughly reprimanded and educated on the values of historical knowledge, the pair searched around the vicinity of the wall. They didn't know what they were looking for, but Natasha hoped that something would jump out at them; all the while, she tried not to let her mind rest on the fact that it might have been a simpler task with three sets of eyes.

'You know, Lucas never told me he was supposed to be deployed,' Natasha said to Lyndsay as they continued their search.

'Yeah, we had a rotation. But some of the guys preferred being where the action was, including Lucas. That was until he met you. After that he would swap out every time, did it with me too.'

'Weren't you surprised he was able to keep his mind on one thing, I mean me.'

'What do you mean?'

'His nickname, "side-track". Didn't he get the name because he doesn't concentrate on one thing and gets distracted?'

'What? No, not at all. You must have seen him when he gets in the zone.'

'I have, that's why the nickname confounded me.'

'The captain got that name at Sandhurst. Most people that go to the academy are what you would call "well off", royals and the like. When Lucas got there, it was under a cloud of mystery. Not only did he miss the first day of training, but he was brought in by top brass from the Ministry of Defence. So, a few of us snooped around and found out his family's criminal background. Basically, he grew up on the wrong side of the tracks.'

Natasha gave him a disapproving glare, but then she recalled what Kallum had said about Lucas's parents. That was two independent sources now bringing up his history. Maybe there really was no smoke without fire. 'Lyndsay, did you ever hear of the name Sebastian Jericho? Lucas mentioning maybe?'

'No, can't say that I have.'

'Possibly a letter from him or a visitor, perhaps?'

'Lucas never got any messages, and no one came to see him, not even at his graduation. Well, actually, there was one letter. A week or so into training, he got a letter saying that his parents had died. He never went into specifics, and I can't say for sure if he actually grieved or not, but he did seem like a changed person.'

'Changed? In what way.'

'It was almost like he'd been holding himself back until that point, and he suddenly felt free to come out of his shell. He really excelled from then on, became an exceptional soldier and a captain in no time.'

'It seems like I never knew him at all,' Natasha said in a low voice. 'We never really spoke about his parents and whenever we did, he'd shut down.'

'Yeah, he kind of built that up over the years. I don't know what happened before Sandhurst, but it certainly left him scarred emotionally.'

The time was coming up to eight at night, and the light was fading as quickly as Natasha's optimism in being able to complete the task set for her by The Baron. There had searched around the park where the wall stood and found nothing. The statue of Emperor Trajan, which Natasha explained to Lyndsay, hadn't been built alongside the wall, but was actually from Southampton, likewise provided no clue as to what Marcus Masterson had hidden here.

'This is hopeless,' Natasha said, and slapped the wall in frustration. She turned and leaned her back against the relic.

'What if someone has already taken whatever it is?'

The thought dawned on her for a moment before she dismissed it. 'No, I don't think so. Marcus wouldn't have gone through so much trouble placing his messages at The Savoy or Freemason's Hall just to hide the key somewhere anybody could find it. The only thing that I can think is that it's not here. I mean, there are other fragments of the Roman wall; it could be at any of them.'

Natasha eased up off of the wall and as she walked along its length, she ran her hand along the edge of the middle row of tiles, literally touching history. During construction, these tiles were laid across completed sections at regular intervals to provide extra strength and stability, but also to make sure the wall was ruler straight. So, when she felt one jutting out from the rest, her suspicions were raised, and she promptly took a closer look.

Not only was the tile an ever so slightly darker shade, only really discernible at close range, but the mortar was also a little different to the touch, as if the materials used to make it were not quite the same as they had in Roman times.

Taking out her car keys, Natasha scraped away at the mortar, much to Lyndsay's surprise. After everything she had said about it, now to see her deface it made her sound a bit hypocritical in his eyes.

'Don't be silly,' she said, defending her actions. 'I'm not destroying the wall; I think this is what we're looking for. You can see, the mortar is a lot softer here and the tile itself has been overly distressed to give the sense of age.'

It didn't take long before Natasha had scraped away enough to pull out the tile. All the while, Lyndsay kept a lookout in case someone saw their suspicious antics. She took out her mobile phone and used the torch feature on it, shining its light into newly opened cavity.

'Well, is there anything there?' Lyndsay asked.

Natasha tentatively reached her slender fingers inside the hole. When they touched the hidden item, she slowly drew them out. It was wrapped in a piece of cloth. Once she had unwrapped it, Natasha discovered that there was a segment of a metallic disk within it. 'Now, what the hell is this, Marcus?'

Chapter 20

When Lucas called Ellen and told her he needed her help, she had said yes almost immediately. He sat in her abandoned factory and explained to her exactly what kind of job The Baron had sent him on. Ellen would be, inadvertently, helping the leader of the terrorist organisation that had killed her brother, but it still hadn't caused her to change her mind about helping Lucas. He was her family now, after all. She did have a proviso, however.

'You have to promise me you'll kill him if you get the chance, Lucas,' Ellen said coldly. 'You know I rarely ask for anything; you call and I'm there for you. But I'm having trouble with this one. It's hard to reconcile with the fact that I'll be helping the man that murdered my brother.'

'Don't think of it as helping him,' corrected Lucas. 'You'll be helping me lure him out. Until I get his ID, find out who he is, I can't act against him; he's a ghost.' He looked at the same vague reports that Natasha had read, for what it was worth.

'*You* can talk about being a ghost.' Ellen's fingers rapidly flew across her keyboard and the Interpol report on The Baron vanished and was replaced by another file on Sebastian Jericho. 'You have to tell her. She deserves to know.'

'I thought you didn't like her?'

'Yeah, and? Besides, you two are all but divorced. Knowing that she was married to the greatest international thief, and not having a clue, will be the final nail in the coffin for that marriage,' Ellen quickly clapped as a smile slowly spread across her face. 'You know something? Seeing the two reports together kind of highlights the similarities in the vagueness of them.'

Lucas took another look and agreed. 'That's the whole reason I came up with the Sebastian persona. He could be anybody. He was a legend, and I acted as his middleman. Clients thought they were talking to his lackey, not knowing that they were talking to Sebastian Jericho himself.'

'So, who knows about you being Sebastian?'

'Only you. Why?'

'It's just a hunch, but I think you should add The Baron to that list. Don't look at me like that, hear me out. Not only has he ripped off your mysterious leader bit, but why else would he come to you with this job unless he knew you had the skill set to pull it off?'

Lucas looked off into the distance, his vision growing blurry. Apart from Ellen, the only other people that knew the truth about Sebastian Jericho had been his parents. What if he had a hand in their deaths? What if the car crash hadn't been an accident? What if he had got the information out of his parents before killing them? 'You have to find out who this guy is, Ellen.'

'I'm already on it. I've been working on a program. It correlates every scrap of info we have about The Baron and his organisation, takes CCTV footage from around the area of their attacks, the day of and a few months before, hopefully catch them doing reconnaissance. Once I get some images, I'll cross reference them with known associates and hopefully, through process of elimination, we'll find out what this guy looks like and who he is.'

Lucas looked sceptical. 'The words needle and haystack come to mind.'

'It's easy to find the needle if you use a metal detector,' Ellen stated. 'You'll see. Besides, you know that the more difficult the problem, the less bored I get.'

The sound of clickity-clacking keys was all that was heard for a few more minutes as she applied the final lines of code. When she had finished, Ellen reclined in her chair and admired her work with a sigh of satisfaction. Then she started the program running.

Nothing happened at first, just the cursor flashing on the screen. Then it booted up into life. Images of people flashed up on the monitor. Green vector lines appeared over their features as the program tried to search for matches using the parameters set out by Ellen.

'So, it's working?'

'Of course it's working,' Ellen said. She couldn't believe that he questioned her ability. 'It's going to take some time to come up with anything, but while it does, we can crack on with your other problem.'

'The Brienne Collection.'

'Exactly.' Ellen rolled, in her chair, to a second computer setup, began typing away, and when she found the right page to read aloud. '"In 1926, a seventeenth-century trunk of letters was bequeathed to the Dutch postal museum in The Hague, currently Sound and Vision The Hague, then as now the centre of government, politics, and trade in The Netherlands. The trunk belonged to a postmaster and postmistress, Simon and Marie de Brienne, a couple at the heart of European communication networks. The chest contains an extraordinary archive: 2600 "locked" letters sent from all over Europe to this axis of communication, none of which were ever delivered." 2600 letters? He really wants you out of the way, doesn't he?'

'Tell me about it. Not only do I have to get over to Holland, break into the museum, then I have to sift through thousands of letters just to find one.'

'Wait a minute, you might be in luck. "... 575 of them even remain unopened. Our international and interdisciplinary team of researchers has undertaken a process of preservation, digitisation, transcription, editing, and identification of letter-locking formats and categories that will reveal its secrets for the first time – even those of the unopened letters." And guess where these researchers are ... right here in London.'

'You're kidding me?' A sudden burst of optimism overcame Lucas. Perhaps this wasn't a lost cause after all; he faster he could get this done, the faster he could get back to Natasha.

'Nope! They're at Queen Mary University, in the dental department. They have some sort of super X-ray there called MuCat. They scan the letters with the machine to see the ink on the page. Scanning each letter takes seventy-two hours, and that's just the first process. It goes to other universities until the image gets to this stage.' Ellen sent a short computer-generated video demonstrating the opening and closing of the Letter-locking process to the monitor in front of Lucas.

'So, they create 3-D images from the scan, which allows them to open the letters and see the contents without actually opening it?'

'Yup, and in turn, preserve the letter.'

The technological process impressed Lucas, more and more, as he watched the over again. 'How do we know if the letter we need is here or not?'

'The ones at Queen Mary all have partial addresses.'

Lucas fished out his phone and showed Ellen the message that he'd received.

'Monsieur T. De Jong,' she read in perfect French. 'Soin de Monsieur F. Dubois, marchand á La Haye. So, this De Jong guy was staying with a merchant named Dubois? Certainly sounds partial to me.'

'Same here. Even if it's not, we won't have wasted too much trying because we don't have the time to formulate an elaborate plan. We'll have to do it off the cuff.'

'You want to wing it? A job like this?'

'Do I really have a choice?'

Ellen shrugged. 'No, I guess you don't. So how we going to this?'

'A very simple plan, which can go wrong at any point; you infiltrate the university as a student, you let me in, and I find the letter. Simple.'

'You have got to be kidding me,' Ellen said, staring wide-eyed at Lucas. 'I thought you were an SAS captain?'

'Unfortunately, we don't have the time to build scale models, check security and come up with a better plan. You can pass as a student, Ellen, so you're up. Once I'm in, you'll wait at the car and feed me directions to the right department.'

'Okay, fine,' she replied as she rolled up one of her special cigarettes and lit it. 'If I'm going to be playing a student, I might as well smell like one.'

• • • •

DURING THE TWENTY-PLUS minute journey to Queen Mary University in Whitechapel, Ellen searched for images and plans of the Institute of Dentistry, giving Lucas the chance to select his point of entry. 'Right there, the education academy entrance. Open that window a crack on the first floor and I'll climb in through there.'

She nodded, went through her tech bag and pulled out a couple of earwigs. She put her own in place and handed the other to Lucas, then gave them a quick test.

'I know this isn't really your thing, but thanks for doing this, Ellen.' Lucas knew that she was a bit antisocial and not really a people person, perhaps even borderline agoraphobic, but he appreciated the fact that she never let him down when he needed her, and he did the same for her.

'Don't be stupid, Lucas, we're family. Maybe not by blood, but I'll always have your back, you know that. Now, let's do this, because I need to get home. I got some anime to watch.'

She grabbed her bag as they left Lucas's car and headed toward Turner Street, where they separated; he remained at the corner whilst Ellen continued on to the entrance. From his vantage point, Lucas could see a security camera sweeping left and right, on the opposite building, covering right where he intended to make his entrance. He counted to find out exactly how much time he would have to get up in through the window before the camera would spot him.

Ellen waited at the side of the entrance, smoking her roll-up and blending in with the other student smokers that congregated in the designated zone. She groaned inwardly at the inane chatter and thanked the stars that she had never needed to debase herself by going through the educational system. The thought of it made her skin crawl.

So deep in her thoughts was Ellen, that she almost missed the opportunity she'd been waiting for, the chance to follow the ragtag group of students and skip through the security barrier, once they'd finished having their smoke.

Because of her small size, a shade over five feet, Ellen was short enough to disappear in the crowd with ease. She still made sure that she was on the far side of the group to avoid the eye-line of the security guard. 'Okay, I'm in,' she whispered, with her finger touching the earwig. 'I'm making my way to the window now.'

'Good, I'm on my way,' Lucas replied. The security camera took twenty seconds to complete its arc, but after ten seconds, it would point directly at the window. He didn't see it as a problem, though. It would take a matter of seconds to get up there, and by the time it would have swung back, Lucas expected to be inside.

In a perfect world, that would have been the case.

Ellen was at the window, which she'd unlocked it and pushed up ever so slightly. She could see Lucas, standing underneath the security cam, waiting for it to reach its apex. Once it did, he was off like a shot. He sprinted and stepped up onto the railing, bounded off, springing himself up into the air to grasp the platform above the education academy. He hung there for a split second before pulling himself up. Lucas made for the window, about to slide it up and enter, when he saw Ellen turn sharply to her right, then he heard a male voice speak to her.

'Hey, I know you,' the male student said.

'What?'

'I've seen you before.'

'Really? Well, uh, I am a student here after all, or haven't you noticed?' Ellen scoffed.

'Yeah, and you're my type of girl.'

Ellen rolled her eyes. She hadn't been rumbled. It was a lame attempt at a pickup, and judging by the scowl on Lucas's face and the way he tapped his wrist, she knew time was running out. She had to get him inside before the camera spotted him. But how could she with this bozo standing here?

She grabbed a handful of the student's shirt, spun him around and pulled him down towards her. Then she kissed him. It was all the distraction Lucas needed to push the window up, with Ellen providing extra moaning to cover the sound, and climb inside just in time, before taking cover in a nearby doorway.

There was suddenly the sound of a loud slap as Ellen struck him across the face, instantly turning it red. 'I'm not that type of girl!' She stormed off, leaving him standing there bemused, with a smile on his face and his eyes welling up because of the stinging pain in his cheek.

• • • •

LUCAS AND ELLEN SEPARATED again. She returned to the car, giving Lucas directions to the right department that housed the MuCat X-ray using her laptop.

The going was relatively easy, Lucas being able to use stealth to reach his destination unhindered. The halls of the university changed in decor as they he left the educational part and entered the sterile research area. The amount of people in lab coats increased as he got closer and closer to his goal. At one point, he could hear voices coming towards him, getting closer. He ducked into a room, hoping to hide until they had passed, only to have them enter the same room. It was a locker room.

Lucas pressed his back against the wall and disappeared into the shadows behind the door. His training kicked in and his breath shallowed. The two lab assistants discussed which bar they'd be going to; all the while being watched by the unseen former trooper.

Luckily, just as Lucas wondered how long they'd be hanging around, they left, it was literally just a case of them leaving their lab coats and heading off for a few pints before going their separate ways home. Once he was sure the coast was clear, he grabbed an appropriately sized lab coat and made for the MuCat room.

'Ellen, I'm at the door. It's got a five-digit keypad.'

'Okay, no problem,' she replied, her laptop open and poised for action. 'We don't have the time to crack it, so give me the make and serial number and I'll tell you how to reset it to the default code.'

He gave her the info she needed. She completed the task and came back with the info in her usual quick and efficient style. Several button pushes and combinations later, Lucas was in.

There was a gentle humming coming from all the electrical equipment, but he wasn't here to admire the machinery. He set about searching for the specific letter The Baron was after.

Lucas found the Brienne letters within a case in an adjoining office. He wasted no time in slipping on the soft-touch white gloves that lay nearby before picking up a few of the centuries old letters to sort through them looking for the letter which only had "Monsieur De Jong, soin de Monsieur Dubois, merchand á La Haye" written on it.

As strange as it was in this day and age, to have a letter with just a name a no address, three-hundred years ago things were different. Oftentimes, it was left to the postal worker to track down the recipient. In this case, they obviously failed since all the letters in the Brienne collection were undelivered.

Either through misdirection, the person having departed elsewhere, or just refused since it was the receiver of the letter that paid the postage, not the sender. They were collected here and not destroyed. It was an incredible insight into historical life, which could be quite harrowing. It brought to mind two such stories Lucas read about; a singer falling pregnant to a patron only for him to refuse the many letters from her. The other one was addressed to a young cadet in the army. His mother lamented that she had heard nothing from him in four months and prayed that he was in good health, not knowing that he was already dead, hence it remained undelivered.

'I've found it,' Lucas said after flipping through a few hundred of the intriguing, locked letters.

'Good,' Ellen replied. 'Now, can we get out of here?'

'I'm on my way,' Lucas said as he quickly and gently slipped the letter into his pocket and dispensed with the gloves. As he headed back into the lab, the X-ray machine's humming suddenly came to a stop, and it let out a series of beeps.

'What's that?' Ellen asked.

'I think the X-ray has finished scanning a letter, which means someone will be here any minute.' As Lucas continued on his way out, the image of the just scanned locked letter appeared on a computer screen on a nearby desk. Although the picture was in a raw form and hard to distinguish, the notes next to it were perfectly legible.

'There's another letter addressed to the same man.'

'You're kidding me? What are you going to do?'

Lucas thought for a moment, then leapt into action and swiped the letter from under the scanner. 'I'm taking it. The Baron only asked for one letter, and one is all he's getting. If it isn't the one he's looking for that's his problem.' He slowly opened the secure door to the lab and looked up and down the corridor before slipping out.

'Why take it at all then?'

'Because I don't have the time to wait for these lab jockeys to send this stuff to MIT and get the 3D rendered images back. I'm a nosey guy and this letter obviously has information The Baron wants. And if it's important to him, then it's important to me.'

'So you're going to open it?'

'Yup. Just don't tell Natasha.'

'My lips are sealed.'

. . . .

BY NOW, THE HALLS OF the Queen Mary University were all but empty. Lucas had no issues exiting the building, even getting a goodnight nod from one of the security team. He got back to his car and jumped into the Alfa, handing the two centuries old letters to Ellen, who turned them over in her hands, comparing them.

'They're almost identical. I mean, this one has that little droplet of ink, but that was a common thing to happen in those days. Apart from that, they're the same.'

'That's the one I picked up from the X-ray,' Lucas replied as he dialled a number on his phone. It rang twice before the other end was picked up.

'Do you have the letter?' The Baron asked.

'I do,' Lucas said, 'but I'm thinking that giving Natasha extra time to find the Eye of Nineveh isn't enough. You want this letter so badly; you're going to have to let her parents go as well.'

'You can't renegotiate the deal.'

'And yet here I am, renegotiating.'

'You will see that I don't play games, Lucas.'

The line suddenly went dead.

'Hello? Hello? The bastard hung up on me.'

'And you say I've got bad social skills.' Suddenly, a series of notifications came through Ellen's phone. 'Uh oh.'

'What is it?'

Ellen frantically typed away at her laptop. 'In my line of business, it pays to keep tabs on your friends as well as enemies, just in case any of them are compromised. So, I have a program running that alerts me if the name of anyone I know suddenly starts spiking on wanted lists.'

'So?'

She turned the computer to Lucas. 'Interpol, NCA, FBI, Mi5. You two are hot! You and Natasha are top of every agency's most wanted list!'

'That son of a bitch!'

Chapter 21

Natasha and Lyndsay remained by the section of the Roman London wall, where she had just found a piece triangular of metal, hidden there by Professor Marcus Masterson. They each turned it over in their hands and had a close look at it, but neither of them could tell what it was, or what it was for. They could discern some lettering on one side of it, a lip and groove on each long edge, but that was all.

'None of makes sense.' Everything that had happened so far that day was making Natasha question what she knew about the man that had fuelled her passion for history.

'What do you mean?'

'I'm just wondering why and how Professor Masterson got on The Baron's most wanted list.'

'No one knows more about the Assyrians than him. You said so yourself.'

'Yes, and he'd been working with the Iraq museum regarding the eye of Nineveh too, I know. But this,' she held up the metal triangle, 'this isn't something you pop into Selfridges and pick up.'

'Well, no, but there are still metal workers. It could be a commission piece.'

'Oh, it definitely is a bespoke piece, of something bigger I'd say, but the point is he's supposed to be a university professor.'

'Okay, so he's a bit eccentric and has time on his hands. What's the big deal?'

'Time and money. That suite he had at The Savoy was around two thousand pounds a night. And his shoes had been there for more than one day.'

'So he's come into a bit of money.'

'He's come into a lot of money. The kind of money that if the person who paid you didn't get what they wanted, they'd kill you for.'

Lyndsay thought a moment about what Natasha was implying. 'You're saying that Marcus was working for The Baron?'

'No, no, of course not. I'm just thinking out loud.' Natasha couldn't believe that her beloved educator would be working for a terrorist. Even if the clues did suggest some connection between the two, she wouldn't believe it until he told her himself. The need to save her parents, find the eye and Professor Marcus, drove Natasha to renewed heights. 'Come on, the next piece of the Roman wall is just around the corner.'

When she told Lyndsay that, she meant it literally. Within two minutes, they had reached their next destination, Cooper's Row. But like what happened with most ancient buildings, modernity had encroached, and a hotel had been built around it.

'Look, there it is,' Natasha said, pointing through the car park. In garden area, at the back, it was possible to see the Roman wall, but within moments of them entering the hotel car park, they were descended upon by a guard.

'Can I have your name and room number please?'

'Excuse me?'

'Your room number, sir. For the valet parking.'

'Oh, we're not staying here,' Natasha revealed. 'We just need to have a quick look at the wall.'

The guard looked over his shoulder and then back at the two of them. 'That won't be allowed. This is private property and isn't open to the public. If you're not a resident of the hotel, you can't be here.'

'Come on, we just need to have a quick look,' pleaded Natasha.

'No, what you need to do is turn around and walk out of here, before I call the police,' he said, taking his radio in hand.

'You're kidding right?'

Lyndsay stared at the man. 'No, he's not, Natasha. Come on, let's go.'

They reluctantly left, under the watchful gaze of the guard. Once they were outside, Lyndsay had a quick look around the building, hoping to find a wall he could scale, but there was no chance. The hotel backed up to an office block.

'There's no other way in,' he explained and shook his head.

'Well, if that's the only way in, then that's the way we go.'

'Has it crossed your mind that there might not even be anything there?'

'True, but there's only one way to be sure,' Natasha said. Her eyes twinkled as adrenaline pumped through her veins. 'You go in, distract the guard and I'll sneak in between the cars and check out the wall.'

'What am I supposed to talk to him about?'

'I don't know, the weather, anything. Just give me enough time to have a proper search.'

'Well, you'd better hurry or I might just knock him out.'

Natasha waited by the side of the car park entrance and watched Lyndsay coolly walk inside. It wasn't long before she heard the guard again, but he was quickly cut off before he could make good on his threats when he was asked questions about his job role and employment opportunities.

This was her chance. She peeped inside and saw that Lyndsay had manoeuvred the guard so that his back was to the entrance. Crouching low, she slipped into the car park.

Natasha had seen Lucas do it plenty of times; stay low, move swiftly on the balls of your feet to reduce noise. She had gotten good at it herself, forced to in fact, considering the amount of times they had found themselves in tricky situations, caught in crossfires that they had inadvertently started, and the like.

When she reached the last row of cars, Natasha found that there was an open space, at least seven feet, between her position and the exit to the wall. She slowly raised her head and looked through the car window to see where Lyndsay and the guard were. She swore under her breath. Their positions hadn't changed. The guard's view of the exit was only obscured by Lyndsay's large frame. Natasha knew it was going to take speed and perfect timing if she was going to make it through unseen.

Then she saw a number on the side of the guard's booth and got an idea. Natasha took out her mobile and dialled the number, only to discover that the last digit was obscured by the cars before her. She paused a moment, then realised that it could only be one of ten possibilities, and rang the number, changing the last digit, in a trial and error.

After having a couple takeaways answer the call, a deadline, and a woman calling herself Snowflake, the phone in the box finally rang at the seventh attempt. As soon as he was inside, Natasha was off and hung up the phone. She saw Lyndsay turn briefly, and they gave each other a quick thumbs up.

Once she was hidden out the back, she was able to fully appreciate the section of Roman wall. It wasn't as tall as what was outside in Tower Hill, but it was still impressive none the less. It had several arched windows, which Natasha knew were part of the medieval extension, the wall having been solid except for the several entry gateways during Roman times.

She checked the lower, original, wall first, slowly making her way up each row, bit by bit. Now that she had some inkling of what she was looking for, and of how the professor had hidden his strange object, it didn't take Natasha long to discover that nothing within her arm's length fit the description.

She needed to get higher.

Natasha groaned. Being a protector and preserver of history, she loathed her next steps. If Robert Jones knew what she had in her mind, he'd have a heart attack. At the farthest corner of the wall, away from the entrance, she climbed up the ten-metre-high ancient structure. Natasha's heart strings pulled as bits of the wall crumbled underfoot with each step of her ascent.

She reached the top, and got to a standing position, but it was no less precarious up there. Not only was it uneven, where she needed to jump down, before climbing up again, some parts were missing altogether, which she had to jump across. Whenever she could, Natasha bent down to investigate the stones of the wall, and finally, near the end of it, when she was beginning to that it had all been a waste of time, she found it.

Natasha scraped around the newer looking piece of stone, until she was eventually able to pull it out, along with a surprising amount of spider webs. She reached inside the cavity until her hand touch on something that shouldn't be there, and she brought it out.

She had found another piece of the mysterious item Professor Marcus had left. Now she just needed to get down.

With the plan of using one of the arched windows to help her down, firmly in her mind, Natasha crouched, shimmied over the ledge and reached down with a leg, until her toe came in contact with it. As soon as she had blindly found the window ledge, she clung to the edge of the wall and brought her other leg down to join the first.

As more of her feet found purchase on the stone, more of her slender weight was added to the weather worn ancient masonry. Natasha crouched again, preparing to repeat the process. She hung over the edge and gripped the stonework.

Suddenly, a brick gave way in her hand.

Natasha landed in a heap on the ground, winded, with her ego bruised rather than physically hurt. But the sounds of her fall had alerted the guard to their ruse.

'Come on, Natasha, we have to go. We've outstayed our welcome,' Lyndsay shouted as he heard the guard call the police.

The archaeologist got to her feet, slightly dazed, but she was aware enough to heed the warning. After checking that both pieces of the object were still in her pocket, she staggered off to join her comrade and they made a swift exit.

'You okay?'

'Yeah, I'll be fine, just a little shaken,' Natasha replied. 'I got this though.' She pulled out the two pieces of metal from her pocket and showed them to Lyndsay.

He took them up for a closer look. The message still made no sense to him. 'These pieces don't fit together.'

'It would have been great if they did, but no problem. We'll head to the next section and hopefully what we find there will bridge the gap.'

'Where to next?'

'All Hallows' Church, funnily enough, on London Wall.'

The pair headed to Fenchurch Street Station, using it as a shortcut to Leadenhall Street. The roads were all but empty at this time of night; the City at 21:00 was far cry from the City at 09:00. Suddenly, two police cars went flying past, then moments later, they came to a screeching halt. With their sirens switched on, they reversed at top speed, flamboyantly skidding to a stop beside Natasha and Lyndsay.

Four police officers jumped out; their guns trained on them. 'Natasha Travers? You're under arrest. Turn around with your hands behind your head!'

'What?' Natasha couldn't believe what she was hearing. 'Look, that guard was overreacting. We just needed to have a quick look at the Roman Wall. We didn't do anything there.'

'We have a warrant for your arrest.'

'For what?'

'Terrorist activities and being a known associate of The Baron. Now put your hands behind your head and turn around!'

Natasha complied with the demands, but she couldn't hide the fear from her face. Time was against her and wasting time proving her innocence to the police, was time taken away from her saving her parents.

Chapter 22

'Well?' Lucas queried Ellen, his frustration mounting. 'Is there anything you can do? Can you get us off the wanted list?'

'Of course there's something I can do,' she replied, totally engrossed in the hacking she was doing on her laptop. She was loading a piece of malware that she had created herself, but the whole process of trying to implant it in all these law enforcement computer systems, wasn't going to be easy. 'The thing is, it's going to take some time. There's a multitude of ways he could have accomplished this, meaning there's a multitude of ways to undo it.'

'I'd better warn Natasha and Lyndsay, tell them to steer clear of the police.' With his phone in hand, Lucas was about to dial her number. Before he could, however, The Baron rang again. 'I hope you know that there won't be much of you left, after I come to collect, if you keep up all these dumbass moves.'

'Don't write cheques your body can't cash, Lucas.'

'I'll cash them, believe me, and I'll have money left over.'

'I look forward to seeing that, but for the moment, I trust you've changed your mind about giving me the Brienne letter?'

Lucas wanted nothing more than to tell him to go to hell, and if it were just himself he had to worry about, he would do just that. But anything he did, also had consequences for Natasha also. And that was something he couldn't deal with. 'Yes, I'll give you the letter,' he said through tight lips.

'Good! I'm glad you've finally seen sense and realised that there's no point going against me. Someone will be with you soon to collect the letter.'

'I'm going to enjoy breaking this guy in half,' Lucas breathed once the call ended.

'I'm sorry you had to do that. If I had been able to ... '

'Hey, don't be stupid, Ellen. If we didn't have a time constraint, I would have told him where to go. I'd have backed you all day long to crack it.'

Ellen appreciated the support and smiled. Then she saw movement over Lucas's shoulder. 'Looks like someone is coming our way.'

'Really?' Lucas turned in his seat. There was indeed a man, in the quiet car park, walking with a strut directly towards them. 'That was quick.'

'Either he was already on his way here ... '

'Or he was staying somewhere nearby.'

'You don't think The Baron runs his operations from around here, do you?'

Lucas had a glint in his eye. He felt like this was an opportunity to take back control. 'There's only one way to find out, Ell.' Before he could explain his plans, however, the man tapped on the window, heavier than Lucas liked. He buzzed the window down, just a touch.

'You got something for me?'

'Nope,' Lucas replied.

The man sneered down at him. 'Don't play games.'

'I've got something for The Baron, not for you. Unless you're telling me that you are The Baron.'

'They said you were a bit of an asshole.'

'They who? The rest of J? I'm glad I've made such an impression.'

'Don't make this any more difficult than it has to be.'

Lucas opened the car door of his Alfa Romeo and squared up to the man. 'And what if I want to make it more difficult?'

When they locked eyes, the man's bravado slowly diminished, seeing that Lucas was no simple mug. 'Uh, maybe I was a being bit rash,' he said, holding his hands up. 'The Baron sent me to pick up a letter for him.'

'See, that wasn't so hard, and I didn't have to make it more difficult for you after all.'

'No, you didn't,' the man replied as he unnecessarily fussed with his clothes.

The action allowed Lucas to notice something that he hadn't, up until that point. Unlike every member of The Baron's organisation he had come across, this one didn't have the familiar snake tattoo. The realisation stunned him for a moment. 'What did you say?'

'Do you have the letter?'

'Yeah, I got it.' Lucas took one of the two letters from out of his inside pocket. He hesitated a moment, undecided if he wanted to hand it over or not.

'The Baron is expecting me to return soon.'

This was music to Lucas's ears. Maybe The Baron was here after all, he thought, and handed over the Brienne letter, feigning reluctance. He didn't want to seem overly eager to please, suddenly, despite the prospect of finally getting his hands on the terrorist leader. He needed this man to think nothing was wrong, so that he would lead Lucas directly to the grand prize. 'You got what you came for, what about the wanted notices?'

'Not my decision, but if I get this safely back, the boss might look favourably on your situation. It was a pleasure doing business with you.'

As soon as the man was out of earshot, Lucas relayed his plan to Ellen. They were both optimistic about the possibility of finally having revenge against The Baron and seeing him pay for his crimes. 'While I'm tailing that guy, I want you to find a way to read the other letter. It must have something important if he wanted it so bad.'

'I guess I could try to source a MuCat,' Ellen thought out loud, then saw Lucas staring at her with a raised eyebrow. 'What? You can buy anything if you know where to look,' she grinned.

'I'll take your word for it. Right, let's get to work, I don't want this guy getting too far ahead. You take the car, Ellen, I'll come pick it up later.'

She nodded, placed her laptop on the dashboard and climbed over into the driver's seat. As she brought it forward to her driving position, a new notification sounded. Ellen checked the computer screen, then showed it to Lucas. 'Natasha's been picked up on Leadenhall Street.'

'She's in custody? Damn it. I need to go help her!'

'What about tailing the man? What about finding The Baron?'

'It'll have to wait.'

'Wait? Are you kidding me? You're not obligated to her anymore, Lucas. You're on the verge of divorce. Have you forgotten that? We stop The Baron; we end it all.'

Lucas was torn. He knew Ellen was right, but he couldn't abandon Natasha, no matter how things were between them. 'I have to go. Besides, what if this guy doesn't lead us to him? Natasha will still be arrested.'

'You said yourself that there's only one way to find out.'

He thought for a moment and came to a decision. 'Okay, Ellen. I know you're not big on field ops, but what if you followed this guy? Just hang back, call me when you got the location and I'll come as soon as I can.'

'I guess I'll have to,' Ellen replied with a frustrated shake of her head. She grabbed her equipment and bag. 'Since it looks like I'm the only one motivated enough to get revenge for Nikos.'

'Come on, Ellen, you know it's not like that,' Lucas called after her, but she was already running off to catch up to her quarry. He let out a huge sigh before setting off.

· · · ·

ELLEN WAS GLAD FOR the chance to put some space between herself and Lucas. She couldn't believe that he had chosen Natasha over finding The Baron; over avenging her brother. But then, the archaeologist was always foremost in his mind. 'The trappings of him being in love,' she muttered to herself.

A feeling she didn't experience too often, thanks to what her foster parents put her through. Her councillor even had a name for it, demiromanticism, the inability to develop romantic feelings for someone unless she had a deep emotional bond to them, which tended to take years to build. It didn't mean she didn't enjoy cuddling, hugging, or having sex, it just meant she did it without being romantically interested in them.

The only person that knew, outside of her doctor, was Lucas. He knew everything about her, just as she knew everything about him. And despite his closeness to Natasha, he had never told her. He was loyal like that. Ellen wasn't ashamed or embarrassed about being demiromantic, she just didn't feel the need to flap her gums about personal details that were none of any bodies business.

Despite him being under Natasha's thumb, as she believed, if he said he'd be here when the time came, then he'd be here. Ellen believed him. She just needed to let him know where.

She had followed The Baron's advocate along Cambridge Heath Road for twenty minutes until they were passing Bethnal Green underground station. It had been quite a difficult task for Ellen to track the delivery guy; the road was long and all but straight. It was almost 22:00, so visibility was impaired, meaning she couldn't stay as far back as she would have liked.

Despite all that, a few short minutes later, Ellen saw the man take a left onto Poyser Street, a road where the many railway arches had been converted into warehouses and industrial units.

Ellen crouched behind a parked car and watched the man stride nonchalantly down the road. She moved from one car to another, always staying low. Then the man she was following came to a stop, and he entered a warehouse, number two-six-three.

She waited a few minutes, just to make sure this wasn't just some pit stop, then when Ellen was satisfied that it wasn't, she text the details to Lucas, who replied with a thumbs up.

Ellen made a roll up, happy with a job well done, before she stood and prepared to make her way home. She lit the unfiltered cigarette and took a long pull before letting the fragrant smoke out of her nose. Just as she was about to bring it to her lips once more, Ellen was suddenly struck heavily in the back of the head, and she collapsed to the ground, unconscious.

Chapter 23

'You're making a mistake. I'm not a terrorist. I'm an archaeologist!'

The female police officer who sat in the passage seat turned to face their prisoner. She glared at Natasha with the look of disdain, like she'd killed her dog. 'Tell it to Interpol,' she said through gritted teeth.

Natasha was taken back by the hostility and wondered when the saying "innocent until proven guilty" had been switched to become "guilty until proven innocent". She was just glad that she hadn't tried to explain why she was working for The Baron. Even though it was to save her parents, she didn't think it would cut it with these two.

She wondered if Lyndsay, held in the other police car which led the way to the station, was having any better luck than she was convincing the officers of their innocence. In her mind, Natasha imagined them suddenly pulling over and being released, and the officer with the resting bitch face apologising, as she undid the cuffs.

That was fantasy. The reality was that they weren't pulling over or being freed, they were on their way to the City of London police station, and she had no idea how she was going to get out of this situation, nor what would happen to her parents, since she couldn't complete the task set by The Baron and find the Eye of Nineveh.

They paused at the red lights at the junction of Fenchurch Street and Gracechurch Street. The lights turned green, and the police cars set off again. As the lead car took the right-hand turn, a van, travelling at high speed, jumped the light and smashed into the side of the BMW, flipping it over onto its roof.

It was like the whole scene played out in slow-motion before Natasha's eyes. The horrific sound of metal crunching into metal and shattered glass rang in her ears.

'What the hell!' The male police officer gasped.

'Do you think they're okay? You'd better call it in!' His partner asked as she unbuckled her seatbelt. She was about to rush to their aid when the back doors of the van suddenly opened and four hooded assailants jumped out, each armed with an automatic rifle. Then two of them opened fire on the overturned police car, whilst the others pointed their rifles at them.

• • • •

LUCAS MADE THE SUPPOSEDLY ten-minute journey from Queen Mary University to Fenchurch Street in less than eight, and he was glad for his lead foot when he saw and heard the carnage ahead of him.

He'd been expecting to have to try and convince the police of their mistake, tell them the whole story, if Natasha hadn't already done so, but this war zone tableau was the last thing he thought he'd see.

Not having time to plan anything, Lucas did the first thing that came to mind; he drove into the gunmen. His Alfa Romeo Giulia GTA had been a gift from Ellen, and he wondered how he was going to explain the damage it was about to sustain as he charged headlong at the armed and masked people.

The first two, the ones standing near the police car Natasha was in, managed to jump out of the way, as did one of the shooters. The fourth, however, was so involved in shooting the police car, as if it had been a lifelong dream of theirs, that by the time they were aware of what was happening, the side of the black Alfa had slammed into them and pinned them to the van, crushing them between the two vehicles.

As he stepped out of the car, the van driver fired at Lucas. He stayed low, using the car as protection. The other three gunners were getting back to their feet, and when they did, he'd be an open target for them. He couldn't wait around.

The moment he heard the driver's handgun click empty, Lucas leapt out from behind his car, scooped to retrieve the dropped assault rifle, and kept moving. He went round to the other side of the bullet riddled police car and checked the occupants. One of the officers was dead, having taken most of the bullets from the shooters. The second policeman was pretty banged up. Lucas saw that the same could be said of Lyndsay, when he saw his friend hanging down from his buckled seat.

With the smell of petrol and gunpowder prevalent in the air, Lucas undid the seatbelts of the two men as quickly as he could. He was just about to pull them out when he came under machine gun fire.

Lucas swore under his breath; any of these shots could ignite the vapours. He shouted at Lyndsay and the officer to get clear, whilst he lay down controlled suppressing fire. Once they were at a safe distance, he used the car as cover and moved along it until he was in a better position to flank the shooter nearest to him.

With unerring accuracy, he stood, let loose two bursts of fire, killing the assailant instantly, before ducking back into cover.

Two down, three to go.

Lucas didn't stop to admire his work; it wasn't over yet. The driver suddenly stepped out, gun raised, but the last of the bullets from Lucas's acquired machine gun thudded into his chest.

He dropped the empty assault rifle and picked up the dead man's Glock. A quick rummage through the deceased's body revealed a spare magazine, and also the tattoo of the J organisation. The snakes head with bared fangs.

Lucas looked at the body art in confusion. Why would The Baron want Natasha dead? She was doing what he wanted – searching for the Eye of Nineveh. That's when the truth dawned on Lucas. They weren't here to kill Natasha; they were here to make sure she continued her hunt.

They were here to kill the police.

The female officer stood behind her open car door, her taser aimed at a terrorist. Her heartbeat raced. Although she had trained for situations like this, facing a gunman, training couldn't truly replicate the stresses of the real-world scenario; the bullets in these machine guns weren't blanks.

She delivered her warning, shouting at them to put down their weapons, just as police procedure textbooks dictated. The only problem with that is, criminals, the true hardened ones, live by a different set of rules. And they take their chances when they're faced by a taser, and they have a machine gun.

He kicked the car door into her hard. Then again. Then a third time. She yelled in agony each time it slammed against her. She clutched at her ribs and was falling to her knees when the door was kicked on her a fourth time, her head going through the glass.

Her partner jumped out and fired his taser. It hit its target, shocking him to the ground. The trouble was, there were two targets, and the second terrorist emptied his clip into him.

Seconds later, two 9mm bullets struck the side of his head.

Lucas put the gun in his bag as he came running up to the police car. 'Natasha! Natasha!' He yanked the rear door open and found her crouched down in the legroom of the backseat. 'Are you okay, Nat?'

Natasha slowly looked up, hearing the familiar voice. 'I'm - I'm okay,' she breathed as she let Lucas help her out of the car. As she looked around at all the devastation and dead bodies, she was on the brink of going into shock, but Lucas shook her out of it, made sure she focussed on him.

'Come on, Nat. We've been in worse scrapes than this. Besides, these guys weren't after you.'

'What do you mean?'

He rolled up the sleeve of the unconscious terrorist. 'They're The Baron's men, probably sent to make sure you weren't delayed.'

'Wonderful. That's hardly going to prove my innocence. I guarantee this will convince the police that I'm a terrorist.'

Lyndsay came over with the injured policeman. Seeing he was still handcuffed, Lucas drew the gun on the officer, who immediately put his hands up. 'Since I just saved you and your fellow officers' lives, I think it's clear to see that these cuffs are on the wrong people. What do you think?' The police officer looked from Lucas to the gun and back to Lucas, then he took out his key and undid the handcuffs on both Natasha and Lyndsay. He cuffed the unconscious terrorist, then tended to his colleague.

The three took the opportunity to leave just as the sound of sirens grew louder. Lucas's car was still drivable, despite the damage to the passenger side. Once they set off, Lucas and Natasha each brought the other up to speed on what they had been doing. She was jealous of the fact that he had got to see the Brienne letters. That jealousy soon turned to disbelief and anger when he showed her the one that he had kept.

'Would you calm down!'

'How can I? You've stolen an important piece of history!'

'But don't you want to know just how important it is? I do. I want to know why The Baron wants it so bad. I want to know why there were two letters. I want to know why he didn't know that. Don't you want to know any of those things?'

Natasha gently turned the letter over in her hands, marvelling at the elaborate calligraphy. She took in a deep breath, as if she were literally smelling the history. 'Okay, I'll admit, I am interested.' Natasha saw the grin on Lucas's face. 'But you have to promise me that you won't open it ... '

'I've already got Ellen looking into it.'

'... and you have to get it back to the collection too.'

'I'll find a way,' Lucas said cheerfully.

Natasha looked sceptical, but she'd give him the benefit of the doubt. 'Since this is show and tell, this is what I've found along Marcus's map.' She held up the two discs, which Lucas quickly glanced at whilst watching the road.

'What's that on them? What do they make up?'

'Don't know for sure and I haven't had the chance to see if they connect together, thanks to that altercation.' Natasha fiddled with the two pieces, sliding them along their lengths until they slotted together. 'Seems to be some sort of inscription and an engraving of something. "Dickens saw their most glorious end. Once".

'Something you could figure out without the rest?'

'It's nice you have such faith in me, Lucas, but no, I don't have a clue what it could mean. Right now, it's complete nonsense.'

'Okay, so we need the rest of this thing. Where do we look?'

'Well, there are nine places where you can still see pieces of the Roman wall. Lyndsay and I have already visited two. The other seven parts are at All Hallows-on-the-wall church, St Alphage Garden, St Giles in Barbican, Barbers Garden, London Wall car park, Noble Street –'

'Wait! Did you say a car park?'

'Yes, I did. Quite a big piece actually, at parking bay 54. There is one problem, though. The last piece. It's in the basement of the Old Bailey and it's not open to the public.'

'What? You're kidding, right? We have to break into the Central Criminal Court?'

Chapter 24

A hush filled the car the moment Natasha made her revelation, with good reason. Located on the street it gets its name from, the Old Bailey had been on that spot, in one form or another, since as early as 1585, and had been the scene of many high-profile cases. It made sense that a piece of the wall was there, a bailey, as Natasha explained to them, was a fortified wall, and the road was built on top of it.

Getting into the criminal court, however, was going to be nothing like sneaking into a university. There would be better trained security and a lot more cameras. This was definitely going to need some planning. 'The good thing,' Lucas added, 'is that we can leave this one until last. Your professor might not have been able to get in there himself.'

'That's true,' Natasha said. 'If we assume that every subsequent piece is the exact same size and shape...' She used the two pieces of the golden disc, moving them around, to imagine what the unknown disc probably looked like when the object was complete. 'It's a heptagon!'

'A hepta-what?' Lyndsay queried from the back.

'A heptagon. A seven-sided polygon. That means seven pieces in total, and we've already got two.'

'So, we're looking for five more pieces out of these seven locations,' stated Lucas.

'Five out of seven? So where do we begin?' Lyndsay asked.

'Right here,' Natasha said as she indicated for Lucas to pull over and park. 'Okay, this is All Hallows-On-The Wall,' she announced as they got out of the car.

Lucas pulled a small torch from his bag, pushed the button, and shone its powerful beam along the length of the masonry. 'That's quite a bit of wall to check.'

'Don't worry, it's not all Roman; just that bit around the side of the church.'

'When I woke up this morning, if you said that by midnight I'd be crawling around a church, I'd have thought you were nuts,' said Lyndsay.

Lucas chuckled. 'Yeah, same here.'

'No, you were probably expecting to be crawling all over Chiara by this time,' Natasha said.

Lyndsay took a sharp intake of air. 'Ouch,' mouthed.

'That's a good one, Nat,' Lucas replied with a fake laugh. 'You go check your wall. I'm going to check in on Ellen.' He took out his mobile phone as he went to stand beside his car.

Natasha rolled her eyes, disappointed at herself for voicing what was in her head. The whole situation between her and Lucas was still so raw. She had bitten her tongue on so many occasions, but she couldn't be expected to catch every barbed comment that came to her lips and suffer in silence.

As she gazed over at him. The thing she hated most was that she was still in love with him; that had never stopped. They were in a good place when it happened, never better. It wasn't as if they were at each other's throats, and he sought the solace of another's arms. It came completely out of the blue. No matter how betrayed and disappointed she might feel, her love for Lucas remained. She just needed to know why he had done it. Then maybe she could heal. And she was sure she knew exactly who to ask to get that answer.

'Ellen's not answering,' Lucas said as he returned, his eyebrows creased in concern. 'She texted me, a while ago, with the address of the guy that took the Brienne letter. I haven't heard anything from her since.'

'Maybe her battery's dead.'

'No, it's ringing. It's just not being answered.'

'You should go have a look. Make sure she's okay.'

'I've checked every part of this,' Lyndsay suddenly announced. 'There's nothing here. I think you'd better start formulating that plan for the Old Bailey, Captain.'

'Where to next?'

'Saint Alphage and Salters' gardens. It was once a churchyard. When the church was demolished in the nineteenth century, they turned it into an urban garden,' Natasha said. 'Come on, it's not far, just a little further down London Wall.'

They jogged the short distance to the hidden oasis. The north edge of the ancient London Wall divided the gardens. Both sections of the garden had various flowerbeds and benches for the workers from the surrounding offices to eat their lunch beside the water feature. It also had a magnolia tree; an oak tree and the southern edge of the garden was defined by a beech hedge.

Natasha smiled, remembering when she came here for the first time when she was a youngster. She had been stunned to find a pocket of nature surrounded by modern buildings. The passage of time and London's rich history was encapsulated in that garden. The Roman wall built in 200AD, topped by medieval masonry, standing next to a church that was first mentioned in the historic chronicles shortly after the Norman invasion of 1066, and converted into a garden in 1872. Over sixteen-hundred years of history open for all to see.

Lucas tapped Natasha, seeing that she was in one of her zoned-out moments, where she was able to visualise and build a picture of the way things were. She used to explain things in such vivid detail that he could see it too. It was like bringing history back to life.

The three of them set to work, searching the wall for anything that looked out of place. With three pairs of eyes doing the job, it was a much quicker process to find the mortar that was softer and ever so slightly lighter than the rest.

Natasha scrapped away at it, not entrusting the precision job to either of the other two, for fear they might not be as delicate during the process as she would be. It was a slower course of action, but no less fruitful. Eventually, she freed the brick and take out the prize hidden within the cavity.

She unwrapped it, and there it was, another golden piece. With a big grin on her face and her heart beating with expectation, Natasha tried to connect it with the two pieces they had already found, but it soon became apparent that they weren't meant to be together; the engraving and the message didn't match up.

Lucas had taken the break time to reach Ellen once again. Still, there was no answer. His levels of worry rose exponentially. He knew she could take care of herself, having dealt with plenty of unscrupulous characters and leaders in her short life. But most of those had been on the other side of computer screens. He stared at his mobile phone, regretting sending her after the man. If he hadn't come running to save Natasha, then Ellen wouldn't have had to tail him and she'd be alright; not that he knew for certain anything had happened to her, but that was the way his mind was veering towards.

Maybe it was time for him to accept that he had messed things up with Natasha. Accept that they were getting a divorce. Accept that he wasn't obligated to her anymore. Accept that she didn't need him.

· · · ·

ELLEN OPENED HER EYES. Her vision was blurred, but with each blink, it cleared. She rubbed her head. Her was brain fuzzy. The last thing she remembered was sending Lucas a text, the address of the guy she was following. Then she made a roll up, took a toke, and was just about to make her way home. And then … She touched the back of her head and flinched. It was sore. At least it wasn't bleeding, she thought, after seeing there was no blood on her hand.

Dragging her legs off of the cot she was laying in, Ellen scrutinised the room she found herself in. It seemed to be a bare office and as she staggered to its windows, she stared out and saw that she was in some sort of warehouse, probably the same one she'd followed that man.

'Damn it!' Ellen breathed. 'The bastard must have known I was following him all along.' She shook her head in disappointment and suddenly felt her stomach clench with the onset of nausea. She knew she was in trouble, big trouble. Ellen was sure that The Baron didn't like people snooping around his organisation. She also knew that he was pretty ruthless when necessary. Her brother had suffered such a fate at his hands, now she was going to suffer the same.

There were a few men out there in the half-empty warehouse, less than Ellen had expected to see, if she were being honest, but did they really need a lot of guards to watch over a cute but vertically challenged girl like her? She shook her head in answer to her unspoken question.

She saw The Baron's advocate, whom Lucas had given the Brienne letter to, out with the guards. One of the men indicated to him that Ellen was awake, and he immediately made his way over, rubbing his hands with a creepy grin on his face.

Ellen backed away, worried by the look he gave her. It was almost the same as the one her foster parents gave her when they would come to her bedroom.

She heard a bunch of keys jangle in the lock and the man entered. 'I'm glad to see you're finally awake. Ellen Paige, right? It's been over two hours. A real sleeping beauty.'

'Yeah, well, thanks for the hospitality, but I should really be going. Tell The Baron I'll drop by another time to say hi.'

'The Baron? You didn't really think he'd be here, did you? Well, to be honest, we kind of hoped that you would but it was supposed to be Lucas that took the bait, not his little sidekick.'

'Sidekick? Dude, I'm the main effing attraction.'

'Of course you,' he mocked. 'Anyway, when the boss found out that you were the one that followed me here, instead of Lucas, plans were changed a bit.'

'What plans?'

'Doesn't really matter now, does it?'

'You don't know that! It could be very pertinent information.'

'If you say so. Maybe it is, maybe it isn't. Basically, you're going home, Ellen.'

'Home? You're letting me go?'

'Sure. Someone's going to come and get the letter and they'll be bringing someone to pick you up.'

'That's okay. I can get home by myself; I wouldn't want to put you or The Baron out.'

'Well, you're not putting me out, and I'm positive you're not putting The Baron out either, because I don't work for him.'

'What?'

'I never said I worked for him. I just never corrected you or Lucas's assumptions.'

'So, The Baron isn't coming to get the letter?'

'Nope.'

'Then who's coming to pick me up.'

'Your dad, of course. Graeme. Apparently, he was thrilled when my boss got in touch with him and told him about finding you.'

Just hearing the name of her foster dad was enough to make Ellen tremble.

Chapter 25

With three of the golden pieces collected, Natasha led Lucas and Lyndsay to their next location, St Giles' Cripplegate. It was a quick five-minute walk, turning off at Fore Street, to reach the church, situated in the middle of the Barbican Estate, the city within a city.

It was said that a church had been on that spot for over one thousand years, a wattle and daub chapel during Saxon times and a Norman church from 1090. But they weren't here to enrich their knowledge of papal architecture.

'And there we have it,' Natasha announced with her hands out wide.

Past the church was a terrace which overlooked part of the Barbican's manmade U-shaped lake. Lucas took out the torch from his bag, once again, and shone the beam across the water. On a bank on the other side was a long section of the wall. There was even part of a tower, which Natasha explained was a medieval addition.

'So, who's going across?' Lucas asked, at which point both he and Lyndsay stared at Natasha. 'I mean, we oafs couldn't be trusted with such a delicate job, we should just stay as far away from the wall as possible.'

'Fine!' Natasha snatched the offered torch out of Lucas's hand. She didn't realise that her words would come back to bite her so soon. She walked further down and tried the gate of the railing, but discovered that it was locked. She had a quick look around, forgetting that it was one in the morning, before she lithely climbed over the short metal barrier. Going down the steps onto the pontoon, Natasha turned and gave them a strained smile. 'I didn't realise I was being accompanied by such gentlemen.' Her words dripped with sarcasm. She stared at the lake and willed herself to step into the queasy green water.

It came up to mid-calf, and she quickly waded to the other side and gave the others a thumbs up before she set to work looking for the next piece. Lucas and Lyndsay looked on, seeing the torch beam moving around and illuminating the building behind the ancient wall.

'She's a great woman, Lucas. You're lucky to have her.'

'Don't you mean had? It's over between us.'

'Who are you trying to kid? Look how you keep running to her aid when you know she's in trouble.'

'Bad habits.'

'Bollocks. It's plain to see, marriage or not, you two are still head over heels for each other.'

'It's too late to do anything about it now.'

'It's never too late. You just have to explain your reasons, your mindset behind your action. You have to come clean about everything, and I mean everything. She's your unicorn, man.'

'The thing is, I know. I got myself in a situation that was hard to get out of.'

'What? Jesus, Lucas. You're telling me it's a tougher situation than being chased through a temple, in Nineveh, by terrorists? Or being shot at by gangsters in Peru? Maybe it's more difficult than climbing a cliff face?'

'Those things are easy. If I fail in those actions, then I'm dead. In this situation, I know I'm going to hurt someone.'

'Who? Natasha or Chiara?'

'Mostly Natasha.'

'Hate to break it to you, but you've already hurt her.'

'And now you want me to add to it.'

'If she really is the one, then you have to lay everything out on the table and if she turns around and says nope, there's too much baggage, then so be it. But give her the chance, don't decide for her.'

Lucas looked at the lake, ever decreasing waves still roiling where Natasha had stepped. His mind was in deep thought as he mulled over where he was, and where he wanted to be in his life. Then he realised he had everything he wanted already, and he almost let it all go because of one thing. Lucas smiled as he finally knew what he had to do.

Before he could tell Lyndsay his plans, Natasha suddenly shouted from across the water. She had found the piece. She had made her way a lot further down the wall to find it, but the search had been worth it.

'Four down three to go,' she yelled.

Just then, they heard a commotion coming from somewhere behind Lucas and Lyndsay. Natasha, as curious as the other two, was about to make her way back across the lake. But Lucas signalled for her to stay where she was and hide. She refused at first, but when his signals became more insistent, she reluctantly relented and hid, switching the torch off in the process.

Once they knew she was safe, Lucas and Lyndsay went off to investigate. They slowly walked past the gothic church once more, the source of the clamour getting closer by the moment.

They heard voices by the lake on the opposite side. As they edged closer, it became apparent that they were somewhere that they shouldn't be. Behind the wall, where the pair hid, down by the water, in the shadows, the moonlight illuminated things just enough for Lucas to make out several thugs, some making it obvious that they were armed, as a drug deal went down. Lucas cursed their luck. They needed to back away as soon as possible, without drawing attention to themselves.

Suddenly, they heard a voice and the familiar sound of a gun being cocked.

'Ray! We got us some nosey bastards, here!'

'Bring them down!' Ray shouted back before turning his attention back to the deal. 'Well, well, well, Ennis. What were you saying about not bringing the feds?'

'I already told you, I haven't gone to the police. And I don't know who these jackasses are,' Ennis said, pointing at Lucas and Lyndsay as they became unwelcome guests at the party. 'I'm just here to make the deal and go.'

Ray took a deep breath and let it out. 'The thing is, Ennis, people have been mentioning your name. Said they've seen you with stiff mofos. Whispering shit. Going into dark alleys and stuff.'

Ennis fidgeted as beads of sweat appeared on his forehead. 'It's ... it's not what you think.'

'Is it not? Then why don't you tell me,' Ray pressed, but when he got no reply, he tried a different tact. 'Or do you want to tell Clive?'

'No, no. I'll tell you. They're not cops. They're ... they're prostitutes. Male prostitutes.'

There was a momentary silence that was broken by an eruption of laughter. 'Shut up,' Ray shouted. 'I said shut up! So, Ennis, you want me to believe that you're into fellas? Maybe you ought to tell your girl, Mischa, that. And what was your boy's name?'

'Jordan.'

'Yes. Jordan, that's it. Well, Ennis, we will honour our end of the deal; we can't have Clive's crew getting a bad rep. Your two cronies can go with the powder to your boss.' One of Ray's associates closed the case and handed it to one of Ennis's men. 'You, however, won't be going anywhere. You know what they say, Ennis, snitches get stitches,' another associate handed a machete to him, which brought terror to the face of Ennis. 'But when it comes to working with Clive's Crew, snitches get dead.'

· · · ·

AS SOON AS LUCAS HAD gone out of her sight, Natasha had crossed the lake, disregarding the instructions she had been given. She low crossing the pontoon and went up the steps up to the point where she could see across the peninsula, but there was no one to see.

But she could hear.

She heard the pleading, which became muffled screams, then gurgling ones. Then silence.

Natasha ducked down and her hand covered her mouth. She didn't know for certain what she'd heard, but her imagination could hazard a guess. When she heard movement again, she slowly popped her head up and saw two men carrying a body sized plastic bundle towards Fore

Street. Moments later she witnessed Lucas and Lyndsay being led, at gunpoint, back to the terrace and up into the two-thousand apartment estate.

She swore under her breath. What was she supposed to do? Call the police? If she did that, she would need to know the apartment number. Natasha was just about to climb the rest of the steps and climb over the railing back onto the terrace when the men returned, one of them heading to the side of the church.

Natasha dropped down again, her heart pumping. She took deep breaths and tried to slow its beating. She prayed they hadn't seen her, and it soon became apparent that they hadn't when she heard the telltale sound of someone urinating. She groaned in disgust.

'This is bollocks,' she heard one of them say. 'Why is it always us on clean up?'

'Probably because we're the newest, we still have to prove ourselves, Raheem.'

'Well, give me something to prove myself then, instead of having to clean up blood and guts.'

'You going to tell Clive that?'

'Well, no, Jace. Of course not.'

Natasha's luck suddenly ran out, and so was the battery in her mobile phone, as it beeped several times to alert her to its condition.

'Did you hear that, Jace?'

'Yeah, of course. Sounded like a phone.'

'Well, go check it out then,' Raheem ordered as he finished.

Jace grudgingly did as he was told, mumbling under his breath; they were on an equal level in Clive's crew, and he didn't see why he should be treated as the lackey.

Natasha could hear him getting closer. Her eyes darted around as she fervently sought a way out of her predicament. There was only one thing she could do, run.

'Hey, it's some bittc –'

Putting her MMA training into good use, she kicked Jace in the side of his head before he could finish his slur, before Natasha vaulted the railing and sprinted off past Raheem, who was struggling to zip up his jeans. That delay didn't last long, and he was soon giving chase.

Natasha headed towards London Wall, the main road, in the slim hope that she might see a black cab she could flag down. She turned onto Noble Street, with London Wall in sight.

Instinctively, Natasha had come to what would have been her next destination, the Noble Street gardens. She stopped on the walkway and looked down into the sunken garden. Faced with an archaeological site, the fact she was being chased quickly left her mind.

In a split moment she had decided and leapt over the barrier into the wildflower meadow, several feet below, being careful not to disturb the beehives, and hid. He came racing around the corner, and immediately slowed when there was no sign of her. He knew he hadn't been that far behind her.

Natasha could hear him walk on the platform she hid beneath. Her heartbeat was thumping in her ears so loudly she was sure he could hear it. But it wasn't the beating of her heart that drew his attention, but the rustling she made when she tried to stay out of his field of vision as he moved off.

Raheem ran to the end of the walkway, looked down into the garden, and saw Natasha underneath the ledge. 'Gotcha!' He walked down the steps into the private garden smiling at the opportunity to present to him; he was in for some kudos when he brought this witness to Clive.

Natasha had slowly stepped out of her hiding place, not seeing the need to conceal herself any longer. She quickly surveyed her surroundings and saw that, although she might be able to jump back up, it wouldn't be an easy task to climb out with someone bearing down on her. The only real way out was up the stairs Raheem had used, but that meant getting past him.

'Damn, girl.' Raheem had gotten close enough to finally see who he'd been chasing. 'You're *fine*. Man, Clive is going to have a field day with you, girl,' he said, then a sadistic smile crept across his face. 'But who says that he has to be the first one.'

As she watched him rub his hands together, Natasha gagged at the idea of him touching her with his filthy hands. The moment he was within range, she unleashed a flurry of blows to his face, and several kicks to the side of his knees, knowing that the cumulative effects would slow him down.

The moment she relented for a split second to catch her breath, he tried to pounce and got a leaping knee to the jaw for his troubles. Natasha grabbed one of his flaying arms and hip tossed him right into the beehives.

The angry bees immediately set upon the intruder, who yelled as he was stung repeatedly. He hobbled off, desperately trying to swat the furious insects. Natasha hung back, waiting until the coast was clear of the bees. Then she came out and began searching the wall.

Unlike the other sections of wall, the Roman remains here were just exposed foundations, without medieval masonry on top of it, those remains were further down. It had also been part of one of the forts that housed the soldiers. Thoughts of what it would have been like, who they were flowed though Natasha's mind as she searched.

It wasn't long before she found what she was looking for. In one of the corners of the fort, under the wildflowers and ragstone, was the fifth piece of Marcus's object. Its golden surface glinted in the moonlight and caught the attention of someone other than Natasha.

'Oi!' Jace shouted. 'I'm going to break you in half, bitch!'

Chapter 26

Jace grinned down at Natasha as he ambled towards the steps down into the garden pit. Her exit would be blocked again in a matter of seconds. There were no bees to aid her this time round, so she attempted the climb out.

Natasha put the artefact in her back pocket as she backed up to the ancient wall. Then she exploded into a sprint and jumped for the viewing ledge.

She made it, but her fingers didn't have enough of a grip, and she dropped back down, landing with a grunt. Jace saw what she was attempting to do and swore at her as he ran.

Natasha backed up again, took a couple of deep breaths and took off again. The fast-twitch fibres in her legs, fuelled by adrenaline, fired and propelled her through the air.

She made it again, this time with a firm grip. Having to make the second attempt at the jump, though, had given Jace just enough time to get to her. He tried to grab her legs. She swung them violently, desperate to fend him off.

Natasha hit Jace several times, but still he kept coming. Then he caught one of her legs. She wriggled, trying to free herself, but couldn't. Then he grabbed the waist of her cargo pants. Natasha let out cries of anguish as, with three mighty pulls, Jace broke her grip, dragging her back down into the garden pit. At that moment, however, she felt like she was being dragged down to hell.

They fell in a heap amongst the wildflowers, Jace winded by having the athletic build of Natasha land full on his chest. His hands were like an octopus. She fended them off the best she could. Then she remembered specific training that Lucas had given her for just such occasions. Although they had been standing during the lesson, the positioning was same, so the principles would likewise be similar.

Natasha bent her head down before throwing it back with all the strength in her neck, cracking the back of her head into his face. She could feel her hair at the back matting. He shouted and swore. Natasha freed herself and took the chance to drive her point home, a knee to the groin.

She sprinted off with his groans of discomfort ringing in her ears. When she reached the stairs, Natasha glanced back and saw Jace struggle to his feet, trying to rub life back into his manhood. Although she couldn't help smirk, seeing him already up spurred her on to get moving again.

Even though Natasha was in relatively good shape, it was gone two in the morning, and the constant running and fighting finally took its toll on her. She needed somewhere she could hide, rest, and catch her breath.

Natasha headed for the London Wall underground car park.

As she went down the ramp and slowed to a walk, Natasha thought she'd check out the piece of Marcus's object she'd just found. She put her hand in her pocket, and when she didn't find it, checked all of her other pockets. It wasn't there!

She hid behind a car in bay eleven and played back recent events in her mind. It must have fallen out when Jace yanked me down, she mused, and cursed the little perv. Hopefully, it was still there, and I'll be able to go retrieve it. I'm due some luck.

But that luck didn't materialise.

Moments later, she heard footfalls echoing through the car park. 'You can hide all you want, but you can't escape, bitch.' Jace's declaration reverberated through the half empty space.

Natasha crawled from car to car, going deeper and deeper inside the building. When she found one of the side entrances locked, she thought maybe he was right.

'I'm going to find you,' he sang in a creepy melody, and went on to describe the things he intended to do to her before bringing her to his boss. '... and he's going to love this little golden thing too, whatever it is. Clive just loves gold.'

'Damn it,' she whispered. Natasha's mind was all over the place; Ellen was missing, Lucas and Lyndsay taken by a gang, a member of that gang had a piece of Marcus's object, and to top it off, a piece of it was in the Old Bailey. Or maybe not. As the thought formed in her mind, she remembered that there were still two pieces to be found, and three locations to be searched, including the one she was already at.

She was so deep in her thoughts that Natasha had zoned out, only to be brought back to her senses when Jace banged on a car in frustration. She almost jumped out of her skin. He was a lot closer than she would have liked. Two, maybe three rows down.

Natasha rose slowly, just enough to look through the window of the Land Rover Defender she was crouched beside. As he moved closer, she worked her way towards the back of the vehicle.

When he reached the front of the SUV, she had made it to the rear. Her heart pounded so much that she thought it would burst right out of her chest.

He swore again. 'You're starting to piss me off!'

The housing of the spare wheel for the Defender was obscuring Natasha's view. She needed to see what he was doing so she could avoid him. The way things were right now, he could come around the car any minute and catch her.

She grabbed hold of the wheel housing and pulled herself up. From her new position, Natasha could see him looking back to the entrance of the car park, possibly thinking that she might have snuck past and doubled-back. Another idea suddenly came to him, and he dropped to ground.

Natasha glared wide-eyed, panic running through her unrelenting. Her feet were up above the bottom of the Land Rover, but it was taking every ounce of strength to keep herself there.

Jace looked as far as he could see, laying on the ground, looking everywhere, just in case she was underneath one of the cars. 'This is bollocks,' Jace said to himself. 'Where the hell is she?'

Natasha's muscles cried out in pain as the lactic acid built up in them. She gritted her teeth, determined to hold on, but she didn't know how much longer she could last. If she slipped now, she wouldn't have the strength left to defend herself. She'd be finished.

Eventually, Jace slowly got to his feet, then he continued to walk further into the underground facility, same way

Natasha needed to go if she were to search the Roman wall that was at bay fifty-four.

She needed to get him going the other way.

Natasha checked her pockets, eventually finding something that might be of use, a two-pound coin. A second later, she quickly popped up from her hidden position and blindly threw the coin before she ducked back down.

In the silence, it was easy to make out the sound of a windscreen cracking.

She swore under her breath. When you've got bad luck, you've got bad luck. Even though she had damaged someone's car in the process, the diversion, at least, was a success.

Jace spun around, hearing the sound loud and clear. With a big grin on his face, he hobbled his way back towards the entrance, still soothing his aching groin.

The moment she was sure he was far enough away, Natasha, still moving from car to car, headed towards the wall. She got there just as she heard Jace's frustrations boiling over.

Although the piece of wall was exposed, they had erected a fence around it, to protect it from would-be vandals. Natasha scaled it, trying to make as little noise as possible. When she dropped down, she paused and listened to make sure Jace hadn't heard her and wasn't making his way back.

Time was against Natasha. She had to find this piece of the gold object as quickly as possible, if it was in fact there, so that she could follow Jace back to his gang. She'd need that information for when she called the police. Not only that, but The Baron's timer loomed large, with only five hours left to find The Eye of Nineveh, and she still had no idea where it was.

You could really get a sense of how thick the ancient Roman wall was from this section, and unlike a few of the others, she had been to, there was a lot of the original Kent ragstone, that was used in its construction, left.

She smiled a childish grin as she touched it, sensing the history in each carefully placed stone. She wondered about the builder; what was his name? Did he have a family? Children? Did he have a long life, or did he die in battle? Bringing history back to life was one of the best things about her career choice.

Marcus was right. She did have a curious nature, but that was what made the difference between her being a good archaeologist and a great one. She preferred being great. Her father wouldn't have it any other way, either.

Having checked all around the lower parts of the wall, as high up as she could reach, Natasha knew what she had to do now, climb another historic wall. She let out a deep sigh and shook her head. She hated having to do it, and she couldn't believe that Marcus had actually done it; he was protective of historical sites as much as she was, and yet here was the proof that he had been climbing another one.

Natasha had found it.

She loosened the ragstone, scrapping away at the mortar surrounding it, until it was able to be pulled out. As she placed it on the top of the wall, before she could make sure it was secure, she heard a car door slam. She jumped, and in so doing, the tentatively placed stone began to topple.

As if in slow motion, it bounced and clunked its way down, chips of stone flying off. Each sound of stone hitting stone was amplified by the echo, and when it finally hit the fence, it was like a crescendo, and came to a rest.

Natasha stared at it in horror.

'Ah ha! I've got you now, bitch,' Jace shouted.

She heard him, and it wasn't long before she could see his elongated shadow coming back. Natasha grabbed the golden piece, the sixth one she had found, and quickly descended. There wasn't enough time for her to climb over the fence. She ducked behind the substantial wall and hoped providence might shine on her.

This time, she did.

Jace took nothing but a cursory look, saw the stone laying by the fence, and turned to leave. 'Stupid bloody wall. Screw this, I'm out of here.' He took another look at the golden piece he'd found and smiled. 'Clive will be more than happy with this; he doesn't need to know anything about the woman.'

• • • •

DETECTIVE CHIEF INSPECTOR Jake Russell sat in his office, with his back to his desk, sipping his cup of Lady Grey tea. He was watching a frozen image of Marcus at the British Museum, standing in front of the Eye of Nineveh, the night of its disappearance. He brought the cup of steaming liquid to his lips once more, not breaking his stare once. Not even when there was a knock at the door. He bid them enter and when he saw it was the young detective, Derek Wilkins, he called him over.

'Working late?' Wilkins asked.

'When criminals start working nine to five, so will I.' The inspector gestured to the screen. 'What do you see there, Wilkins?'

'Well,' the detective had a look at the screen. 'That's Professor Masterson, the night of the gem heist, right sir?'

'Yes, it is. But what do you make of this?' DCI Russell pointed to the professor's hand. Wilkins was stumped and shrugged his shoulders, saying it was too blurry, at which point the Russell directed him to an image he had blown up by the tech heads.

Wilkins had a look at the picture, rotating it a few times. 'It kind of looks like it might be an inhaler pump.'

'Exactly. Yet I've asked around, Robert Jones, his colleagues at Cambridge, they all said he wasn't asthmatic.'

'Then why does he have it?'

DCI Russell took a few more sips of his tea, letting the detective wait for his answer. 'There could be a simple reason. It might not be his or he could have found it. But that wouldn't explain this.' He rewound the DVD of the security cam footage a little and played it. Nothing seemed out of the ordinary to Wilkins, so Russell played it again, this time pointing out three small distortions. 'No, Wilkins, they're not dust particles. He pumped the inhaler three times. At three different angles, the third one being the most visible, just.'

'To what end?'

The DCI shrugged and finished the last of his tea. 'Who knows? What was in the inhaler? Why was that man following him and why was the professor so terrified? Where is he now? Too many unanswered questions make me think he is a distinct person of interest. More so than Lucas Redmond. I'd gather.'

'Funny you should mention him. That's why I'm here, actually. There was a shootout near Fenchurch Street.'

Jake Russell sat up, hearing the news. 'City of London jurisdiction.'

'Yes, they were involved. They responded to the arrest warrant that was put out for Natasha Travers, and they picked her up.'

'Have you discovered the origin of that request yet?'

'No, and the agencies that I have spoken to so far have all denied it was them.'

'I see.'

'Before they could bring her back to the station, they were hit. Officers were killed, two survived. Thanks to Lucas, apparently. Saved them and took out the shooters.'

'Who hit them?'

'The J organisation apparently.'

Russell whistled. 'Now how is a terrorist group mixed up in all of this?'

'I wish I knew. What do you want me to do about these warrants for Travers and Redmond?'

'Forget them. I want confirmation of who issued them before any of the officers follow through.'

'Are you sure? There's no doubt that they were involved in this shooting.'

'And from what I heard, they saved lives. If City of London police want to question them, then they can do their own legwork; I can't spare the officers. The only person

I want this task force actively searching for is this man right here.' Inspector Jake Russell pointed to a picture on his desk. 'I have a lot of questions for the eminent Professor, Marcus Masterson.'

Chapter 27

Natasha hugged the wall as she carefully made her way up the entrance of the London Wall car park. Up ahead she could see Jace, now fully recovered from the earlier introduction of her knee to his groin, walking without a care, flipping in the air, the piece of the golden object she'd dropped.

Natasha knew she had to keep her distance, because there was nowhere for her to hide or people to blend in with.

He turned onto Wood Street. He was headed back to the Barbican, just as she had hoped. Without him leading the way, finding the right apartment, amongst the thousands, would literally have been like searching for a needle in a haystack.

Natasha stayed back and let him enter St Giles Terrace, let him go up the staircase to Andrewes House estate, and waited. She waited for the moment Jace went out of sight, so that she could make her move and get after him again.

As he made his way up the stairwell, every time his back was turned, Natasha got closer, ducking into an ingress or behind a parked vehicle, when he was about to turn and go up the next flight of stairs.

At the top floor, the seventh, he came out, walked along the balcony and turned off. Natasha was just about to set off after him and sprint up the steps, when she was suddenly caught in the high beams of a car.

She squinted, shielding her eyes against the bright light. It must have been another member of the gang Jace was a part of, she thought. Natasha was so drained and fatigued that she had no clue where they had come from, or if they had been there all along, watching her, just as she had watched their gang-mate.

The headlights were switched off and Natasha heard the car door open and slam shut. This was her chance. To get rid of the white spots that obscured her vision, thanks to the dazzling light, she blinked her eyes until they vanished and was turning to run when she heard someone say her name.

'Natasha Travers, The Baron would like to speak to you.'

'What?' The bloody Baron?' She turned to see a man holding out a mobile phone towards her. She duly snatched it from his hand. 'What the hell do you want?' Natasha was more than a little put out by the fact that his man had made her lose Jace.

'I've been trying to contact you, Natasha. I wanted an update of your search,' The Baron said.

'Yeah, well my battery died.'

'That's unfortunate and inconvenient.'

'You want to know about inconvenient? Inconvenient is your lackey making me lose the man that's stolen a piece of the clue to finding the Eye of Nineveh.'

'I'm sorry to hear that.'

'I don't need your apologies. I need your lackey to help me get it back.'

The Baron told her to hand the phone to his follower, which she did. After a brief conversation, he handed it back before he took a gun out of his inside pocket and offered it to her, which she refused.

'What the hell is this?'

'A gun. You wanted help to get the piece back? Well, there's your help.'

'I don't like guns.'

'Then you're shit out of luck,' The Baron replied. 'Get a move on. Time waits for no woman, man or parent, Natasha. Goodbye.'

The J terrorist held out his hand and Natasha slapped the phone in it, then he headed back to his car. She couldn't believe it. If he wanted the gem so badly, he should have offered her some sort of assistance. Her having to waste time does neither of them any good. 'What an asshole,' she said under her breath and walked off.

She turned off into St Giles' Terrace, heading to the stairwell of Andrewes House that Jace went up. Natasha knew it was a long shot, but she hoped that once she got to the seventh floor, she might hear or see something that might tip her off.

There was one minor detail that Natasha had overlooked, however. She had forgotten that when she had first been discovered on the terrace, there had been two gangsters, Jace and Raheem.

As Natasha took the first step, a fist landed on the right side of her back. Then again. She crumpled over, coughing. A wet arm went around her throat and squeezed.

'Oh, I'm going to make sure that when Clive is finished with you, the rest of the boys do things to you you never even thought possible,' Raheem whispered in her ear. 'You'll pay for what you did.'

Natasha noted that his voice sounded different, and when he turned her around, her eyes went wide. His face was covered in bee stings. It was swollen in places and red. Even his lips hadn't escaped the onslaught.

'I had to jump into that damn lake to get rid of those bees. Look at what they've done to me!' His anger rose rapidly, and he unleashed two swift punches to her stomach and then dragged her limp body upstairs.

• • • •

THEY ARRIVED ON THE seventh floor with Natasha worse for wear. Every time she had made any little attempt at resistance, Raheem had stopped it sharpish with a punch or a slap.

Natasha hadn't seen the number of the door she had been pushed through, but right now; she couldn't care less. She was terrified. The smell of drugs hung heavy in the smoky air.

As Raheem manhandled her through the penthouse property, the gang members they passed whistled and jeered, male and female alike, knowing that she didn't belong, wanting to make her as uncomfortable as possible.

She felt unseen hands on her, accompanied by drug fuelled hysterics. One of the girls, a blond, stroked Natasha's hair, as if she were a new doll to be played with. But when she then tried to kiss her too, the gangster found this one was not to be toyed with, and solid kick empathised that point.

More laughter erupted at the girl's expense. She didn't like it, felt slighted, and tried to swing at Natasha, but Raheem fended her off. The girl was tenacious, kept trying to get to her.

Until a door was opened, and dark-skinned man appeared. His stern look was enough to bring silence to the proceedings. Gold filled his mouth and on each of his fingers, a gold sovereign. This had to be none other than Clive, thought Natasha.

Just as she thought things were about to go from bad to worse, Natasha's heart leapt, and her hopes were bolstered when she glanced past the imposing man and saw Lucas and Lyndsay. Not only that, but in Clive's hand, was the sixth piece of the professor's object. She just needed to figure out a way to free themselves and retrieve it.

'Another one of my soldiers doing good work,' Clive bellowed. 'One brings me this golden trinket, and another brings me this fine woman. This is what I like to see from new recruits. Bring her in.'

Thankfully, this room of the penthouse was much less smoky, and Natasha noted that in any other situation, particularly ones that didn't involve drug dealers, she might have been able to appreciate the space more.

Part living-room, part office. It was bright, airy, and tastefully decorated, as if an interior decorator had set up a showroom. From her initial meeting with Clive, a room like this was the last place she'd expect to see him in.

'Sit her down on the sofa,' Clive ordered Raheem as he went to the large desk, which had two multi-screen setups displaying the stock markets that were at the back of the room, and sat in the black leather chair there.

Lucas and Lyndsay were sat facing him, their backs to the entrance, and as Natasha was brought closer, she could see that their wrists were bound at the back by cable ties. When she was dragged pass them, and dumped on the plush sofa, see saw their feet were too.

'How you holding up, Nat?' Lucas asked.

'Not bad. Better than you by the looks of things.'

'You sure?' he challenged as he saw her clutching her right side.

'So you know each other?' Clive piped in. 'This makes things all the more interesting. Are you ready to tell me what I want to know yet, or do I have to extend my hospitality to this lovely lady?'

'We've already told you, we're not the police,' Lyndsay said. 'How many times do we need to tell you before it penetrates that thick skull of yours?'

'I was just thinking the same thing,' added Lucas. 'He does have the look of the Neanderthal about him. You're the archaeologist, Nat, what do you think?'

'Well, he does have the exaggerated cranial structure associated with cavemen, to be fair,' she replied, examining Clive with a scientific eye. 'You can see it especially in the brow, it has the same protuberance –'

'Enough! You want to make jokes? Well, here's a joke. Tell me the truth or I start cutting things off. What? Not laughing? Raheem, take the girl, keep her under guard. I'll come and see to her later.'

· · · ·

THE FOUR WALLS OF THE room Natasha found herself in now were dismal compared to the last one. It was almost like it was in the middle of a refurb, but she was more than certain that this was the actual look they were going for.

Exposed floorboards and walls with what looked like dried blood.

Natasha was still nervous about the whole situation; she couldn't see a way out of their predicament. But at least she knew that Lucas and Lyndsay were okay, for now. Natasha hoped they were having better luck planning than she was. But then again, that was their forte.

Just then, the door opened, and the blonde Natasha had encountered earlier entered carrying a bottle of water, which she offered to the captive. Reluctantly, she took it, not wanting to be indebted to any of these people, but it had been several hours since she had anything to drink.

She opened it and gulped it down. As she did, the blonde closed the gap between them and stroked Natasha's hair once more. Natasha cringed at her touch.

'Look, no offence, but that's not my thing, okay?'

'It could be, though. I like you. After the others get done with you, you'll be glad for the feminine touch,' she said as she cupped Natasha's cheek.

That was more than enough, and she slapped the hand away. 'You're not very good at listening, are you?'

'And you're not good at taking a hint. There's two ways this is going down; the easy way, or the hard way. I'd prefer the easy way, because I don't want your pretty little face getting damaged.'

'Well, I'd prefer the third way,' Natasha said. 'No way.' She grabbed hold of the blonde and slammed her against the door before a scuffle ensued. The banging soon brought others to break it up.

'Get her out of here,' Jace said as they pulled their gang mate away. 'I'll stay and keep watch of this one.' The others left and Jace paced back and forth, watching Natasha closely.

'You come any closer and you'll get the same beating she got.'

'Look, I'm sorry about before,' he said in a hushed voice.' I'm sorry about some of the things I said, but I had to. He has people, spotters, eaves droppers, everywhere.'

Natasha scowled at him. 'What are you talking about?'

'I tried to tell you before when I pulled you down at the Noble Street garden, but you busted my nose and damn near my groin too.'

'Tell me what?'

'I'm a police officer.'

Chapter 28

Clive had grown frustrated with the answers he was getting from Lucas and Lyndsay and had resorted to violence to relieve the stress that was building within him. Each punch he gave them was like being punched with knuckledusters, thanks to his sovereign ringed fingers.

Just as Clive was about to punch Lyndsay again, a notification sounded from his computer, and he hurried round his desk to check. 'Wicked! My buy-in for the yen/dollar market has activated!' He started clicking away with his mouse as if he had completely forgotten what he had just been doing. 'And my shares in gold have gone up too!'

There was a knock at the door and Ray entered, carrying Natasha's bag. 'You're going to love this, boss man.' He poured the contents of the bag on Clive's desk.

His eyes lit up when he saw five more golden objects in front of him. Reaching for his drawer, Clive pulled out the one he already had and put it with the others. They made a pleasant clinking sound as he rearranged them on the desk. He picked up and examined each of the six golden segments, in turn, grinning from ear to ear. 'What are these?' Clive asked his two captives. 'Templar gold? What do the police want with them? And what are these markings?' He got no answer. 'Well, if you won't say anything, maybe your fellow officer will. Bring the girl.'

Several minutes later, a lot longer than the drug dealer was expecting, Ray returned with Natasha in tow. 'What the hell is going on out there?' Clive demanded, referring to the commotion outside of his office. Ray threw Natasha down on the sofa and went to whisper in Clive's ear. 'You're certain?'

'I heard it with my own ears.'

'The little bastard. You know what to do.'

'Some of the men are teeing off on him as we speak. What about these three?'

'You mean two. She won't be going anywhere. She's going to be my new plaything. As for these two? Get the room ready for three.'

'Sure thing, boss man,' Ray turned and grinned at the two seated and bound men, then left to make the ominous preparations.

Natasha barely heard any of the conversation. Her attention was focussed on the pile of Marcus's gold objects on the desk. It was the first time that she had seen all six pieces together, and she couldn't help getting up and walking over to them as if in a daze.

She picked up each piece, stared at them with a fixed gaze, as she turned each one over in her hands. Then she licked her lips and slotted them together. They clicked securely in place. In a short time, she had the heptagon complete, except for the single missing section that was in one of the last two locations.

'Well?' Lucas watched Natasha the moment she went over to desk. He was just as eager to see it complete as she was, hoping that they wouldn't even need the last piece. 'What's on it? Does the text make sense now?'

She read out all of the message that was available, rotating the disc as she did. '... which Turner and Dickens saw their most glorious end. Once divided now never apart. Where we saw enlightenment and welcomed the dark.' She read it several more times in her head, but she still couldn't figure it out.

'What about the engraving?'

'It kind of looks like an island and possibly a coastline.'

'An island? You're kidding me. How much time do we have left?'

'I don't know. Three or four hours maybe.'

'So, this disc thing is part of some bigger treasure then?' Clive had been watching and listening. If there was any more gold to be had, he wanted it.

'No, a single gem, the Eye of Nineveh.'

'Is it worth a lot?'

'Priceless.'

Clive stroked his chin. 'It would seem that the two of you weren't lying after all,' he admitted. 'You're not feds. Turns out that we had a mole. Jace apparently is an undercover police officer, isn't that right, babes?' He patted Natasha on the backside and both she and Lucas fought to keep their cool. 'Ray just heard him spilling his guts, and guess what? Soon I'm going to spill them for real.'

'Okay, no hard feelings,' said Lucas. 'We forgive you for the misunderstanding. These things happen. So, when will you be cutting us loose?'

'That's not going to happen. You see, no one outside my crew knows I'm here, and I intend to keep it that way. Which means you two and the pig need to vanish, permanently. Come on, babe. It's time we got to know each other better. And don't forget to bring my gold.'

'So that's it, Nat?' Lucas said to Natasha as she placed the partially completed disc into her bag before she slung it over her shoulder. 'You're just going to go off with your new guy and leave us to die?'

She furrowed her eyebrows and stared at him. Where was this coming from? 'You can't seriously think that I'm okay with all of this.'

'Yeah, whatever. You sure look okay with it. I'm sure your dad will be ecstatic, too. He always thought you could do better than me, that I would bring you down. Well, when you bring this guy home, he'll probably disown you.'

'Screw you, Lucas! Any opinion my family has about you is down to one person, you. No one told you to jump into bed with that Australian tart. Leaving her damn makeup on the sheets. There was no gun put to your head.'

'I don't see a gun put to your head, right now.'

'That could be arranged,' Clive interjected.

'Screw you, Clive.' Natasha and Lucas replied in unison.

'At the end of the day, if you can live with yourself, do what you want. You've always been a bit of a balteum fibula.'

Natasha was incredulous. 'What did you call me?'

'You heard! I said balteum fibula! Do you want me to spell it out for you?'

During their years together, when they faced troublesome situations, much like this one, it was sometimes necessary to get messages across without being overheard. They had tried Aramaic, but Lucas hadn't picked it up as quickly or easily as he had Latin, so they'd stuck with that. And it had worked like a charm, except for that one time when they were in Bali and they first encountered Juergen, a South African arms dealer who specialised in antique weapons, but also just happened to speak Latin.

Natasha knew what balteum fibula meant, but she didn't know why Lucas would be calling her a belt buckle. Not until she looked down at his.

It was a solid circular shape with partial ellipticals; one on either side. It was like a full moon on top of two smaller moons, making them seem crescent. It had been custom made in Cambodia. She had never been a big fan of it, to be honest, but right now, it was the best-looking belt in the world.

Natasha slapped Lucas hard across the face. Even Lyndsay felt the sting of that one. 'How dare you call me that?'

'Ouch,' Lucas said, his face the image of shock, as much for the strength of her strike as it was for her hammy acting.

'Oh, I'm sorry, darling,' she continued and dramatically threw herself onto him. Out of the sight of everyone, Natasha fished a hand in between their bodies, reaching for the belt buckle.

'That's not it,' Lucas whispered in her ear.

Natasha felt her cheeks heat up as she made the necessary directional adjustment. She rotated the circular part of the buckle, which in turn released the hidden catch holding the two ellipticals.

'Okay, that's enough of that,' Clive said. He pulled her away, but she broke loose and kissed Lucas.

It had all been an act up until then, the argument, the slap, though it had felt good to Natasha, not so much to

Lucas, but there was nothing fake about the kiss. It started softly at first however, the ardour quickly rose.

To their audience, it just looked like two people passionately making out. What they didn't see was Natasha sliding one of the elliptical shapes out, revealing its hidden stiletto blade. Then, she cut the cable tie binding Lucas's wrists.

'You always were a good kisser,' Lucas said.

Natasha smiled. 'I know!'

Deciding he'd seen enough, Clive yanked Natasha off of Lucas, causing her to drop the short blade. 'I said that's *enough*.' He leered at her and licked his lips before he dragged her to the door. 'I can see that I'm going to have a wicked time with you, girl.'

'Don't worry, Nat. I'll be seeing you soon.'

'You'd better bloody well hurry up!'

· · · ·

AS SOON AS THE DOOR was closed, Lucas went into action; he knew it wouldn't be long before someone came for them. Although Natasha hadn't been able to cut through the cable tie entirely, it was just enough for him to use brute strength to snap it apart. He cut the one around his legs before he retrieved the other off the floor.

Just then, the door creaked open. Lucas jumped back into his seat moments before Raheem entered. 'Right, it's time for you two to join that copper, or what's left of him. We went to town on him,' he stated, admiring his bruised knuckles.

Raheem went over to Lucas, intending to cut his legs free before taking him to the killing room. As he neared the prisoner, he felt something crunch underfoot. He looked down and saw the cut black plastic tie. By the time Raheem's mind processed what it was, Lucas had driven his two blades up into his neck. His blood gurgled in his throat as he died.

'That was one hell of a show you two put on,' Lyndsay said as Lucas cut him free.

'Yeah, well, we've had plenty of opportunities to practise in the past,' replied Lucas. 'It's good to see can still roll with it, but jeez, that slap.'

'I think your ancestors heard that one.'

'Yeah, whatever! You ready to get out of here?'

'I'm on your six.'

Lucas eased the door open as quietly as he could. There was a guard, but his neck broke before he had any time to react to their escape for freedom. The former soldiers stuck to the wall, moving as one, honed skills they would never lose.

As they passed each door, they paused and listened, desperate to find Natasha. At the fourth door they tried, Lucas could hear muffled voices. Thinking that he was too late, thinking that it was Clive about to rape Natasha, Lucas stepped back, and the door flew open as he kicked it.

He scanned it quickly. The walls and floor were covered in plastic. It was the kill room. Jace was in the centre, still being worked on, his face a bloody mess. As he reached for his gun, the gang member started hollering, calling for help when he saw Clive's two captives standing at the door. Lucas got to him, before he could put his hand on the pistol, and ran him through several times, but it was too late. Clive's crew had been alerted.

After cleaning his blades on the dead gangster, Lucas slipped them back into his buckle, picked up the gun and searched the body for any spare clips, but didn't find any. 'Check on the officer while I cover the door.'

Lyndsay followed Lucas's ordered. 'He's in pretty bad shape,' he reported. 'But he says that Clive would have taken her to his residential penthouse. Apparently, he owns all the apartments on this level.'

'Hopefully, our stuff will be there too. Can he walk?'

'I can walk,' Jace said, his voice weak. 'I need a phone, need to call in backup.'

'There's one on the stiff,' Lucas said.

Gang members were responding to the call for help, just as Lucas and Lyndsay's escape was discovered. They hoped that Jace's responders would turn up equally quick, but they didn't intend on hanging around waiting.

Lucas stepped out, gun extended, with Lyndsay assisting Jace behind him. They moved swiftly, but cautiously. Now wouldn't be the time to be careless, not when they were so close to getting out.

As they moved towards the exit, some members of the Crew were lined up like a shooting gallery, not having the skills or the knowledge of how to tackle urban combat. Even the way they were firing their guns, sideways like they'd seen in the movies, gave Lucas the edge. Whilst they missed wildly, he would triple-tap them, two in the chest and one to the head. He'd rummage through their pockets, pick up more ammo, and managed to arm Lyndsay too.

They eventually reached the front door and immediately came under fire as they opened it. 'Whoa! Looks like we won't be going out that way.'

'The residential penthouse is at the far end of the floor,' explained Jace. 'The ones in the middle are for the Crew.'

'More numbers than the two of us could handle, Lucas.'

He nodded in agreement. Just as Lucas was formulating another plan of escape, he heard the welcome sounds of police sirens and smiled. 'I guess they don't hang around when it's one of their own in trouble.'

The arrival of the police shook up the gang members. This separated the boys and girls from the men and women; one set would run, the other would stand and fight. Luckily for Lucas and Lyndsay, there weren't many of the latter, and the ones that did were easily picked off.

They continued to move along the seventh floor, doing a quick sweep of the crew penthouses, to make sure there wasn't anyone hiding, before heading on to Clive's residential rooms.

Lucas and Lyndsay lined up on either side of the penthouse's front door. On the count of three, the breach the room like the consummate professionals they were. Slow, soulful music blasted over the sound system as they edged inside the penthouse. They had heard nothing from the outside, suggesting that the whole place was sound proofed. All the rooms were empty, except for one.

In one bedroom, Lucas had seen the chained leg of a woman sticking out from underneath some silk bedsheets, and immediately rushed over. He pulled back the sheets and found she was dead. Her complexion was so similar to

Natasha, he had thought it was her. Neither of them could tell if it was the drugs paraphernalia or the long-term beatings she obviously suffered that finally ended her life.

'It's like a seedy boudoir,' Lyndsay whispered as they zeroed in on the room they believed to be the master bedroom.

'Probably runs prostitution here too.' Lucas's lip curled as he thought about the atrocities the gangster was committing here. He could almost hear the screams of abused women being lost, cut short by the sound proofing, only to be heard by Clive for his sick pleasure.

They listened at the door of the main bedroom, but couldn't hear anything, so they gently turned the handle and slowly opened it. They soon discovered the reason they had heard nothing; the room was empty. They found Lucas's bag during their search, and they also discovered Clive's escape route. In the corner of the wardrobe, someone had cut a hole through the floor into the lower apartment.

'Damn it,' Lucas shouted as they rushed out of the penthouse onto the balcony. They looked over the railing, saw all the flashing lights of the police cars. Members of Clive's Crew that had decided to run for it were chased by the officers. Neither Lucas nor Lyndsay could see Natasha or Clive.

They ran to the balcony that overlooked the lake, and there they were, Clive and Ray dragging Natasha. She wasn't making her abduction easy for them, wriggling and writhing, desperate to break free.

'Come on. We'd better move if we're to catch them!' Lyndsay said.

Lucas looked over the railing, directly at the ground below, handed his bag to his friend and climbed over it.

'What the hell are you doing?'

'What I do best ... living dangerously! Who dares wins.' With those last words, the motto of the SAS, Lucas let go of the railing.

Chapter 29

DCI Jake Russell was making his way home, looking forward to having a few hours shut eye before renewing his investigation. Then the call about the disturbance at the Barbican came through. He sighed; something always came up. It wasn't until he heard that Lucas Redmond and Natasha Travers were on sight that his mood lightened, and he put his foot down on the accelerator.

Detective Inspector Derek Wilkins was already on the scene when Russell arrived, when the action was already in its last throes, but still hectic all the same. The flashing red and blue lights of the police cars illuminated the night, casting their brilliance on the faces of residents woken by the disturbance.

'Wilkins,' Russell called to the detective inspector, who was in conversation with a constable. 'Any sign of them?'

'No, sir, but the PC's have been informed that if Lucas or Natasha should be sighted, they're to be brought to me.'

'Good.' Wilkins was shaping up to be a good right-hand man, intelligent, proactive. Russell had more than his fair share of working with fresh detectives that needed too much handholding and coddling; he was impressed by this one, he might just keep him around. 'So, where's the undercover officer?' he asked, squinting from all the lights.

'Over there, being seen to in the ambulance,' the detective replied and led the way.

Jake Russell followed, trying to hide a yawn. As he fought the involuntary action, he briefly caught sight of a man with a bag. It jogged something in his tired memory, a flash of recognition. Before he could act, a member of Clive's crew decided he didn't want to be arrested after all, and in his break for freedom, ran headlong into the DCI.

Wilkins was surprised when he saw his commanding officer tackling the hoodlum. 'What?' Russell asked, seeing the look on his subordinate's face. 'You didn't think I had it in me, huh?'

'Well ... '

'When you're a DCI, it doesn't mean that you can't leap into action when the need arises. It just means that you use your brain more, so that you don't have to.' Russell grabbed a nearby constable and sent him running to the corner he had seen the man. The officer soon indicated that there was no one there.

'What is it, sir?'

'I don't know, probably nothing.' He put the thought to one side as they arrived at the ambulance and found Jace sitting up on the gurney. 'Are you up to answering a few questions?' Jake asked. He was given the go ahead and continued. 'Your report stated that a Lucas Redmond and Natasha Travers were here?'

'Yes, and another one. A guy called Lyndsay.'

'Damn it! That was who I saw. Lyndsay Alperton. He was in the photo of Lucas's regiment. Do you know what they were doing here, Jace?'

'Not specifically. I think they just got caught up in Clive's shit. But I know they were collecting pieces of some golden thing.'

'Golden thing?'

'Yeah. They were searching the Roman wall when Ray killed Ennis. That's how Clive got hold of them, and the two things that guy loves more than anything are gold and girls.'

'That girl happens to be Lucas's wife, though, and he's not your regular run-of-the-mill hoodlum. Do you know what happened to them?'

'Well, after Lucas and Lyndsay saved me, they took off after Clive to rescue Natasha.

'Thank you, officer. Come on, Wilkins. Let's hope they're still in the area.'

· · · ·

AS LUCAS PLUMMETED, the wind whistling pass his ears. He could admit to himself, and the Celestial Being, that this probably wasn't his best idea. But it was the best he could come up with in a pinch. He didn't want to lose sight of Natasha and he didn't have time to run back and take the stairs. Lucas needed to reach the ground, fast. And there was no faster way of getting from A to B.

He dropped the three-metre distance to the next floor in a split second, all the time he had for his reactions to fire, allowing him to catch hold of the railing, breaking his fall. He took a moment to steady himself, then Lucas repeated the process until he had reached the last floor of Andrewes House. He let go, twisted in the air, so that when he landed in a crouch, he could see the two gangsters running further into the Barbican complex with Natasha.

Lucas drew the gun from his back and set off after them, shouting Natasha's name. Hearing him gave Natasha renewed hope and more fight, which she put to good use, finally freeing herself of Ray's grasp.

He became panic-stricken the moment she kicked him away. Being close to her had offered protection, their pursuer wouldn't risk taking the shot with her being so close. Now he was out in the open, he was fair game.

Ray reached for his gun but, whatever he had planned was cut short, as three slugs from Lucas's gun slammed into him.

'Let her go, Clive,' Lucas demanded, as the gangster stopped running and turned around. One of his arms was wrapped around Natasha, pinning her arms. His other hand squeezed her throat, holding her off the ground like a human shield.

'What are you going to do?' Clive mocked as he slowly backed away. 'Shoot me? Through your woman? Doubtful!'

'You don't know what you're doing, do you?' Natasha said.

Clive squeezed her throat tighter. 'Shut up, bitch!'

'You're just digging a deeper hole for yourself.' She struggled to get the words out with his hand clamped around her neck.

'Back off!' Clive shouted at Lucas. 'Back off or I'll break her neck!'

'There's no end to this situation where you come out on top, Clive. It's just a matter of how many bullets you get.'

Lucas glanced down briefly and fired his gun. 'Starting with this one.'

Clive howled in pain as the slug ripped through his shin. He staggered, unable to continue holding up Natasha. She was released and ran. His shield, his protection gone. Shots rang out. Each bullet finding their target.

Lucas walked over to the drug dealer, stood over him and watched the dark patches on his shirt grow as blood posed from the bullet holes. 'This is for all the women, all the people whose lives you've destroyed,' Lucas said before he emptied the cartridge into Clive.

It took Natasha several attempts to bring Lucas back, but finally she did. 'Come on! Snap out of it. We need to go; the police are here and we're running out of time to save my parents.'

'You okay? Lucas asked, gently rubbing Natasha's arm.

'Um ... yeah,' she replied. She suddenly felt self-conscious, uncertain how to react to the unexpected tenderness, and turned her body to the side, rather than face Lucas directly. 'Um, yeah, I'm good.'

He noticed her shy away from his touch, but Lucas didn't have the time to broach it as he heard police coming their way, drawn by the gunfire. 'We should go. Where's the next piece of wall?'

'Around the corner at Barbers Garden,' revealed Natasha as they walked away from the scene.

'Damn it. It'll be kind of hard to investigate it now whilst the area is crawling with all these police.'

'I know, but we can't hang about waiting for them either; time's not on our side,' she reminded him.

'So, we move on to the next piece.'

'The last piece, at the Old Bailey.'

'I've got a plan, but I need to find Ellen first. It's been too long; I'm worried about her.'

'Yeah, of course. No problem.'

As if on cue, Lyndsay suddenly pulled up in Lucas's battered car. 'Need a ride?'

• • • •

EVEN THOUGH ELLEN HAD desperately tried to stay awake, she had failed. She rubbed her eyes and rolled over on the cot. It was hard for her to tell how long she had been sleeping, but it was still dark, so she knew it had only been a few hours. She stretched and yawned. That's when she saw the glowing ember of s cigarette. Someone else was in the room.

'You don't know how many times I've watched over you whilst you were sleeping, Ellen.'

She shuddered at the sound of his voice, and chills ran up and down her spine. She tucked her knees under her chin, clapped her hands over her ears, trying to shut him out.

In the darkness she couldn't see him, but Ellen knew he was smiling. She could hear it in his voice. All these years later, without seeing him, without thinking about him, he still had an effect on her, and she hated that fact.

Before she even realised it, Ellen whimpered, rocking back and forth on her haunches. Exactly as she used to do when she was under his care.

'I've missed you so much, Ellen,' Graeme said. 'It broke my heart when you were taken away from me. I want you to know that I never stopped looking for you, though, Ellen. Changing your name made it hard, but I knew that one day you would come back to me, come back to the Collective.'

'I wasn't taken,' she said in a hushed tone. 'I was rescued.' Her eyes had grown more accustomed to the darkness, but even in the moonlight she could barely see his outline, just glimpses of his face when he puffed on the cigarette.

'Rescued? It was destiny that brought you to me, Ellen. I had rescued you from this godforsaken world. I had purified you. Cleansed you from the inside out. Prepared you to be the vassal of the messiah. You were chosen for this great deed.'

'I was *fifteen*.'

'Just the flesh, your soul is ancient.'

'You disgust me.'

'And you disappoint me. You were a believer. Your word was as good as mine amongst the Collective.'

'I said what I had to say to keep you happy. I did … I did what I had to do to survive.'

'Is that the story you tell yourself at night, Ellen?' Graeme scoffed. 'Did I ever threaten you at any point? Threaten you with violence?'

He hadn't. But Ellen knew as well as he did that his followers, the Collective, did his bidding. Anything their spiritual leader wanted; they were more than eager to do.

'Don't you get it, Ellen? I love you. I loved you the moment I saw you. We were meant to be. That's why you were brought to me. It was fate.'

Ellen recoiled. 'You're sick!'

'Six years amongst the heathens is a long time, Ellen. It must have tarnished you; they must have touched you. I will have to purify you once again, deeper this time, so it lasts with you, so you know your role and position next to me. You're older now, but still the chosen vassal. All the five leading religions are still waiting for the one individual that will unite them and usher in a one-world religion. That individual will be our progeny. But you must be cleansed first, Ellen,' Graeme said as he stubbed out his cigarette. 'And there's no reason we shouldn't start now.'

Ellen heard the scrapping of his chair as he got to his feet. His steps were slow, deliberate. But that ominous sound of her abuser drawing near was more than enough to give her flashbacks of the times it had happened before, and the subsequent feelings of disgust, self-loathing, guilt, and shame. But above all else, fear.

She heard something fall to the floor, like an item of clothing, then the unbuckling of a belt. His heavy breathing made her shudder and break out in a cold sweat. 'No, no, no, this isn't happening! Not again,' Ellen repeated between hyperventilated breaths.

Then she felt his touch, felt him stroke her cheek.

Ellen became faint, dizzy, stressed by the terrifying ordeal which she'd thought she had put behind her, compartmentalised it and locked it away in the recesses of her mind. But here she was, his hands on her again, unable to cope, and she blacked out.

Then she heard gunshots in the distance. Then more. Shouting, screaming. More shots, closer.

'Seems like we'll have to postpone our reunion, little Ellen,' Graeme said, and bent down to kiss her. 'Don't forget, daddy loves you.' Then he was gone.

Ellen passed out, hearing Lucas calling her name as he desperately searched for her.

Chapter 30

By the time Ellen had recovered consciousness, she found herself in a bed at Natasha's apartment. She could see Lucas sitting in a chair nearby, with a forlorn face, fiddling with one of his Montecristo cigar tubes. 'I wouldn't light that in here if I were you. She'd have your hide.'

'Ell, you're awake!' Lucas slumped back in his chair, the tension in his body suddenly released.

'I'm not dead you know, sitting there looking like you're at a funeral.'

Lucas smiled slowly, but still averted his eyes from Ellen. 'I'm sorry. I'm sorry it took so long to come and get you. I'm supposed to be looking out for you, protecting you and I let you down, Ell.'

'You know something? I knew you would come. Even when Graeme was touching me, I never stopped believing that you'd come, Lucas.'

'Graeme? Your foster dad? How the hell did he find you?'

'Whoever that bastard I followed works for. They called him. Wait, didn't you see Graeme when you rescued me?'

'No, I wish I did. I would have finished him once and for all.'

'I can't believe he's gotten away again,' Ellen said, trying to hide not only her disappointment but also her fear. 'The Collective at work, huh?'

Lucas suddenly came and sat next to Ellen. He scooped her up and hugged her, completely taking her by surprised with his moment of tenderness. She'd been putting on a strong, brave face but, without warning, she completely broke down.

. . . .

LYNDSAY SAT IN THE living room, where he had been speaking to Natasha, whilst Lucas had gone to tend to Ellen. She had played the good host and gotten them both a drink, but it wasn't long before the night's events took its toll on her, and Natasha's head bobbed. Before she knew it, Natasha had fallen fast asleep.

He gently took the glass out of her hand before the contents could spill and set it down on the table. It had been a long and hard day for her, and Lyndsay had to admit that he was surprised that she had gone this far. Lucas and himself had been trained to endure hardships like sleep deprivation, but Natasha was just an archaeologist. Lyndsay was almost certain that what drove her on was the fact that her personal stakes were high, the lives of her parents.

Picking up the golden disc, the former SAS soldier examined the artefact closely. They had been trying to figure out the cryptic message without the final piece, but he had made a comment that its toothed edge reminded him of a cog, a cog with a small gauge.

This had made it all but clear that they needed to find the final piece, not just for the message or the engraving, but for the likelihood that it may serve an additional purpose, too.

Just then, Lucas returned from Ellen's bedroom. Seeing Natasha sleeping, he motioned Lyndsay over to the balcony.

It was coming up to five in the morning, and London was just beginning to stir. But night workers, such as office cleaners, were already well into their shifts.

'Look, I can understand why you'd want to change things. Ellen's been through a lot and you're looking out for her, but you know the alternative, right?'

'A frontal assault. We force our way in.'

'Exactly! A two-man assault team on the central criminal court. Do you hear how crazy that sounds?'

'We don't have any other choice. We only have two hours until The Baron's deadline. There's no time to prepare another plan.'

'You could have at least asked me,' Ellen said, stepping out onto the balcony as she lit one of her fragrant roll ups.

'I knew you would have said yes,' Lucas responded.

'You don't know. I might have said no.'

He looked at her with a disbelieving gaze. 'Really?'

'Okay, maybe I would have said yes, but still, it's my decision to make.'

'You're right. I'm sorry.' Lucas put an arm around Ellen and gave her a squeeze. 'Well, if you're sure you're up for it, here's the plan ...'

· · · ·

DESPITE LUCAS'S INITIAL concerns about Ellen, knowing that she wasn't as tough on the inside as she led everyone to believe, she could still do what they needed without a hitch. Lucas and Lyndsay arrived at the court, knowing that their cover, as supervisors from the cleaning company working at the Old Bailey, was intact.

'That's right, it's our first time here. We're pretty new on the job,' Lucas explained to the intercom.

'It's not just that,' the security guard replied. 'The regular supervisor came a few weeks ago. Your company wouldn't be checking up on your cleaners again so soon.'

'Have you checked your system? We've been getting some complaints from some of our bigger contracts, so they increased the frequency of inspections.'

'Well, I think you're going to have to reschedule it, because I don't remember seeing anything about a cleaner inspection when I signed on last night.'

'Wait a minute, Taiwo, I think I've found something,' one of the four other guards announced from behind a computer screen. The intercom was switched off whilst Taiwo went to see what his colleague had discovered.

Lyndsay turned to Lucas, who just smiled back.

'Don't worry, Ellen has everything under control. Isn't that right, Ell?'

'I'm disappointed in you, LA,' said Ellen over their earwigs. 'Did you seriously think I'd let you guys down?'

Taiwo came back to the intercom. 'Well, um, I don't know how, but it seems like we somehow missed it. I'll just need to see your ID passes.' The security guard unlocked the doors after seeing the hastily produced cards.

Lucas and Lyndsay stepped inside, and each immediately put on a pair of cotton gloves. Which drew suspicious looks from the security. 'They're not taking any chances. They want us to check the quality of the work they've done.'

'I see,' replied Taiwo. 'Do you want me to call someone up?'

'No, no. It's supposed to be an unannounced visit, to catch them in the act, so to speak.'

'Well, as I'm sure you're aware, your cleaners are working on all levels right now.'

'What we'll do is work our way up from the basement, if that's okay with you guys?'

'Sure,' Taiwo acknowledged before giving them a security briefing. When it was over, and the pair had gone down in the lift, he returned to the security counter and picked up the phone.

'What are you doing?' the second guard asked.

'This all sounds very dodgy, Matt. I'm going to call their firm, just to be on the safe side.'

• • • •

AS SOON AS THEY STEPPED out of the lift, Ellen was on them, squeaking in their ears. 'You need to move! That Taiwo guy has been trying to ring the cleaning company. Good thing you put that looper in their switch box, but I'm sure it won't be long before he tries a mobile phone.'

'Not with what I've got here at sleeping beauty's place, so you'd better move quick.'

'Okay, Okay, we understand.'

At that moment intercom at Natasha's apartment went off. The sudden unexpected sound made Ellen jump. She had a nervous smile as she realised what it was, but then her mind raced. 'It's Graeme!'

Lucas stopped dead in his tracks. 'What did you say?'

The intercom buzzed again.

'How did he find me?' Ellen said to herself more than anyone. She could feel herself hyperventilating as she backed away from the door. She clenched and unclenched her fists.

'Ellen! What's happening? Ellen. *Ellen.*'

She couldn't hear Lucas's worried yells, as her levels of concentration were entirely consumed by the buzzing intercom, and the possibility of Graeme breaking in to get hold of her again; it wouldn't have been the first time he'd done so.

Lucas turned to Lyndsay. 'I have to go.'

'What? Your kidding, right? What about the final piece?'

'I have to go,' repeated Lucas. 'I will not let her down again. You go find it; we'll link up later.'

Suddenly they heard Ellen scream over the earpiece, followed by her quick shallow breathing. She was still unresponsive to Lucas's shouts, then he heard Natasha's voice in his ear.

'Lucas? What's going on? Ellen's in a bad way, like she's having a panic attack or something, mumbling about someone called Graeme.'

'Is anyone else there?

'What?'

'Is there anyone there?'

'What are you talking about?'

'Who rang the bell?'

'Oh, that. The concierge said it was Kallum Taylor.' Hearing Lucas's sigh of relief, Natasha felt she needed to know more. 'What's going on, Lucas? Who's Graeme?'

'Ellen's foster dad. Could you keep an eye on her for me? Comfort her and help her calm down.'

'Yeah, sure. Of course I will.'

'Thanks, Nat. We won't be long. We're in the basement of the Old Bailey now.'

'What's this other chatter she's listening to?' Natasha asked, as she had trouble separating the two audios in her head. 'I don't know how she does it. It's just so ... wait a minute! It's the police band. They've been alerted to you and Lyndsay.'

'Damn it.' The two former soldiers set off, jogging down the green-floored hallway. Air ducts, wiring and piping flew by as they picked up speed down the bleak corridor. They eventually came to the three-metre section of wall.

It was raised on a plinth which helped their search and saved them from having to crawl the length of the wall on their hands and knees. They started at opposite ends, working as quickly as possible, the imminent arrival of the police looming in the back of their minds.

'Wait, I think I found it,' Lyndsay said as he scraped away the mortar between two of the red tiles.

Then they heard the ding of the lift as it arrived in the basement. The police were here quicker than either of them had hoped. The clock was ticking, barely sixty seconds before the officers would be upon them.

'We've got the final piece,' Lucas said with a gleam in his eyes. 'But we need an exit. Can you see anything on Ellen's screen? Blueprints, security cams or anything?'

'No, her laptop's closed, and I don't really think she'd be much help right now,' Natasha reported, glancing at the dozing Ellen.

'Damn it.'

'We're screwed, Lucas.'

'Not necessarily. Nat, what about St Sepulchre?'

'Of course, the church entrance.'

Lyndsay was baffled. 'Church? What the hell are you two on about?'

'It's the church across the road from the court,' Natasha explained. 'Back in the day, when a chaplain was needed to perform the last rites, they would use the tunnel to avoid the baying, macabre crowds outside the Old Bailey. The tunnel went from the church to Newgate prison, then the condemned was led to the old court for public execution.'

'Okay,' Lyndsay said and clapped his hands together. 'Sounds like we've got our exit.'

'There's a catch though.'

'Why am I not surprised? Things never seem to be easy with you two.'

'When the prison was eventually knocked down, the Old Bailey was rebuilt and extended on top of where it once stood. The entrance should be somewhere down in the labyrinthine basements, and it's most likely bricked up.'

'No problem,' Lucas said to Lyndsay with a wink. 'We just need to find something heavy to use as a battering ram.'

'And what about the police that are coming? You expect them to wait for us to smash through the wall?'

Lucas, still with his confident smile, took the gun from his bag and tossed it to Lyndsay, who immediately checked the cartridge.

'It's empty.'

'Yeah,' nodded Lucas, 'but they don't know that.'

Chapter 31

The pair ran deeper into the basement corridors of the Old Bailey, each white tiled passage looking identical to the last, even down to the discolouring due to age and mildew.

'Come on, L.A.,' Lucas urged, sensing by Lyndsay's silence that his friend still wasn't completely sold on the idea as it was laid out. 'Trust me, the first responders won't be armed police. They'll just be beat cops; threaten them a bit and they'll stay back and radio for an armed unit.'

'I just hope you're right.'

Me too, Lucas said to himself. They had found a tensa-barrier stand, which they hoped could take on the role of battering ram; they just needed to find the part of the tiled wall that was once a doorway to a tunnel.

They continued to knock sides of the corridors they passed through until they finally came across a bit that sounded distinctly hollow compared to either side of it.

'This has got to be it,' Lucas said, beaming with excitement. He immediately set to work, going back as far as he could, holding the heavy metal stand under his arm, the smaller end towards the wall, before charging it. The sound of metal hitting brick and tile echoed throughout the basement.

The first couple of strikes had little effect. The third time, however, saw a chunk of a tile crack and fall away. Two more times and more debris fell away to join the rest on the floor.

Although they had found the means of their exit, the repeated banging drew the security guards and police to them all the quicker. Soon, from the other end of the junction, they heard the first set of demands. 'Armed police! Stop what you're doing!'

'First responders would be beat cops, huh?'

'Well,' Lucas began sheepishly, 'they were probably in the area. Just tell them you have a gun; they won't risk rushing in.' As Lucas finished, he put the stand down before picking it up again, this time with the wider, heavier base at the forefront. Now that he'd weakened the wall, he intended to batter it down.

Sweat beaded on his forehead and the muscles in his arms flexed and rippled as the force of each juddering blow ran up them. His urgency increased after Lyndsay, who did as Lucas suggested, and declared he had a gun, only to have gunfire from an automatic rifle answer him.

Lyndsay ducked back around the corner, narrowly avoiding the bullets. 'Don't you get tired of it?'

'Of what?' Lucas asked before ramming the wall again.

'Of being wrong!'

Lucas feigned dismay. 'It doesn't matter. You can believe me when I say we're out of here. One more strike ...'

And the wall came tumbling down.

Dust and debris kicked up as the bricks and tiles crashed to the ground. Lyndsay was already hotfooting it to the newly created hole the moment he saw the police advancing in response to the commotion.

As soon as Lucas had climbed through, he grabbed the torch out of his bag. Their footprints in the untouched layers of dust, was evidence that the tunnel remained unused for decades.

Lucas brushed away the thick cobwebs, which made him feel like he was back in a hidden cave, deep in the Amazon; but this was deep under London, just one of the many secrets the ancient city held.

It wasn't a long passage, and they soon reached a wooden door at the end. Lucas covered the torch with his hand, giving Lyndsay just enough light to kick the door open, whilst smothering the beam so as not to give the armed police a target when they stared into the darkness.

Something was blocking the door from inside the church. Then illumination came from the opening as the police used their own torches. Sensing the imminent danger, Lucas ran into the back of Lyndsay. Gunfire suddenly rang out. They both bundled through the door, falling onto the floor, toppling over the oak table that had been placed there many years ago.

Taking no time to stop and reflect on their near miss, Lucas and Lyndsay sprinted to the entrance of the church. A priest, who had been startled by the banging and their sudden appearance, called after them, and seconds later, when the police came through the door, he pointed in the direction the two men had run. But it was too late. Lucas and Lyndsay had made their escape with the final piece of Professor Marcus Masterson's object.

• • • •

'HOW'S ELLEN?' LUCAS asked as he and Lyndsay arrived back at St Katherine's dock. Her welfare was the most important thing to him in that moment. It was a side of him that Natasha hadn't seen for a while.

'Well, she woke up in a panic, thinking that something bad had happened to you when she had her episode, but I told her I'd helped out. It took me some time to convince her of that, then she went back to sleep.'

'I can just imagine that,' Lucas smiled, relieved that Ellen was okay. He put his hand into his bag and pulled out the golden object. 'Here it is, the final piece.'

'And not a moment too soon; we're almost out of time,' Natasha was desperate. If The Baron was true to his word, her parents had barely an hour left to live.

She took the last segment of Professor Marcus Masterson's puzzle from Lucas. With the others looking on, and a gleam in her eyes, Natasha licked her lips as she slotted the final piece into position, completing the gold-plated disc.

It had been a crazy night. Natasha took a moment to reflect on the trials she had endured over the last twenty-four hours; being arrested, shot at, chased, and God alone knew what Clive had intended to do. But now the object that she and Lucas had been searching for lay before her.

She looked deeply at the object, studying it hard, lost to thought as she twirled a loose strand of her hair. Natasha rotated the gold disc as she read the now complete inscription, silently mouthing the words as she did so. Occasionally she'd pause. Her eyebrows creased as she thought for a moment before she would continue.

'Well?' Lucas asked as his patience waned. 'Are you going to read it out or not?'

'What? Oh, sorry!' She hadn't realised that she'd zoned out. After clearing her throat, Natasha read the cryptic message out loud. '"An inland coast beyond that of which Turner and Dickens saw their most glorious end. Once divided now never apart. Where we saw enlightenment and welcomed the dark."'

He waited for that nugget of information that would give Lucas that lightbulb moment, but it never came. 'That's it? That's all the information he's given us? We've been running up and down across London to find out about Turner and Dickens' happy ending? What a complete waste of time.'

'It's "glorious end".'

'What?'

'You said happy ending. But the inscription is glorious end.'

'Whatever. The fact remains the same, we have no idea where to look.'

'Margate, Ramsgate, or somewhere in that region,' Lyndsay suddenly said.

'Thanet,' stated Natasha.

'What makes you think it's there?' Lucas asked Lindsay.

'"The skies over Thanet are the loveliest in all Europe".'

'Who said that?' Lucas asked.

'Joseph Mallord William Turner.'

'Well, well, well. When did you become such an art boffin?'

'You know, I think he's onto something there, Lucas,' Natasha chimed in. 'Dickens loved Broadstairs. The area influenced his novel, *David Copperfield*. And there's also evidence that Julius Caesar landed there, so that keeps Marcus's Roman theme going.'

'Well, it looks like we're off on a road trip. I think we should take your car though, Natasha, mines a bit beat up. I'll go wake up Ellen and we can make a move.'

As Lucas left, Natasha's phone rang. It was a video call. She answered it and the first thing she saw were her parents slumped over in their chairs. She shot up out of her seat, thinking them dead.

'Tick tock, tick tock,' The Baron's voice chided. 'Your time is up, Natasha. Do you have the Eye of Nineveh, or do I have to make your parents sleep permanent?'

'They're only sleeping,' Natasha breathed a sigh of relief.

'Yes, but I can change that in a second,' he said. 'Now, do you have the gem?'

'No ...'

'What a shame.'

'... but I know where it is. I just need more time.'

'Time is one thing you don't have.'

'Well, if you had helped me with the drug dealers, like I asked, I wouldn't have been delayed.'

'True, a mistake on my part.'

'And if you hadn't sent Lucas on some little side mission, it would have been done quicker. And don't get me started on you putting us on global Wanted lists.'

'I don't know what you're talking about; I sent my men to rescue you. And as for Lucas, I didn't send him anywhere.'

Natasha looked puzzled. She couldn't tell if he was telling the truth or not, but why would he lie now? And it brought up another pressing question; if it hadn't been The Baron then someone had impersonated him? But who?

'Well, it appears you've had a long, busy night. If you're certain you know where it is, I am going to give you time to retrieve it. You have until 1000 hours and not a minute longer.' With The Baron saying all he had to, the phone was disengaged.

'You're sure you don't want to come with us, Ellen?' Lucas and his young friend returned with him desperately trying to get her to change her mind, but to no avail.

'I know you're just trying to look out for me. Keep me close so you can look out for me, but it's seven o'clock. What's going to happen? Besides, I've had enough of this field work for a while. I just want to go home and chill out for a bit. And I need to check on that algorithm I programmed, see if it's had any hits.'

'Yeah, but I just don't like the idea of you going off on your own.'

'What if I take her home?' Lyndsay suggested. 'I'm sure you two have things in hand from here on. I could do with some rest too, to be honest.'

'If you're sure, I'd appreciate it.'

With handshakes and hugs all round, the party of four headed for the underground car park, where Ellen made a devastating discovery.

'You have got to be shitting me! This is how you treat my gifts? Do you know that car is a limited edition? Only five hundred made. Well, I hope you enjoyed it. You won't even get a Hot Wheels car out of me next time!' She got into the passenger side of the beat-up car and badly wanted to slam the door shut, but it wouldn't. It just creaked and groaned.

Ellen sat there with a face like thunder, as at the fourth attempt, Lyndsay got the car started. They pulled off, Lucas and Natasha following in her Range Rover, but neither of them noticed the car that followed as they entered the main road, nor did that driver take note of the car tailing them.

Chapter 32

Lucas was giving Natasha's SUV another workout, zipping in and out of slow-moving cars as they flew through the morning traffic. He knew time wasn't on their side; the journey to Ramsgate was almost two hours, and he intended to get there as fast as possible.

Tires screeched and car horns blared out as he ran another red light, swerving and narrowly avoiding an orange Honda Civic coming across the junction. Lucas took a quick glance at Natasha, half expecting her to be having a heart attack, but she was deep in thought, studying the disc again.

'Everything okay?' Lucas asked as he momentarily tested the Range Rover Evoque's off-road capabilities, before re-joining the tarmac, having overtaken several cars.

'I think I made a mistake.'

It was a statement he hadn't heard her utter on too many occasions. 'What do you mean, "mistake"?'

'We were so focussed on Thanet and the connection with Turner and Dickens that we didn't consider the other clues. This bit, for instance. Thanet isn't an inlaid coast; during Roman times, it was an isle. Before the silt build-up, the coast was from Reculver to Richborough.'

'And now it's an inland coast, once divided now never apart. And what about the last part?'

'Where we saw enlightenment and welcomed the dark refers to the Roman invasion and their departure. They brought culture and civilisation to these wild barbarian lands and when they left, the Dark Ages soon followed.'

'So where do we need to go if it's not Ramsgate?'

'Even though there's a Roman fort in Reculver, it was Richborough where the Romans landed for their decisive invasion in forty-three AD, and where they departed at the end of their occupation. It's an important Roman Britain site.'

'So Richborough it is then. The only problem is, we've already passed the turning.' They were entering the village of Cliffs End when the new destination was decided upon. 'I should warn you, you're probably going to get quite a few speeding tickets,' Lucas declared.

'Oh, thanks for that,' Natasha scoffed. 'I'll be sure to forward them onto you.'

'Well, you're about to get another one.'

'For what?'

Straight ahead, in the distance, Lucas could see a train hurtling towards London. They skidded onto Foads Hill, a residential area, at the end of which was a level crossing.

'You're not seriously thinking of ... you won't make it!'

The engine of the Evoque HST roared. It's 395hp, powered by both a turbocharger and supercharger, was pushed to its limit as Lucas pushed the accelerator as far as it would go.

The warning lights at the crossing were already flashing, signalling an oncoming train, the bell was sounding, the barriers coming down. Lucas's eyes were intense. Natasha's forearms rigid as her fingers dug into the armrests.

The speedometer edged towards the HST's 140mph top speed, with Lucas hoping that it was enough. The crossing raced towards them as the train raced towards it. It was a dash to the finish line, where failure would have dire consequences for Lucas and Natasha.

He was beginning to think it might have been a tad foolish on his part to attempt such a thing, but it wouldn't be the first time, and it certainly wouldn't be the last if he survived this one.

The barriers were fully down, blocking the left lane of either side of the track, but the Range Rover hurtled onwards, regardless. Lucas drifted to the right lane. Out of the corner of his eye he could see the train ever closer. It was going to be close.

From the clear lane, they flew across the train tracks. Natasha closed her eyes, seeing the train charging towards her for the split second they were in front of it. The horn from the train drowned out her screams. The Range Rover was buffeted by the cross wind as the train passed behind, barely missing them.

They both let out cheers of celebration at the avoided devastation. 'Just like old times, huh, Nat?'

'You always did know how to show me a good time,' Natasha replied, and immediately regretted her words when she saw Lucas's smirk. The double entendre wasn't lost on her.

As they continued on to their destination, the Lucas and Natasha had yet to notice the two cars that had to wait for the train to pass.

. . . .

THEY PULLED INTO THE car park and ran to the Roman fort ruins, knowing that they only had one hour left to find the Eye of Nineveh. Natasha didn't really know what they were looking for, but that had been her thinking at the beginning of this quest, and yet she had found the pieces of Professor Masterson's little disc. With a bit of faith in her abilities, and a touch of luck, Natasha believed that they'd be able to find whatever it was.

Natasha suggested that they each work on one side of the massive fort wall surrounding the site. As she watched Lucas run off to the opposite end, her eyesight fell on the rectangular foundation at the centre of the fort, which was once the site of a huge marble, monumental gateway. In antiquity, it would have dominated the skyline, being some twenty-five metres tall. The focal point of the burgeoning town.

She wandered over to the foundations, at its centre a raised intersection, and pictured what it would have looked like to see the grand four-arch building towering above her. She could imagine the bustling streets, filled with merchants and new arrivals from across the empire.

Natasha inspected the site closer, getting a more detailed idea of its size in her head. Then she saw what looked like the edge of a circle on the side of the intersection. Pushing aside the overgrowth, to get a better view of it, Natasha uncovered a round circle cut into the mortar.

As she traced her finger along the circumference, she could feel the small like those on the disc. 'I think I found something, Lucas,' Natasha yelled as she took the disc out of her bag.

Lucas sprinted over, just as Natasha was about to place the disc, slowly rotating it so that the teeth lined up, then it slotted into place. She let out a slight gasp and looked up at Lucas.

'Now what?' he asked.

She looked back at the disc of golden, as it gleamed in the morning sun, and shrugged. 'I wonder...' Natasha pushed her hand against the circle of gold and rotated it.

There was a click, then the sound of gears working. Lucas pulled Natasha back as part of the intersection suddenly fell into the earth, then another and another, stopping at staggered heights, creating a staircase leading underneath the ancient site.

'This is amazing.' Natasha could hardly contain her excitement.

'Yeah, it is. For a professor to do all this; they must get paid a pretty penny.'

'What are you trying to say?'

'Nothing that I'm sure you haven't been thinking yourself,' Lucas countered. 'That your professor isn't as squeaky clean as you think. Maybe he double-crossed The Baron? That's a sure-fire way to earn the ire of a terrorist.'

'No way. Just because you think it doesn't make it so.'

'Okay, okay, I was just playing devil's advocate.' He took his torch out. 'So, you ready to solve this quest?'

'Damn right I am.'

'So am I,' Kallum Taylor announced as he approached the two startled treasure hunters. 'Caught in the act of moving your stolen goods. Is this the fabled hideout of Sebastian Jericho, The Ghost?'

'You've got to be kidding me.' Natasha shook her head in disbelief. 'Following me again?'

'Don't worry, Nat, after I've finished with him, he won't be following anyone anytime soon. If it wasn't for him, Ellen would have been safe. I would have followed that J terrorist right back to The Baron, unless, of course, you are him.' Lucas's determined walk was halted when a gun was unexpectedly pointed at him. 'Now what kind of insurance investigator carries a gun?'

'The kind that has to deal with people like you.'

'Or the kind that aren't insurers at all,' Natasha added. 'Because I'm beginning to believe that you're not particularly good at your job. I mean, you can't still honestly believe that we had anything to do with the disappearance of the eye? Why would we be running all over London trying to find it if we knew exactly where it was? And while we've been doing that, what have you been doing?'

'Judging by how fresh and catwalk-ready he looks, I'd say he's had a nice night off.'

'Oh, I investigate. I investigate my suspects. I watch them, knowing that eventually they will lead my straight to my prize.'

'And where are the police?' Natasha asked. 'Aren't you supposed to be working in collaboration with them?'

'Don't worry, they'll be here to arrest you both. And while you two languish in prison, I'll be enjoying my healthy finder's fee. Now, I think it's time you took me to the Eye of Nineveh.'

Kallum waved them on with his gun. Lucas and Natasha slowly took the steps down into the unknown, with their captor bringing up the rear.

Chapter 33

Lucas turned on his flashlight as the further they descended, the more the light from the entrance diminished. They eventually came to level ground and continued to push on down the tunnel.

'Well?' Natasha said expectantly to Lucas.

'What?'

'Look at the walls. These were hewn with hand tools. If Marcus did this, like you were implying, don't you think he would have used modern equipment?'

'Yeah, maybe you're right about down here, but can you explain the disc and steps?' Lucas took her silence as her answer. 'Anyway, let's not worry about that right now. Let's just hope that the gem is here after all this.'

As the crept along the cold, damp tunnel, it began to curve. 'I think we're heading towards the amphitheatre,' Natasha speculated. 'This could have been an escape route for dignitaries, if the subjects got rowdy at the games, or the barbarians breached the walls.'

Lucas came to a stop as the passage widened. 'There's something up ahead, a cavern maybe.'

'This must be it,' Kallum declared and ordered the pair to move on.

The passage opened out to a ten-metre width and, as Lucas shone the light around, they could see a bridge crossing what seemed to be a bottomless chasm, leading to another passage on the other side. Natasha asked him to point the torch at the wall she stood at.

'Forget about that,' Kallum commanded impatiently. 'We're here for Eye of Nineveh, nothing else.' He walked on, and his eagerness almost cost him his life when he went to cross the bridge and the large paving stone he stepped on gave way beneath him.

Kallum yelled as he barely managed to stop himself from plummeting by catching the top of the ledge, relinquishing the gun to do so. After handing the torch to Natasha, Lucas reluctantly helped him up.

'If you want to get through this, maybe you should listen,' Natasha chided. She went back to looking at the wall, which had taken her interest. On the rough surface were four, five by five grids, a few of the squares were blacked out, randomly, as all four had different patterns. They didn't even have the same amount of black squares.

Having dumped Kallum on the ground, Lucas came over to join Natasha. 'What have we got here? A chess game?'

Natasha mumbled a no.

'Wait a minute.' Lucas grabbed her wrist and aimed the torch at the ground where Kallum had almost lost his life. 'The paving stones on the bridge are five by five.'

Natasha looked back at the wall. 'Then these black spaces must be the safe route.'

'Maybe not,' Lucas added, and pointed at the images. 'Look, this is the one Kallum stepped on, but it's only black in two of the grids.'

She studied each image intently, then something came to her. 'Maybe...'

Natasha sauntered over to the floor grid and stood in front of the two square paving, to the right of the missing one.

'Whoa! What are you doing?' Lucas's concern was clear as he strode over and grabbed Natasha's arm.

'What I have to do to save my parents.'

'This is dangerous, let me do it.'

'No more dangerous than some of the other things we've done. I'm Danger Girl, remember?'

Lucas chuckled. 'I knew I couldn't talk you out of it, but I wanted my concern noted for the record.'

'They are,' she smiled up into his brown eyes. 'Besides, you were already too late.' Lucas followed Natasha's gaze down and saw that she was standing on the stone.

'So, you solved it? What's the solution?'

She beamed with pride. 'Quite simple, really. You said the one that this idiot stepped on was on two of the pictures, an even number. The one I'm standing on is in three of them.'

'An odd number. How many are there?'

'Four others.'

'And where's the next one?'

'One across and one up.'

'Okay, take these.' He handed her some glow sticks. 'This will help us follow you.'

Natasha made the first step. Each stone being a one metre square, it wasn't too difficult to make, even under torch light, especially since it was the immediate diagonal stone. To reach the next one, she had to leap over a false one. At each step she landed on, Natasha would crack the stick and place it in the centre of the paving stone, like a glowing bread crumb.

The third safe landing spot was two up. Lucas came around to illuminate the zone. 'Okay, where's the next one?'

'Three across.'

'Three? Are you sure? That means you'll have to clear two metres from a standing start.'

'I'm well aware of that. It's no different from the plyometrics I've been doing in the gym.'

'Except,' Kallum butted in, 'if you under cook it, or overpower it, the consequences will be more than a consoling pat on the back from your Chelsea tractor driving girlfriends.'

'Shut up, Taylor.'

'You're a bit of a wanker, aren't you, Kallum?' Lucas snarled.

'I'm not here to make friends. I'm just doing my job.'

Natasha took a few breaths and went through the motions: swinging her arms and crouching into a squat. Then, without warning, she explosively propelled herself forward through the air.

She made it, landing with her feet on the edge of the paving stone. But as Natasha attempted to stand, her right foot slipped, and the stone it touched fell away.

Lucas yelled out her name, agonising because that was all he could do, as she planted her hands to stop herself from falling off. After catching her breath, and letting her heartbeat return to something like normal, Natasha pulled herself up. She left the glow stick, took the last step, again immediately diagonal of where she was, and collapsed against the wall, waiting for the others to catch up.

• • • •

AFTER REUNITING, THE party continued their quest for the Eye of Nineveh through the second passageway. It wasn't long before they came to another chamber, smaller than the last, but then it didn't need to be large, as, after Lucas swept around the space with the flashlight, the only thing present there was a plinth, on top of which sat the eye of Nineveh.

'We found it, Lucas! We've found it!' Natasha clapped her hands with glee.

Lucas grinned. 'Yeah, we did. And just in time, too. We can get your parents back from The Baron now.'

'Are you sure this is the real thing?' Kallum queried. 'I mean, it's just sitting here. A priceless jewel, right there with no protection. Anyone could just walk away with.'

Natasha was incredulous. 'Are you some sort of idiot? How did you become an insurance investigator? For your information, Lucas and I have been searching for the eye all night, running all over London, following clues, being shot at, and arrested to get to this point. There's no way anyone could just walk away with it.'

'Well, I'm about to do just that!' Kallum charged Lucas, barging him into Natasha, slamming the both of them into the chamber wall. Then he grabbed the Eye of Nineveh and rushed out, picking up the torch as it rolled on the ground.

Natasha tended to Lucas, who had banged his head due to Kallum's cowardly act. 'I'm going to kick his ass,' she fumed. 'How are you feeling?'

'I'll be alright. Good thing I've got a tough head. What about you?'

'I'm fine. Come on,' Natasha said, getting to her feet. 'We can't let him get away.'

They sprinted after the investigator. Like survivors of near-death experiences, they could see light at the end of the tunnel. Then it bobbed up and down as Kallum traversed the bridge puzzle.

'He's almost at the other passage,' Lucas yelled. 'We're going to have to hurry across.' But those plans were scuppered when they arrived at the bridge. They came to a skidding halt as they saw that Kallum had removed all the glow sticks.

'That's hardly going to stop me,' Natasha scoffed.

'But it will me,' added Lucas. 'Forget it. We'll jump it.'

'What? It's five metres!'

'You'll do fine. We've got a run-up this time. Don't worry about it. Besides, we're running out of time. Come on, I'll go first.'

They took a few steps back, then Lucas exploded into a sprint. As he reached the edge of the pit, he slammed his foot down and propelled himself through the air, almost gliding, landed, tucked and rolled.

'See, Nat, simple. Now it's your turn.'

She psyched herself up, rocking back and forth on her heels. Then she broke into a sprint. Natasha liked risk-taking as much as Lucas. Base-jumping, free rocking, she enjoyed it all. But unlike him, she always had that healthy dose of fear to overcome before fully immersing herself in the fun factor.

Suddenly, a distant gunshot rang out.

Natasha missed a stepped, but she was too close to the edge to stop. She had to jump. Making the adjustment just before she planted her foot to propel herself forward, Natasha aimed for the first paving stone she had stepped on.

It was a great call! Natasha landed on it, but awkwardly. She was losing her balance and toppling towards the hole created by the stone that had crumbled away under Kallum.

She flailed her arms, trying to regain her balance as she teetered on the edge. Just as she felt herself going, Lucas grabbed the waist of her pants and yanked her to safety, ending up in his arms.

Natasha's chest rose and fell due to her exertions, strands of her curly hair stuck to the sweat on her face. She could see a certain something in Lucas's face, as she looked up at him, a look she'd seen many times before. She licked her lips in anticipation.

But then she remembered why they were there, remembered that Kallum had run off with the gemstone, the same gemstone she needed to save her parents from the terrorist. 'Um, maybe we should ... uh ... get after Kallum, don't you think?'

'Yeah, yes, uh, for sure. Let's go.'

Natasha cursed under her breath as she chased after Lucas.

* * * *

AS LUCAS AND NATASHA emerged from the hidden underground tunnel system, they found Kallum nursing his head. Before they could question him about what happened, now that they were back on the surface and could get a signal, Natasha's phone rang.

'Hello.'

'Ah, Miss Travers,' The Baron said. 'I wanted to thank you for doing the right thing and getting me the Eye of Nineveh. You were wise not to double cross me like Professor Masterson.'

'What have you done to him?'

'Nothing. Marcus was paid an extremely good sum of money to oversee the creation of an identical Eye of Nineveh. I intended to exchange the fake one with the real one when it was on route to London. But I didn't know that Marcus had secretly had a second fake made and took the real one for himself.'

'You're lying!' Natasha couldn't believe what she was hearing and took it all with a grain of salt. Sure, Marcus Masterson had been a Cold War spy, but that was then, in his youth, now he was in his seventies. Doing something as dangerous as fleecing a terrorist was crazy. 'What about my parents?'

'Rest assured; your parents will be returned unharmed. Thank you once again for all your assistance. We will not speak again.' The Baron hung up the phone.

Rage bubbled up in her hand when she saw Kallum get to his feet. She lashed out and gave him a right hook, sending him back down to the ground. 'You are such an idiot! We wanted to follow The Baron's men back to him. We had no intention of letting him keep the Eye of Nineveh. Now you've put this power in the hands of a terrorist!'

'What power?' Kallum asked, rubbing his jaw. 'I wasn't going to give it to them, but their warning shot changed my mind.'

'Shut up,' Natasha snarled at him. 'Did you at least see which way they went?'

He shook his head.

'Come on, Nat. We'll head back to London, hopefully, with any luck, that's where they've gone.'

• • • •

IN NO TIME AT ALL, they were once again thundering down the road in Natasha's Evoque HST. She had tried to get hold of her parents at their home, but no one was picking up. Lucas could feel that she was becoming anxious.

'Whatever else The Baron is, he is a man of his word; if he said they'll be unharmed, we can believe that. They probably just haven't arrived yet.'

'Yeah. Yeah, you're right,' she sighed.

'Whoa, look at that.' Further down the quiet country road, a plume of smoke rose up into the sky. As they approached, Lucas could see a black BMW wrapped around a tree. An identical model to the ones that had chased them to Vauxhall Bridge, The Baron's men.

Lucas and Natasha looked at each other as he pulled over so they could investigate the wreckage. They couldn't believe their luck and speculated as to what might have happened. Overeager to get back to The Baron, losing control in the process, was the common consensus. However, neither of them guessed the terrorists had been attacked, but the bullet holes in the car and their bodies confirmed this.

And there was no sign of the Eye of Nineveh.

They barely had time to contemplate the implications of what had happened, the consequences for her parents and the population as a whole, when several police cars arrived at the scene, sirens blaring, and surrounded Natasha and Lucas.

Chapter 34

To say the previous day was one of the worst Natasha Travers had experienced would have been an understatement.

This day was continuing on in the same vein. 'Surely, things can only get better?' She sighed as she sat in the interview room of the local police station, waiting to be questioned by them.

Although the local police only wanted to conduct routine questions about the accident, to build a picture of what happened, but since neither she nor Lucas had actually seen anything, they were due to be released. However, when their names were entered into the police database, it flagged a hold order issued for both of them. She had been told that DCI Jake Russell was on the way from London.

For two hours she had sat in a holding room, away from Lucas, stewing in her own thoughts, before she had been moved to the interview room. Eventually, the door opened.

'Hello again, Miss Travers,' DCI Russell said as he stood in the doorway. 'Wilkins, would you get me a cup of tea. Would you like one, Natasha?'

'Milk, two sugars.'

'Make that two, Wilkins.'

The DI nodded and closed the door behind himself. Russell took his coat off and hung it on the back of his chair before sitting down. He took the time to make himself comfortable, taking out his notepad in preparation, but didn't say anything until the teas arrived.

'Mmmm, that's not a bad cuppa,' DCI Russell said after taking a sip. 'It's obvious what stations get the good tea.' He took another sip before putting his cup down and taking a pen from out of his pocket. Flipping open his notebook, Russell wrote some additional lines before finally addressing Natasha again. 'Quite the adventure you and Lucas have had, wouldn't you say? First, being a suspect of the Eye of Nineveh disappearance, then the shooting at The Savoy, and let's not forget the high-speed chase. Your implication with a terrorist group, and a drug dealer, who we found dead, by the way. But my favourite part is when Lucas fakes his way into the Old Bailey and escapes.' Jake Russell finished reading from his notes and closed the pad.

'I'd personally say it's been a very inconvenient day, to be honest.'

'I can imagine. Whilst you two have been running all over London, and now Kent, I've continued my investigations, and a lot of inconsistencies have popped up.'

'At least someone is investigating something.'

'What's that supposed to mean?'

'That Kallum Taylor, he's been following us.'

Russell and Wilkins gave each other a knowing glance. 'He's actually one of the inconsistencies. Barrington's has never employed an insurance investigator by that name.'

'What? Who the hell is he then?'

'We're still trying to find out.'

'I can't believe it. And that bastard had the gem in his hand.'

'He did?' Jake opened his notepad again, making some quick scribblings. 'So Kallum had the eye all along?'

'No. Lucas and I found it, following Professor Masterson's clues. We were supposed to find the eye and give it to The Baron.'

'Wait, so you're working for the terrorists?'

'Not by choice. They'd kidnapped my parents and threatened to kill them if we didn't.' Then the realisation that The Baron never received the gemstone hit Natasha. 'Oh my god! His men never made it back to him. He probably thinks I double crossed him.'

Suddenly, the door was opened and a black-haired man in a cobalt-blue, three-piece suit, confidently marched in. 'This interview is over,' he declared.

'Who the hell are you?' Jake Russell asked as he abruptly stood up.

'David Evans, Section 7.'

'Well, Mr Evans, I've never heard of it. So, if you'd please, this is a closed interview.'

'My credentials,' David said and handed the DCI a card.

'SIS? Now why would the Secret Intelligence Service be here?'

'That's above your pay grade, I'm afraid.' Just then, there was a knock at the door and a police officer brought Lucas in. 'Now, if you'll excuse me, this *will* be a closed interview.'

The detectives gathered up their things and reluctantly left. 'We'll be waiting outside,' Jake said over his shoulder, as he left slamming the door open behind them.

Lucas went over to Natasha and gently squeezed her shoulder. 'Are you okay?'

'Yeah, I'm fine. You?'

'Not as good as you, no one brought me a cup of tea.'

'Would you like one?' David offered as he closed the door.

'No, but I would like some answers.'

'As would I,' Natasha added. 'What does Mi6 want with us?'

'To offer you both a job.'

Lucas and Natasha looked at each other and burst out laughing.

'Do we look like spy material to you?' Lucas said between laughs.

'You won't be doing cloak and dagger stuff ... well, not so much. Section 7 has its own mandate. It's not all about spy-craft.'

'Then what is it about?' Natasha asked, more than a little intrigued now.

'Treasure hunting.'

'What?' they both exclaimed.

'To be specific, the finding and retrieving of specific artefacts deemed too dangerous to be left out in the world. Artefacts such as the Eye of Nineveh.'

'Wait a minute! So, you know about its mystical powers?' Lucas asked.

'Of course. We had the preeminent Assyrian antiquities scholar working for us.'

'Professor Masterson!' Natasha gave Lucas a smug look. 'See, I told you.'

Lucas shrugged. 'So, shoot me! You said *had*. Does that mean he's ...?'

'We don't know. He's vanished, dropped off the radar. After swapping the eye with the fake one, he was supposed to bring it back to S7, but he hid it instead.'

'Why would Marcus do that?'

'The only reason I can think of, is that he had this idea that an outside influence infiltrated S7. It was all just speculation, though, he couldn't provide any hard evidence.'

'The Baron did say that Marcus had an extra gem created.'

'So he gave a fake eye to The Baron, and a fake one to the British Museum and then hid the real one?' Lucas mused.

'That's our hypothesise. How The Baron found out it was fake so quickly, we don't know.'

'It's obvious,' Lucas stated. 'You've got a mole. Someone connected to your organisation must have told him about the fake. Revealing the museum fake was his insurance policy. It let them know he had the real gem, and they couldn't kill him.'

'Recently the old fool didn't trust anyone.'

'Except you,' Natasha pointed out.

'And you,' David replied. 'Marcus always said that you were a bright spark, Natasha. Said that we should recruit you. And now that he's missing, we could use your help.'

Natasha glanced at Lucas, hoping to gain some help in deciding. He nodded, but she wasn't so sure. She had gotten used to working for herself, being her own boss, and Natasha wasn't sure if she could give up that autonomy. But then again, there was the bigger picture involved, keeping ancient powers out of the hands of the wrong people. 'What about our business? What about The Acquirers?'

'What about it? You continue as normal, of course. If you accept my offer, you won't be working in an office. You'll only be contacted when a credible lead comes up. Besides, your business is a good cover, just like Marcus being an archaeology professor. And there are other perks.'

Lucas narrowed his eyes. 'Such as?'

'Well, all these misdemeanours you've stacked up during the last day can disappear for a start. The shootings, the speeding, the trespassing.'

'I'm in,' Lucas said enthusiastically.

Natasha looked at him with wide eyes.

'What?' Lucas asked with a shrug. 'I don't see any issue with accepting. It'll be like doing what we do, but with government backing. What's not to love?'

'The fact that they have a leak in the organisation, for a start. That doesn't concern you?'

'To tackle that, you'll be reporting to me and me alone,' David interjected. 'Which means that some things may have to be sourced from outside of S7. But I understand that you have an excellent fixer.'

'Yeah, Ellen does well for herself, and it wouldn't be the first time she's done off the books work for agencies. So, you got any other issues, Nat?'

'Apart from having to work with you more than I'd like? No.'

'Then I take it you're both on board?' As they nodded, David took two plastic cards from his pocket, placed them on the table and pushed them towards Lucas and Natasha. 'Welcome to Her Majesty's Secret Service.'

She picked up her card and looked at the photo; it was the same one from her passport. 'You already had these made up? What if we refused?'

'I'm not sure you really want to know, to be honest,' Lucas said.

Natasha creased her brows, puzzled by the statement, then she turned to David. He didn't elaborate on it, leaving her dumbfounded. 'You're kidding me, right?'

'Trust me, Nat, this is how things run around these parts. I should know, the Russians aren't the only ones that eliminate their own.'

The tension was palpable as Natasha contemplated the full extent of what she was getting herself into.

'Well, thanks for that, Lucas. I can see why she's divorcing you. Don't worry, Natasha, the Official Secrets Act is not as dramatic as he makes it out. It just means that it's a criminal offence for current, that's you, or former government employees, to leak certain types of information considered damaging. There's nothing about assassination in there,' chuckled David.

'Fine. Whatever. Can we just move on?'

'Sure. So, we need to find the Eye of Nineveh, again.'

'And how do we do that?' Natasha asked. 'We have no idea who took it.'

'We have a few suspects as to who could be behind that little smash and grab in Richborough. But one name stood out from the rest.' David flipped through the images on his mobile phone until he found the one he was after, a surveillance picture of a stylish black woman, her face half obscured by a well-placed newspaper, as if she knew she was being photographed. 'You know, they say use a thief to catch a thief. Well, Lucas or Sebastian, tell me, how do we catch your mother?'

Chapter 35

Natasha picked up the phone and examined the photograph. 'You're trying to tell me that this is Angela Redmond? Lucas's dead mother?' She wasn't buying it and pushed the phone back towards David. 'This could be anybody.' She turned to Lucas, expecting to get his confirmation that it wasn't the woman that gave birth to him, but the look on his face suggested there was something in it. 'Lucas?' Natasha watched him abruptly stand up and begin pacing back and forth, his fists clenched so tightly his veins throbbed.

'We weren't one hundred per cent sure if it was her or not. There's very few photos of Angela Redmond, but judging by his reaction, I'd say it's a safe bet it's her.'

Lucas shot David a look of murderous intent that shot shivers up his spine. 'Leave us.'

'Maybe you two need to chat. I'll have them prep the chopper to leave, don't be too long.' He knew it wasn't nice what he'd just done, blindsiding Lucas like that, but David Evans wasn't afraid to do the things that needed to be done. And from what he'd read in Lucas's redacted files, he was of the same ilk; the ends justified the means. Separating himself from the situation would give Lucas time to calm down.

Once David had left, Natasha considered how she should broach the subject. She had so many questions built up over so many years. But there was no straightforward way to deal with it, except to rip the plaster off. 'So that woman is your mother, isn't she? You told me she was dead.'

'Because that's what I was told,' he replied as he came back to his seat. 'When I was at Sandhurst, they told me my parents died in a car crash in Capri. There was even a funeral.'

She looked back at him with wide eyes. 'Who is she?'

'She might as well be the devil.' Lucas sighed deeply. He knew that the time had come. He had let this secret control his life for too long. It had even cost him his marriage, now he had no reason to hide it. 'You know I've always been a little shady about my past.'

'That's an understatement. You always skirted around the subject.'

'Because it's nothing like yours, Nat. It wasn't about which top university I'd go to. It was about how big a score I could get, which house I could break into, what museum or art gallery I could steal from. I was afraid I'd lose you, lose your respect if you knew everything.'

'You really think I'm that shallow?'

'No. But my pride wouldn't let me take the chance. Someone like me isn't supposed to be with someone like you. That's why your dad hates us together.'

'And probably why my mum is always fighting your corner,' she smiled.

'Your mum's a good woman.'

'Tell me more about yours.'

'Well, there are thieves, and there are master thieves. Then there's Angela Redmond. She stole everything and anything. For herself and to order. If you could pay you could play, that included government contracts too.'

'So, Angela, is this Ghost person?'

'No, I am.' There it was, the look he had been dreading to see on Natasha's face, but as quickly as it appeared, it was gone. 'I created the persona of Sebastian Jericho, The Ghost. He was the faceless spectre of the underworld. Feared and revered but never seen, which was perfect. I was a teenager acting as the go between for Jericho, his mouthpiece, and nobody messed with me because they never wanted to face the consequences of the bogeyman.'

'And nobody ever found out? That this master criminal was just a kid?'

'Nope. Only Angela knew the truth. That's how I knew she was still alive.' Lucas said as he took a folded piece of paper from his pocket and handed it to Natasha.

She unfolded and read the piece of paper. 'Sebastian Jericho.' Natasha shook her head slightly. 'I don't get it. What is this?'

'It's in her handwriting.'

Then it struck her. 'Wait ... this is the letter you got? The one that started your ...'

Lucas nodded.

Natasha returned her gaze to the page, admiring the flamboyant handwriting. perplexed that someone with such beautiful calligraphy could be a criminal mastermind, but then creativity would be a useful trait for someone following that career choice. 'I understand the feelings you'd have finding out that Angela faked her death. What I don't understand is why it made you do what you did. What happened between the two of you?'

'We were on a job together, like we did most of the time. We were supposed to steal a formula from a pharmaceutical company, except there was no formula. It was a setup. Our escape was blocked but Angela usually had a secondary exit planned, just in case, but that was blocked, too. This time she had a third escape plan, which involved using a zip line she had installed to a neighbouring building. She got across, then she cut the line, waved and disappeared, leaving me stranded.'

'Are you serious?'

'Hard to believe, huh? The queen and the sacrificial pawn. Your mother is supposed to be the one woman that you can trust and believe in. Safe to say I was pretty scarred after that betrayal. If my own mother could do that, who was to say that any other woman wouldn't do the same? I never got emotionally attached to any women after that. I'd seduce them, have fun with them and get out before they could double-cross me.'

Natasha didn't know how to respond. She'd never seen Lucas be so open and vulnerable before. The tricky thing for her to deal with was that it was making her fall in love with him all other again.

'The day I found out that she had died, the dark cloud that had been hanging over me was lifted. But of course, the bitch couldn't have just stayed dead. The moment she returns, I revert to type, and ruin every good thing we'd built. I'm damaged goods. It's probably for the best that you left me, Nat.'

She reached out her hand and placing it on his. 'I'm not so sure it is.'

Just then, David Evans opened the door. 'Are you done yet? We're wasting fuel here.'

• • • •

NATASHA LET THE SOOTHING water from her power shower wash away all the tension, aches and pains that had built up since the Eye of Nineveh vanished from the British Museum. She had been on the go for over twenty-four hours, and now that she was no longer running on adrenaline, having a relaxing shower was a welcome respite. She could do with some pampering.

As soon as David had brought Lucas and herself back to London, Natasha had headed straight to her parents. She was more than happy to see that DCI Russell had been true to his word when she discovered two officers at her parent's home.

The possibility of The Baron's retaliation for losing the gemstone had been a very real one. She had feared for the safety of her parents. This was the first time that her activities had an adverse effect on them, had put them in danger. If she was being honest, it had all been a bit too much stress for her. Natasha decided that she'd leave the whole saving lives thing to Lucas from now on.

As she stepped out of the steamy shower and, with a towel wrapped around her wet hair, entered her bedroom, Natasha thought back to what Lucas had revealed about himself, all these things that he had kept secret from her were now out in the open. It took their relationship to another level, and as she rubbed coconut oil into her skin, she couldn't believe how much she wished it were him doing it.

Suddenly, the phone rang, and to Natasha's delight, it was Lucas. She grinned like a teenager as she answered the call.

'I just wanted to check up on you,' he said, 'make sure that everything was okay with your parents.'

'Yeah, they were fine. My mum wanted to thank you for everything you did.'

'Don't worry about it; family, you know.'

'I want to thank you too,' she said softly. 'You felt able to share things with me, and even after filing for divorce and everything, you were there when I needed you.'

'Of course I was, Nat. I always will be.'

'And what if I said that I needed you now?'

Just then, Natasha heard the familiar Australian lilt of Chiara Harris in the background, and immediately regretted what she had implied. She hung up the phone and hid her embarrassed face behind her hands. The phone rang again, startling her. She had half a mind to ignore it, but she felt she had to apologise, blame it on the time of the month or something. 'I'm really sorry, Lucas. Think nothing of it. You know how I get when ...'

'Hello, Natasha. It's me, Philip. Philip Armitage.'

'Philip? Oh, hi!' she replied in a pitch so high, nearby dogs would have heard her as she narrowly avoided being twice embarrassed. 'How are you doing?'

'I've had a meeting cancelled, so I was wondering, if you're at a loose end, perhaps you'd like to go for that lunch. Well, it would be a late lunch now.'

This was a sign, an opportunity to look for a new relationship. If Lucas could do it, why shouldn't she? 'You know what, Philip, I think that would be a wonderful idea.'

Chapter 36

When Peter had asked Natasha if she liked sushi, she had said, 'yes, of course, doesn't everybody?' Little did she know that, when he picked her up in his white, chauffeur-driven Rolls Royce Phantom Extended, he would bring her to Berkeley Square in the heart of Mayfair. Their destination, Sexy Fish; the restaurant and bar that oozed glamour and opulence, decorated with artwork from Frank Gehry, Damien Hirst, and Michael Roberts.

When they arrived, all manner of super cars lined the streets. The driver opened the Phantom's rear-hinged doors and allowed them both out. Passers-by looked at them, knowing that famous people often frequented the restaurant. They quickly lost interest, however, when they saw that the pair weren't movies stars or singers, not knowing that Peter Armitage could buy several times over, and still have change.

After straightening her mauve coloured summer dress and fixing her untied hair, Natasha took Peter's offered hand. She had been close to wearing a smart casual ensemble of a pair of jeans and blouse, but decided that she'd make a little more of an effort, and as they walked into the restaurant, she was glad that she did. There was a real nightclub feel, not what she would have expected from Peter, to be fair. There was more to him than she originally thought.

He caught her looking and smiled. 'What? Shocked that I'd be in a place like this?' Peter asked, his voice raised so she could hear him over the DJ's pounding dance music.

'Well ... I'm not going to lie. When I saw you with my dad, I thought you looked a bit stiff.'

'Indeed. The thing is, the bar here has the world's largest Japanese whiskey collection, some four hundred bottles, and the cocktails are something else. Besides, I wanted to impress the lady and angle for a dinner date.'

'I would be just as happy going to a Wetherspoons for a pub lunch.'

'Really? That's not what your father tells me.'

'My dad has an idea of how he wants me to be. Unfortunately, for him, that dream, and the reality, don't match up. If you want to get to know me and have that dinner date, don't use tips from him, ask me.'

The maître d' glided up and greeted them warmly. It was obvious by the way he spoke to Peter that he was a frequent patron of the restaurant. He announced that the private dining space was ready and led the way.

The door they were eventually brought to had the title The Coral Reef Room on it, as it was held open and Natasha ushered inside, she could immediately see why; she saw two live coral reef tanks embedded in the walls. The maître d' informed her they were two of the largest in the world. There was a custom-built bar, with an off-white veined marble top and antique brass detailing. Flowers and candles lined the long table which Natasha quickly counted could seat forty-eight.

'You didn't, did you?'

'Of course I did. I didn't want to share this experience with anyone but you, Natasha.'

It was an unexpected gesture, and she felt her cheeks warm up. But it wasn't the obvious high amount of money spent that made her feel this way, it was the fact that he wanted her to be the centre of attention. The way Lucas used to make her feel.

'I hope you don't mind,' Peter said as he pulled a chair out for Natasha. 'But I've already arranged a menu for us.'

'No, not at all. It'll be an interesting surprise.' She smiled. 'I know you have a certain style when it comes to dress code. Now I get to see if that extends to gastronomy.'

It did.

For the starter, they had beluga caviar served with steamed buns and tiger prawns grilled with chilli and lime. The main was Japanese wagyu fillet with grilled tender stem broccoli and spicy quinoa. Dessert, coconut semifreddo with mango and passion fruit compote, all washed down with several Pin Up Coladas, their signature cocktail, a combination of a pina colada and strawberry daquiri.

Natasha found the whole spread delicious, and she was enjoying the company too. The conversation flowed, his knowledge of history and ancient cultures impressed. Although she remembered seeing some artefacts in his office, Natasha had no idea that information about the subject went so far beyond that of a hobbyist.

'I totally agree with Rudolph Kuper and Stefan Kröpelin, the Sphinx was underwater hence the erosion pattern it displays,' Peter stated with passion. 'Now, if that has something to do with Atlantis, then that's another thing.'

'Well, there's only one way to find out,' Natasha replied playfully, as the Pin Up Coladas had an accumulative effect on her.'

'Are you planning an expedition?' Peter leant forward, hoping to get some breaking news.

'Chance would be a fine thing.'

He sat back once again. 'You never know, something might come up.' Suddenly getting up and excusing himself, Peter headed to the cloakroom.

Instead of sitting and waiting for her host to return, Natasha got up herself and went to have a closer look at the coral reef tanks with all the brightly coloured fish. It was a therapeutic, watching fish swimming this way and that, without a care in the world.

She heard the door of the VIP room open behind her, and a blurred reflection in the glass. 'You know, Peter, we used to have a fish tank when I was a kid. I used to love sitting there watching them, hearing the pump bubbling away, but cleaning the tank was a real pain in the ass. Oh!' Natasha turned around to see a tanned man with jet-black, shoulder length hair and a trimmed beard standing there, hands behind his back. 'Sorry, I think you've got the wrong room.'

'No, Natasha Travers, this is the right room.'

'That voice ... I recognise it ... you're ... you're The Baron.'

'I am. Now, where is the Eye of Nineveh?'

'I don't know,' Natasha admitted as she tried to keep her composure in the face of the terrorist. 'Kallum Taylor took it from us, and your men took it from him and were killed on the way to you, I suppose. Whoever did the shooting has the eye.'

He scrutinised her with his hazel eyes. 'Very well, I believe you. I needed to see if you were telling the truth for myself. Things are not over between us. The deal was your parents for the gemstone, yet you are the only one that got what they desired.'

'That's not my fault. Don't you touch my parents!'

'I won't, but if I find out that you or Lucas double crossed me, my next visit won't be so cordial.

• • • •

IN THE CENTRAL LONDON district of Fitzrovia, on Bolsover Street, is a grand, red-brick Edwardian building, home to several different offices, including that of The Acquirers. Lucas Redmond had tried to get a little rest at his apartment, but after coming clean about his past to Natasha, and then her surprising phone-call a bit later, left him in a quandary. His mind was spinning, did he actually have a chance of a reconciliation with Natasha? Or was he misreading the signs? Reading into something that wasn't there.

With any chance of sleep gone, Lucas had headed into the office. Even without either of her bosses around, Venice Jones, their more than capable personal assistant, had kept things running smoothly, but with potential clients stacking up, she was extremely happy to see Lucas. Especially since the clients in question were offering the kind of jobs he had expressly told her to bring to him only, and that Natasha was not to have any wind of them.

'Well, Mr Baggera.' Lucas held the door of his office open to allow a short, overweight man to exit. 'As soon as your first payment clears, I'll get to work. And as usual, we will expect the rest of the fee on delivery.'

'That won't be a problem, Mr Redmond,' the client replied as he shook Lucas's hand. 'I look forward to hearing from you.' He nodded to Venice, left the reception area with Lucas, who called a lift for him. After a final goodbye, he was gone.

'That shouldn't be too difficult a job to pull off,' Lucas said, returning to Venice.

'Forget about that. Carry on with what you were saying,' she urged.

Lucas leaned against her dark oak desk. 'Yes, so we are now at the beck and call of Section 7, or S7, for short. It does come with its benefits though.'

'You know damn well that wasn't what I was talking about,' Venice replied as she pushed her glasses back up the bridge of her nose. 'I meant you and Natasha. Come on, spill it.'

'I don't know. It just felt like we had a moment, that's all.'

'Her telling you she needed you now is more than a moment. That's a green light to come over and do the business.'

'That was before she heard Chiara and hung up.'

Venice looked pained. 'When are you going to get rid of that cockblocker?'

'She's not a cockblocker. She's my girlfriend.'

'And before her, you had a wife, a wife that's still into you.'

'She said that?'

'No, but I see things.'

Before Lucas could reply, his mobile phone rang. He showed the screen to Venice.

'It's a sign,' she whispered.

'Hey, Nat,' he said after answering the call. He tried to sound natural, and not like someone that had just been talking about her. 'How you doing? It sounds like you're at a nightclub. You're where? Sexy what? I'm at the office. Oh, okay, see you soon.'

'Well, what did she say? Did she want to carry on from earlier?' Venice asked with a cheeky wink and a smile.

'She's coming in, said something happened.'

'No! No, no, no, she can't come in. You've still got the other client in the waiting room.'

'No problem, I'll take care of him before she gets here.'

'Well, you'd better hurry then. She's at Sexy Fish, right?'

'Yeah, how d'you know?'

'Good listener, anyway, it's just around the corner ... uh oh, too late.'

Lucas followed Venice's gaze towards the lift and saw Natasha stride out. His jaw dropped. It had been some time since he'd last seen her in a dress. 'You look amazing, Natasha,' he breathed.

'Oh, thanks,' she smiled shyly and fluffed her hair. 'I was having lunch.'

'He's right, you know; you do look great. You should wear dresses more.'

'I don't know. I'm used to wearing cargo pants. I don't think this look is really suitable for the field.'

'Well, you're not in the field now. Why don't the two of you go for a drink or something, celebrate becoming agents and stuff.'

'That's not a bad idea, Nat. What do you say?'

'What? No! The Baron is here. He's still after the eye and he thinks we double crossed him.'

Suddenly, the door of the waiting room was opened and a slim Arab man with a thin moustache stepped out. 'Ms Jones, how long am I expected to wait? Ah, Ms Travers and Mr Redmond! I am so pleased to finally meet you. I'll get straight down to business; I won't waste your time. My name is Nabil Hussein ...'

He was interrupted as Lucas's phone rang again. When he saw it was Ellen, he answered it immediately. 'Are you okay? Is anything wrong?'

'Hey, chill out. Everything's okay. You're not going to be super overprotective now, are you?'

'No,' Lucas lied.

'Good. Because I've found the Eye of Nineveh.'

Chapter 37

Even though his meeting had been cancelled, Nabil Hussein had been more than happy to hear Lucas say that the Acquirers would, not only, accept the job without hearing all the details, but also give him a ten per cent discount.

As they made their way to Ellen's place in Natasha's car, which David Evans had arranged to be delivered, she mulled over Lucas's business practice, and she wasn't too pleased about it. 'Jeez, Lucas. That guy's request could be for anything.'

'Could be.'

'You're very blasé about this.'

'Why not? It's Casablanca. You love Casablanca. I love Casablanca. What could go wrong?'

Natasha groaned. Something always went wrong.

'Anyway, enough about work. What kind of lunch gets you all dressed up.'

'I am not "all dressed up" thank you very much. You make it sound like I usually dress like a slob.'

'Well, no, but it's been a while since you've shown anything above your ankle. We're not in the Victorian age anymore, hon; this is the age of dresses barely covering butt cheeks,' he smirked.

'Up yours, Lucas.' Natasha had never explained to him how his affair had made her feel. Like he was no longer attracted to her, and it made her feel undesirable. Her self-confidence took a bit of a hit, and unconsciously she began to dress modestly.

She was intelligent enough to know that her own self-worth shouldn't be dependent or anyone else, but when that person was someone you loved, that rule was a little harder to follow.

'So, who did you have lunch with?'

'Peter.'

'Armitage? Really?'

'Something wrong?' She had seen his mood change.

'No, nothing at all. So how was it? Boring probably?'

'It was actually really good. He's a remarkably interesting man.'

'Hmmm, I bet.'

'It's a shame I had to cut things short, but he was kind enough to drop me off at the office.'

'I can drop you off here if you want to get back to him.'

'What is wrong with you? Aren't I allowed to move on like you? Am I supposed to be frozen in time, pining for someone that doesn't want me?'

'No, I'm not saying that.'

'Then what are you saying?'

'I'm saying that I was going to end things with Chiara, but she had to go to the office because Peter was unavailable.'

'Oh.' It was a bombshell that she hadn't seen coming, or how she was supposed to react to. 'Oh, I see.'

Luckily, the awkwardness didn't last long, as they were soon pulling up at Millennium Mills, and the respite of Ellen's big news.

'So, as you know, I was looking into X-Ray machines,'

'X-Ray machines?' Natasha looked at her cockeyed. 'What for?'

'Supply and demand,' came her curt reply, and quickly changed the subject before they could ask more questions. 'Anyway, whilst I was traipsing through the dark web, I came across a black-market bazaar happening tomorrow evening, in Teddington.'

'Okay, so what's the big deal? You planning on getting me a new car?'

'After what you did to my last present? You can forget that. No, the big deal is the feature auction.'

Ellen sent an image to the large OLED screen. Both Lucas and Natasha's eyes went wide when they saw the Eye of Nineveh sitting on a red cushion.

'They're not wasting anytime getting rid of it,' Lucas mused.

'Almost like they know what they have on their hands,' nodded Natasha. 'The question now is, how do we get it out of theirs and into ours?'

'It won't be easy,' Ellen revealed. 'This bazaar is no joke. The buy-in to attend is one million dollars alone.'

Lucas whistled. 'With that kind of money bandying about, you can bet that the security will be pretty tight around the place and the buyers will no doubt have their own armed bodyguards.' He thought for a moment as he tried to devise a plan, producing one and then rejecting it just as quickly. 'Do you think you can get the plans of where they're holding the sale?'

'Yeah, sure. It'll take a bit of time though.'

'What are you planning to do?' Natasha questioned.

'Steal it, tonight.'

'What? By yourself? What about the security you were going on about? And, besides that, we don't even know it's there yet.'

'She does have a point. I wouldn't store it there overnight.'

'Well, the only other thing I can think of is to call S7 and get them to raid the place ...'

'There you go! And you don't get put in danger.'

'... which will result in a massive shootout.'

'And I wouldn't advice that anyway,' Ellen added as she looked at some of the munitions and armoury that would be going on sale, some of which tempted to purchase herself.

It was frustrating that the Eye of Nineveh was in touching distance, but there was no viable way of retrieving it, as every plan was shut down, one by one. 'Well, why don't we just bloody walk through the front door and bloody take the damn thing then?' Natasha said.

Lucas rubbed his chin for a moment as he thought. 'Like Peru?'

'Like Peru.'

'Wait! What happened in Peru?' Ellen asked as she looked from one childlike grin to the other.

'Our honeymoon.'

'I'll tell you about it sometime, Ell, but right now, I need you to create a little cover-story for Natasha. Nothing too elaborate, it shouldn't need to stand up to anything strenuous, it's only if someone gets a little curious.'

'Okay. What if she's the slapper of a gunrunner that's recently died?'

Natasha wasn't sure if she had heard Ellen correctly, and said nothing.

'That could work,' Lucas nodded. 'She could have got a piece of his pie when he popped his clogs. You got anyone in mind?'

'Yeah, I do. I heard on the grapevine that Oleg Ivanov bought it a few weeks back, and that guy had plenty of slappers.'

Natasha folded her arms across her chest and tapped a foot. 'I heard that. I'm nobody's slapper.'

'Well, you are now, princess, to this guy.' Ellen pressed a few keys and an image of a short, bald, obese man appeared on the screen. Natasha balked at the sight of the larger-than-life picture. His skin was shiny, but she couldn't tell if it was sweat or grease dripping down his face.

'I'm not being arrogant or big-headed here, but there is no way that anyone is going to believe I was shacked up with this guy.'

'Oh really? Do you see those four women behind him?'

At Ellen's behest, Natasha had another look at the pic and nodded. 'Yeah, they're beautiful, like supermodels.'

'Yeah, those are his girlfriends, his flavours of the month.'

'Okay. People *are* going to believe I was shacked up with this guy.'

'If you look the part, that is. This Doris Day thing you got going on isn't going to cut it.'

'I've got stuff, don't worry about that.'

Satisfied everything was moving in the right direction, Lucas grabbed his phone and dialled the latest number added to his contact list, that of David Evans. He brought the director of Section 7 up to speed, telling him what they'd found out and what they planned to do, before going to say what he needed from the agency.

'Well, he wasn't overly excited about giving us free rein with their budget, but when I told him they wouldn't get a penny, and that it was all for show, he gave in. Just make sure the cash is safe, Ell.'

'Not a problem.'

'Good. In that case, we got the green light. Let's get this gem back.'

Chapter 38

The next day arrived and David Evans had insisted on being a part of the operation. Lucas nodded and gave him the role of driver. The director's excuse was that he wanted to make sure that the operation went smoothly. But Lucas had a niggling feeling that the idea of letting people with not so wholesome backgrounds, such as himself and Ellen, loose in a criminal's playground, with governments funds, no less, gave him a sleepless night.

'Look, if it would make you feel better, we'll make Nat the only one that'll have access to funds,' Lucas said to David as they stood next to a wine-red Mercedes Maybach S-Class.

'Quite frankly, yes, it would. But you know as well as I do, that these people are going to want to see evidence of her funds and the million-dollar entry fee from an account that your friend, who has no issues with working for anybody from dictators to arms-dealers ...'

'To the British and American governments. Let's not get it twisted, you people have been getting into bed with unsavoury types, long before Ellen.'

'But we were doing it out of loyalty to our respective countries. Where does her loyalty lie? With herself?'

'I vouch for her loyalty.'

'And who vouches for yours?'

'Natasha.'

'The woman you cheated on?'

He knew the stigma would follow him. Like a stain on your shirt, you can never get out, no matter how many times you washed it. Even when it became faint and hard for people to see, you know it's still there. It's something you have to live with.

It didn't mean he had to like it when people whose opinion didn't matter decided to voice that opinion.

'Look, David, just remember that it was you that came to us. We didn't seek out your little clandestine department. I'd happily call Natasha and tell her that the op is off, then go find Jake Russell and sit through his evidence. If you want the eye of Nineveh, you need us, or else there'd be more agents here than just yourself.'

'Alright, alright! It's just that it's a lot of money. If it goes missing, I'd have a hard time explaining it all.'

Lucas was exasperated and slapped his hand to his head. 'You do know that Ellen is pretty rich, right? Bitcoin is her bitch. Who's car do you think this is, anyway? And she doesn't even have a license. You wait here, I'm going to go see what's keeping Nat.'

He had taken just two steps when he saw the vision that was Natasha walk out of Ivory House. 'Fucking hell,' Lucas breathed.

As Natasha walked over the bridge, his eyes devoured her from head to toe. Although it was all one piece, from the front, the top half of the sand-coloured dress, gave the impression that it was merely a strip of fabric used as a crisscrossed halter-neck, which covered her breasts, went behind her back, wrapped around her waist and was secured at the side. The bottom half was a maxi-dress that had a high split up the left leg, all the way to the waist where it was fastened. Open-toed, heeled sandals and a matching clutch completed the outfit.

'How do I look?' Natasha asked as she sashayed past an open-mouthed Lucas.

'Yeah ... you look ... Yeah.' He was completely flustered.

'You know, if you're supposed to be playing my bodyguard, Lucas, I don't think it's appropriate that you should be looking at your employer like that,' she said with a mischievous grin.

'Unfortunately, your bodyguard isn't a eunuch,' came his response as he held the car-door open for her enter gracefully.

Once they were all inside, David started the car and set off. Lucas opened the glove compartment and took out a box of earwigs from Ellen, which he handed out. 'How's the signal, Ell?'

'Perfect! I've wired the fee to the bazaar, and they sent the address. I've forwarded on to you Lucas. They also sent a unique code that you must show at the entry.'

'Got it,' he replied and entered it into the car's satnav. 'What about blueprints?'

'Still searching, should hopefully have something by the time you arrive there.'

'Will you be able to keep track of the funds?' David asked.

'Your money is safe, if you want, I could digitally redirect all their money ...'

'That won't be necessary.'

'Okay, just saying. I've finished Natasha's cover, too. Your name will be Natasha Anyabaek.'

'Natasha On-your-back? You are joking, right?'

'It's Anya. An-ya. I thought I'd keep it simple because of your limited brain cells.'

'Yet you're the one without any qualifications.'

'I don't need a piece of paper to tell me I'm the smartest person in the room.'

'Chill out, you two,' Lucas demanded. 'Right, let's go over the plan for what it's worth. David?'

'I'll be outside keeping an eye out on the perimeter, unless things go south, then I'm the cavalry.'

'Good. Nat?'

'Once I'm in, I play the diversion, buy big, flirt a bit, and create an opening for you.'

'Excellent! When I see my chance, I'll slip behind the scenes and hopefully find what we're looking for, then I'll find you, hand it off and you head for the exit. Job done.'

They travelled the rest of the way in relative silence as they all prepared their thoughts and steeled themselves for the coming events. Several times, Natasha caught Lucas looking at her in the rear-view mirror, eyeing her legs – one of her best features – as she crossed them.

• • • •

THE LOCATION OF THE black-market bazaar was nothing but extraordinary. It had the appearance of a little Gothic castle complete with pinnacles, battlements and a round tower. The white clad masonry was quite a sight to behold as they drove up the horseshoe driveway. As were all the super, hyper and luxury cars ahead of them.

'You ready for this, Nat?'

'Of course. Are you?'

'Always.'

'Just in case anyone is wondering, I'm ready too,' Ellen said in their ears. 'And I've got the plans. There's quite a large storage space in the basement, so it might be worth starting your search down there when you get the chance.'

'Got it.'

The entry process was a slow one as each buyer had to show that they had the funds to be partake in this exclusive club. Eventually, it was Lucas and Natasha's turn. He stepped out and opened the door for her to exit, which she did just as elegantly as she had entered it. Once the door was closed, David drove off to find his parking spot.

A man dressed in a black suit with matching shirt and tie stood at the podium, waiting patiently. 'Your code?' Lucas reeled it off without looking at the text. 'Ms ...'

'Anyabaek,' Natasha completed with an impressive Russian accent. 'My dear Oleg's favourite. I'll save you from butchering my name so that I don't have Luka here butcher you, eh?'

Lucas met the man's gaze, and with just as an impressive accent but with a lot more menace, questioned the doorman. 'Do we have a problem? Have you never met a Black Russian before?'

'No, no problems here. Everything seems to be in order. I hope you enjoy your bidding, Ms Anyabaek,' he said and offered her a bidding number, which she ignored before striding off, leaving it for Lucas to take.

'We're in,' Lucas whispered, giving Ellen and David the progress report.

The stunning Georgian gothic architecture of the exterior continued inside; large stained-glass windows, pointed arches, ribbed vaults, flying buttresses, and ornate decoration were everywhere. The gilded vaulting of the ceiling in the Grand Hall reminded Natasha of the vaulting in Henry VII chapel in Westminster Abbey. If only the occasion could match the surroundings.

'This place is amazing, Lucas.'

'Yes it is,' he agreed as he took a couple drinks off of a passing waiter's tray and gave one to Natasha.

'As my bodyguard, are you supposed to be drinking?' She downed hers to calm her nerves, then swapped her empty glass for his. 'How long do you think it'll be before things get started?'

'I'm not sure, but it's getting pretty tight in here. I'm going to have a quick walk around. Don't go anywhere.'

'*You* don't be too long.' She watched him disappear into the throng and sipped her champagne, trying her best not to look nervous.

'You look nervous, chérie,' a man with a French accent and slim moustache approached her. 'Perhaps I can help to calm those nerves a bit. My name is Alain Mercier, art dealer.'

'Natasha Anyabaek.'

'Here, have some of this,' he took a hip flask from his pocket and poured a green liquid into his glass, before offering to do the same to Natasha's.

'No, thank you. Absinthe does not agree with me.'

'That's the point of it, chérie,' he smiled and took a mouthful. 'So, what brings you to this little soirée?'

'What everyone is here for, I suspect. The Eye of Nineveh.'

'Really? Do not tell me you believe all of this nonsense the seller has posted about it? Having mystical powers and such.'

'I take it you do not? If everyone here is like you, then I may just get it cheaply.'

'You would do better to put that money in art, like me. Rembrandt's The Storm on the Sea of Galilee painting will be on sale here,' Alain revealed gleefully. 'They will be taking us downstairs at any moment for a preview of the lots soon.'

'What do you know of the seller?'

'Absolutely nothing, chérie, but I have heard that it is none other than Sebastian Jericho.'

'Really?'

'Judging by some of the items on sale, I could well believe it. We might even see the man himself.'

She smirked. 'You never know.'

Suddenly, gasps of astonishment moved through the crowd. They wondered what the cause of it could be. Alain speculated it might be their host. As they craned their heads, Natasha found out that it was something much worse.

Oleg Ivanov was alive and well.

Chapter 39

Natasha didn't know what to do. Things were turning out to be a little bit too much like Peru for her liking.

'Is something the matter?' Alain asked, seeing her look around in all directions.

'I am looking for my bodyguard,' she responded.

'Don't worry about him, I will more than happily guard your body, chérie.'

She gave him a thin smile and wondered what it was about the criminal underworld that made all the men seem a bit sleazy. 'Neh, neh. He is paid to attend to me. Let him earn his wage.'

Natasha was surprised that she hadn't heard any communication from the others and only now realised that her earwig wasn't working or had some fault. She got even more agitated when she saw the doorman talking to men who Natasha assumed were security. He seemed to be giving them a detailed briefing and directing them around the hall, no doubt looking for her.

Where the hell are you, Lucas? Natasha thought to herself. Then, almost as if he heard her, Lucas crept up beside her and announced his presence by tickling her hand. She spun around and hit him in the chest.

'Where—' Natasha began, then remembered to apply her Russian accent. 'Where have you been?'

'Sorry ma'am, I've had some technical issues.'

'Really? You will have to tell me more and I have news of my own. If you would excuse me, Alain.'

'Of course, chérie. I will come and find you when the auction starts.'

'Oh, you do not have to.'

'But I insist.'

'Of course you do,' she replied and gave him the thin smile again before walking off with Lucas.

'Quid est quod de?' Lucas asked in Latin. He didn't want their conversation being understood, as he indicated to Alain.

'Nothing at all. Forget about that,' Natasha answered in the same language. 'Where have you been?'

'I've been trying to get a look around, but I couldn't get too far. Both the downstairs and the upstairs were blocked off by guards. I'll have to find another way.'

'Apparently, the Lots are downstairs, and we'll be taken to see them before the auction begins.'

'This is good! If everybody is going to be down in the basement, it'll be the perfect time for me to try and check upstairs and you can check down; hopefully one of us will strike it lucky.'

'Got it! But my earwig isn't working.'

'Neither is mine. They must have some sort of frequency jammer. I guess they don't trust their clients.'

'I was starting to think that, when no one responded about Oleg Ivanov.'

'What about him?'

'He's here!'

Lucas was quiet as he thought for a moment. 'Okay, that's not a problem.'

'I'm supposed to be one of his girlfriends!'

'And we'll just keep you out of his way then.'

'Easier said than done.'

He reached out and squeezed her hand. 'Don't worry about it.'

But Natasha *was* worried. Worried that the greasy man with the overdeveloped appetites for food and women would get his hands on her. Just the thought of it made her spine shiver.

• • • •

THE POTENTIAL BUYERS were directed downstairs to preview the goods on offer, but Lucas held back a moment, and watched Natasha meld into the crowd as they were led away.

As waiters cleaned up, three of the black-suited security guards remained at the foot of the stairs leading to the upper floors. Two of them eyed him suspiciously. They were expecting everyone to be downstairs, including bodyguards.

'Shouldn't you be with your employer?' one of them said, the bulge of a firearm evident under his jacket.

'And I will be,' Lucas replied, reverting to a Russian accent. 'She has very particular eating habits. She wanted me to inspect the menu and make sure that it is up to her standard. If not, she will not be happy, and I will get blame. Ever since she get money she treat me like dog!'

'I'd bark at her feet anytime,' one joked.

'I'd even let her scratch my tummy,' another added.

'Maybe I will elevate myself and make her the dog, yes?' They all laughed. 'Now, which way to the kitchen?'

Exactly as he was told, Lucas walked down the hall, took a left, and followed the scent of delicious smelling food. The kitchen was a hive of activity, much more animated than things had been out front. The head chef walked around, tasting this and that, barking out orders like a kitchen dictator.

Nobody said anything to Lucas as he passed through, even after snatching up a few of the hors d'oeuvres left over from earlier. It was a welcome respite from his growing hunger, and wished he could have gone back for more, but he had found an exit of the gothic manor, and if he couldn't get upstairs from inside, then he'd have to get up there from outside.

. . . .

NATASHA HADN'T SEEN such an array of weapons before. In her opinion, a military base would have been hard pushed to beat this collection. And then, she wasn't sure if they had the kind of gadgetry on display; this would have been right up Ellen's Street.

It wasn't only weapons and armaments that was being shown off, just as Alain Mercier had said, Rembrandt's one and only seascape painting was there, and the art dealer stood in front of it transfixed, muttering to himself, in French, saying he couldn't believe that it was the real thing.

There was a general murmuring filling the basement, as one Lot after the other brought sounds of astonishment from the viewers. It was soon Natasha's turn to ooh and ahh when she saw two Romanov Fabergé eggs and a diamond, emerald and ruby brooch said to be the Diamond Star of the

Grand Master of the Order of St Patrick, stolen from Dublin castle in 1907. They were all wonderful pieces. Pieces that shouldn't be here if Natasha were being honest. But no sign of the Eye of Nineveh.

Something did catch her eye, though. A gold mechanical model of the solar system. An Orrery. Also known as a Planetarium, it demonstrated the motions of the moon and planets around the Sun. The fact that it only had six planetary arms, and one for the Earth's satellite, gave Natasha a hint of its age, pre 1781, the year Uranus was discovered.

The workmanship of the mechanism was exquisite, in particular the engraving on the planets. She looked at the third one orbiting the Sun, and as she expected, it said Earth. Out of the corner of her eye, Natasha caught a glimpse of the fourth sphere, but instead of Mars, it said Nergal.

She was perplexed and looked at Mercury, which read Nabu, then Venus, which was labelled Ishtar, Jupiter read Marduk and Saturn, Ninurta. 'These are all Mesopotamian deities,' Natasha whispered. 'Weird that they'd be on something like this.'

Natasha took one last longing look at the gold machine and was just moving on when she Alain Mercier ahead of her. Not wanting to endure the Frenchman's lasciviousness again, she turned around with a mind to avoid him, but in doing so, walked right into another problem.

'Ah, we meet at last, but according to what I have been told, we already know each other. Perhaps you'd like to reacquaint yourself with me?' Oleg Ivanov, face shiny with oily-sweat, grinned broadly.

• • • •

AS SOON AS LUCAS STEPPED outside, he could hear Ellen and David chattering over the earwig. 'It's actually good to hear your voices again,' he said with some relief as he scouted around the back of the manor, searching for a potential entry point.

'There you are! What the hell happened?' Ellen screamed in Lucas's ear.

'Our host must not trust anybody. They must have installed a jammer somewhere inside.'

'Have you found the eye?' David asked.

'No, not yet. Natasha is in the basement checking, and I'm about to check upstairs.'

'You should know that I think I saw someone that looked a lot like Oleg arrive.'

'Natasha said the same thing.'

'It's him alright,' Ellen confirmed. 'When David told me what he saw, I dug a little deeper and found no hard evidence of his death, just a dodgy death certificate that his doctor was probably paid to write. It's not the first time sometimes faked their death. Apparently, it was a ruse to flush someone out. I don't know if he got the person or not, but there was no way he was going to miss an event on this magnitude.'

Lucas knew that for sure. 'Well, as long as Nat stays out of his way, things will be okay.'

'I hope so. He's a bit of a sadistic bastard.'

'Right, I've found a way up, I'm going back in,' he suddenly had the urge to get things over and done with as soon as possible and get Natasha out of there.

'So, what are we supposed to do when comes go dark again?'

'I don't know, Ellen, talk amongst yourselves, get to know each other.'

'He's not the cheeriest of fellas, you know.'

'You know I can hear you, right?' David responded.

'You know I don't care, right?'

Lucas sighed. 'Play nice, Ellen.' Using one of the drainage pipes fixed in a corner around the back, he began to scale the wall. It was an easy, straightforward climb for someone of his capabilities, and in no time, he had reached the top and was climbing over the battlements.

· · · ·

NATASHA WAS SHAKEN by the sudden appearance of the man, like a deer in headlights. 'Well ... I ... uh ... I didn't see any harm in a little name dropping,' Natasha finally said in Russian. 'I thought that being a woman in this environment, saying that I was associated with you, would open more doors for me.' The words made her skin crawl, but she'd learnt from Lucas's actions in many situations that the ends justify the means. These were just words she was telling him, words with no meaning, just to stroke his ego. If they got her out of the sticky situation, she'd tell him anything he wanted to hear. And then have several showers later.

'Well, being the premier guns smuggler, I'm not surprised. But you didn't ask me, so when I turn up here to be told that one of my women is here, I end up looking the fool. You didn't show me the proper respect.'

'I can only apologise.'

'Oh no, you can do so much more than that, milaya.' Coming out of his mouth, the term of endearment had an ominous menace behind it.

Chapter 40

Lucas was in his element; sneaking around, staying close to the walls, sticking to the shadows, moving around silently. Skills he had learnt as a thief and perfected in the special forces were never more useful than now.

He had climbed through the first unlocked window he found and had searched every room on the top floor. It wasn't easy. There was a veritable army of black suited security for Lucas to avoid. But he was doing just that. There were a few times, when he was hiding in alcoves or on a corner, hearing the footsteps of a guard getting closer, he would cock his fist back, ready to knock them out if they got into range, but at the last minute they would turn around or change direction, and Lucas would slip away.

Slowly working his way down, passing rooms with four-poster beds, Lucas eventually came upon the impressive library, located in the centre of the manor. It had been set up with rows of seats and a podium, an ideal location for an auction. The bookshelves and the two doors at the end of each wall of books had the pointed arch associated with gothic architecture.

He listened to the one on the right and heard muffled voices. Through the keyhole, Lucas could indeed see more guards and lots for the auction. He checked the other door. Hearing nobody or seeing anybody through the hole, he gently opened it. It was a spacious office, with more books and a marble topped desk, on top of which was a red velvet cloth. He lifted it up, and there it was, the Eye of Nineveh, sitting on the red cushion, exactly as shown in the picture. Lucas quickly pocketed his prize.

Laid out next to gem were an assortment of other papers and a photo. He looked at the photograph. It was of the stone slab, covered in cuneiform, he and Natasha had seen back in the temple of Sammu. Next, Lucas read the sheet of paper and soon realised it was the phonetic translation of the prayers; he remembered the sounds when Natasha had read it, when they first encountered The Baron. 'Not only are these bastards selling a nuke, they're giving them the instruction manual too!'

• • • •

NATASHA SMILED AS BRIGHTLY as she could, maintaining her mask, even though inside she wanted to scream. 'I don't know what you mean.'

'Of course you do,' Oleg replied. 'You told people you were one of my women, a lie, but now I will make you one of them. Then it will no longer be a lie. You have an exotic look and as you can see, I do not have a Black woman among my entourage of ladies.'

'I'm not just Black, I'm Latino too; I embrace both sides of my heritage.'

'Really? Well, milaya, soon you will embrace some Russian as well.' Oleg grabbed Natasha's wrist and twisted her arm behind her back, then he whispered into her ear. 'You know the best thing about getting a new woman? It's breaking them in. Like having a disobedient dog; you just have to keep beating them, and beating them, until they cower at the sight of a raised hand. I can see it in your eyes, you're going to take a lot to break in.' He licked his lips at the prospect.

Suddenly, the man that had checked them announced that the auction was ready to begin and gathered then everybody before leading them out of the basement, and then up to the first floor.

Slipping the translation into a pocket, Lucas stepped out of the office and headed for the exit of the library. He came to a sudden stop. People were making their way upstairs. He tried the window behind the podium, but he couldn't open it. He tried the one in the office, that one wouldn't budge either.

He was trapped.

Lucas paced back and forth. There was nowhere to hide in the library or the office. But he could smash the window and get out via the ledge, even if it might alert the guards to his presence. He was about to pick up a chair when he thought he heard a faint repeated tapping. He stood stock still, held his breath. There it was again. 'Morse code?' It sounded like it was coming from behind the fireplace.

He desperately searched around for the mechanism that would open the hidden door. Time was running out. He could hear people taking their seats next door in the library. Throwing the chair through the window and taking his chances was looking like a very viable option, with every passing second.

Then he noticed something about one of the bronze candlesticks on the fireplace. A part of it was shiny. It reminded him of when he and Natasha were in Milan, at The Duomo. On its huge bronze doors one of the panels on the left, which depicted the last time Mary held the hand of her son, Jesus, before he was crucified. Visitors that have lost a loved one often rub the hands in memory of the ones they have lost. And as such, it had become shiny over time. The candlestick had likewise been handled.

Lucas took hold of it and pulled it towards him like a barkeep pulling a pint of Guinness. There was a click and the catch holding the bookshelves on the right, released. He quickly opened the secret passage and closed it behind him.

The knocking was louder now, definitely morse code, an SOS. Lucas carefully crept down the spiral staircase. Then he heard the familiar voice of Kallum Taylor.

'You can bang all you want, you old fool. No one here will come running to your rescue, Marcus. They're too busy outbidding each other on my hard gained prizes.'

'You don't know what powers you're messing with. The Eye of Nineveh is not some simple trinket.'

'Powers? You really are senile, aren't you? But I don't care. The more people believe it, the more money I'll make; it's a fabulous selling point. I mean, you couldn't make up this kind of provenance. Now, I need to go and make sure all my overseas buyers are ready. The Chinese in particularly want to be sure that we're working on a secure network.'

Lucas waited a few seconds as he heard Kallum leave, then he came down to the cell himself. 'Professor Marcus Masterson?' It was evident that the old man had been roughed up quite a bit.

'Yes, that's me. Wait, is that you, Lucas?'

'Yeah, it is. We've been looking all over the place for you.'

'And Natasha?'

'She's upstairs, at the auction. David is here too. I've got the eye. I just need to find a way to get you out of here, then I can go back for her.'

'You must get the stone out of here. They forced me to translate the prayer to activate the power within it.'

'Do you mean these?' Lucas showed the professor the paper and photo.

'Yes, excellent. You must destroy them.'

Lucas did what he was told, taking a lighter out of his pocket and setting them on fire.

'Good,' the professor smiled. 'With the original tablet split in two, plus separated and now my translation gone, only two people have a chance of activating the Eye of Nineveh, myself and Natasha.'

Lucas shot the professor a look. 'You've just put a target on her back.'

'I warned her not to get involved.'

'She was involved the moment you double crossed The Baron. What made you get into bed with terrorists?'

'He came to me, not knowing about my ties to Section 7. I went to David and the agency devised a plan to give The Baron a fake. It was working until he was tipped off.'

'David mentioned something about that. Any idea who it is?'

'No, but it's definitely someone connected with S7.'

'How can you be so sure?'

'The Baron's phone was on the desk when he got the call about the fake. I saw the area code before he snatched it up; 0207 009. It came straight from Section 7.'

Suddenly, there was a noise from the top of the stairs. The hidden door was opened, and a couple of guards sniffed the air. Lucas could hear them discussing the possibility of a fire and finally deciding to investigate.

'Shit! I've got to go,' whispered Lucas. 'But once I've got Natasha, we'll come back for you.'

'Forget about us, just get the gem to safety.'

Lucas gave the professor a stern look before heading off down the stairs. There was no way he was leaving here without Natasha.

• • • •

THE AUCTION PROGRESSED at a healthy pace, with Alain Mercier missing out on the Rembrandt to someone representing an oil sheik but picking up other pieces he had his eye on. Natasha had her eyes closed most of the time and tried with all the strength of her will to ignore Oleg Ivanov's hand as it slid higher and higher up the inside of her thigh.

She couldn't do it. Natasha shot up out of her seat, which brought a round of guffaws from the attendees.

'Miss, there is no need to stand up to lodge your bid,' the auctioneer stated. 'A raised number will suffice.'

As Natasha sat back down, she heard someone from the back mock Oleg about not being able to control his woman. This brought a grimace to his face, which was purely for her benefit.

'Well ...?' the auctioneer urged.

'Oh, sorry.' She was about to decline her bid when she realised two things. First, the Lot on offer at the moment was the Orrery she had admired and second, winners of a

Lot were taken into a side room on the right, no doubt to go through the final purchasing details. But maybe there was another way out of the room without coming back into the library. It was worth a try, even if it wasn't her money, and held up her number.

Natasha couldn't see who she was bidding against, as they were seated somewhere in the back. There had been others, but it eventually came down to just the two of them. And whoever they were, they weren't ready to match Natasha's winning bid of five hundred and seventeen thousand pounds.

She stood up triumphantly, Oleg's slimy hand slipping off her thigh. Natasha didn't turn back as she walked confidently to the room, where arrangements were made for the Orrery to be brought to her car.

'Thank you very much, Ms Anyabaek,' the financier said once the transaction was complete. 'I'll have someone bring you purchase to you driver immediately. You may return to the auction.'

'If you do not mind, I would much prefer to go down with your employee. My driver can be somewhat clumsy.'

'As you wish.' The golden mechanism was packaged into a glass case, and boxed up securely, before being loaded onto a six-wheeled hand trolley.

She couldn't help smiling as they set off. The sense of relief enveloped her as they turned a corridor, bypassing the library altogether. Her joy was short lived however, as before they could reach the stairs down, Oleg and his entourage of women blocked their route.

'Leaving so soon, Natasha? The night is still young, and we have so much things to do.' He let the worker pass but grabbed Natasha when she tried to slip by too. 'Not you, milaya.' He dragged her to room, but discovering that it was just a lounge, he tried another and found what he was after, a bedroom.

Oleg threw her down on the four-poster bed as his four women followed him in and closed the door behind them. 'Now, how should I begin your treatment?' He slowly took a short length of rubber hose from his jacket pocket.

• • • •

LUCAS CRACKED OPEN the second door to the secret passage and found that he was back on the ground floor, in one of the halls of the gothic manor. Part one of his mission was complete, retrieve the Eye of Nineveh. Now he had to find Natasha and escape.

He stepped out into the hall and walked with an air of confidence, since he was meant to be there. If anyone did happen to stop and question him, Lucas knew those guards at the stairs could vouch for him since they had sent him to kitchen. He came to an area he recognised. To the right was the kitchen, so he headed left towards the foyer and a staircase up.

As he neared the hall where everybody had entered and, on arrival, had their first drinks of the night, Lucas heard four controlled, muffled explosions, followed by the sounds of suppressed gunfire and the clinking of empty bullet shells falling on the hardwood floor.

Lucas flattened himself against the wall, as he heard several footsteps pounding their way upstairs. He chanced a quick glance and cursed his luck; it was The Baron's terrorist organisation. Seconds later, the first shots from the library rang out.

• • • •

AS NATASHA LOOKED AT the four women, all their will to defy beaten out of them, she feared what was to come as Oleg stood there, licking his lips, with a crazed look on his face.

He slapped the rubber hose into the palm of his hand over and over, not taking his eyes off her for a second. 'Take off your underwear.'

'What?' She hoped that she had been wrong in her hearing, but she hadn't.

'I said, take off your underwear.' He grinned. 'Personally, I prefer it when they refuse, because it's so much sweeter when I rip them off.'

Not wanting to give him anymore pleasure than he was already gleaning, Natasha did what she was told, despite every fibre in her body telling her to resist. But in her head, Natasha knew that was exactly what he wanted. He was a sadist, pure and simple, and she could tell that humiliation was barely the tipping point of what he wanted.

'Give them to me,' he said and held out his hand.

She held them out at arm's length, not wanting to get any closer to him than necessary. 'I hope you choke on them,' Natasha snarled.

Oleg snatched them from her, laughing. 'Don't worry, I will give you something for you to choke on.' He leant his head back and draped the underwear across his face. She felt violated and embarrassed when she heard him taking deep breaths and moaning.

Then they all heard gunshots.

Before she knew what she was doing, Natasha had taken that moment of confusion, and charged at Oleg and kneed him in the groin. He took a sharp intake of breath, which wasn't a lot, as he had sucked the underwear into his mouth.

Natasha pounced on him, forcing the rest of the obstructing item into his mouth. Some of it was caught between his teeth as she covered his mouth and nose. He fought ferociously, landing blows on her stomach and ribs, but she held on until he lost his balance, and Natasha fell on top of him.

The four women of Oleg's entourage woke up from their cowed state, finally seeing a chance to free themselves from their tormentor. Each of them held down one of his limbs, as he looked on with wide eyes, shocked that they would turn against him.

Eventually, with his oesophagus blocked, Oleg Ivanov twitched a few times as life left his body, then he was still. The death certificate wouldn't be faked this time.

Chapter 41

Natasha opened the door slightly, and she likened what she saw to a war zone. The black-suited security and the bodyguards of the black-market buyers were in a firefight with hooded assailants who Natasha recognised all too well as J Organisation.

She couldn't stay there, she had to get out. Natasha glanced back at the four kept women of the recently deceased Oleg, hugged each other, tears streaming down their faces as they came to terms with being free once more. Right now, they were in no state to leave. Natasha closed the door behind her as she made a break for it.

It was a stop start motion, bullets striking the walls around her forcing Natasha to halt and duck before sprinting again. Bodies dropped everywhere as she ran with her hands over her ears, desperately trying to block out the constant sound of gunfire ringing in her head.

She was approaching the staircase, when suddenly, one of the auction buyers was riddled with bullets, the force of which pushed them into Natasha and she toppled over the banister, along with the man who clung to her, as she hung on for dear life.

Her screams of distress alerted Lucas, who was slowly making his way up, dispatching all in his way. When he heard Natasha and saw the situation she was in, he swiftly changed his focus.

Natasha's grip was slipping with the extra weight of the man. Even after Lucas fired two shots into him, and he finally let go, her arms were too fatigued to get a firmer grip. One arm released. Lucas sprinted down the stairs but seeing he wouldn't make it in time, he jumped over the side of the railing, cutting out vital seconds, the seconds he needed to slide under Natasha and catch her as she plummeted, finally losing the strength to hold on any longer.

They embraced longer than they should have, given the situation, as the gunfight had spilled out throughout the manor. Neither of them cared at that moment. The passion they had for one another was beginning to boil over. Their heads moved closer; they could feel each other's hot breath on one another's lips.

Then something happened which turned the heat down to a simmer. Lucas saw a terrorist behind Natasha, creeping towards them, and emptied his clip before in the assailant before he knew what hit him.

Lucas could see that Natasha was shaken by the chaotic scene, and now his priority was to get her to safety. 'It's time to go, Nat. Here, take this,' he said, giving her the Eye of Nineveh, and replacing his empty clip. 'Head for the exit and I'll give you cover.' She nodded, but he could see the concern in her eyes. 'Don't worry, Nat, I'll be right behind you. Now get moving.' As he said it, he let off shots at oncoming terrorists.

Natasha clutched the gem tight and ran towards the half blown off doors, dodging and ducking as she heard the zigging of bullets. Off to the side, she suddenly saw the familiar figure of her tutor, being led towards another door by Kallum Taylor and one of the black-suited security. 'Professor Marcus! Professor!'

Marcus turned and saw his former student running towards him. 'No, Natasha. You must get out of here!'

Lucas turned and saw Natasha heading the wrong way. He called after her, but she was already out of earshot, or she simply ignored him, hoping to rescue her old tutor. 'Damn it,' Lucas cursed and was about to give chase when a figure staggered through the door. David Evans collapsed into Lucas.

'I'm sorry,' he strained to say, 'he got the drop on me.'

Lucas laid him down and inspected the wounds. David had been shot twice, once in the side of his stomach and once in his shoulder. 'Who are you talking about?' Lucas did his best to try and stem the flow of blood, then he felt the blow of a gun butt on the back of his head.

'That would be me, Mr Redmond,' The Baron said as he dragged the dazed Lucas after the escaping Natasha.

• • • •

IF THE CHAOS WITHIN the gothic manor was like the shootout at the Okay Corral, the tableau in the rear courtyard was more akin to a Mexican standoff. Kallum Taylor stood behind his henchman, who used Professor Marcus Masterson as a human shield. The Baron hid behind Lucas whilst holding a gun to his head. Natasha stood in the middle, looking from one to the other.

'Miss Travers,' The Baron called out from behind Lucas. 'It is time to conclude our business. I released your parents for the gemstone, now it is time to fulfil your end of the bargain.'

'The eye is mine now, Natasha,' Kallum said. 'Give it back! His men had it, but the merchandise was too hot for them to handle. His goons had it, and that completed your transaction; you don't owe him anything.'

Natasha looked at all the people involved, struggled with the dilemma of what to do, who to choose, knowing that whoever she didn't choose would more than likely be shot. It would just have to be another decision she would need to learn to live with, as despite everything, she slowly leaned towards Lucas.

Then a gun was fired, and Lucas fell to the ground.

Natasha screamed and ducked down.

The Baron's gun blasted in the floodlit darkness. Two shots hit Marcus in the chest, and he dropped to the ground. The terrorist leader rolled to the side, avoiding the retaliatory fire, then fired three more times, ending the life of the henchman.

Slippery Kallum had made his escape the moment his guard had squeezed his trigger. The Baron let off a speculative round after him, just to make sure he didn't change his mind and decide to come back.

'It's time to go, Miss Travers.'

'No! Lucas!' Natasha wriggled in his grasp until she felt the hot barrel of his just fired gun pressed against her abdomen.'

'I don't want to, but I will if I have to, Miss Travers.'

Natasha could see in his eyes that he was deadly serious. She relented and let him take her. A time would come when she might have a better chance of escape. She needed to be patient and ready for it.

They walked through the tree line of the manor grounds, where a helicopter waited. The pilot stood by, smoking a cigarette, until he saw his boss coming with a woman in tow. He immediately threw away the smouldering butt, jumped in the cockpit, and started the engine.

The whirring of the blades picked up as they rotated faster and faster. The Baron pushed Natasha into the helicopter and fastened her in before taking a seat himself. Then they began to take-off. He smiled as he admired the Eye of Nineveh, his at long last. The first step to bringing about a New World Order had been taken.

As the helicopter rose above the trees, Natasha looked back at Lucas's body in the distance, unable to hold back the tears. Then he moved, slowly at first, with a struggle, but he eventually got to his feet. 'Lucas!'

The Baron looked back in astonishment, but he had little to worry about. Victory was within his grasp.

Lucas watched the helicopter gain altitude. He'd seen both Natasha, and The Baron seated in the back. But this wasn't finished yet. He looked at the shoulder he'd been shot in. There wasn't much pain, just a numbness, courtesy of the adrenaline pumping through his veins. 'Natasha! Can you hear me?' He hadn't noticed that his earwig had dropped out until now. He was on his own, no backup, no tactical, just him, alone. Lucas smiled. 'If that's how the universe wants this to play out, then let's play!'

• • • •

THE FIRST CAR HE FOUND with a set of keys still inside were those in a Fiat 695 Abarth; not the first car he would have picked, but the 140mph would more than do right now. He slammed his foot down on the accelerator and gave chase, following the flashing lights of the helicopter.

Lucas swerved in and out of traffic, doing his best to keep an eye on the road and the direction of the helicopter. It was a difficult task; they could go in a straight line, whereas he oftentimes lost sight of them as he was forced to follow the roads. When he wasn't having to taken necessary route detours, it was having to avoid traffic. On more than one occasion, he was glad he had the small but big punch Fiat to slip through gaps in between cars that larger vehicles wouldn't have been able to.

Sooner than he'd realised, Lucas arrived at the ExCeL centre at Royal Victoria Docks in east London. The helicopter had continued to pull away from him and was already making its descent. Lucas knew it must be landing at London City Airport, which was along the southern edge of the Thames. If The Baron had a waiting private jet there, then he'd be in big trouble. The chances of getting across the bridge in time would be slim, but there was no way he'd pull out of the chase now.

He skidded around the corner of the huge exhibition centre, hitting the backend of the car, forcing him to put it in opposite lock to maintain control. He tore through a hotel car park and saw something that both bolstered his resolve, but at the same time made his heart sink. The Baron had disembarked the helicopter and, with Natasha in tow, climbed aboard a speedboat to cross the Thames towards a yacht named The Rites of Spring.

As soon as the passengers had left the speedboat and were safely onboard, the yacht's engines were fired up. Luckily for Lucas, there was a speed restriction along this part of the Thames, but he was able to floor the accelerator, smash through the fence and along the dock. He skidded to a halt, leaving long tire marks on the tarmac, and vaulted over the barrier onto the pontoon. He sprinted for all he was worth. The only thing on his mind was saving Natasha, at all costs, no matter the consequences.

He leapt and caught hold of the impressive yacht. Lucas was about to climb aboard when he heard two men talking close to the railing. They eventually finished shooting the breeze and returned to their sentry duties.

Lucas pulled himself up and followed the terrorist that was heading to the starboard side. The former Special Forces soldier came up behind him and despatched the armed guard quickly, breaking his neck, before arming himself with the dead man's weapons, a HK MP5 and a Glock 19.

He returned to the port side and crept up behind the other sentry, getting rid of him in the same manner, collecting more ammo and a knife and then heading down into the luxury yacht.

With the knife in hand, Lucas slowly walked, looking for Natasha. Another one of The Baron's men was coming, and he got a knife in the heart for his troubles. Unfortunately, Lucas was unaware of the other terrorist, further down the galley, who opened fire.

No longer having the advantage of stealth on his side, Lucas turned to his acquired machine gun, ripping through the bodies of three more terrorists before he felt a bullet go through his thigh.

'You have been quite the opponent, Mr Redmond,' The Baron gloated, 'but this is where your adventure comes to a shuddering end. No rewrites, no sequels, no do-overs. Just the end." He aimed his gun at Lucas and prepared to fire. 'Goodbye, Mr Redmond.'

Natasha, using all of her strength, hit The Baron's arm with a fire extinguisher. His shot missed wildly, giving Lucas precious time to hobble away. The terrorist leader fired again. Unable to aim properly with his damaged arm, he only grazed Lucas as he rounded the corner.

Angry at her interference, The Baron aimed at Natasha and pulled the trigger, but the gun was empty. Even more frustrated now, he grabbed her head and slammed it into the wall, knocking her out cold.

Once he had made it back topside, Lucas had gone to draw the Glock, but it wasn't there. He ready himself to face The Baron and end things once and for all. He had made promises. Promises that he intended to keep. This man had to pay for the innocent lives he had taken and had to be stopped before he could take anymore.

Lucas tried to focus. He was losing it. He could see the horizon; they were approaching the Thames estuary. His head was dizzy as his heart raced, and he blinked the sweat out of his eyes.

The Baron approached a gleeful smile on his face. 'Are you trying to tell me you get seasick? This is going to be easier than I thought.'

Lucas didn't see the first three punches that hit him, but with his arms up, hands by his head, he blocked and countered the next two. His comeback was cut short, however, as the terrorist leader targeted Lucas's wounds, punching the bullet hole in his shoulder repeatedly, until his fist was dripping with the blood of his enemy.

'That's enough,' Natasha yelled. She came up the stairs, pointing Lucas's dropped gun at The Baron.

He turned around and faced her, his hands at his side. 'I would be more scared if it were Mr Redmond holding the gun rather than you, Miss Travers, but as you can see, he's not in the best shape to hold anything.'

'It's his thesslophobia; fear of oceans.'

The Baron look down at Lucas and stamped on his injury leg. 'He faced his fear to save you but came up short. Well, that's a shame, for you mostly. No one to come to your rescue. It is a shame you don't like guns.'

'Who said I needed rescuing?' Natasha fired three bullets in quick succession, all striking the centre mass. 'Just because I don't like guns, doesn't mean I don't know how to use one.' She fired a fourth bullet, for good measure, hitting him in the centre of his forehead.

The Baron collapsed to the ground, dead.

The Eye of Nineveh popped out of his pocket and clinked across the deck as the terrorist collapsed. Natasha bent over and picked up the gem, and stared into it, wondering if an artefact like this should really go back on public view.

Epilogue

Natasha arrived at St Dunstan in the east, the church ruin that had been turned into a beautiful garden, an oasis in the city. It was a place she loved, so quiet, despite being a stone's throw away from the often busy Lower Thames Street.

She could hardly believe that it was only a few days ago that she was in the area, sprinting for her life and searching for parts of the Roman wall that once surrounded the City of London.

Now she could take things easy and enjoy nature, barely taking any notice of the black BMW that parked across the road.

Natasha sat on one of the benches and sipped her salted caramel iced coffee as she crossed her legs. It was a beautiful day; the birds chirped, and the trees rustled in the gentle breeze. It was idyllic. However, she couldn't help but wonder how things would have turned out if Baron had obtained the Eye of Nineveh. The consequences didn't bear thinking about.

Beside her was a discarded copy of latest Metro newspaper and Natasha picked it up hoping to find something to take her mind off the narrowly avoided disaster. She opened it and immediately groaned. They were still reporting the recovery of the stolen gemstone. About how the endeavours of DCI Jake Russell, DI Wilson and consultants, Natasha Travers and Lucas Redmond had not only saved the reputation of the British Museum but also averted a certain international incident.

It wasn't the story that annoyed her, that was exactly how David Evans and Section 7 wanted the story spun, the involvement of the secret government department was completely kept under wraps and out of the news. What annoyed Natasha was the photo.

The picture had been taken when she was talking to Lucas, and whilst he had his usual beaming smile plastered over his face, she was caught in some sort of inhuman scowl. She was reminded of the infamous photograph of then-Labour Party leader Ed Miliband eating a bacon sandwich.

Natasha threw her head back and groaned again. It wasn't every day you were in the newspaper.

'Come on,' David Evans suddenly said as he sat down heavily next to her. 'It's not that bad.'

Natasha looked at the strapped-up arm of the S7 head. 'Shouldn't you be in the hospital?'

'I haven't got time for that.' He looked around briefly, making sure no one was taking any particular interest in them, before he continued in a lower tone. 'I had to make sure that everything went smoothly with the transportation and deposit of the Eye of Nineveh.'

'What do you mean, deposit? Isn't it going back to the museum?'

'Not a chance,' David replied matter-of-factly. 'The retrieval and storage of dangerous artefacts is the remit of this department. We can't run the risk of having this fiasco happen again; the next terrorist might succeed.'

'So what's on display in the British Museum?'

'A perfect replica. As long as no one performs any carbon dating tests, which I doubt they will, since it would involve drilling into the gem, everyone will be none the wiser.'

'To be honest, I had the same concerns,' Natasha admitted. Although she would always prefer to have the real objects on show in museums, sometimes it just wasn't possible. But never did she think that a reason for showcasing fake artefacts would be because the real McCoy was a danger to humanity. 'So where is it?'

'Somewhere safe.'

She gave him a cockeyed look.

'It's a secure site that doesn't exist on any government document, except one, and that's in Downing Street. Like I said, somewhere safe. Extra precautions were taken.'

'Still no closer to finding the leak, Marcus mentioned, then?'

'No, but they'll slip up, eventually. I'm a patient man, I don't mind playing the long game.' At that moment, David noticed that Natasha's demeanour had changed since mentioning her mentor. 'Marcus was a good man. He'll get the send-off he deserves, Natasha.'

She nodded and wiped away the tear that was forming. 'I need to get back to the office,'

'As do I.'

She stood up and finished the rest of her iced coffee. 'And thank you for the update.'

'Right now, you and Lucas are my most trusted agents, so you deserve to know the outcome of all your hard work, Natasha.' David got to his feet and adjusted the strap of his sling so it wasn't cutting into his neck anymore. 'I can't wait to get this bloody thing off. Take care, I'll see you at the funeral, unless something comes up before then.'

They walked together to the exit and, after saying their goodbyes, went their separate ways, David to the left, Natasha to the right, heading to Lower Thames Street. She dropped her empty bottle in the nearby bin and suddenly got the feeling that she was being watched.

Natasha glanced around and relaxed slightly when she saw no one looking in her direction. But as the sun peeked out from behind a passing cloud, its rays glinted off something that drew her attention. She turned her head sharply and saw someone watching her from within the black BMW.

She moved slowly, cautiously towards it. As she got closer, Natasha could see that it was a woman, closer still, and she could recognise that it was Chiara Harris. 'What does she want?' Natasha wondered.

When Natasha was close enough to see Chiara's face fully she came to a stop, the glare she gave her was full of murderous intent.

To her credit, after the initial surprise, Natasha returned the look with almost as much intensity; there was no love lost between them. She was fired up by the fact that this was the woman that had played a part in the breakdown of her marriage, something she never thought that she'd be able to reconcile.

It was a stare down, a battle of wills, like the samurai masters of old that were said to be able to determine the outcome of a duel, just by staring into the eyes of their opponent.

They persisted to lock eyes, the world continued to move around them, unaware of the battle that was taking place. The contest only ended when Chiara revved the engine of her car and took off at high speed, in a cloud of smoke, wheels squealing.

As Natasha watched the car go, she took out her mobile phone and called Lucas. 'You'll never guess what just happened,' she said after their initial greetings.

• • • •

'WELL, THAT EXPLAINS why she's late,' Lucas said. 'She must be on her way here now.'

'Maybe. She certainly took off in a hurry. So, how are your injuries?'

'I'm fine, Nat, but more importantly, how are you?'

'The S7 therapist that David is sending me to is helping a lot.'

'That's great. I'm happy to hear that. I know that it's never easy to take a life.'

'No, I guess not. But it came down to a choice, either you or him, and if I had to, I'd make the same choice again.'

'Thank you, Natasha.'

'Come on, Lucas. You annoy the heck out of me sometimes, but I still...' Natasha caught herself before she declared her feelings, covering it up by clearing her throat.

Lucas smiled. 'I feel the same way.'

Just then, Lucas is given a note by a waitress at the restaurant he is at. He opens it thinking that it's from Chiara, who he was waiting to see. On the paper is written SJ. He hangs up the phone on Natasha and calls the waitress back. 'Who gave you this?' He asked her urgently.

'That gentleman over there.' Natasha pointed.

Lucas immediately went over, using his crutch, to find Kallum Taylor sitting and looking pleased with himself. 'I should break you in half right now,' Lucas said to him.

'Well,' Kallum looked the wounded Lucas up and down, 'that would be quite a feat in your current condition. I might just like to see that.'

'Be careful what you wish for.'

'I'll get straight down to business then. Your mother wanted to thank you for the Brienne job.'

'What?'

'Yes, Kallum works for me,' a voice from behind Lucas said. 'As you can see, reports of my demise have been greatly exaggerated.'

He knew the voice but couldn't believe that it was her. Lucas's phone rang, but he switched it off and let it go to voicemail. 'No shit! You faked your death.'

'Don't turn around,' Angela Redmond said.

Lucas thought it was a strange request, considering they hadn't seen each other for so long. It was even more weird when you throw in the fact that she was supposed to be dead. Yet here she was, still not wanting to see him. He fought to control the angry twitch in his lip.

'It's for your own protection, Lucas. I have some associates that would gladly use you as leverage against me if they knew you were my son.'

'So, you thought it would be better to let me think you were dead?' Lucas scoffed. 'What happened to dad? Is he alive too?'

'No, he's very dead,' her voice trailed off. 'I needed to trim the fat off of my operation, get rid of the chaff. If it's not serving a purpose in the grand scheme of things, not pushing things forward, then get rid of it.'

Lucas was taken aback by what he was hearing. 'What about the woman in the car? Who was she?'

'Someone that fit my height and build just enough.'

'How can you be so callous?'

'Self-preservation can give you the strength to do extraordinary things. I had to get rid of some unwelcome attention, and this was the perfect way. Don't think that you and I are all that different, Lucas. From what I've read, you are more than willing to do what it takes to get the job done.'

'Who are you talking about? My military record is confidential.'

'Not to everyone. There are a lot of people out there with their own agendas, Lucas. Powerful people. Your goal should be to secure a seat at the high table and not be one of their pawns. Follow my example. Be careful who you associate with.'

'What's that supposed to mean?'

'It was the government that told you I was alive, wasn't it? Was it before or after they got you to join them? A little snippet of information to do their bidding? To reward you?' Angela heard Lucas push his chair back. 'Don't turn around,' she repeated. But he did more than that. He got up and sat in the seat opposite her.

Seventeen years had passed since he had last seen her, and she looked exactly the same as she did then. Angela was young when she gave birth to Lucas, barely eighteen, and her lifestyle kept her that way; being a cat burglar was a strenuous career.

'I told you not to turn around. Not one for following instructions, I see.'

'Wonder where I got that trait from. So, you're telling me not to trust the government?'

'Why? Why don't you want me to see you? Scared you'll develop some maternal feelings? I shouldn't be surprised by anything you do. It's not like you've been the best mother, much less human being.'

'I resent that! Maybe not the best, but certainly good enough. I said don't turn around.'

'You left me on the Skipton job! Your own son! I got arrested, and you got off scott free.'

'It was a calculated risk. You were just underage at the time and I had the insurance policy to make sure you didn't get a rough ride.'

'Sandhurst was a rough ride.'

'Character building, I'd say. Trust me Lucas, it could have been a lot worse.'

'So you're saying you left me for my own good?'

'That's exactly what I did. The job was a setup. Our luck was never that bad. The person I got the job from sold me out. If I got caught, I wouldn't have seen you for a long-time. Maybe never, considering the things I know.'

'You never saw me for a long-time, anyway.'

'Haven't I? I was there at all your most important moments. Your graduation from Sandhurst. Your acceptance to the SAS. Your wedding. To be honest, I never thought that it would last this long with that Travers girl, different backgrounds and all that. Glad you haven't made me a grandmother yet though.'

'As if I'd let you see any child of mine.'

'Of course you would. Family comes first. That's why I'm bringing you back into the fold. That's why I sent you on the Brienne job, to see if you still had the talents I taught you.'

'That was just a test?'

'Well, no. The letter was needed.'

'Why? What's in it?'

'What is in any letter. Knowledge. And that is power, information. That is how I am where I am. That is why I had to disappear. That is why I am feared. Come with me, Lucas. Join the organisation and you'll learn everything. You'll be at the high table.'

'That's alright, you got a pretty good lapdog here.' Lucas thumbed at Kallum and then did a double take, looking closer at him. He'd become deathly pale and sweated profusely, his eyes so red that it looked like he was about to cry blood.

'As you can see, a vacancy will be opening soon. He fumbled with the ball. He had the Eye of Nineveh and he let it slip through his fingers. As I said, you have to get rid of the chaff,' Angela said coldly. 'Oh, and by the way, be careful what passes through your hands, Lucas. Physical currency is so contaminated these days. You'll be hard pushed to find any that doesn't have coke, speed...or something far worse on them. I told him, but he didn't listen. Perhaps you will. A friendly warning from mother to son.'

'Warning about what?'

'Ask your friend, Ellen, about the Georgia Stones.'

'The what?' Lucas was so focussed on Kallum that he didn't see when his mother left. He pulled out his phone, switching it back on. The screen lit up with multiple calls from Ellen and Natasha.

He called over the waitress to get an ambulance for Kallum, whilst he listened to the first message from Ellen.

'I can't believe you're ignoring my call, but I'll let you off since you kept your promise to me and killed that bastard. So, speaking of that former terrorist, the algorithm came up with some stuff. I know it's a bit late and that he's dead and all, but you've got to hear this. The Baron wasn't his nickname or anything. That was his actual name, Baron. Baron Harris,' Ellen's messaged paused for effect. 'As in Chiara Harris, as in they were brother and sister. As in, you just killed your girlfriend's brother ... well actually, your wife just killed your girlfriend's brother. Jeez, your life is like a soap opera.'

'Oh, fuck,' Lucas exclaimed.